SWORD OF THE NORTH

LUKE SCULL was born in Bristol and lives in Warminster with his wife. Luke also designs computer roleplaying games and has worked on several acclaimed titles for Ossian Studios and Bioware.

Luke's first novel, THE GRIM COMPANY, was shortlisted for the David Gemmell Morningstar Award, 2014.

Visit his website at: www.lukescull.com

THE GRIM COMPANY

'The writing is incredible... *Sword of the North* is everything I'd hoped it would be, a deserving sequel to one of the finest fantasy novels of recent times – a rich and rewarding read told by a true storyteller.' SFBook

'Paced like a race, never a dull moment, extraordinary set pieces, bold and brilliant. A stellar exemplar of what the genre has to offer today.' Tor.com

'An enjoyable romp at the heart of the genre.' Interzone

'Scull spins a gripping tale with expertise and relish.' Guardian

'Packs an impressive amount of violence, hazy morality and betrayal, crafting an energetically cynical read. Showcasing thrilling action sequences alongside effective plot twists, it'll please fans of the darker edges of epic fantasy... An entertaining page-turner.' SFX

'If you like your gizzards glistening and your mages mean, this rollicking debut will suit. Hugely enjoyable.' Daily Mail

'One of the bright new voices in epic fantasy.' Speculative Book Review

'A deftly crafted work that covers politics, betrayal, assassination, war, and frighteningly believable battles against enormous magical monsters.' We Love This Book

THE GRIM COMPANY
SWORD OF THE NORTH

LUKE SCULL

HEAD
of
ZEUS

For Mum

Contents

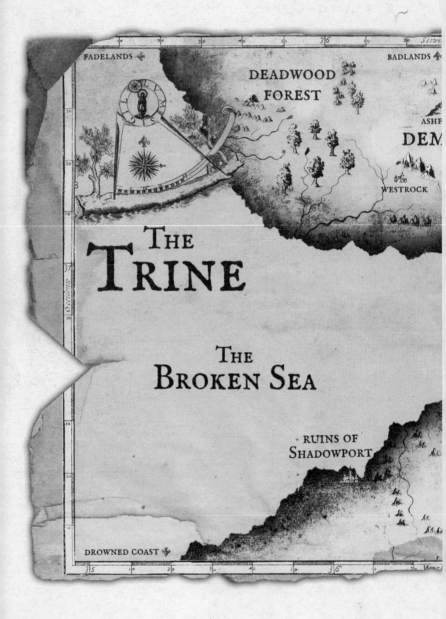

FADELANDS

DEADWOOD
FOREST

BADLANDS

ASHF

DEM

WESTROCK

The
TRINE

The
BROKEN SEA

RUINS OF
SHADOWPORT

DROWNED COAST

SWORD OF THE NORTH

Thirty-six Years Ago

H E COULD HEAR them crashing through the trees behind him. He half-skidded down the slope, ruined boots finding little purchase on snow frozen solid. His feet were numb with cold, felt as dead as the lamb flopping wildly over his shoulder. Blood still leaked from the slit throat of the beast and soaked the filthy rags that covered his body.

There was a curse from one of the men chasing him, followed by an angry yell. He shifted the carcass on his shoulder and allowed himself a grin. He was losing them, even weighed down as he was. He reckoned a few had given up already. They were old men, most of them. Well past thirty.

He would get some distance on them and find somewhere to hide. Lie low for a bit and get a fire going. His stomach gave a mighty growl, a reminder that this winter had been desperate. Harsher than any he could remember.

He leaped a fallen tree, managing to keep his balance despite the thick patch of ice just beyond. Moments later he heard a thump and a fresh flurry of curses turned the air blue – he guessed one of his pursuers had blundered into the log and landed flat on his face.

He wondered what had become of Leaf and Red Ear – or Dead Ear, as he decided he would take to calling his hapless friend. Red Ear was supposed to be keeping watch while he and Leaf raided the farm. They were just done slaughtering the first lamb when someone raised the alarm. It turned out Red Ear was about as useless a sentry as he was a cook. How he'd survived in Skarn's gang as long as he had was anyone's guess.

The trees finally parted. He could see the river now. Once he was across the Icemelt's surface the stubborn bastards would surely admit defeat. He ran on, rapid breaths throwing up clouds of mist – but approaching the bank he realized he had things all wrong. The Icemelt had yet to fully freeze over. Massive chunks of ice churned in the surging rapids, grinding together with enough force to crush a man to pulp. There wasn't a chance in hell of swimming across that raging deluge.

Listening for the sounds of the chase, he swerved, intending to head downstream and circle back into the forest.

Two men emerged from the trees, blocking his path.

'You've gone far enough, boy.' The nearest of the pair was panting, but there was no mistaking the grim resolve in his voice. Nor the glitter of cold steel at his waist.

He didn't waste time replying. Instead he dashed forward and drove his forehead into the speaker's face. He heard bone crack, felt cartilage break beneath the force of the blow. He spun immediately, shrugged the lamb off his shoulder and raised it as a makeshift shield. The other man's sword thrust wedged in the animal's flank, and his assailant's surprise lasted just long enough for him to get in three quick blows, dropping his opponent to the ground.

He retrieved the lamb and was tugging the sword free when someone barrelled into him from behind, knocking him down and sending both the sword and the abused carcass flying from his grasp.

He twisted around to grab the newcomer. This one was a real piece of work, as tall as he was and a good bit heavier. Though he'd always been unusually strong for his age he couldn't get the bastard pinned down for a solid hit. He took a glancing blow to the mouth and spat out blood. The other man grabbed him in a headlock and forced him down. He pushed back desperately and narrowly avoided getting his skull dashed against a rock.

He lost all sense of time as he struggled with the big Easterman. A minute or an hour might have passed as they battered each other on the bank of the river, neither able to get the upper hand. Finally they broke apart and his opponent stepped back, breathing hard.

Slowly he became aware they were being watched and he turned. Half a dozen faces stared back. One he knew well, beneath the bruises that had turned his boyish features into a discoloured mess. Leaf.

One of the men held a long dagger at Leaf's throat. Two others had arrows nocked and drawn. The meanest-looking shook his head and spat on the snow. 'Where the rest of you hidin'?'

'The rest of us?' He knew whom the man referred to, or reckoned he did. And if that was the case, he was as good as dead.

'Your gang. Been raiding the settlements near the Borderland for the last year. Left a family murdered in their beds, mother and children and all.'

The memory made him wince. He wiped his face with the back of his hand and examined the bloody smear it left. He glanced up. The sky had grown dark as an old bruise.

'I'm waiting for an answer, boy.'

He narrowed his eyes and stared at the dead lamb lying skewered by the side of the river. 'It wasn't me what did that. Nor Leaf nor Red Ear.'

'You gonna tell me the three of you split from the group when it started killing folk?'

'It's the truth.'

The leader of the Eastermen spat again. 'We'll do this the hard way then.' He gestured at the man holding Leaf. 'Drown him in the river. Slowly, mind. Give our friend here time to ponder whether there's anything he should be telling us.'

Leaf began to struggle as he was dragged to the river. His friend was little more than a child in truth, and his efforts to wriggle free were hard to watch, but he didn't turn away. Not even as Leaf's head was forced under the churning water.

'How old are you?' the leader asked, once Leaf's head was dragged back up again.

'Sixteen,' he replied. He could see Leaf's teeth chattering uncontrollably. The wiry youngster was struggling to catch his breath and his skin had turned a nasty shade of blue.

'Huh. Hardly more than a boy and yet you knocked two of my men senseless. Butchering that woman and her kids must've been easy work.'

He was growing angry now. 'I told you – we didn't do it! All we ever did was steal some livestock. We left Skarn and the others before they reached Eastmeet.'

Leaf went into the water again. When he came back up his eyes had rolled back in their sockets. He wasn't struggling any more.

The leader gestured at the limp figure. 'He's done. Finish him and throw the body in the river.'

Rage surged through him. He liked Leaf, who was smart and had a cheerful nature despite the fact he'd cut his uncle's throat rather than spend another night in his bed. Leaf had watched out for him when he had joined Skarn's gang; saved him from a bloody confrontation or two when his pride wouldn't let him back down.

'You drown him and I'll kill you.'

The men with bows shifted slightly, their arrows nocked and ready to loose. Their leader gave an ugly little chuckle and nodded at the man holding Leaf. 'Drown him.'

He charged.

The next thing he knew he was lying on the ground, staring up at the leaden sky. Snowflakes fluttered down to melt on his face. He reached for his knee and felt the arrow protruding there. A face loomed over him.

'That was stupid. Brave, but stupid. Men!'

He felt himself being dragged across the snow towards the sound of rushing water. They turned him roughly and held him out over the river. He stared out across the Icemelt, watching as

4

Leaf's body twisted and spun like its namesake before it finally went under. Then someone took hold of his hair and his head was pushed down, down towards that freezing maelstrom of ice...

'Wait.'

His would-be executioners hesitated and his head came to a halt an inch above the water. He stared into its savage depths.

'What's your name?' asked the voice. It was deep and powerful and sounded like it was directed at him. He turned his head a fraction and saw the speaker was the big bastard he had fought earlier.

'What does it matter?' The leader was clearly annoyed. 'He's a brigand. Kill him and be done with it.'

'The boy's got fire in him. Fire and steel. We could forge him into something with purpose. The spirits know we need fighting men at the Keep.'

'He's a cold-blooded killer. A child murderer. Besides, he's just taken an arrow in the knee. Few ever recover from a wound like that.'

There was a brief silence. He held his breath, the roar of the Icemelt raging below him.

A strong hand pulled him up, almost gently, and turned him around. 'I've never met a boy who put up as much fight as you did. Especially not half-starved. I'll ask again: What's your name, lad?'

He stared back at his saviour. The man's face carried a few minor injuries from their earlier struggle, but his eyes betrayed no malice or anger. Only a certain curiosity.

'My name...' he said slowly, trying not to pass out from the pain. He blinked snow from his eyes. 'My name...' he said again.

'... is Kayne.'

Wild Country

'Kayne.'

The gruff voice snapped him awake like a bucket of ice-cold water over the head. The Wolf could rasp his name any number of ways fit to freeze the blood. One glance at Jerek's bald, fire-scarred visage was all the confirmation he needed that things were about to turn ugly.

'Bandits?' he mouthed silently. Jerek nodded and scowled into the receding night. The grim warrior's twin axes were already unharnessed, brutal implements of death that had taken more lives than Kayne could count.

The old Highlander pushed himself painfully to his feet, rubbing sleep from his eyes. They hadn't bothered to light a campfire. It was the height of summer and, besides, they'd hoped to avoid drawing attention. Hoped to avoid a situation like this.

He unsheathed his greatsword and squinted into the darkness. Not a damn thing, he thought sourly. His eyesight was getting worse.

Jerek's senses, on the other hand, seemed as sharp as ever. His friend did the lion's share of the sentry duty, and though neither man had spoken of it, Kayne was beginning to feel guilty. There was only so much guilt a man could take. And the older you got, the more difficult it became to bear the weight.

A twig snapped somewhere nearby. An arrow hissed through the air and thudded into the grass six feet from where the horses were tethered. They snorted and shifted nervously.

Kayne sighed. He hated archers. They were little better than wizards, in his estimation, though at least most had the decency not to prance around in what was, when it came right down to it, a glorified dress. A sliver of the dream he had just woken from flickered in the dark pits of his mind, and he glanced down at his left knee. The memory of that ancient agony made him wince.

Jerek motioned to his left and stalked off, crouching low and weaving from side to side. Kayne followed his lead, though the effort of bending caused his back to complain something fierce.

He thought he saw the shadows shift ahead. Bandits normally travelled in small groups, the better to strike hard and fast and make a quick escape. There were unlikely to be many of them. If they could take out one or two, the rest would scatter soon enough.

Suddenly, he sensed movement to his right. Careless of his creaking knees, he dived into a roll, coming out of it with his greatsword raised high, prepared to cleave whoever it was in half.

But it was only Jerek, his eyes glittering in the ghostly light. The Wolf spat on the grass and shook his head. 'They fled,' he said. 'Best we get moving. No sense waiting to be picked off in broad daylight.'

Kayne nodded. Bandits were always a risk when crossing the Badlands, as the two men knew all too well from recent experience.

They returned to camp to find their packs missing.

'Pricks stole our bags,' growled Jerek, never one to mince his words. He reached up and began tugging at his beard, the way he always did when he was on the verge of flying off into a rage.

Kayne closed his eyes and leaned on his greatsword. This was an inauspicious start to their journey. Three weeks had passed since they'd departed Dorminia, and the wounds they'd suffered during the battle for the city had forced them to rest for a time. Jerek's injuries in particular were nasty – at least two broken ribs and a cracked cheekbone. But the Wolf would rather pass out in the saddle than delay another week. Jerek hated crowds. He hated soft, Lowlander comforts. He hated pretty much everything, truth be told.

'At least we still have the horses,' Kayne grunted. He walked over to the mounts, shaking his head ruefully. 'We could ride back to Ashfall and resupply,' he suggested, though he already knew what the answer would be.

Jerek shot him a dark look. 'I ain't going back there. Place is a shithole.'

Kayne couldn't argue the point. Ashfall was appropriately named. The black dust got everywhere, blown in by swirling winds from the Demonfire Hills to settle on Dorminia's northernmost vassal town. Ashfall wasn't a place either man wanted to return to in a hurry.

'Guess we ride on,' Kayne said, sheathing his sword and pulling himself onto his mount. The sky was lightening, midnight blue fading to iron grey as night gave way to morning. He studied the area as Jerek climbed onto his own horse, a black stallion that accepted his scowling burden with an ease that would have surprised the stable master who sold them the beast. Jerek had a way with animals he lacked with people.

The land ran flat for miles in every direction. Wild grasses warred with small copses of oak and elm and beech. The daylight would soon reveal their brilliant shades of gold and green.

Farther north, Kayne knew, these vibrant colours would become muted. The grass would grow dull and sparse, and scrub would replace tree until the Badlands truly began – a vast stretch of barren country once home to the nomadic Yahan horse tribes before the Godswar broke the land. The last time he and Jerek had passed through, the place had been fair crawling with bandits. Given the trail of corpses the two Highlanders had left behind, Kayne figured the Bandit King would be in no mood to welcome them back with open arms.

As they rode, he watched Jerek with concern. The Wolf looked in some pain. Likely he was nursing one of his injuries.

8

Kayne's own wounds still hurt, especially the knife slash in his stomach that had threatened to turn rotten. The flesh was clean and had knitted back together, but the scar was still raw. He paid it little mind. There were some wounds that never healed, wounds that festered deep in the soul and ultimately did more to break a man than any bodily hurt. The spirits knew he carried enough of those scars himself, but the news he'd received back at the Grey City lent him hope that the largest of them might not follow him to the grave. For the first time in many months, he had a purpose. Something to live for.

He let go of the reins and squeezed the coin purse hanging at his belt. Forty golden spires and a handful of silver sceptres – a large sum of coin by anyone's standards. He and Jerek had been through hell to earn it. It wasn't every day you helped liberate a city from a tyrant. He'd made friends down in the Trine, met some good men and women – and a few some way off good, but interesting nonetheless. In different circumstances he might have been tempted to stay. Instead he and the Wolf had left Dorminia as soon as they had collected their pay. The other treasure nestled inside that pouch had changed everything. It was the reason he was riding back north. Back to the High Fangs. Back to the place he had once called home.

'Kayne.'

Jerek pointed at the thicket of trees just ahead. Kayne leaned forward on his brown mare and squinted, but saw nothing save an indistinct green blur. He shook his head in frustration. He could remember a time when he had thought thirty was old. By forty, a man was past his prime. A man's fighting days should be ancient history by fifty, stories to tell the grandchildren. Yet here he was into his sixth decade and still doing the same old shit, except now his body was falling apart and taking a piss was a tougher battle than killing a man.

He pulled back on his reins and fell in behind Jerek. They turned away from the stand of trees and urged the horses to a run. A moment later a group of armed men on horseback burst out from behind the trees. He counted five, and Jerek grunted to draw attention to three more emerging from a thicket ahead.

'We're not getting by those without a fight,' Kayne said, eyeing the men warily. The two Highlanders spurred their horses on, wind streaming through Kayne's grey hair and dancing around Jerek's hairless scalp. Kayne risked a glance behind him. The riders giving chase were gaining fast. 'Shit,' he muttered.

They were never going to outpace the bandits; the Highlanders' mounts were of reasonable stock, but the horses of these steppes were renowned the world over. The sudden disappearance of the vanished Yahan tribes had gifted the Bandit King the finest horses in the land.

Three of the riders pulled alongside them, easily keeping pace. The leader raised a hand with what looked suspiciously like a flourish. 'Surrender!' he called out in dramatic fashion. 'Flee and your lives shall be forfeit.'

Jerek narrowed his eyes and spat over the side of his horse. Surrender was the last thing on his mind, Kayne reckoned. More likely the Wolf intended to cut a bloody path right through them.

He lowered his voice so he hoped only Jerek could hear. 'Better we do this on the ground. We're outnumbered four to one, and I'm not much for fighting on horseback.'

For a moment he thought his companion would ignore him, but a few seconds later Jerek tugged at his reins and brought his stallion to an abrupt halt. Kayne did the same, hoping he hadn't just made a terrible mistake.

They dismounted as the bandits moved quickly to surround them. The leader slid off his mount with an easy grace, even seeing fit to sketch a quick bow, to Jerek's evident annoyance.

'Well.' The bandit leader stroked his thin moustache; his jet-black hair was bound in a ponytail and the hilt of a fancy sword stuck out from the belt at his waist, which was cinched tight around grey leather armour. Kayne swallowed a sneeze as the fragrant scent of the bandit tickled his nose. The man smelled faintly of perfume.

'Well,' the dapper outlaw repeated. He flashed a smile, revealing bright white teeth. 'I believe we have ourselves a robbery. I would like to say you gave us quite the chase, but that would be a lie.'

Kayne watched Jerek out of the corner of his right eye. The Wolf's teeth were grinding together, explosive rage mere seconds away. This dandy was rubbing him the wrong way something fierce.

'I'm gonna make a suggestion,' Kayne said carefully. 'We pay you a few coin to buy safe passage. Then you bid us a pleasant journey and we part ways, all peaceful-like.'

The bandit leader raised a gloved hand to stroke thoughtfully at his chin. 'I see you are familiar with our customs. That pouch at your waist will indeed do nicely. As will your weapons – there is always need for good steel in these parts.'

'Go fuck yourself.'

Every man present immediately turned to stare at Jerek.

'I ain't handing my axes over to some faggot,' the Wolf explained unhelpfully.

Kayne tried not to let the despair show on his face as steel whispered from sheaths all around them. To his credit, the bandit leader kept his sword at his belt. 'I do not believe', the moustached outlaw said slowly, 'that you are in a position to refuse.' He pointed at the purse hanging from Kayne's belt. 'What's in the bag, old fellow?' he asked amiably.

Kayne's blue eyes narrowed at the insult, but he untied the pouch nonetheless and tugged it open to expose the glittering contents for all the bandits to see. 'Forty golden spires,' he said, trying his best to keep his tone friendly. He gave the purse a shake to demonstrate, but in his annoyance he misjudged it and the real treasure he kept hidden within spilled out onto the grass.

Shit. He didn't know whether to laugh or cry, so he settled on a manic grin.

'Forty golden spires – and what else? A collection of precious gems, perhaps?' The bandit chuckled, a rich throaty sound. He gestured at the small bundle that lay wrapped in cloth. 'What are you trying to hide? Hand it over.'

'I can't do that,' replied Kayne. There was iron in his voice now, a hard edge he couldn't will away, though he knew where it would lead. Jerek met his eyes and in that moment they both understood what was about to happen.

The bandit leader sighed again, clearly savouring the drama of it all. He shook his head in mock regret. 'Then we shall take it by force.'

'Uncle,' a small voice piped up. It was the youngest of the bandits, the lad nearest the leader. Kayne studied him with a frown. He was little more than a boy, a wiry figure with green eyes and bright red hair. Too young to be keeping such company.

'Hush, Brick.' The leader waved a dismissive hand.

'But these men…' Brick tried again. The older bandit leaned across and cuffed him around the back of the head.

'I said hush. Where are your manners? I didn't raise you to be a barbarian. Not like these brutes.'

'That's a bit harsh, boss,' said one of the bandits, a hint of reproach in his voice.

Their leader raised an eyebrow. 'I was talking about the Highlanders.' He placed a gloved hand on the hilt of his sword. With his other hand he drew his forefinger dramatically across his throat. 'Kill them.'

Brodar Kayne tossed the coin pouch into the air.

It sailed across the circle of bandits; their hungry eyes were drawn to the gold spilling out of it like flies to a corpse. The distraction lasted only a moment, but in that short time several things happened.

Kayne reached behind him, tugged his sword free of its sheath, and beheaded the brigand nearest him. An axe arced through the air, spinning end over end, and thudded into the chest of the bandit opposite Jerek. The impact dropped the bandit like a stone, blood painting the shocked faces of the men on either side. The Wolf was on them in an instant, his remaining axe cleaving through leather and bone.

Only the bandit leader reacted to this surprise turn of events, vaulting quickly onto his horse. He kicked down and sent his mount racing away without so much as a backward glance.

One bandit ran at Kayne with his scimitar raised, yelling in that pointless way that men who'd never been in a real fight often did. Kayne knocked aside his awkward swing, drove a boot into the man's stomach and sent him sprawling. He was still fumbling desperately for his weapon when the old warrior finished him off.

An arrow whistled over Kayne's shoulder. He ducked low, gritting his teeth against the spasm of pain that shot down his back. The youngster, Brick, was reaching for his quiver again, utter terror in his emerald eyes. The other bandit was already sighting down his bow. It was aimed straight at Kayne.

He caught the glint of metal in the corner of his vision and the archer's head suddenly burst like a melon, an explosion of gore and chunks of bone. The body tumbled to the ground, the handle of Jerek's axe sticking out from the broken mess that had been the man's head.

And only one bandit remained.

Kayne met Brick's eyes and held them as the lad's freckled hand fumbled with the bow. There were thirty feet between them. 'You any good with that?' Kayne asked conversationally, wiping his greatsword dry on the corpse at his feet. Jerek was inching closer to the axe buried in the chest of the first man he'd killed.

'Good enough,' replied Brick with admirable conviction. He got the arrow nocked and drew his bowstring.

'You already missed me once,' Kayne replied evenly. 'Best make your next shot a good one. Don't reckon you'll get another chance.' He nodded pointedly at Jerek, who was bending down slowly to retrieve his weapon, face grim with the promise of death.

He could see the boy's resolve beginning to waver. 'I don't want to die,' he said, sounding awfully young. He stared around wildly at the bodies of his comrades. At the ruin of a man's head, mangled brain leaking through his shattered skull.

'None of us do. But it's an ugly business, robbing folk.'

Brick's eyes jumped from Kayne to Jerek and back again, the bow in his hands twitching one way and then the other as he tried to keep both men in his sights. 'I know who you are. You're the Highlanders who killed dozens of Asander's men. The Bandit King has a bounty on your heads.'

Kayne sighed. 'Aye,' he replied. 'That's us.'

'I'll ride away and won't look back,' Brick said, desperation in his voice. 'I won't tell anyone you're here. I give you my word!'

Bit late for that now, lad. I let you go free, you'll bring every bandit in the Badlands down on us.

His heart sank at the knowledge of what had to be done. He steeled himself and walked slowly over to the boy, then thrust out a bloodied hand. 'Give me the bow and we got ourselves a deal.'

Brick hesitated and let the string go slack. Brodar Kayne took the bow with a grateful nod.

With his other hand, he punched Brick hard in the face.

'We should kill him. Get it done quick.'

Kayne rubbed at his bristled chin. He glanced up at the stars overhead, then down at the groaning figure strapped to the saddle on the horse beside him.

'He's just a boy.'

'You'd killed a man at his age, Kayne, and you know it.'

Jerek had been less than impressed to find Brick still breathing. The Wolf had calmed down now, furious rage replaced by sullen anger. In Kayne's experience the latter tended to linger a fair old while.

'Best not to use me as a yardstick, I reckon.'

Jerek spat. They rode on in silence, heading ever northward

into the wilds that lay beyond the Trine. Another day or two and they'd be well inside the Badlands.

'The Bandit King ain't forgotten about us,' Jerek finally said. 'Chances are his cousin Fivebellies ain't either. You heard the kid. There's a bounty on our heads.'

'I know. Not much for it now.'

'Kid's uncle will come looking for him too. You thought about that?'

'Aye.'

'And?'

'Not much for it now.'

Jerek shook his head, the moonlight casting a shine on his bald scalp. 'You're turning into a right old pussy and that's a fact.'

Kayne sighed. 'Age will do that to you.'

Jerek snorted in reply.

An hour later they reined in their horses and set up camp. They bundled Brick off his saddle and onto the ground. The boy had a big purple bruise on his cheek, but no permanent damage. Kayne shook his head ruefully. There had been a time when his right hook was guaranteed to break a man's jaw.

'You awake?' He gave the waterskin he was holding a shake, sprinkling a few drops over Brick's face.

'Urgh! Leave me alone.'

Jerek jabbed a booted foot none too gently into Brick's ribs. 'Shift, you lazy prick.'

'Ow! Where… where am I?'

Kayne took a bite out of a chunk of bread and gave it a good hard chew. 'I'd like to say among friends,' he said, around mouthfuls. 'But the truth is that you're our captive and you'd best do what we say or we'll more than likely kill you.'

He gave Brick a moment for this to sink in. 'Where's my uncle Glaston?' the boy asked.

'First hint of trouble and he fled like a startled deer. A right coward, your uncle.'

'He's no coward! He's the smartest man I know.'

'He was smart enough to save his own skin, I'll give him that.'

'You don't understand,' said Brick. 'Asander the Bandit King would have killed me if it wasn't for him.'

'You're not on good terms with the Bandit King?'

Brick shook his head and touched his bruised cheek. 'We were fleeing south to escape him. We only wanted your food and whatever coin we could steal. We're not murderers.'

Kayne raised a thick eyebrow but decided to let that pass. He was silent for a moment, trying to see a way forward that didn't involve murdering the lad. 'Right, Brick,' he said. 'Here's how it's going to be. You'll ride with us, act as our guide through this land. Do as you're told and you can have your horse back when we reach the Purple Hills.'

'Uncle Glaston won't abandon me.'

'Then you'll just have to explain the situation when he shows his face again. I'll untie your legs but your wrists are staying bound for now.'

He cut through the rope around Brick's legs and then handed him a heel of bread and the rest of the waterskin. The boy tore hungrily into the bread, the right side of his mouth doing all the work. Kayne felt a moment of pity for the young bandit. He shook his head sadly, remembering a small body disappearing beneath the Icemelt all those years ago.

Jerek was seeing to the horses. Kayne lowered his aching body to the ground and settled back against the trunk of an oak. Then he reached into the coin purse at his belt and rummaged around inside. It felt lighter than before – they'd lost a handful of spires and sceptres during the fight with the bandits. He figured it was coin well spent.

With great care he removed the items wrapped inside the bag. The protective cloth had become stained with blood during the fight, but he was relieved to find none of the contents were soiled.

He stared down at them, cradling them delicately in his palm. His three most precious treasures.

A lock of Mhaira's hair, chocolate brown.

The ring she had presented to him for their joining ceremony: a plain band of silver. It was still bright despite the passing of the years.

The small knife he had fashioned for Magnar: the traditional gift a father presents to his son on his fourteenth naming day, when a boy officially becomes a man. He ran a finger softly down the dull blade.

Jerek walked over, and Kayne noticed that he limped slightly. The Wolf must have taken a wound in the fighting earlier that day. He hadn't mentioned it. He never did.

Kayne felt a fresh wave of guilt, the terrible burden of truths he had kept hidden for so long.

Jerek watched him, his scarred face unreadable. If the Wolf noticed the tears threatening Kayne's eyes he betrayed nothing. 'We'll find her,' he said simply. He kicked off his boots and was snoring almost as soon as he hit the ground.

Kayne rewrapped the objects in his hand and placed them carefully back inside the pouch. He glanced over at Brick, who was staring out into the night, no doubt wondering when his uncle might return and attempt a rescue.

He got himself as comfortable as he could, and then he too settled back to watch the wilderness. Time and again his failing eyes were drawn to the north.

A thousand or more miles away, the wife he had until recently thought dead waited for him. He would find Mhaira; put things right between him and his son if he could. Then he and the Shaman would have their reckoning.

After two long years, the Sword of the North was coming home.

The More Things Change

THE WHARF WAS crowded with people – a big stinking mass of humanity sweltering in the noon sun. Most appeared to be poor and desperate, though Eremul the Halfmage wondered if a few of the 'volunteers' packed onto the docks weren't in actual fact bored merchants' sons seeking the thrill of adventure.

The city folk who would remain behind watched mournfully as their loved ones shuffled down the gangplanks towards the huge ships floating listlessly in the harbour. They would shortly be sailing west, out over the Broken Sea to the Celestial Isles. The majority looked terrified at the prospect. One or two seemed strangely eager. Eremul's thin lips twisted in contempt.

They believe they are going to return from the Isles rich men. It takes a special kind of moron to place his head in a noose and expect the hangman to make him a prince.

A month had passed since Salazar's assassination. During that time it had become clear to Eremul that Dorminia's new ruler was no saviour, no great deliverer compelled by altruistic desires. As far as he could see the city had merely swapped one tyrant for another. The White Lady of Thelassa was every bit as totalitarian as Salazar had been. Only subtler in her methods.

'Are you the Halfmage?' someone drawled behind him. He twisted his neck and frowned into the unctuous grin of a round-faced fellow – a merchant judging by the extravagant purple doublet straining over his corpulent frame. The gold buttons alone must have been worth a small fortune, enough to feed dozens of starving mouths down in the Warrens.

Eremul wheeled his chair around and pointed a slender finger at the robes hanging over the stumps of his legs. 'Know any other horrifically maimed wizards?'

The merchant's watery eyes narrowed slightly. 'No.'

'In that case, you have surmised correctly: I am indeed the Halfmage.' He shifted uncomfortably in his chair. The fabric of his robes clung damply to his arse in the sweltering heat. He would need to wash again before his visit to the Obelisk.

'You're a hero,' the merchant said, refusing to take the hint and piss off. 'I heard they had to scrape the Tyrant off the streets once you were done with him.'

Eremul sighed. He was beginning to tire of his new status – not least because it was based on an outrageous lie.

'Look at all those brave pioneers preparing to sail,' the merchant continued. 'A testament to the indomitable spirit of this great city.'

They watched the line of men and women filtering down the gangplank into the carrack currently docked. The ships were all Thelassan vessels, boasting names like *Maiden Voyager* and *Mistress of the Seas*. Their flags hung slack in the afternoon sun.

'I almost wish I could go with them,' the merchant declared. 'They say the Celestial Isles are filled with riches.'

'Riches this city will not see a copper of.' Eremul couldn't keep the anger from his voice. 'The White Lady has already helped herself to a generous slice of Dorminia's wealth, as evidenced by the dispossessed nobles furiously plotting rebellion.'

'You are against those privileged parasites having their assets stripped?' The merchant sounded surprised.

Eremul frowned. 'On the contrary, I fucking *love* the idea. But I note that none of the confiscated coin has filtered down to the proverbial man on the street. The poor are worse off than they were under Salazar.'

The merchant shrugged and waved a dismissive hand at the

scattering crowd. 'Then they have only themselves to blame. Some of us are doing rather well under our new Magelord. I've always believed in an honest day's pay for an honest day's work.'

'And if there is no "honest day's work"?' Eremul asked softly. 'What do you suppose became of those who served the nobles? The maids and the cooks and the gardeners? The White Lady imposes heavy taxes while food shortages grow worse. One might almost suspect her of intentionally starving the city to force people to take the Pioneer's Deal.'

The merchant's bluster was replaced by the anxious look of a man not at all keen on the direction the conversation had taken. 'You shouldn't talk like that,' he said, glancing around nervously.

Eremul's expression twisted into one of mock confusion. 'Whyever not? Are you suggesting we still have reason to fear speaking the truth?'

The merchant wiped sweat from his face and adjusted his collar. 'You of all people should be glad the White Lady now rules here. Good has triumphed over evil.'

Eremul sneered unpleasantly. 'This is the Age of Ruin. There is no good and evil.'

There was a sudden commotion north of the harbour. A score of men in chains were shuffling towards the docks, as motley and sinister a bunch as the Halfmage had ever seen. A handful of the White Lady's spectral handmaidens shepherded them along.

Eremul watched the group with interest. He found his eyes drawn to one prisoner in particular: a tall figure wearing a black coat that must have been grand once upon a time but was now a tattered thing, too large for his gaunt frame. The way he carried himself was different to the others; where they slouched, he strode along proudly. For some reason, the sight brought to mind a great bird whose wings had been clipped.

The prisoner turned his head towards Eremul, who flinched and shrank back in his chair. The prisoner wore a red cloth covering his eyes, and his jaw was clenched so ferociously that he looked like he might bite through his tongue. Despite the fact he couldn't possibly see through the cloth, the Halfmage had the unsettling sensation the man was somehow staring straight at him.

The strange prisoner was led into the hold of a ship a little apart from the others, and Eremul remembered to breathe again. He felt suddenly embarrassed. Getting spooked by a blind old jailbird was a troubling reminder of just how badly Isaac's betrayal had shaken him.

'You look like you've seen a ghost,' said the merchant next to him.

Eremul had forgotten the blustering idiot was even there. 'It's nothing,' he replied irritably. 'Did you see the prisoner in the black coat? There was something odd about that man.'

'Huh.' The merchant scratched his head. 'Just another criminal who deserves whatever he has coming to him.'

'Indeed.' Eremul was already pushing his chair past the portly fellow. 'Let's hope we all get what's coming to us,' he muttered.

The Halfmage wheeled himself through the maze of narrow streets that coiled out from the harbour, deliberately avoiding the broader avenues. His newly found fame ensured that he was no longer the subject of casual mockery. Instead, despite all evidence to the contrary, the people of Dorminia now insisted on treating him as the resident friendly wizard.

Why let the evidence of one's own eyes get in the way of a good narrative?

The stream of folk arriving at the depository seeking some magical boon had almost driven him mad. He had threatened to curse the next idiot that came knocking with the cock-rot. Petty stuff coming from a man celebrated for having slain a Magelord in a wizardly duel, he had to admit, but it seemed to have done the trick.

The sheer absurdity of it all still tickled him. The tyrant Salazar – arguably the most powerful wizard ever to have lived – defeated by him, the Halfmage?

He sniggered and immediately regretted it as the stench of old shit filled his nostrils. The brief conflict with Thelassa had plunged Dorminia's infrastructure into a miserable state. Piles of decaying rubbish blocked a drain in this particular street. Thick black flies and teeming maggots crawled all over the resulting tower of filth. The Halfmage held his breath and cursed silently as he accidentally rode over a stray turd with a *squelch*.

He was dripping with sweat by the time he reached the depository, a nondescript building that housed the city's largest collection of books outside the Obelisk's great library, which had thankfully escaped unscathed from the recent damage to the tower. Eremul found pleasure in very little. Books were amongst the few things he still held close to his withered heart – as was the scruffy little creature that wagged his tail happily at him as he pushed open the door.

'You've been waiting for me,' Eremul exclaimed, lifting the brown-haired mongrel onto his lap. Tyro proceeded to lick delightedly at his face. The animal had made a miraculous recovery from his near drowning on the night Salazar had obliterated Shadowport, taking to his new master like a duck to water.

Though that is perhaps an unfortunate analogy in the circumstances.

He smiled, enjoying the dog's simple affections. It felt good to smile – a brief respite from the ceaseless barrage of misfortune he had endured over the years.

Horribly maimed by the city's former Magelord. Forced to become an informant, ratting for the Crimson Watch. How quickly things can change.

His eyes settled on the broom leaning in the corner of the room, beside a stack of books. His smile twisted into a frown.

Betrayed by my own manservant. Who were you, Isaac? What were you?

Those particular questions were the subject of his latest obsession. He needed *something* to fill the void Salazar's death had left. The desire for vengeance had kept him going during his lowest moments; he felt strangely empty without it.

The great poets are full of bullshit. Love has nothing on hatred's capacity to give a man purpose.

He had been offered a new manservant, a perk befitting his status as a member of the new Grand Council. After giving it some thought, he had declined. He was bereft of the dual crutches of his hatred and the thing that had been Isaac, and yet to his own surprise, he found himself managing reasonably well. He doubted his optimism would last – but for now, he would attempt to stand on his own two feet. Metaphorically, at least.

Eremul lowered Tyro gently to the floor. The dog yelped twice and darted off to wriggle under a table. The Halfmage wheeled himself through the archives towards his washchamber, eager to scrub away the stench of the city. He paused when he noticed something awry with the book on his desk. It was an ancient text that detailed the major races of the northern lands during the Age of Legends. When he'd left earlier that morning he had been reading about the elder race known as the Fade. Somehow the book now lay open on a page depicting a brutish green-skinned humanoid.

He summoned his magic and probed the invisible wards guarding the building against intruders. They ought to have alerted him if anyone had attempted to break into the depository. He found the wards undisturbed.

He inspected the room, finding no sign of any interloper. Tyro poked his head out of his hiding place and yawned. Eremul raised an eyebrow. 'It would appear you've developed a taste for ancient history. My thanks for not covering the book in drool.'

Tyro watched him stupidly. Then he bolted out from under the desk and attempted to crawl up onto Eremul's lap again, eyes bright with excitement, head bobbing up and down, desperate to have his ears rubbed.

'I trust you won't defecate on anything valuable while I'm at the Obelisk,' the Halfmage said. He tried to sound disapproving – but he was smiling as he spoke.

The Grand Council Chamber was uncomfortably warm despite the late hour. Between the stifling heat, the waffle spilling from the mouths of the magistrates to either side of him, and the incessant banging of the hammers from far above, Eremul's head was beginning to ache. To add to his annoyance, the city's Grand Regent had decided to keep them all waiting.

He frowned down the length of the great darkwood table that dominated the chamber, running his gaze over the robed figures seated there. Chancellor Ardling was one of the few magistrates to have survived the previous regime; the grey steward of the city's finances met his eyes briefly and then glanced away. To his left, Remy argued with a magistrate whose purpose Eremul struggled to recall. Whatever dark deed the new Master of Information had performed to earn his place on the Council, it evidently gnawed at him. He could smell the drink on Remy's breath. It wasn't the first time the ratty spymaster had attended a council meeting half drunk.

Of all the qualities for a city magistrate to possess, a conscience is perhaps the least desirable. It will undo a man faster than any nefarious plot from a rival.

Eremul was well aware of the farcical nature of his own elevation to the Council. Someone had to take the credit for Salazar's death following the mysterious disappearance of his true killer. It fell on Eremul's shoulders to play the part of the hero – a role it was tacitly understood he must accept, if he didn't want to vanish without explanation, or be found floating face down in the harbour. As Master of Magic he had no real say in the running of the city. But then, in truth, neither did anyone else around the table.

We're all actors in a mummer's farce. Puppets dancing to the strings of the White Lady of Thelassa.

There was a bustle of activity near the great iron doors and

24

Dorminia's new Grand Regent finally sauntered into the chamber. At his side was one of the White Lady's handmaidens – the Magelord's eyes and ears in the city. Like the rest of her kind, she was pale of skin, onyx-dark pupils at the centre of otherwise colourless eyes. She drifted along in her spotless white robes, casting no shadow despite the lurid orange flames that lit the room.

The Grand Regent's shadow on the other hand was as conspicuous as the insufferable look on his thin face. The man who had until recently served as Salazar's right hand had swapped his black robes for those of a flashy golden hue. Much to Eremul's disgust, he had also donned a circlet of silver in the manner of the Ishari princes of his homeland to the east. It looked ridiculous perched atop his balding head.

Grand Regent Timerus paused briefly beside the obsidian throne at the head of the table, favouring the assembled with a regal smile. Then he lowered himself slowly into the chair with the assurance of one whose bony arse was born to fill its cushioned seat. Eremul felt a flash of annoyance; it was one thing to endure the whims of a Magelord capable of drowning an entire city, quite another to be treated with utter contempt by this treacherous lizard of a man.

'I trust you are all comfortable,' Timerus began, knowing full well the magistrates he had kept waiting were sweating like pigs in their thick ceremonial robes. He steepled his fingers in front of his face in that infuriating manner of his. 'I understand the Thelassan vessels departed harbour without incident.'

'Almost without incident,' corrected Marshal Bracka. The newly promoted commander of the Crimson Watch, such as it was, glanced nervously at the White Lady's handmaiden. An outsider might have found the notion that the big marshal was intimidated by a woman half his size ridiculous, but all present had heard the stories of the massacre that had occurred at the western gate during the taking of the city. The handmaidens had scaled sheer walls and snapped the necks of the city's defenders

25

like dry twigs. Bracka himself was still nursing a broken arm from that encounter.

'Do continue,' Timerus drawled. He smiled, no doubt relishing the other's man's discomfort.

'Rioters set fire to a warehouse on Kraken Street. They were chanting for the leader of the rebels, the woman calling herself Melissan. I had the Watch execute a few and arrest the others.'

Timerus arched an eyebrow. 'I trust you will discover this Melissan's whereabouts soon.'

Bracka frowned and rubbed at his bushy red beard. 'Ain't easy in a city this size. Especially not with all these new arrivals.'

Chancellor Ardling cleared his throat. Eremul found him to be among the less odious of those present, partly because he was at least competent in his role as Master of Coin, and partly because he simply lacked the imagination for genuine cruelty.

Before Ardling could speak, there was a loud crash from above followed by a piercing scream that grew louder and was then abruptly cut off. 'One of the construction workers,' said Remy with a small hiccup. 'Maybe working them through the night wasn't the wisest idea.'

Timerus smiled that humourless smile of his. 'This isn't a *tyranny*, gentlemen. They agreed to the terms. These are difficult times for us all.'

Eremul frowned. *You smug bastard*, he wanted to say. *You wouldn't know hardship if it buggered you up the arse with a rusty spear. How much of the city's wealth have you already embezzled?*

Ardling cleared his throat again in order to get their attention. 'Speaking of difficult times, I am sorry to say our finances are in a precarious state. The damage wrought by the siege weapons was quite extensive.'

There was a chorus of nods around the table. Eremul had spent much of his adult life near the harbour and was therefore used to less-than-sparkling streets. For the other magistrates, the sight of rancid sewage and fallen masonry near their homes in the wealthier parts of the city was a new and wholly unwelcome experience.

Lorganna raised a hand. Timerus had made her Civic Relations Minister following the fatal poisoning of half the Council months past. Timerus himself had been one of the participants in that particular plot, an act of treason that had only come to light after Salazar's assassination. The elevation of a woman to the Council had provoked a few disgruntled voices of dissent. As far as Eremul was concerned she was unlikely to prove any worse than the men, and in any case he had always considered himself an equal-opportunity misanthrope.

'The city's liberation cost the lives of many conscripts from the farming towns,' Lorganna said. The new Lord Justice stifled a yawn, and Bracka raised his eyes towards the heavens as she continued. 'The hinterland settlements are at risk of starvation. The villagers flock here, yet with rising food shortages our own poor can barely afford to eat.'

Timerus shrugged a narrow shoulder. 'They have been offered the Pioneer's Deal, have they not? Those who volunteer to explore the Isles will be fed and provided clothes and other amenities. Their husbands and wives will be paid a silver sceptre each week in their absence.'

'A silver hardly stretches to a loaf of bread, my lord. Prices are rising day by day.'

The Grand Regent sighed. 'The poor shall have to abide. The White Lady has invested much in Dorminia already.'

The simmering resentment that had been festering inside Eremul for weeks suddenly bubbled over. 'To hell with her investment! What of the sacrifices we've already made? Thousands dead. Hundreds more packed off to the Celestial Isles. This Council will soon rule over a dying city. And famine is not the worst of it,' he added, immediately regretting those last words.

Timerus sat back in his throne. He had an angry glint in his eyes, but his interest was piqued. 'To what do you refer?'

27

Eremul took a deep breath. He had been waiting for the right moment to broach this subject. Now was decidedly not the right moment. Still, he would gain nothing by delaying any longer. 'I believe we are in great danger,' he said carefully. 'On the night of Salazar's assassination I returned home to find my servant waiting for me. At least, I had thought him my servant. He spoke of judgement. Of returning to his homeland to prepare for a crusade. I assure you, this man, Isaac – he was not human.' He glanced around the great table. Polite interest warred with incredulity on the faces of the magistrates. 'I have spent the last month studying every text in the city that even fleetingly refers to the race we call the Fade. It is my belief they will shortly return to these lands, sailing east across the Endless Ocean.'

Timerus raised an eyebrow again. 'For what purpose?'

Eremul leaned forward and fixed the Grand Regent with his most foreboding stare. 'They intend to destroy us all.'

Silence greeted his pronouncement. He had expected laughter or at least a snigger or two. Timerus shook his head. 'I do not believe you a stupid man,' he said slowly.

That took Eremul by surprise. 'I appreciate your generous assessment of my intellect.'

'No... you are not stupid. You are broken. Delusional.'

'Hang on a gods-damned minute—'

'It all makes sense,' Timerus cut in smoothly. 'You have lived in fear for so long that you are simply unable to accept your sudden change in fortunes. You cling to your paranoia like a babe to its mother's teat.'

Timerus's words poked something raw inside him. Something raw and ugly. 'Don't you patronize me, you son of a bitch.'

The White Lady's handmaiden twitched. 'Watch your tongue,' she said in a voice as passionless as stone. 'Or be forever silenced.'

He knew discretion was the better part of valour, but at that moment he couldn't help himself. 'I've heard similar before,' he sneered. 'You should take care when threatening a wizard. Even a mad fuck like me.'

'Enough,' ordered Timerus. The hint of concern in that arrogant voice was strangely satisfying.

So he fears I am not bluffing. If I take nothing else from this disaster of an evening, I shall forever treasure that at least.

'You are hereby stripped of your position on the Council,' the Grand Regent proclaimed. He pointed one slender finger towards the double doors. 'Get out.'

Eremul looked around. The assembled magistrates refused to meet his gaze, save for Lorganna who gave him a tiny nod.

'Good evening, my lady,' he said. Then he wheeled himself from the chamber.

Night of Fire

HER HANDS SHOOK. She stared at the man strapped to the chair in the middle of the room. He slumped there, head covered by an old sack pulled tight around his neck. The blood crusting the top of the sack was a dark stain against the filthy canvas. The man's breathing was slow and laboured, every inhalation a painful struggle for air. She glanced at the knife in her hand and swallowed hard. Ambryl would be back soon. She was running out of time.

She walked over to the prisoner. The sheer stench of the man almost stopped her in her tracks. He had been here for over a month and had soiled his breeches countless times. The whole building stank, a foul odour of piss, shit and death.

The room seemed to rock around her, the early evening bustle from outside growing louder. A woman's laugh mocked her. A beggar's cry carried an edge of concealed menace. A dog barked, once, twice, and then a third time, wilder with every yowl, and suddenly her heart was beating fast and the knife felt slippery in her sweating palms.

She squeezed her eyes shut and blocked out the sounds, taking a few deep breaths to calm herself. She gripped the sack that covered the man's head and dragged it upwards. The dried blood and filth caused it to stick against the side of his face. She pulled harder, feeling the coarse material scrape his cheek raw. Ignoring his grunts of pain, she yanked the sack free and tossed it aside in disgust.

'You're an ugly bastard,' Sasha said, after a moment. Three-Finger's head wound had healed to form a scabby mess. Beneath a brutish brow, piggish eyes blinked away crust accumulated over days spent in perpetual darkness. He had a month's worth of beard on his face, but it was erratic, growing only in the spots where the disease that ravaged his skin failed to reach. Tufts of coarse, greying hair sprouted between patches of purple flesh layered with dirt.

Three-Finger tried to utter something, but succeeded only in spraying saliva over his chin. She narrowed her eyes at him. 'What did you say?'

This time he managed to spit the words out. 'Go fuck yourself, whore.' The look he gave her set her heart to hammering again.

Sasha raised the knife and held it in front of his face. 'Remember when you told me I had a dirty mouth? You won't hurt anyone ever again.'

'Untie my wrists and we'll see about that.' He strained against the rope that secured his hands to the back of the chair and unleashed a torrent of curses. She watched him, waiting calmly until he ceased struggling. Eventually he went limp and sagged forward until his head rested on his chest. The wound Ambryl had given him had almost split his skull in half. It was a miracle he was still alive.

'We made it through the chaos at the gates,' she said softly. 'We were the lucky ones. Creator knows you didn't deserve it, but you had the opportunity to make something of your life. Better men than you died that day. Better women too.' She remembered the wizard Brianna, torn apart by Salazar's magic. 'You deserve this,' she said. *He does deserve it*, she told herself. *He does.*

'Do it then. Get it over with and run back to that preening cock you're so hot for. Does the kid even know I'm here?'

It took Sasha a moment to understand what Three-Finger meant. Then the blackness surged up, threatening to overwhelm her. 'Cole hasn't been seen since the night the city was taken,' she said numbly.

The prisoner gave an ugly little chuckle. 'So he's dead, that it? Kid wanted to be famous and instead he's lying in an unmarked grave somewhere. Life rewards the good guys, don't it just.'

'He was a better man than you'll ever be, Three-Finger.' She placed the edge of the knife against his scabrous neck.

'Moryk,' the prisoner replied. 'My name's Moryk. If you're gonna slit me open like a hog at least call me by the name my ma gave me.'

Sasha stared down into the man's beady little eyes. He didn't look dangerous or predatory or even particularly sinister. He just looked pathetic. Her hand wavered, anger replaced by sudden despair.

'To hell with you,' she spat. She jerked the knife away from Three-Finger's throat and stumbled over to the desk in the corner of the room. She fumbled around for the drawer pull, struggling to see through eyes blurring with tears. She found the handle, pulled open the drawer and removed the tiny pouch within, then slammed it down on the desk. Ignoring the cord, she jabbed the end of the knife into the pouch and slit it wide open, watching anxiously as the contents spilled out.

Sasha bent over the desk and let the silvery powder carry her away to sweet oblivion.

She couldn't say what the hour was when Ambryl returned. She thought she heard the door open, but it hardly seemed important enough to demand her attention. Not until she was dragged up from the floor by her hair and slammed against the side of the warehouse.

Her older sister stared at her, hazel eyes betraying nothing. Sasha grinned stupidly in response.

Ambryl slapped her across the face.

'... That hurt...' she mumbled, raising a hand to rub at her stinging mouth. She stared at her palm in confusion. It looked whiter than she remembered. 'Am I a ghost?' she wondered aloud. The absurdity of the question made her giggle.

Her sister slapped her again, harder. 'You are a fool. Gather your senses.'

It dawned on Sasha that her hand was covered in *hashka*. So was her face. She could taste it in her mouth, along with the bitter metallic tang of blood. 'I'm sorry,' she said. She didn't know why she was sorry. Only that it seemed the right thing to say.

'The rapist is still alive.' Her sister gestured at the figure slouched in the chair. 'You promised me you would kill him.'

Sasha rubbed her nose. It was beginning to burn. Ambryl had lit candles near the door, but the illumination failed to reach Three-Finger, who was a dark silhouette in the middle of the room. Sasha was glad she couldn't see his face. 'Murdering him won't change anything,' she said slowly. 'It won't bring back Cole. Or Garrett. Or the rest of my family.'

She had discovered the remains of her foster father inside the temple of the Mother. She had fallen to her knees and sobbed until her eyes were a red ruin. Then she had hurried to Cole's apartment, and from there to Garrett's home, and then to the address of anyone connected with her old rebel group whose name she still recalled. Most wanted nothing to do with her. None knew what had become of Cole.

'I'm your family now,' said Ambryl. Her older sister took her chin gently in one hand. 'Your true family.'

Tears dampened Sasha's eyes. 'How could I not know you were alive all these years?'

'Forget that now. It is in the past.'

Sasha sniffed and wiped at her tingling nose. 'Ambryl—'

'Hush.' Her sister's grip tightened slightly. 'I asked you not to call me that. Ambryl was a different woman.'

'It's who you are. My sister. Not... not Cyreena, or whatever you call yourself now.'

'That which is weak must be purged! Purged so that men like this one cannot hurt us as they did all those years ago.' Her hand

33

closed around the knife resting on the desk. 'Ambryl was weak. Cyreena is not.'

Sasha stared numbly at her sister. 'What are you doing?'

Ambryl walked across to their prisoner. 'Fixing what is broken,' she said.

Three-Finger must have seen the look in her eyes, as he renewed his struggles with greater effort than before. There was real fear in his voice now. 'Get away from me, you crazy—'

His words became an agonized scream as Ambryl thrust the knife into his thigh, right up to the hilt. She pulled it free and stabbed him again in the shoulder. This time she gave the blade a cruel twist.

Sasha winced. The *hashka*'s effects were wearing off. She watched with dull horror as her sister slowly butchered their captive, one thrust at a time.

Suddenly there was an almighty roar from outside. The warehouse shook, raining down dust. 'What was that?' Ambryl demanded, blinking grit from her eyes. A woman screamed somewhere out in the night. The smell of sulphur was heavy in the air.

Sasha felt as if she were going to faint. She knew that evil stench. Dark memories of the massacre at the Wailing Rift wormed their way into her mind. 'Someone's using alchemy,' she whispered. 'Explosive powder. We should go.'

Ambryl stared down at the wretched figure of Three-Finger. Spreading pools of blood gleamed in the glow of the flames from outside. 'First I will dispose of this animal,' she said coldly. She raised the knife.

Something small and round smashed through the window. Sasha watched with growing dread as it rolled a few times before coming to a halt near the door. 'Get down!' she screamed. Ambryl only gave her a puzzled look, so Sasha charged across the room and shouldered her to the floor.

An instant later the firebomb shattered.

The heat was extreme, enough to singe the hair on Sasha's

head. She struggled to her knees, dragging her dazed sister up beside her. Half the room had become a raging inferno. Flames licked at the rafters high above, threatening to bring the whole building crashing down on them.

'Come on,' Sasha gasped, pulling Ambryl towards the door. They staggered out of the warehouse and into the night. Sasha coughed wildly, gagging so hard she vomited up her lunch.

'Are you hurt, sister?' Ambryl still clutched the bloody knife in her hand. Sasha wiped her mouth and shook her head.

'What about me?' rasped Three-Finger's despairing voice. Sasha squinted through the haze of grey smoke now billowing from the doorway and spat the last of the bile from her mouth. 'To hell with you,' she whispered.

They hurried away from the burning building. The storehouse opposite was ablaze – fire was spreading down the entire row of warehouses east of the Hook. The world seemed to spin around Sasha as they ran, the glow of hungry flames blurring with the random flares of imaginary light that still sizzled through her drug-addled brain.

The sisters lurched into the plaza, almost barging into an elderly man who had his hands pressed over his face. Blood dribbled between his fingers. Other city folk gathered nearby, some terribly burned, a few sobbing or wailing uncontrollably. A woman cradled a small body in her arms. Sasha saw the blackened thing that was all that remained of the woman's son or daughter – it was hard to say which – and almost vomited again.

Ambryl grabbed one man by the shoulder and spun him around. He noted the knife she held and flinched back. 'What's going on?' Ambryl demanded.

'Rebels,' he spluttered. 'Melissan's fanatics.'

Sasha was about to ask how the fanatics had got hold of alchemical powder when a commotion broke out. Two men and a woman sprinted into the plaza. The nearest man hurled something at the Watchmen chasing them. There was a flash, and then one of the guards was rolling over and over on the ground, smoke rising from his smouldering tabard. The remaining Watchmen quickly backed away.

'Tell your Magelord this,' shouted the female rebel. 'The sons and daughters of Melissan will not rest until the White Lady withdraws her claim to the city!' She reached under her cloak, grasping for something—

And then suddenly froze, eyes wide in confusion. Her comrades were similarly paralysed, bodies held in contorted postures.

Sasha recognized the heavy tingle of magic in the air. Her eyes swept the plaza. There he was – the Halfmage. He was focused on the rebels, his thin lips working silently. Without thinking she turned to Ambryl. 'Give me that knife.'

He didn't notice her until she was right beside him. Sweat beaded on his olive skin to run down a surprisingly youthful face. He was barely into his thirties and yet the wizard's green eyes held more cynicism than the death gaze of the bitterest spinster.

'I want answers,' she said, looming over him, the point of the knife angled threateningly towards his head.

'Not now,' he hissed. His eyes flickered to her, widened when they saw Ambryl beside her. 'You!' he exclaimed.

Whatever spell he was working faltered in his surprise, and the female rebel lurched back into motion. Before she could toss her firebomb, one of the White Lady's handmaidens crossed the plaza in a blur and casually snapped her neck.

Suddenly free of the magic that held them in place, the two men made a break for it. There was another streak of movement and then one was flying backwards through the air, his killer clutching his beating heart in one porcelain hand. The lone survivor stared around wildly and changed direction, heading straight towards Sasha.

Lightning crackled from the Halfmage's extended digit, striking the rebel dead in the chest. He jerked for a few seconds and flopped to the ground just in front of them.

'Are you trying to get us killed?' the Halfmage spat, voice thick with anger.

Sasha looked down at the rebel's sizzling body and swallowed when she saw the ceramic ball he clutched in his death grip. *It's the moon dust*, she realized. *I'm not thinking clearly.*

Ambryl was staring at the Halfmage with a queer expression. 'I'm not surprised to find you here. You seem to show up whenever some disaster befalls the city. Like a maggot drawn to death.'

The wizard sneered. 'I could say the same for you. This night could hardly get any worse. I need only return home to find Isaac pleasuring himself in my bed and my evening would be complete.'

'Isaac?' Despite the anger she felt, Sasha was intrigued at the mention of the strange manservant.

'Better you don't ask.' The Halfmage frowned at the body of the rebel. 'What's that?' He leaned forward in his chair and pointed at the corpse. The man's shirt had burned away, leaving his ruined chest exposed.

Sasha knelt down and examined the corpse, grateful that her drug-abused nose was deadened to the stench of charred flesh. 'There's a tattoo on his neck. Some kind of script.'

'What does it say?'

'I don't know the language,' she snapped. 'And you're mistaken if you think I'm doing you any favours. I came to you asking for help. You slammed your door in my face.'

The Halfmage glanced around. Sasha followed his gaze. More Watchmen were arriving, clutching buckets of water drawn from cisterns beneath the city. Small groups were banding together to put out the fires that still raged to the east. A physician tended to the wounded, implements neatly arranged beside him.

'Fine,' the Halfmage said wearily. 'Come with me to the depository and I'll answer your questions. I have some of my own.' He frowned down at the smoking body. 'First I must ask you to do something for me.'

She narrowed her eyes. 'What?'

'I need that tattoo.' His eyes went to the knife and lingered there.

Sasha looked down at the corpse, and then at the blade in her hand. 'You don't mean...'

'Yes. Try not to make a mess.'

With a heavy sigh, she bent to her task.

Dreams of the Dead

*H*E DRIFTED ON *a river of stars; stared at a vast blackness stretching for infinity.*

Who was he? He thought he might remember if he concentrated hard enough, yet something about that idea struck him as dangerous. Better to forget. To embrace dissolution.

He closed his eyes – or at least stopped seeing. It didn't matter who he was or might have been. He was at peace now, a weightless vessel pulled along by the cosmic torrent below, surrounded by an endless sea of perfect tranquillity.

And yet…

There was something. *Discordance – a ripple in the absolute calm. He tried to ignore it. To let awareness slip away, become one with the emptiness.*

But it was persistent.

'Bastard's alive.'

'What?'

'He's alive. I just saw him twitch.'

'You sure? I've never seen a man that pale still drawing breath.'

'Me neither, mate. But his chest is moving. See?'

'Well, bugger me.'

'Come again?'

'Bugger me, I said.'

A heavy pause.

'Did you mean that literally or... what's the word... figuratively? It's just... we've been stuck on this ship for days now. A man has *needs*.'

'The fuck you talking about?'

'Forget it. We gonna take his boots or what?'

'Yeah. You grab the left foot. I'll take the right.'

'Hang on. There's something leaking from his stomach.'

Another pause.

'Kid's bleeding pretty bad.'

'Yeah. Someone shanked him good. Nothing worse than a gut wound.'

'Let's grab his boots and get the hell away. Before those ghost women discover we're down here...'

And then only silence.

'You came,' Tyrannus rumbled in a voice seething with spite. The Black Lord had been staring down at the world below, his divine gaze piercing the vast divide between the celestial plane and the mortal realm with an ease that only the gods could ever comprehend.

The newcomer was unmoved by the hatred in that divine voice. The Black Lord Tyrannus was one of the oldest Primes, birthed when the earliest of men first walked the earth.

But he was the Reaver, and he was older still.

'I came,' he agreed, his own voice as cold as the grave, deeper than the hidden abysses at the bottom of the greatest oceans.

They stood together in silence and watched the circle of the world far below. Armies clashed; magic flared; men died.

'We are winning,' the Black Lord growled eventually. Such was the bitterness in his voice that his words might well have elicited confused laughter from another god.

The Reaver did not laugh. There was little in all the cosmos in which he found amusement. 'The wizards of the Alliance retreat before the Congregation's armies, that much is true. The gholam has left a trail of devastation in its wake. But the

Mother's treacherous high priestess may yet swing the balance again.'

Tyrannus snarled. The black leathery skin of his hideous face wept venom that dribbled from his chin and plummeted from the heavens. Moments later a dark storm gathered on the battlefield far below. The skies opened, unleashed a torrent of acidic rain so caustic it stripped flesh from bone, killing hundreds on both sides.

The Reaver shook his head, yet his skull-visage remained impassive. 'You let your emotions rule you. Your fury will not aid our cause. No god may sway events in the world below through direct intervention. It is the one rule that binds us all.'

Tyrannus turned away, clenching ebony claws into boulder-sized fists capable of prodigious acts of violence. 'I know well the rules that bind us, Bone Lord. It is why I summoned you here.'

The Reaver raised one rotting arm and rubbed absently at his fleshless cheek. 'I am intrigued. I would never have acquiesced to your outrageous request otherwise.'

The Black Lord met his gaze, eyes of furious black fire meeting those worm-eaten and rheumy with age. 'I am considering freeing the Nameless.'

He had thought emotion something long lost to him, but at the other god's words the Reaver felt a flicker of something close to the memory of fear. 'You speak of madness. The Nameless is a thing without purpose in the Pattern of Creation.'

Tyrannus smashed a huge fist down into his palm, creating an explosion of sound that would have shattered the eardrums of any mortal within a hundred miles. 'Humanity has grown arrogant!' he hissed. 'They abandon us as their forebears once did. Even in the brief passage of their short lives, they believe themselves elevated above the need for worship.'

'And so, in response, you would unleash the Nameless upon them?'

'*I would restore humanity to its rightful place! Trembling in the shadows! Praying to us for their salvation! The mightiest among the gifted are a threat even to the Pantheon. That was never a part of the Creator's design.*'

The Reaver stared down at the battle raging below. Every death was an affirmation of his efficacy, in its own way a silent prayer. True, freeing the Nameless and its kin would serve him well – they would bring death to the world in catastrophic numbers. Yet the Reaver was ancient, the oldest of the Primes save for the Mother. Millions had already passed through his gates. Patience was ever his greatest virtue.

'*I will not help in this,*' the Reaver declared, with the finality of a heart beating its last. '*The Nameless would wreak devastation on an unknown scale. We may not be able to imprison it again once its purpose was fulfilled.*'

'*Then you doom us all!*' Tyrannus snarled. He took a step towards the Reaver. The heavens shuddered beneath the weight of his divine fury.

'*Not all,*' the Reaver replied. His skull face twisted into a humourless grin. '*I have made plans should the impossible come to pass.*'

'*And if I choose to end you now?*' Tyrannus roared. He raised his brutal hands and suddenly clutched a great flail forged of utter darkness.

The Reaver laughed then, a grating sound like a thousand tombstones grinding into place. '*You threaten to kill death itself? I will still be here when you finally pass through my gates, Black Lord. Until there is nothing left to die and my purpose is fulfilled. It was written in the Creator's Pattern...*'

'*... in the Creator's Pattern...*'

... Pattern...'

'He's twitching again.'

'Shit! I was sure he was done for. He's a stubborn one.'

'What's that in his hand?'

42

'Looks like a dagger. Is that a ruby in the hilt? Quick, grab it.'

'I can't. He won't let go.'

'What do you mean he won't let go? He's near dead! Cut off his fingers if you have to.'

'Wait – who's *that*?'

The sound of clanking chains growing closer.

'Hey, you! What are you doing down here?'

No answer.

'Ha – he's blind! Probably went looking for a piss and wandered in here by mistake.'

The other voice. Louder now, and slightly amused. 'Best turn around, old fellow. This place isn't safe.'

No answer. The footsteps did not slow.

'I said turn around, you deaf old—'

A brief flash of light and the beginning of a scream abruptly cut off.

Then silence once more.

He was floating again. Back on the river of stars. The pain was still there, but it was beginning to fade.

The incandescent stream that carried him along seemed to gather speed. He was moving faster now. He smiled faintly. His journey was almost done. Soon the suffering would end. He could finally sink into oblivion.

A voice called out a name somewhere in the endless depths of space. There was something familiar about that name, but he closed his mind to it. Recognition would only invite more pain.

He was racing along now, the stars beneath him a blur. The voice repeated that word again, louder this time.

A colossal shadow seemed to envelop him.

It was a skull, so massive it filled the emptiness like a small planet. A yellow orb the size of a moon shifted slightly to regard him, and he realized with utter horror that it was an eye, rotten and filled with malevolence. The river of stars had turned a sickly colour now, a festering effluvium bleeding into the skull's cavernous maw.

Sudden terror. He tried to scream but no sound emerged. He struggled desperately to resist the stream's pull, to no effect. The skull would claim him at any moment.

And then he heard that voice a third time. It was quieter now, distant, but he willed himself to understand, to turn the sound into meaning.

Caw. It sounded like caw. *The sound a bird makes? No, that wasn't it. It had to be something else. It had—*

The sound of beating wings; the unexpected feeling of air buffeting his face. Enormous talons closing around him. He caught sight of a great bird above, lifting him up and away from the skull-planet. That terrible, luminous eye swivelled upwards, watched his escape with deathly fury.

The giant bird squawked again. 'Caw,' it seemed to say.

Except that it wasn't 'caw'.

At last he remembered who he was.

He opened his eyes, whimpering in pain. He could see only darkness. Someone was holding him up. He felt a hard object being pressed against his lips. Cool liquid rushed into his parched mouth, and he almost choked before swallowing it down.

He became aware of the quiet whisper of water lapping against the side of a hull, the gentle swaying motion of a ship at sea. He had been on another voyage not long past, though it seemed a lifetime ago now.

'Lie still,' commanded a voice with an edge of steel.

'Who—' he began, but a rough finger pressed against his lips, silencing him.

'You will live. But the next time you awaken, you must be prepared to fend for yourself. Do you understand?'

'Yes,' he croaked.

'Good. Rest now.'

He listened to the sounds of slow, steady footsteps and metal shackles scraping against wood fading into the distance.

This time, when sleep finally came for him, he did not dream.

Thirty-six Years Ago

THE OXEN HAD stopped moving again.

Kayne stared up at the iron sky and watched his breath mist. Any moment now the open-top wagon would resume its rickety journey west, sending fresh eruptions of agony stabbing through his injured leg. His captors had snapped off most of the shaft but the head remained wedged deep in his knee. The furs beneath him were soaked through with blood.

He had lost consciousness on three separate occasions. Each time he had awoken to a world of fresh misery. He figured a fortnight had passed since the disaster on the banks of the Icemelt, but it was hard to be sure, what with the pain clouding his brain. His stomach growled and he reached down, felt his ribs poking out through the woollen tunic he'd been given. His captors fed him meat and bread of an evening, but it wasn't enough. He had been hungry before his capture; now he was damned near starving.

Footsteps crunched on snow nearby and a familiar face stared down at him. It was the big bastard who had saved his life back at the river.

'We're here,' the burly Easterman grunted. His beard had grown bushier and was flecked with ice. Kayne felt embarrassed by his own wispy growth. He was a man grown, or close enough. Past time he wore the truth of it on his face, as a Highlander ought to.

'Here?' he repeated, trying to hide the pain in his voice.

'Heartstone.' The warrior reached down and placed one meaty hand on his shoulder. 'You'll meet the King soon enough. Best keep that temper in check.'

Two Eastermen hauled him out of the wagon and lowered him to the ground. One moved to support him. As Kayne threw an arm around the man's broad shoulders, the boot of his wounded leg accidentally scuffed the snow and he almost howled. The Easterman grinned nastily.

He half-hopped and was half-dragged along a dirt track that was barely visible beneath the blanket of white. Desperate to take his mind off the raging fire in his knee, Kayne focused on Heartstone. The capital dwarfed the small village he had once called home. The sprawl of huts and smaller homesteads around the walled perimeter quickly gave way to larger structures of two, even three floors. Painted signs announced taverns and smithies, fletchers and whorehouses. There was even a shop dedicated to witchcraft. He had only ever known one sorceress, his aunt Namara, who'd kept an eye out for him following the tragic accident that had claimed his mother.

Curious faces watched the Eastermen and their young captive as they made their way towards the centre of town. Grim warriors in hides and furs and bristling with steel looked up from sharpening their weapons or patrolling to scowl at the newcomers. Womenfolk bustled around performing errands, a few giving Kayne sympathetic glances when they thought no one was watching.

Sweat stung Kayne's eyes despite the frigid morning air. He was burning; his skin felt hotter than a furnace. He gritted his teeth and clutched the shoulder of the warrior beside him until his knuckles turned white.

After what seemed like an eternity a great clearing opened up ahead of them. Just beyond the clearing, looming out of the mist, was the grandest building Kayne had ever seen. He craned his neck, staring up at the summit far above. Whether by fate or chance the sun chose that moment to peek through the clouds and reveal a majestic figure staring down at them, arms folded across his chest. He quickly faded from view as the sun disappeared again.

There was a large crowd gathered in the clearing. It parted as they approached, and a half-dozen warriors stepped forward. Each wore identical armour and carried steel of the finest quality. All moved with the ease of veterans.

Even near delirious with pain, Kayne felt a thrill at the sight of the Six. As a boy he had dreamed of growing up to become one of the King's champions. He had passed many a summer day practice-fighting with his father and old Renek the Lame, who knew how to wield a sword even though everyone made fun of his club foot.

One hard winter the village of Uthreft had launched a raid. His father had decided that if he was old enough to swing a blade, he was old enough to kill a man. The sight of the thief lying there, the haft of the spear Kayne had just plunged through his neck quivering like an accusation dying on his tongue, had soured him against the warrior's life for a good while after.

'King Jagar approaches,' boomed one of the Six from behind his great helm. The Kingsman moved to one side and went to stand by two of his colleagues. The other three did the same, forming a small guard of honour.

The warrior supporting Kayne went down on one knee along with the rest of the Eastermen. 'Get down, boy,' he whispered harshly.

Kayne swallowed and, summoning his courage, tried to lower himself onto his good knee. He was halfway to the snowy ground when his wounded leg buckled and he almost pitched forward, crimson agony exploding in his brain. There was a ripple of laughter from the onlookers, who quickly fell silent as a shadow descended on Kayne.

He blinked tears from his eyes and stared into the thoughtful gaze of Jagar the Wise.

The King of the High Fangs was every inch the man Kayne had imagined him to be. A mantle of red velvet covered his broad shoulders, parting slightly at the front to reveal an iron cuirass underneath. Jagar's thick head of hair and impressive beard were peppered with hints of grey, but he remained a robust man, still at his physical peak.

The King inspected the Eastermen with a considered expression, his eyes eventually settling on Kayne and lingering on his wounded knee. 'Remain as you are, boy. Who leads here?'

'I do, my king. Orgrim, named Foehammer by my peers among the Wardens.' The warrior who had spared Kayne's life at the Icemelt bowed and brought his left fist up towards his chest.

'You are a Warden?'

'Yes, my king.'

'Tell me, Foehammer. How do we fare in the Borderland?'

'The East Reaching is besieged by giants and wild creatures down from the Spine. They are a menace but nothing we can't deal with. The demons are a different matter. We've lost twenty Wardens this last year alone.'

'Their sacrifice will not be forgotten.' The King nodded gravely at Kayne. 'This one is too young to be a Warden. What is your purpose in bringing him here?'

'The boy is Brodar Kayne, formerly of Skarn's band. We caught him near the Icemelt.'

The King rubbed at his impressive beard. 'The punishment for brigandry is death by the noose,' he said slowly. 'Yet the trail of blood left by Skarn and his gang has spread to the Lake Reaching. The survivors say their actions could easily be the work of demons. Women, children... babes... they make no distinction. There is only one punishment befitting such crimes.' The King raised a hand and gestured to the men behind him. 'Bring the prisoner.'

There was a brief disturbance near the entrance to the massive lodge as a wagon was hauled forward. Kayne watched it dully, not at first comprehending what he was seeing.

A wicker frame was secured to the wagon platform. The cage was barely bigger than the man pinned inside it; there was just enough room for him to twist his head slightly and stare out at the jeering crowd. Weeping sores covered the prisoner's face and chest. His strength was clearly spent, but there was no space in which to collapse; the wicker frame forced him upright, cutting deeply into his exposed flesh. The sour stench of shit and piss wafted from the cage as the wagon was pulled closer.

Kayne gasped as he finally realized who was inside the cage. Poking out from a gap between two bars was an oversized ear the colour of meat left too long in the sun. 'Red Ear,' he croaked.

'You know this boy?' asked the King. 'He was captured near Watcher's Keep.'

'Red Ear didn't harm no one,' protested Kayne. 'We only joined Skarn the autumn just past. We didn't know he was a murderer.'

The King frowned. 'Yet you were a brigand nonetheless. What crime did you commit to be cast out from your village?'

'I weren't cast out,' Kayne replied hotly. He was growing angry now – at the injustice of what had been done to Red Ear, at the mocking faces in the crowd. 'My village was attacked by demons. Everyone died. My pa and my aunt and my younger brother. Everyone except me. And I ain't never killed a man save the one my pa made me.'

The King raised an eyebrow. 'What was the name of this village?'

Kayne felt tears threatening his eyes. He blinked them away angrily. 'Riverdale.'

The King glanced at Orgrim, who nodded slowly. 'Riverdale was overrun three years past, my king. There were no survivors.'

'This young man appears to suggest otherwise.' The King stroked his beard again, staring into the distance as if wrestling with a difficult problem. 'It's the noose for you, boy,' he said eventually. 'Justice demands you suffer the cage, but I cannot discount your youth or the possibility you may be telling the truth.'

Orgrim cleared his throat loudly. 'My king, forgive me, but I would beg pardon for young Kayne. He shows some promise. The Wardens have need of good men.'

King Jagar shook his head sadly. 'A Warden must be strong of mind as well as sword arm. At best this boy has demonstrated poor judgement in his choice of comrades.'

'Then let him prove himself.'

The voice seemed to echo all around them, as deep as a mountain valley. All present dropped to their knees immediately, save the King who inclined his head. Striding into the clearing was a figure who looked as if he had stepped out of the great sagas of Fordor and Grazzt Greysteel, a legend made flesh.

The Shaman was among them.

He was shorter than Jagar and several of the Six, but none of them could match the Magelord for sheer bulk. His massive arms were folded over a hairless chest as thick as a log. The Shaman wore only a pair of tattered breeches, and though he carried no weapon there was not a warrior alive who could stand against him. In the High Fangs that marked the far north of the world, his word was law.

'A trial by combat,' the Shaman declared in a baritone voice that carried the length of the clearing. He pointed a thick finger at Red Ear inside the cruel prison atop the wagon. 'Release him.'

At the Magelord's command, a handful of men began to hack at the cage with axe and sword, breaking through the thick wicker and pulling it apart. It took a few minutes, and there was a great deal of grunting and cursing, but eventually the remains of the cage fell away from Red Ear, who wobbled and would have flopped right down onto the snow had two burly warriors not grabbed hold of his arms.

51

'A trial by combat,' the Shaman repeated. 'One of you will kill the other and prove himself worthy. The loser will perish, as the weak must.'

Kayne shook his head. 'Red Ear's my friend. I won't fight him.'

The Shaman's eyes glinted dangerously. 'Fear has no place in the heart of a warrior.'

Kayne stared right back. 'I ain't scared of no man. Not even you.'

There was a gasp from the crowd, which seemed to melt away from the hulking Magelord as if he were one of the great fire mountains in the Black Reaching threatening to erupt. For his part, the Shaman seemed unperturbed. 'Hand them each a dagger,' he grunted.

A jagged blade was pressed into Kayne's hand. Red Ear was handed a similar weapon. The gangly rustler was a year or two his senior, of similar height but slighter build, though with them both half-starved it wasn't much of a difference.

'I ain't doing this,' Kayne whispered. He tossed the dagger away.

The gesture didn't meet with the response he expected. There was a strange look on Red Ear's face that reminded Kayne of an afternoon long ago. One of the family hounds had suddenly turned on him for no reason. His pa had taken the hound out to the woods and returned alone an hour later, hands flecked with blood. All he would say was that the dog had gone bad.

As Red Ear staggered towards him, dribble running down his chin, Kayne knew something inside his friend had broken, just as it had with his dog that day.

Red Ear lunged at him, dagger raised. Kayne tried to hop backwards, away from the probing blade, but he stumbled and fell face first onto the snow. The pain was excruciating, but he managed to roll onto his back in time to see Red Ear skittering towards him. He stuck out a desperate arm, grabbed his crazed friend around the ankle and pulled. Red Ear crashed down next to him.

'It's me,' Kayne gasped. 'The hell you doing—'

Red Ear stabbed down with his dagger. Kayne stopped the thrust with his forearm, grunted as the steel sank deep into flesh. He pulled his arm away and the dagger was wrenched from Red Ear's grasp, and then they were rolling around on the snow. Kayne was the stronger, but his opponent fought like a rabid animal. Red Ear rolled onto the arrowhead in his knee, and Kayne bit down so hard he almost severed his tongue.

Sudden rage took hold. He thrust an elbow into Red Ear's nose and then head-butted him in the chest. That brief flurry stunned Red Ear long enough for Kayne to roll on top of him, and then he was punching and biting the other man, lost in fury. He spat something out, caught a glimpse of it glistening bloodily on the snow and realized it was his friend's cauliflower ear. He tasted gristle in his mouth and almost gagged.

That proved fatal to his sudden momentum. Out of nowhere a handful of filthy fingernails scraped a series of gouges down his cheek. Red Ear jabbed him in the eye, temporarily blinding him.

Fury surged back.

Kayne batted Red Ear's clawing hands away. In a moment of terrible clarity he spotted a rock half-hidden by snow. He reached for it, prised the rock from the ground and smashed it down into Red Ear's skull. His friend jerked beneath him but Kayne didn't hesitate. He hit Red Ear again and again, lost in rage, oblivious to everything except the steady crunching progress of bone caving beneath stone.

Slowly the red mist receded. He stared down at hands crimson with gore. Then he rolled off Red Ear's body and vomited up what little food he had in his stomach.

A dark shadow fell over him. He turned his head to stare up into the Shaman's pitiless gaze. 'You', the Magelord rumbled, 'have proven yourself strong of spirit. I will fix your body so that you may serve your king at the Borderland.' The hulking figure bent down, placed palms dancing with yellow fire over his injured knee. The arrowhead wedged there began to smoke, and then caught fire.

Kayne screamed until darkness came for him.

Savages

NINE DAYS AFTER leaving Ashfall, the heavens opened.

One minute they were following a ridge of naked hills, sweltering in the afternoon heat. The next the sun seemed to drop out of the sky and the horizon turned black. The first drops of rain fell hesitantly, throwing up lazy puffs of rust-coloured dust, but it soon became a raging deluge that soaked them all to the bone.

Kayne hunched in his saddle and listened to the roar of the rain battering the hot stone and the sloshing of his horse's hooves as the animal struggled against the torrent. Brick rode nearby, freckled face filled with misery. Five days had passed since they had last spotted his uncle watching them far in the distance. Brick's expression suggested he thought Glaston might well have given up the pursuit.

Kayne suspected otherwise. There was no shortage of hidden gullies and sharply rising ridges this far west. A skilled tracker could easily conceal himself from view, particularly if he knew the lay of the land.

For his part, Brick seemed to be guiding them well. They had avoided running into any more trouble, though there was little reason for bandits to venture this close to the coast. The Unclaimed Lands to the east provided plenty of opportunity for daring raids on the smaller, poorly defended settlements.

Kayne glanced at Brick again. The young bandit's face was so glum that he couldn't help but feel a trifle sorry for him.

'All right?' he grunted, just loud enough to be heard over the storm.

Brick mouthed something in response, but it was lost between the thundering downpour and the water running into Kayne's ears.

'What's that? I didn't catch it,' he yelled back.

'I said I'm all right!' Brick shouted. The boy's unruly red hair was plastered to his forehead. Kayne was surprised to learn that Brick was barely into his thirteenth winter. He was tall for his age.

'Oh.' Kayne shook his head from side to side, attempting to drain his ears without much success.

The two of them rode on in silence at a slow trot. The rain had made the ground slippery; the last thing they needed was for one of the horses to fall and break a leg.

Further ahead, Jerek's horse came to an abrupt halt. Without turning the Wolf raised a hand in warning. Kayne immediately reined in his mount, as did Brick. They had untied the boy's wrists the day after his capture. He was a skilled rider and might have escaped the two Highlanders if he was of a mind, but Kayne had seen something in the lad he reckoned he could trust.

'Saw something move up there,' Jerek growled, nodding at the rain-shrouded hills behind them.

Brick flicked hair out of his eyes and stared up at the rising ridge. 'Hill-men,' he whispered.

Kayne squinted. He couldn't see a damned thing. 'Hill-men?'

'Wild people. They live among the hills, sometimes under them.'

Kayne's brow furrowed. 'Are they dangerous?'

'Yes.'

Kayne scratched at his stubble. 'And you didn't think to warn us, or have us keep a safe distance? Bit of an oversight, that.'

'They shouldn't be this far west,' Brick explained. 'Maybe they came here fleeing Asander. He killed many of their kind.'

Kayne reached behind him, placed one hand on the hilt of his greatsword and the other on his horse's rein. 'Nothing we can do about it now,' he said, blinking rainwater from his eyes. 'We'd best get moving before—'

A large rock suddenly tumbled down the hillside, missing Brick's horse by a whisker. The beast snorted nervously. Before anyone could act, more rocks clattered down. One struck Brick's mount on the flank and caused the beast to begin bucking wildly. The young bandit held on gamely but a mighty kick sent him flying from the saddle. His head bounced once on the ground and he didn't move. Brick's horse bolted off and disappeared behind the veil of rain.

There was movement up ahead of Jerek. The Wolf spurred his horse forward and then the rain swallowed him up, leaving Kayne alone with the fallen boy. 'Shit,' he said.

He leaped down from his horse, ignoring the sharp pain in his knees, and rushed over to Brick. Rocks were still ricocheting down the hill. A pebble struck him just above the eye and he found himself blinking away blood as well as water.

'You all right?' he grunted.

Brick stirred and sat up. The young bandit winced, rubbed at the back of his head and then examined his hand. There was a dark smear on his palm. 'I'm bleeding,' he said weakly.

'You'll live. It's surprising how tough it is to break a man's skull.' Kayne glanced around, but saw no sign of Brick's mount. 'Looks like you're riding with me. Here, let me give you a hand.'

They were climbing onto his brown mare when Jerek burst back into view, standing straight up on his stirrups, axes trailing beads of blood. 'They got us surrounded,' the Wolf snarled. A fist-sized rock suddenly flew past his bald head. Jerek shot Kayne a look the older Highlander knew all too well.

Brodar Kayne dismounted again and this time he unsheathed his greatsword. Brick was rummaging around in the saddlebag, looking for his bow. Kayne thought about warning him to leave the weapon alone, but in the end he decided to keep quiet. Sometimes you had to trust your instincts.

'Here they come,' Jerek spat. With murder in his eyes and his scarred visage flecked with blood he looked like something out of a nightmare. In that at least, the half-dozen savages who suddenly emerged through the relentless sheets of rain were every inch his match.

The hill-men were as naked as the day they were born. Filthy hair adorned with finger bones and other strange devices reached halfway to their waists. One was noticeably smaller than the others, and it took Kayne a moment to realize she was a woman, sagging breasts swaying wetly as she inched forward beside the men, whose shrivelled cocks were mostly concealed beneath extraordinary bushes of hair. Each of the savages clutched a thick cudgel of wood or stone in an oversized hand.

'Nargh,' growled the closest savage, his jaw jutting out further than any man's ought. He shook his club at the Highlanders and their guide. The female hissed.

Jerek spat right back at them. 'Fuck off. I killed one of you pricks already. Shake that at me again and I'll shove it up your arse.'

Kayne placed a hand on his friend's shoulder. 'Let's see if we can't do this the easy way,' he whispered. He lowered his greatsword, resting the tip on the ground. 'We mean no harm,' he shouted affably. He pointed towards the north. 'We were just riding by.'

'Nargh,' said the largest of the hill-men again. He bared oversized teeth and thumped his hairy chest.

Kayne turned to Brick. 'What's he saying?'

The young bandit shrugged his narrow shoulders. He already had an arrow nocked.

'Right then,' shouted Kayne, taking a step forward. 'We don't want any trouble and besides, it's shitty weather for a fight. Sorry about your dead friend. We lost a horse, so I guess we'll call us even, eh? What do you say?'

The savages looked at one another, then began to hoot and holler and beat their weapons on the ground. The female raised a hand and they all fell silent except for the largest. She snarled and cuffed him around the back of the head and he quietened with a whimper.

Kayne relaxed a fraction. Even among these wild savages, it seemed a man knew when to listen to his wife or mother. Likely one and the same around these parts, he reckoned, noting the uncanny resemblance between the brutes.

The hill-woman scrutinized him thoughtfully. Then she shrank back, squatting down on her haunches as if preparing to grovel.

Kayne shook his head ruefully. 'There's no need for that. It was our fault for intruding—'

The woman suddenly thrust an arm forward and launched something at him. It connected with an ominous squelching sound. Kayne's eyes narrowed as he stared at the fresh shit splattered over his hide shirt. The other savages began to howl and then they too were hurling slimy brown turds or smearing excreta across their bodies.

'Fucking unbelievable,' rasped Jerek in disgust. Before Kayne could respond the savages rushed towards them. Brick's arrow struck one in the eye, dropping him lifeless, and then two of the stinking bastards were right in Kayne's face, swinging with terrible strength. The cut he had taken above his eye still leaked blood, leaving him half-blind as he blocked blows powerful enough to shatter bone, driving him back against the ridge. He parried a cudgel aimed at his head. The impact almost knocked the greatsword from his hands, which were quickly growing numb.

'Fine,' he spat between gritted teeth. 'I tried to be reasonable.' He lashed out with a boot, hitting the nearest savage firmly in the groin. The hill-man's eyes took on a distant look and his feral face twisted in agony. Kayne responded by wiping blood from his wounded eye with the back of one hand and then cleaving the dazed savage open from neck to sternum. It was a good kill, and would have merited a satisfied grunt had not his greatsword got stuck in the dead man's chest.

'Shit,' he said, giving the weapon another tug. It didn't budge.

The remaining savage slammed into him like a runaway wagon. Kayne's back crunched into the rock face behind him, the air knocked from his lungs and the greatsword torn from his wet grip.

The hill-man pressed huge palms around Kayne's throat and forced him back against the embankment, shit-smeared mouth and brown teeth straining to take a bite out his face. Kayne struggled to pry the savage's fingers loose but the brute was as strong as hell. Seemed everyone he fought was stronger than him lately. Here he was again, overpowered by a younger and more powerful man.

Still. He was Brodar Kayne, and he wasn't once named Sword of the North for nothing.

He let go of the hill-man's wrist and reached up to the savage's filthy mane. The savage squeezed harder but Kayne ignored the terrible pressure as he tugged hard on the bone charm hanging there. It came away in his hand in a tangle of slimy black hair. He turned it slightly in his shaking palm, angling the sharp point upwards.

Then he stabbed with all his remaining strength. Shoved the bone right up the bastard's left nostril.

The savage howled in agony and reached for his face. Kayne threw himself into him and both Highlander and hill-man crashed down into a great puddle. Kayne raised the sliver of bone again and thrust it down into the savage's throat. He grit his teeth as he felt it pierce flesh. Then he gave the bone a good hard drag.

It wasn't as easy as cutting with a blade. It took a while to open the savage's throat, and for the screams to become gurgles and then fall silent.

Kayne rolled away from the body. Close by, the corpse of

another savage flopped face down, a broken arrow protruding from his chest. Brick had his bow aimed at the female savage, who was edging towards him.

'Shoot her, lad,' Kayne tried to shout, but it came out as more of a ragged wheeze. His chest was hurting and he couldn't seem to catch his breath.

'She's a woman!' Brick yelled back. He sounded confused and more than a bit afraid. The wild woman hissed at him, raising a cudgel studded with nails and broken glass.

Brick wavered and then suddenly Jerek was there, muscular arms covered in blood. He caught the swing aimed at the boy's head between his axes, gave them a twist and yanked the club out of the savage's hands. She spat and snarled and tried to bite the scarred warrior, eyes filled with hatred, spittle spraying around her chin.

He head-butted her in the face.

'Mad cunt,' he muttered as she went down with a splash.

Kayne stumbled over. The woman was still alive, judging by the way her drooping breasts rose and fell, but the rest were deader than dead.

'Kayne. You okay?' Jerek had a queer expression on his face. Almost like he was worried about something.

'Fine,' the old warrior lied. His chest had stopped hurting, but now he felt light-headed – as if he needed to lie down.

They stood in silence for a time. 'Brick's horse bolted,' said Jerek eventually.

Kayne nodded. The light-headed feeling was beginning to pass. 'He can ride with me.' He walked slowly over to his mare. The beast waited patiently, unperturbed by the carnage. Jerek went to fetch his stallion, which was tossing its head skittishly.

Brick wandered over, a haunted look in his green eyes. Likely this was the first time he had killed a man, Kayne thought. He shook his head sadly. The realities of the world caught up with everyone sooner or later. He hesitated, and then placed a hand gently on Brick's shoulder. 'Lad.'

The young bandit blinked. 'Yes?

'I could use some help in wrenching a sword out of a body.'

The downpour finally stopped later that afternoon, to everyone's great relief. Every clop of the horses' hooves sent up great splashes of water, but they didn't dare slow their pace. They wanted to be out of sight of the hills before nightfall.

The cut above Kayne's eye had finally stopped bleeding, though it stung something rotten. Behind him, Brick sat Kayne's horse in silence. He had a lump on his skull the size of an egg. Between their respective wounds and the threat of savages attacking at any moment, neither had much appetite for conversation.

That changed when Brick sighted something to the east.

'Your uncle?' Kayne asked. His own eyes couldn't make out more than a faint blur, but the sudden change in the boy's expression told its own story.

Brick grinned. 'I knew he wouldn't abandon me.'

'I never doubted it. But remember, we have us a deal.'

The youngster gave him a reproachful look. 'I'll keep my word.'

'That's what I figured. Or I'd never have given you your bow back.'

'I... I've never killed anyone before.'

Kayne nodded. He'd been expecting this. 'You did what you had to do,' he said levelly. 'Those savages didn't give us much choice in the matter. There's a lot of dubious reasons for killing, but self-defence ain't never been one of 'em. I hope you never need to learn about the others.'

'How many men have you killed?'

Kayne stared into the distance. 'I try not to think about it.'

They travelled in silence for a time, Jerek riding some way ahead. The darkening sky was as clear as the surface of a lake. Tomorrow promised to be glorious.

'I hope you find them. Your wife and boy, I mean.'

Kayne glanced back at Brick, surprised. There was a wistful

look on the bandit's face. Likely he was remembering his own family. 'I hope so too,' said Kayne. 'You got a mother or father?'

'No. They're both dead.'

'Sorry to hear.'

'They were murdered,' Brick added. 'During the Unification War, when Asander united all the Badlands under his banner. I was only a babe then. My uncle Glaston raised me.'

'I ain't never met a bandit like your uncle.'

Brick's face lit up and Kayne couldn't help but grin, knowing he was in for a story. Magnar had been the same once. He would run to greet his father, eyes shining with excitement, bursting to share all the mischief he and the other lads had got up to without their mothers knowing. Kayne remembered the moment his son had stopped confiding in him. Had clammed up whenever his father entered the room. The smile slowly faded.

'You might not believe this,' Brick began, youthful voice full of enthusiasm, 'but my distant ancestors were nobles from Kingsport.'

'Kingsport?'

'The capital city of Andarr. It was the most powerful kingdom in the north. Well, except for Mal-Torrad.'

'Andarr's twenty feet under water. Has been for the last five hundred years.'

'Not everyone died when the sea flooded the land. My ancestors escaped and helped settle the Unclaimed Lands.'

'Aye?'

'They helped fund the construction of Emmering. But after it was built the settlers chased them out of the city.'

Kayne grunted at the young bandit to continue. He raised a hand to shield his eyes from the sun. There was no sign of the boy's uncle.

'The townsfolk rejected my ancestors' rule,' Brick explained. If he noticed his uncle's sudden disappearance, he gave no indication. 'They declared that no man of the Unclaimed Lands would ever bend knee to another.'

'That don't seem very grateful,' Kayne said, though privately he thought those settlers had the right of it. He'd spent a few months in Dorminia and seen some things he wasn't much fond of. As far as he was concerned, any system of rule where kids starved on the streets while a handful got fat needed a good fixing.

'My family has noble blood,' said Brick. 'That's why the Bandit King had my parents murdered. The Seer foretold a prophecy about the scions of Andarr.'

Kayne raised an eyebrow. 'A prophecy, eh?'

Brick nodded. 'The Seer foretold that one day the true rulers of the north would return and scour the land in a storm of blood and fire. She said I would be the catalyst. Or at least that's what my uncle told me. I was only four and I hardly remember.'

Kayne said nothing. The boy's story sounded improbable: more than likely a flight of fancy dreamed up by this Glaston fellow.

Fifty yards ahead of them Jerek slowed his stallion to a walk. The Wolf turned in his saddle and pointed at something on the side of the scratchy path they followed. It was the body of a hill-man, his legs shattered and his head mashed into a bloody pulp.

They rode on in silence, passing two more bodies. One had been savagely beaten with a blunt object. The other's legs splayed unnaturally, his pelvis split from the impact of whatever had struck him. Kayne frowned at the sight. 'You ever get giants this far south?' he asked Brick. The red-haired youngster shook his head and fidgeted nervously.

A moment later they spotted the architect of the carnage.

'Wait here,' Kayne grunted to Brick. He exchanged a look with Jerek and then the two Highlanders slid from their horses, faces set in grim masks.

The killer stood unmoving in the middle of the path. Kayne had seen some big bastards in the last few months – none bigger than the monstrous Sumnian general who had led the assault on

Dorminia – but he reckoned the stranger that regarded them on the road just then could match any of them for sheer strength. Huge muscles rippled below green skin, ham-sized fists clutching a spiked club big enough to make even Kayne's greatsword look like some noble fop's fencing steel. The odd humanoid looked even more savage than the hill-men, what with his jutting jaw and two tusks protruding above his upper lip, but Kayne noted a keen mind at work behind those amber eyes.

'You heading north?' Kayne said casually. The stranger made a sound halfway between a growl and a moan.

'He asked you a question.' Jerek took a step forward, axes raised.

The stranger's yellow eyes narrowed dangerously but eventually he nodded. Then he glanced at the sack resting on the ground nearby. There was something round and bulky within.

'Mind telling us what's in the sack?' Kayne asked.

The stranger made another moaning sound. He shifted the massive club in his hands, giving it a threatening shake. Scraps of flesh clung to the iron spikes studding the wood. One scrap shook loose, a piece of scalp with oily hair still attached.

'He doesn't have a tongue,' Brick piped up suddenly. 'That's why he moans. He can't speak.'

Kayne looked from Brick to the big green warrior. 'Those savages attack you too?'

The stranger nodded again and a made a series of movements with his left hand, ending with a clenched fist.

Brick turned to Kayne. 'He says he had no choice but to kill them. The hill-men thought he was a demon.'

'How'd you know that?'

'The Bandit King cuts the tongue from any man who dares speak against him. Raff and Slater taught me the mute language.'

Kayne turned back to the stranger. 'You got a horse?'

The stranger shook his head, gestured towards the hills and drew a thick thumb across his throat.

'So they killed your mount. Now you're forced to go it on foot.' Kayne pointed at the sack. 'Must be heavy work, hauling that thing around.'

That got a suspicious look, but eventually the stranger nodded.

Kayne looked from Brick to Jerek. The boy seemed intrigued. Jerek shook his head grimly and shot him a look the older man knew well.

Kayne hesitated. 'We could travel together,' he said eventually, knowing what he was letting himself in for. 'Until we're out of the Badlands. Ain't much farther now.'

Right on cue, Jerek heaved a disgusted sigh. 'Fucking knew this would happen,' he rasped. 'Not even a quarter of the way to the Fangs and already we're collecting orphan bandits and green bastards like some kind of travelling circus. Might as well go back to Dorminia, find us a one-legged whore, maybe a troupe of midgets. Fuck's sake.'

'Calm, Wolf,' Kayne whispered to his friend. 'We could use the help if any more of those savages try their luck. And I've got a mind to know what's in that sack.'

'I'll tell you what's in the sack,' Jerek grated. 'A chopped-up corpse or some other shit we're better off not knowing about. Always is.'

'Could be that you're right. But let's give him a chance.'

Jerek spat. 'Bastard stinks worse than those hill-men. Make sure he keeps out of my way.' Having released some anger, the Wolf turned his back on them and stalked over to his horse.

Kayne walked up to the green-skinned warrior. 'My name's Kayne. The lad here is Brick. My comrade over there is Jerek. Don't mind him, he takes a while to warm to new faces. What's your name, friend?'

The stranger replied with a series of groans that sounded like a cross between a cow dying and a bear taking a shit.

Kayne listened politely. Then he looked questioningly at Brick, who shrugged and shook his head.

'Er, well met then.' He stuck out a hand towards the stranger, who after a moment's hesitation grasped it in his own. The crushing grip made the old Highlander wince. He cleared his throat uncertainly. 'I, ah... don't suppose you mind if we call you Grunt?'

The Butcher King

THE TOWN REEKED of death.

Yllandris hurried towards the western gate, the hood of her purple shawl pulled tight around her head. The silk garment was filthy, stained with old blood and still wet with tears. The sounds of battle grew audible as she neared the gate. The cries of dying men and the howls of the Brethren echoed from beyond Heartstone's walls.

Even with her hood pulled up, Yllandris had to raise a hand to her mouth as she skirted the edge of the great pit just outside the gates. Bodies had been piled within, Highlander and beast and even the odd demonkin, foul creatures the colour of raw meat that putrefied hours after death. Though thick black flies swarmed over the corpses of the fallen warriors and Brethren, even they steered well clear of the liquefying remains of the demonkin.

Yllandris caught a glimpse of the small pile of bones stacked in the corner of the pit and stifled a sudden sob. She glanced away, struggling to hold back fresh tears. The faces of the three children she had been forced to round up for the Herald forced their way into her mind.

'Are you crying?' asked a young voice. Yllandris quickly wiped her face and saw that the speaker was Corinn, a girl of around twelve winters who had recently been orphaned after her father had perished fighting the Shaman's forces a week earlier.

'Just dust in my eye,' Yllandris lied. 'What are you doing here? This place is not safe for children.'

'I'm not a child,' Corinn said. 'I'm a woman near grown.'

You're a girl, Yllandris thought angrily. *You have no idea what it means to be a woman. The sacrifices we must make.*

'You have experienced your first blooding?'

At Corinn's hesitant shake of the head, Yllandris pointed towards the south and east. 'Then you are a child. You should be at the Foundry.'

The ancient factory had become a refuge of sorts for Heartstone's increasing population of orphans. The forges burned day and night, churning out weapons and armour to supply the warriors that continued to flood into Heartstone from the Lake Reaching. The orphans had found new purpose within the Foundry's smoky walls, offering their assistance to the smiths that toiled within. It was hard and dangerous work, but it earned them a meal of an evening and a spot on the floor at night. Even during the short summer months, sundown in the Heartlands saw temperatures fall to near freezing.

'I went to help our men,' Corinn said. She dropped her blue eyes to the ground and bit her lower lip. 'My mother taught me how to clean and stitch a wound.'

Yllandris stared at the girl, noting the blood on her dress, which was tattered and torn. Even so, Corinn, with her warm eyes and blonde hair, was pretty. She reminded Yllandris of her younger self. 'You should leave the healing of the wounded to the sorceresses,' she said sternly.

Corinn pushed a strand of hair from her face and frowned. 'No one helped my father,' she said, her voice trembling slightly.

Yllandris knew what the girl was thinking. *The men Krazka spared when he seized Heartstone have been sent out here to die. They are sacrificial pawns, a distraction meant to slow the Shaman's forces while Krazka marshals the Reachings that have declared for him.*

She searched for words, something to soothe the obvious

hurt in this young woman's eyes. This was unfamiliar territory. She had never given much thought to how others might feel before now. 'Your father was a brave man,' she ventured. 'Honour his memory by staying out of harm's way.'

Yllandris hurried past Corinn and the scowling warriors guarding the gate and ascended the hill that rose just beyond the high wooden palisade. This distraction had cost her precious time. She would be punished severely if she were late for Shranree's summons. The leader of the King's circle and most powerful sorceress in the High Fangs took great pleasure in chastising Yllandris at every opportunity.

The hill was steep, quickly rising to provide the best view of the King's Reaching for miles around. Heartstone sprawled beneath her to the east, the waters of Lake Dragur beyond shining golden in the sun. Rolling valleys spread out to the south, eventually giving way to the Green Reaching, where winter's grip was shorter and less severe than elsewhere in the High Fangs.

It was to the north and west that the attention of the women atop the hill was now focused. Battle thundered between the Shaman's forces and Heartstone's defenders, bolstered by demonkin summoned from the Devil's Spine by their gigantic master. While the King's Reaching was currently a focal point for the fighting, the civil war that had erupted since Krazka had stolen the throne from Magnar raged throughout much of the Heartlands.

As she ascended the hill the huge bulk of the Herald suddenly rose above the Great Lodge and hung ominously in the air. Bat-shaped wings the width of a field beat a susurrating rhythm, twenty feet of scaled horror turning slowly to stare with a triumvirate of burning eyes right at her, seeming to strip her soul bare. The demon lord's snaking tail probed the air. Its slavering maw, filled with teeth like ivory daggers, almost seemed to *grin* at her, and Yllandris wanted to turn and flee back down the hill screaming.

Having surveyed the town, the demon lord shot up into the sky and soared eastwards, casting a colossal shadow below as it passed. Nothing would impede its passage; nothing would dare seek to challenge it. The Shaman himself had tasted the Herald's power during their brief struggle in the skies north of town, and even that immortal godkiller had been found wanting.

It took Yllandris a minute or two to recover herself enough to resume her climb, moving unsteadily on legs that felt like jelly. It cost her precious time, a fact that didn't go unnoticed by the stout little woman in command of the sorceresses gathered on the top of the hill.

'The prodigal daughter finally graces us with her presence,' Shranree declared as Yllandris scrambled to join her sisters. The thirty sorceresses that formed the King's circle turned to regard her. Yllandris tried not to wilt under their scrutiny.

'My apologies,' she said. 'I lost track of time.'

Shranree raised a perfectly shaped eyebrow. It looked strangely out of place on that pink, fleshy face. 'You seem distracted of late. Is there something on your mind?'

Something on my mind? My lover has been mutilated. All that was once promised to me has been torn away. The foundlings... Yllandris swallowed another sob, forcing herself not to react to the woman's provocation. 'Nothing, sister. I apologize for my tardiness.'

Shranree appeared mildly disappointed. Yllandris thought she might leave matters there, but then the rotund little sorceress beckoned at her with a stubby finger. 'Come here.'

Yllandris did as she was commanded. She could feel the other women watching her.

Shranree studied her for moment or two. 'The last few weeks have been unkind to you.'

'I'm sorry?'

'Why, you carry bags under your eyes, girl. Your hair is frankly a mess. And as for that complexion... I am beginning to wonder what the menfolk ever saw in you.'

71

Yllandris's lower lip quivered. She reached up to her face and ran chewed fingernails over her skin. She hadn't painted her eyes or lips in days. There didn't seem any point now. Her fingers brushed the rough patch on her cheek. It itched constantly. Sometimes she lay awake at night, scratching at it until it bled.

Shranree tutted softly, a ghost of a smile in her cruel eyes. 'You poor creature. You are like a snow-flower wilting in the harsh light of the sun. You had best toughen up. There is no cunt-struck fool of a king to shelter you now.'

Yllandris reeled back as if struck, shocked at the venom in the woman's words. In her mind she saw Magnar's mutilated body again. At first she had wanted him for the power that he represented, but now she realized that somewhere deep down she had loved him. At least a little. What had Shranree called him? *A cunt-struck fool of a king.*

'You evil hag,' she whispered. 'I hate you.'

This time Shranree made no effort to conceal her contempt. 'Silly girl. Your whorish behaviour shamed the circle. Those days are over. You *will* learn to obey.'

The senior sorceress raised her hands. Yllandris took a step back, suddenly afraid. A familiar tingling sensation filled the air. Everyone who possessed the gift could sense magic being evoked. 'What are you—'

Her words were torn from her mouth in a gasp of agony. Her joints suddenly felt like they were on fire. Every muscle in her body seemed on the verge of ripping apart. She collapsed to her knees, clawing at the mud, tearing up great clumps of grass in her fists. She opened her mouth and screamed until her throat was raw.

'Sister... is this necessary?' queried one of the sorceresses from the Black Reaching in a small voice.

'She must be disciplined. I take no pleasure in this.'

Yllandris managed to twist her neck to stare up into Shranree's satisfied gaze, which exposed the lie for what it was. She could hardly breathe; her body felt as though it was going to implode.

Seconds passed and the magical assault did not relent. In desperation Yllandris prepared to evoke her own magic and unleash it against Shranree. She knew such an act would force the elder sister to kill her, but she would rather die struggling than meekly accept death.

'What's going on here?' boomed a male voice.

Shranree's eyes narrowed. 'This is none of your concern, Kingsman.'

A big warrior Yllandris recognized – his name was Yorn – had arrived on the hilltop and was watching the spectacle with a deep frown on his bearded face. She had never much liked him, for he had never shown her the attention she was accustomed to from men, but just then Yorn seemed like a blessing sent by the spirits. 'Please,' she mouthed at him through the agony. 'Please... help me.'

'Last thing the King needs is to waste any of his sorceresses,' Yorn rumbled. 'Release her.'

Shranree huffed and tutted but eventually snapped her fingers. Instantly, the magical pressure vanished. Yllandris gulped in air, wiping at her bloody nose with her shawl. Yorn walked over and reached down a weathered hand. Yllandris grasped it and he pulled her to her feet with surprising gentleness. Her limbs felt as heavy as lead.

'I trust you will heed this lesson,' said Shranree. The leader of the King's circle dabbed at her perspiring face with the sleeves of her robe and gave Yllandris a look that chilled her blood. 'Do not force me to rebuke you again. I will not be so forgiving next time.'

The harsh cry of a horn thundered up the hill. Yorn placed a hand on the hilt of his broadsword. 'The King comes.'

The gathered sorceresses fell to their knees as the self-proclaimed King of the High Fangs crested the summit, moving with the grace of a dancer, his magnificent white cloak billowing behind him.

King Krazka placed a gloved hand on the hilt of the sword at his hip and grinned. His dead left eye wept and rolled madly in its socket, but it was the right that unnerved Yllandris, leering at the assembled women as if they were meat rather than the most powerful practitioners of magic in the land.

Behind the Butcher King trailed his Kingsmen. Krazka's champions made a mockery of a tradition that had endured for centuries. The Six were expected to be the most stalwart men in the Heartlands; warriors of renown who had proven themselves in battle countless times. The ragtag collection of killers the usurper King had brought with him from the Lake Reaching looked formidable, but they seemed as likely to stab the King in the back as take a sword thrust for him. They weren't even wearing the ceremonial armour and closed helms. Most likely Krazka wanted to be certain the armed men who spent countless hours in his shadow were who they said they were. After all, he had seized the throne by dint of a similar deception.

Yllandris felt her skin crawl as the King's roving eye settled on her. 'Huh. You used to be a pretty little thing. Looking rougher than a dog's arse these days.'

Shranree's voice was sickly sweet. 'My apologies if her screams displeased you, my king.'

Krazka drew his sword and stared at his reflection in the grey metal. A few spots of blood ran down the blade, which appeared to have seen recent use. 'Ain't the first time I've heard a woman shriek,' he said wistfully.

That drew sharp intakes of breath, followed by an uncomfortable silence. Shranree's smile stayed fixed on her face but now there was something like fear there. Yllandris remembered the severed head of the sorceress Thurva rolling on the ground, seeming to take forever to come to a halt. Krazka's deadly sword had devoured her magic like a hungry wolf. Slid through her neck with hideous ease.

'We await your command,' Shranree said quietly. The blustering leader of the largest circle of sorceresses ever assembled in

Heartstone appeared cowed, as if she were a young maid seeing her lover's exposed cock for the first time.

'I'll make this short and sweet,' Krazka growled. 'I've just received some unfortunate news.'

'My king?' queried Shranree.

Krazka scowled and pointed his sword towards the north. 'The Shaman has won the support of the Black Reaching.'

There were gasps from the circle. 'But Mace already declared for you,' said Shranree. 'He sent six of his sorceresses.' She gestured behind her, where several women now wore very worried expressions.

'He changed his mind.'

There was an explosion to the west and smoke rose from a large hole that had appeared in the ground. Bodies were strewn around the hole, though it was hard to be certain of the identities of the dead at this distance. Krazka stared at the carnage for a moment. 'How many sorceresses has Carn Bloodfist got?' he asked conversationally.

'I believe there may be upwards of twenty in the West Reaching,' Shranree answered.

Krazka nodded. 'And how many do you reckon are out there now?'

Shranree shook her head. 'I cannot be certain. They cloak themselves in magic. Samaya, the leader of their circle, is a skilled illusionist.'

Krazka turned and faced the circle, finally sheathing his magic-devouring sword to sighs of relief. Yllandris watched it all with dull eyes. She felt empty. It would scarcely have mattered to her if the Butcher King had strolled over and cut her throat right then.

'The Herald's returning to the Spine,' Krazka grunted. 'He won't be back for a while.'

Shranree looked flustered. 'But, my king, the Shaman...'

'Aye, he's out there somewhere.' Krazka cracked his fingers absently-mindedly. 'I reckon our one-time Magelord will see this as a good time to show his ugly face again.'

Shranree's double chin wobbled nervously. 'This is ill news. We are thirty in number, the greatest circle ever assembled in my lifetime. But between the Shaman and Samaya's own circle, we may yet be overwhelmed. I fear they will marshal their forces for an all-out assault once they learn of the Herald's departure.'

The Butcher King grinned suddenly. 'I'm counting on it.' He turned and beckoned to his Kingsmen. They stepped forward, and Yllandris saw that one carried a small bundle wrapped in cloth. Krazka gestured and the Kingsman – a pale-faced warrior with bloodshot eyes who seemed vaguely familiar – tugged the bundle open, revealing an assortment of rings. They glittered grey in the sun.

'The Herald brought me these,' said Krazka. 'They're abyssium, same as my blade. They can only absorb so much magic before they break, but I reckon they'll serve the purpose I have in mind.'

Yllandris watched as the King's Six each took a ring from the pile. There was something else there, a larger steel object with a strange cylindrical barrel, but Krazka quickly folded the cloth back and it disappeared from sight.

Yorn walked over to join the Six. She noticed Vard was missing and recalled that he been sent to the Black Reaching and was due back any time now. As she stared at Krazka and remembered the fresh blood on his sword, it was then she realized what had happened. *The mad bastard killed his own Kingsman. Vard brought him the news about Mace and he murdered him in a fit of rage. Yorn is his replacement.*

The King was facing his men now, his back to the sorceresses. The sun was beginning to set, bathing the hill the colour of blood. 'When the Shaman makes his move,' Krazka said, 'we're gonna spring a nasty surprise. Mace wants to throw his sword in with that fucker? I'll burn his entire Reaching to the ground. Just as soon as I'm done with Carn Bloodfist.' He turned slowly, and the look in his eye pierced even the apathy that had settled over Yllandris.

'First we need to test that these rings work,' Krazka announced. 'All you sorceresses from the Black Reaching, raise your hands.'

None of the women did so. Krazka sighed and gestured at Shranree. 'How about you just point them out? Save us all some time.'

Shranree hesitated for only a moment, then spun and began pointing at women and calling out names. 'Henetha. Marella. Quinell...'

Krazka's Six moved forward, weapons raised. The circle parted, sorceresses stumbling away to leave the women from the Black Reaching utterly exposed.

Don't watch, Yllandris told herself. She met Yorn's eyes for a moment. Was that disgust on his face? She remembered his words. *Last thing the King needs is to waste any of his sorceresses.*

A monster of a man barged past her, taller than Yorn and near as wide as an ox, face split in a wide grin. He was joined by another of the Six, a middle-aged man wearing heavy plate-metal armour like the knights of the Lowlands her mother used to tell her stories of.

A moment later the screams began as the Six went to work. Yllandris focused on Krazka, at the bloodlust in that lone eye. She had hated the Shaman once, plotted to end his life so that she and Magnar could rule free of the whims of a ruthless immortal. It had been a childish notion. As she stared at Krazka, the man who had disfigured her lover and taken his throne and sacrificed innocent children to a demon, she would have given her own life to watch the Magelord crush this mad king.

Krazka caught her watching him. He shot her an obscene wink. 'At least they'll die fast,' he drawled. 'Better than the fate your boy's stuck with.'

Yllandris swore then that she would see Krazka dead.

Whatever it took.

Cold Truths, Warm Lies

THE COLLECTORS WERE out in force, wraith-like in the early-morning mist with their charcoal robes and featureless hoods. Corpse wagons strained under the weight of dozens of bodies. Some were blackened things charred beyond recognition, but it was the corpses that still had flesh clinging to them that really made the Halfmage's stomach churn.

Jobs might be scarce, the poor desperate enough to volunteer for a voyage into the unknown just to fill their bellies. But the Collectors, the shepherds of the dead, they never want for work.

He glanced at the women beside him as he wheeled himself over the cobbles. Sasha had offered to push his chair for him, the earnestness in her voice surprising him enough that he forgot to feel patronized. It was an easy journey to the harbour from the depository and the road sloped gently downhill much of the way. Though he was tired from the night's activities, he thought it better than to sit back and catch some sleep, lest he never wake again. He knew the mind of the older sister scowling at him all too well.

Imagine the awe on the faces of the drunks who witnessed the three of us entering the depository together in the early hours of the morning. I would help spread a scurrilous rumour, but I suspect my legend is already stretched to the very edge of plausibility.

'What are you smiling at? I'm still not sure I buy your story, Halfmage.'

Eremul's amusement drained away. He frowned back at Cyreena or Ambryl or whatever she was calling herself these days. He was still struggling with the bizarre circumstances in which the sisters had been reunited – a turn of events that could rival any of the hero's tales he had read for sheer absurdity.

'You've seen the evidence,' he replied. He patted his robe, where the page he had removed from the tome back at the depository lay carefully wrapped beside the grisly trophy they had cut from the rebel's corpse earlier that night.

'I've seen an illustration in a dusty old book. A book that is more than likely a flight of fancy, intended to mislead gullible fools into believing in some mythic past rather than facing the mundane truth.'

Eremul frowned. 'Mundanity is a matter of perspective, especially when one is a wizard. Besides, Saltierre was no Kenats.'

Kenats had been a historian who had gained fame for presenting previously unknown facts about the Age of Legends. Later it had been discovered that he had fabricated almost everything he had written, employing an army of stooges to 'corroborate' his research. The fraud had ended up in a prison in Kingsport, and was eventually stabbed to death by a disgruntled inmate distraught to learn that the many-breasted wandering succubus did not in fact exist.

'I distrust the word of any man who chooses to isolate himself with nothing but a quill and his imagination for company,' Cyreena stated. 'I can think of no vocation quite so emasculating.'

'Then *you* of all people should have no issue with scribes of every stripe,' Eremul snapped back. The woman was starting to grate on his nerves. 'We have irrefutable evidence that the rebels are connected to the Fade. The script on that tattoo is a perfect match with the ancient Fade script Saltierre transcribed in his book. I only wish he had recorded the meaning. With any luck, the White Lady will possess the means to translate it.'

Sasha blinked a few times, disentangling herself from the

dark thoughts Eremul knew preoccupied her. She had said little since they had left the depository. 'I believe you. I knew there was something strange about Isaac.'

Eremul grimaced at the mention of his erstwhile manservant. 'The legends state certain among the Fade possessed an ability to beguile that is akin to magic. I believe Isaac manipulated me for years. You recall I sent him to the Wailing Rift with you back in the summer? No doubt that was his intention all along. He wished to guide events towards his own ends... whatever they were.'

The pain that flashed across Sasha's face at his mention of the Rift surprised the Halfmage, and he said nothing more for a time. He watched the harbourside sprawl, noting once again the sorry state in which the city found itself. Dorminia was still reeling from the destruction caused by the catapults and ballistae the Thelassan army had unleashed. Last night's arson attacks had hit hard; the damage was extensive. He watched as a Collector hauled the body of a woman from the husk of yet another burned-out building.

Sasha shook her head. 'The common folk can't take much more. I thought the worst was behind us.'

'Trust me when I say the worst is always to come. Be grateful you weren't visiting Shadowport when Salazar dropped a billion tons of water on the city.'

'I heard the White Lady is sending ships to look for survivors,' Cyreena said. Her mouth twisted angrily. 'A wasted gesture on her part, when there are many in Dorminia that require her aid.'

'Be sure to raise the point *after* you've relayed to her my warning,' said Eremul. He knew Cyreena despised Thelassa's Magelord – the White Lady had after all succeeded in offing her master – but he didn't want the woman jeopardizing the delivery of his message. The one-time Augmentor had lost none of her self-assurance following Salazar's death. For that, he had to admit to a grudging admiration. Augmentors that had been severed from their bondmagic often went insane.

Though, I suppose one might ask how you can break the mind of someone who is already a thousand glittering shards of crazy.

He was suddenly reminded of the Grand Regent's words – the accusation that he himself was a loony, and his subsequent ignoble departure from the Grand Council Chamber. He would never be permitted to return to the Obelisk. Furthermore, if he didn't keep a low profile, a permanent visit to the tower's dungeons seemed a distinct possibility. Timerus was known to be a petty, vengeful little man.

In that, I suspect, we are alike.

'Are you sure the harbourmaster's office will be open?' Sasha asked. She looked decidedly worse for wear. Her eyes were blurred from lack of sleep and, if Eremul was any judge, moon dust comedown. He had experimented with narcotics himself during his lowest ebbs but found them all wholly underwhelming. Nothing could compare with the thrill of magic dancing through one's veins.

'I've lived here for thirteen years,' the Halfmage replied. He swallowed the barbed comment he was about to make, a reminder about the boat he had arranged for her and her unlikely band of companions scarce two months past. There was no need to bring up the Wailing Rift again.

A few minutes later they arrived at the docks. The harbour was ghostly quiet compared with the previous morning. The Thelassan ships had all departed and were now sailing west, crossing the Broken Sea towards the Endless Ocean. The few ships that were left, the remains of Dorminia's once-great armada, were a sorry sight to behold.

'It stinks of fish,' Cyreena complained.

'I can't smell a thing,' Sasha replied, rubbing at her nose. Eremul looked from one sister to the other. It was easy to see the resemblance now. Cyreena was ten years older, her hair blonde rather than the dark brown of her sister's, but the similarities were obvious. It was the eyes where they truly differed. Sasha's held a sadness unaccountably deep for one so young, yet there was also a sparkle there that even recent events had not entirely dulled. Cyreena's stare, on the other hand, carried nothing but deep malice. By Eremul's reckoning, she was a sociopath.

'Those warehouses store the fishermen's haul,' the Halfmage explained, gesturing to a huddle of huge wooden buildings covered in bird shit. 'Whatever they can dredge up from the Broken Sea. The fishermen's catch grows smaller with each passing year.'

'There are men up there,' Sasha whispered, pointing to the roofs of the warehouses. Figures milled around, crossbows at the ready.

'Crimson Watchmen,' Eremul said. 'Famine is coming. Fresh fish will soon be a luxury only the rich can afford. There will be rioting in the streets.'

Even as they made their way towards the harbourmaster's office, they passed beggars covered in rags and streetwalkers soliciting the handful of longshoremen that worked the docks this early hour. Cyreena's expression suggested she would like to drown the women in the harbour.

The offices were located in a smaller building set back a little from the waterfront. 'Let me do the talking,' Eremul said, allowing his gaze to linger sternly on Cyreena.

He pushed open the door and wheeled himself into the reception area. This early in the morning it was thankfully deserted, with the exception of a stern-faced secretary sucking a cigarillo and a dark-haired woman sitting on a wooden bench pushed up against the far wall. She peered over her reading lenses as they entered.

Eremul approached the receptionist's desk. Sasha and Cyreena waited just behind him. The secretary was a large woman, fair-skinned and sporting an unruly mass of red hair that indicated Andarran heritage.

The secretary plucked the cigarillo from her mouth with one chubby hand and heaved a dramatic sigh at the sheer temerity of the public in disturbing her smoke. 'Yes?' she asked, voice full of righteous indignation.

Eremul forced his mouth into what he hoped passed for a smile. 'A good morning to you! I would like to speak with the harbourmaster if possible.'

'Come back later.' The receptionist waved a hand dismissively and stuck the cigarillo back in her mouth.

'This is a matter of some urgency.'

'Are you deaf? I said come back later.' The receptionist noticed her cigarillo had gone out. She tutted and began to fumble for her tinderbox.

The Halfmage reached forward and grasped the end of the cigarillo between his fingertips. He evoked slightly, teasing the magic out, shaping it into a fire spell. The tips of his fingers glowed red for a brief moment. Then he pulled his hand away and fixed the secretary with his most imperious stare. She looked at her cigarillo in astonishment. The end was now burning brightly.

'Who are you?' she whispered.

'They call me the Halfmage. You may have heard of me.'

The woman on the bench turned to stare at him. The secretary's mouth quivered, her chins wobbling. 'You... *you* are the famous Halfmage? The wizard that killed Salazar?'

'That's right,' he said. He wasn't too big a man to accept a little adulation now and then.

'But you're a cripple!'

The smug smile on Eremul's face evaporated. 'And you're a fat cow,' he snapped back. 'Why the fuck do you think I'm called the Halfmage?' He glared at the secretary. 'You tell the harbourmaster I want to see him this instant. Or else I'll show you exactly why the Tyrant of Dorminia begged for death come the end.' The last part was an afterthought. If he was going to bullshit his way through this, he might as well commit to the performance.

The receptionist reached under the desk with a shaking hand and withdrew a large iron key. She pushed it over the counter towards him. 'This is the key to his office,' she said, voice trembling. 'It's just down the hall, first door on the left.'

Eremul took the key from her unresisting fingers and nodded at the sisters. Then he manoeuvred his chair awkwardly around, accidentally bumped into the desk, somewhat spoiling the moment, and sped off down the passage beyond the reception area. He found the room he was looking for and placed the key in the lock. It clicked open with a twist, and he entered. Sasha and Cyreena followed behind him.

Sitting beside a table stacked high with paperwork, half-empty bottles of wine and what looked suspiciously like a pile of moon dust, was an ugly little man with a bandage around his right hand. His eyes were closed; he apparently wasn't yet aware he had guests. Eremul and the sisters watched him for a moment or two. The rhythmic wet noises from beneath the desk were the only sounds in the room.

'I'm going to assume that woman hanging off your cock isn't the wife you spoke so fondly of.'

Lashan's eyes shot open. 'What the fuck!'

A head emerged, dirty brown hair and a dusting of white powder covering a face that had seen better days. The hooker wiped her mouth and smiled stupidly. 'You want me to carry on, milord?'

'No! Get the fuck out!' Lashan cried. The whore scrambled out from beneath the desk and hurried from the room. Lashan began to fumble with his breeches, fixing Eremul with a stare of utter loathing. 'What are you doing here, you bastard half-man?'

'I'm looking for the harbourmaster. Mardok, I believe.'

'He's dead.'

'Dead?'

'Coughed up his guts. I'm the new harbourmaster.'

Eremul frowned. Several influential figures had been strategically poisoned by agents of the White Lady months ago. The poison could replicate the effects of a common cold for months before necrosis occurred. While Timerus had assured the council that all traces of the black lung toxin had been destroyed, hardly a week passed without another high-ranking official turning up dead.

'I need a ship chartered to Thelassa,' Eremul said. 'Today.'

Lashan was still fiddling with his breeches, the act greatly complicated by his injured hand. His pupils had the dilated look of someone high on *hashka*. 'You're asking me for a favour? After you broke half my fingers? I never found that shit-eater Isaac or the gold he owed. I couldn't even afford a physician for my hand. You can suck my—'

Cyreena walked over to Lashan, grabbed a bottle of wine, and smashed it over the edge of the table. Red wine sprayed all over the man's face and tunic. Before he could react, Cyreena placed the broken end of the bottle right up against his naked manhood.

'You'll have a ship ready to sail within the hour,' Cyreena hissed. The expression on her face could have killed the passion of a thousand raging cocks stone dead. 'If you don't, I'll slice off your balls and force them down your throat until you choke on them.'

Eremul raised an eyebrow. 'She'll do it,' he said. 'If you think I'm irascible after our last encounter, let me tell you – you haven't seen anything yet.'

'I hate you,' whispered Lashan.

'I trust you have everything you need.'

Sasha nodded. She clutched the satchel Eremul had given to her back at the depository. It contained a map of Thelassa, a pouch filled with coins, and enough food to last a week.

Cyreena had already boarded the small caravel that had been hastily commissioned for them. The dusky-skinned captain scowled down from the forecastle. He was a wine merchant, and had agreed to stop off in Thelassa on the way back to Djanka, a small nation on the west coast of the Shattered Realms to the south.

Eremul handed Sasha the papers authorizing the ship to dock

at Thelassa. Lashan had required little in the way of persuasion to put his signature to the document; Cyreena had drawn blood by that point. For a brief moment Eremul had thought he might be required to intervene. Lashan was a pathetic creature, but there were certain things you just didn't do to a man.

'How did that odious fellow know you?' Sasha asked. She seemed about to say something else only to change her mind at the last moment.

Eremul glanced up at the sky. Dark clouds were starting to roll in and a wind had picked up. A storm would break soon. 'He came looking for Isaac. Just before the city fell to the White Lady. I didn't appreciate his tone. Before he fled, he mentioned a contact of Isaac's going by the name "the Crow". I don't suppose you've heard of him?'

Sasha shook her head, causing her brown hair to dance around her face in the sudden breeze that swept across the harbour. The caravel swayed on the rippling water and the captain coughed loudly, clearly impatient to depart.

'Time to go,' Eremul said. He reached into his robes and took out the parchment with the transcribed Fade script. Then he withdrew the glass jar containing the tattoo they had cut from the rebel's body. The jar was filled with salt to preserve the flesh.

'Bring these to the White Lady,' he instructed. 'Repeat to her exactly what I told you.'

'What if she doesn't believe us?'

'Then you had best pray your sister is right and that my suspicions are but the crazed delusions of the mentally unstable.'

'You could come with us.'

It was Eremul's turn to shake his head. 'As I've already articulated, Thelassa is no place for a wizard. The White Lady would not tolerate me in her city.'

Sasha hesitated again, and this time Eremul decided to take pity on her. 'Look, I'm sorry about Davarus Cole. I have told you all that I know. The city was in a state of chaos that night. Anything might have befallen him.'

'No one will ever know what he did for us.'

'Fame is overrated,' Eremul replied. 'The fact of the matter is that the Council, and more specifically the White Lady, do not want it known that a boy slew the mightiest wizard in the north. Why, the wrong sort might start getting ideas.'

'So that's it?' Sasha's jaw clenched angrily. 'Cole is just forgotten about?'

The Halfmage stared at the girl. 'I'll make sure people learn the truth,' he said eventually. 'Not now, but someday. You'll just have to trust me.'

Cyreena appeared on the caravel's deck, a deep frown of irritation on her face. 'Are you coming, sister? We've already spent more time in this charlatan's company than is healthy.'

Sasha gave Eremul a slow nod as if to say that she did indeed trust him – a gesture that for some reason he found strangely gratifying. Then she climbed the gangplank to board the ship.

'You should arrive at Thelassa by nightfall,' Eremul called up. 'Hurry to the palace. As fast as your legs will carry you.'

'That's rich coming from you, Halfmage,' shouted Cyreena as the sails unfurled and the ship slowly turned to face the south.

Eremul was surprised to find that he had a faint smile on his face. 'Just bring my message to the White Lady. Do it for Dorminia, if not for me.'

It was hard to be sure, but he thought Cyreena might have raised an eyebrow at that. 'You've grown,' she said grudgingly, the words almost swallowed by the wind.

He watched the ship drift slowly out of the harbour, gathering speed as the wind buffeted the sails. He was taken aback by Cyreena's final words. They had sounded almost complimentary. He thought about giving the sisters a wave to send them on their way, but decided that would be a conciliatory gesture too far. Instead he turned his back on them and began to make his way across the docks.

What a night that was. The screams. The stench of scorched flesh wafting on the air. Alarming discoveries made in the middle of the night. All in all, some remarkable similarities to the night Salazar had had him taken to the Obelisk dungeons and burned his legs away.

He yawned and decided that he would return to the depository before paying a visit to the morgue. Tyro needed feeding.

'Excuse me! Hello?'

It was a woman's voice, slightly accented. He ignored it. No woman ever hailed him unless the salutation also included a curse of some kind.

'Please! Wait for me! I would like to speak with you.'

He heard footsteps behind him now, the *tip-tap* of a woman's heels hurrying towards him. He turned his chair to see who approached.

It was the lady from the reception, reading lenses perched on her delicate nose. She slowed before she reached him, smoothed down her skirts and fiddled with her sleek black hair. 'My name is Monique. I saw the way you handled that awful secretary. She kept me waiting almost an hour before you arrived. Those two ladies with you – they were your mistresses?'

Eremul became aware of the woman's perfume. She seemed to lean into him slightly, or perhaps that was that just his imagination. 'My mistresses? I fear you are mistaken. They were but friends,' he lied.

Monique favoured him with a smile, a quirky twist of the mouth that he couldn't help but find agreeable. He noticed her lips were painted a striking shade of violet. 'Well... a man like you, a hero, it is hard to know if a female companion is a friend or a lover, no? You must be surrounded by beautiful women.'

'That... may be a slight exaggeration.'

'Ah, but you are modest.' Monique leaned forward, giving him a perfect view of her bosom, the tight corset she wore highlighting her slender yet shapely body. He felt himself respond, and glanced down in rising panic.

'You saved the city from the tyrant.' She seemed to caress the words, her accent turning every sentence into something musical.

'I did what I had to,' he mumbled. 'With magic comes a certain responsibility.' He cursed himself even as he spoke the words, knowing he sounded like an utter buffoon. The woman's fragrance was overpowering. He felt as though his brain was smothered in it. He folded his hands strategically over his lap. 'Well, I should really be getting back now.'

Monique seemed to blush, her high-boned cheeks reddening slightly. She bit her top lip softy, watched him nervously from behind her glasses. 'I wonder if you might wish to join me for dinner one evening?'

'Er, what? I mean… ah…'

'I am but a simple florist, hardly worthy of the attentions of a man such as yourself. Yet I am also lonely, and my mother always taught me a woman must be bold. I am sorry if I offend you.'

'No… ah… no offence taken.'

'Excellent! Then let us say… the Rose and Sceptre, near Artifice Street, two weeks hence?'

'I will check my diary.' Eremul's mouth was so dry he could hardly speak. 'But I'm sure I could fit it in.'

Monique's long nails brushed his arm. 'Then it is a date,' she said, giving him another smile. She turned and sauntered away, the heels on her shoes *tip-tapping* across the street. Eremul watched transfixed until she disappeared from sight.

Then he heaved a ragged sigh, repositioned his treacherous wizard's staff beneath the folds of his robes, and wheeled himself back to the depository as fast as his arms could manage.

Newharvest

H E AWOKE TO the sensation of rain sliding down his cheek.
Memories flooded back to him: a chaotic torrent of
images. Dancing flames in the night; an old man's dying gasp;
the *tick tock tick tock* of a pocket watch in his trembling palm.

*Hard steel driving into his gut. Blood everywhere. Running
down his legs, through his fingers.*

He reached gingerly for his stomach. It felt strange beneath
his fingers. He probed some more, pushed and prodded until he
realized his stomach was wrapped in a stiff dressing. The wound
beneath still burned, but the pain was nothing compared with
the searing agony he remembered from the night he was betrayed.

He stared up at a grey sky ruptured by dark clouds and let
the rain run into his mouth. It tasted foul. Slowly he became
aware of other sounds besides the soft roar of the downpour. He
turned his head and bright lights exploded in his vision. Once
the scattershot bursts of colour finally cleared, he blinked rainwater from his eyes and took stock of his surroundings.

He was lying on the side of a grassy hill. Closer inspection
revealed the grass to be blackened and brittle. Leafless trees dotted
the side of the slope, their trunks white and sickly-looking.

At the bottom of the hill, spreading over the plain like a viru-
lent skin disease, was a small town that resembled something from
a junkie's nightmare. Broken-down buildings cobbled together
from wood and tar leaned against each other, looking likely to
collapse at any moment. Great cracks split the earth the length of

the town, a cobweb of fissures that belched up noxious fumes. Even at this distance, the stench of sulphur was heavy on the air. Sulphur and something else. Something that stank of death.

'Have I died?' he croaked. 'Is this hell?'

'Not hell,' someone whispered right beside him. 'The Blight.'

He made a strangled sound and would have jumped out of his skin had he the strength to do anything except piss himself a little.

The speaker was sitting on the hillside just below him. Big watery eyes bulged from below a heavy brow and bald head that looked oddly misshapen in the murky light. 'Sorry, didn't mean to startle you. Didn't think you'd pull through. Had old Bessie ready just in case.'

'Bessie?'

The strange fellow gestured to a huge metal cleaver resting on the grass next to him. It was stained with old blood.

He shuddered again and tried to roll away, but the sudden pressure against his wounded stomach sent fresh waves of pain pulsing through him.

'Easy. You almost died. Here, let me help you up.' The bug-eyed fellow moved to take his hands and helped him slowly to his feet. 'What's your name?'

'I...' He thought he heard a bird cawing, somewhere far away. The bird from his dreams? It couldn't be. That was impossible. 'Cole,' he said at last. 'My name is Davarus Cole.'

'Pleased to meet you. I'm Derkin.'

Cole took a hesitant step and almost fell. Derkin reached out to steady him and Cole saw that the man's hands were gnarled and twisted, his legs unnaturally short and bowed. Derkin wore a big overcoat, but beneath it Cole could make out the odd curvature of his spine, the way his back hunched over as if he carried a great weight on his shoulders.

'I'm glad you pulled though,' Derkin said. 'My wrists have been bothering me the last few days. Didn't fancy cutting you up.'

'Sorry?' Cole wasn't sure he had heard the man correctly.

'I'm a corpse-carver. Here in the Blight the dead don't stay dead for long unless they're dismembered. Last thing we need is a bunch of shamblers wandering through town.'

Cole frowned. He felt as if he were stuck in some kind of twisted nightmare, but the pain in his midriff was real enough. 'I thought no one lived in the Blight. It's inhospitable.'

Derkin grinned. He had good teeth considering the rest of him was so bent and crooked. 'Newharvest was the first mining town to be founded here. We've been doing the Mistress's good work for a year now.'

'The Mistress?'

'You know. The White Lady. The Mistress decided the magic in the Blight was too valuable to ignore. Course, now the Celestial Isles are hers she doesn't want to give up Newharvest either. That's wizards for you.'

At the mention of magic, Cole recalled his confrontation with Salazar atop the Obelisk; the moment Magebane had slid into the ancient wizard's wrinkled body. 'Have you seen my dagger?' he asked. 'The blade is curved slightly, and it has a ruby in the pommel.'

'A ruby?' Derkin looked doubtful and shook his head. 'Someone must've stolen it while you were unconscious. There were thirty men aboard the ship that brought you down from Thelassa.'

'Thelassa,' Cole repeated. 'I need to get back there. Take a ship across the channel to Dorminia. There's someone I need to find.' He began to climb down the hill. The effort was extraordinary, but the image of Sasha's face in his mind drove him on until finally he reached the bottom, sweat and rainwater running down his filthy, bloodstained leathers.

'Wait! You can't leave!' Derkin called down.

'Why not?'

'You're Condemned.'

'I'm what?' Cole paused and stared back up at Derkin. The

corpse-carver retrieved his huge cleaver and began to descend the steep incline, but his stunted legs slipped on the wet ground. He thudded painfully down onto the blackened grass and proceeded to roll all the way to the base of the hill.

Cole hurried over. 'Are you hurt?'

Derkin grimaced and rolled onto his belly. 'No harm done. No, don't help me, I need to do this for myself.'

Cole's stomach rumbled loudly and he became terribly aware of just how hungry he was. 'What did you mean by Condemned?' he asked, once Derkin was back on his feet.

'A big group of you were transported across the channel from Dorminia. They brought you here in chains. You're a criminal.'

'I'm no criminal! I'm a—'

He stopped before he could say *I'm a hero*. He wasn't a hero, he was a bastard raised by a merchant kind enough to take pity on him. His true father had been a ruthless assassin; his mother a street whore. He would never allow himself to forget that. 'I don't understand why I'm here,' he said instead. 'I did what the White Lady wanted. I killed Salazar.'

Derkin's laugh sounded uncannily like a horse braying. 'Ha ha, that's a good one. And I'm the White Lady's secret lover!'

Cole stared at the corpse-carver, at his mud-covered face and bulging eyes. 'That doesn't seem very likely,' he said slowly.

Derkin gave him a puzzled look. 'I was being sarcastic. Are you feeling okay? You're very pale.'

Cole examined his hands. It was true, they were paler than he remembered. He ran his fingers over his face and scalp, surprised to find how little his hair had grown. 'How long has it been since the night Salazar died?'

Derkin shrugged. 'About six weeks.'

Sasha will think I'm dead. Or worse, that I abandoned her. 'I need to leave,' Cole announced.

Derkin shook his head. 'That's not a good idea. The Whitecloaks or the Trinity will catch up with you, and when they do... I don't want you to end up like Mockface.'

'Who's Mockface?'

'You'll find out soon enough. The execution is due to start any time. Come on, let's find you something to eat. You look half-starved.'

Cole hesitated. He was wounded and in no shape to attempt to cross the Blight alone and unarmed. Getting himself killed acting the hero wouldn't help anyone. 'You're right,' he said dejectedly.

Derkin gave Cole a friendly pat on the shoulder. 'It's a short walk to the centre of town. I'll keep the pace slow. You're probably still a bit unsteady on your feet.'

As it turned out, after the first handful of uncertain steps Cole was surprised at the strength in his legs. Soon he was forced to check himself to avoid surging ahead of Derkin, who walked in an ungainly hobble that was painful to watch.

'How are you holding up?' asked Derkin for the third or fourth time as they made their way down the muddy road into town.

'Fine,' Cole replied.

'Not far now.' It scarcely seemed possible but somehow Derkin slowed another step. 'Phew, I didn't realize I was moving at such a fast clip. I'll leave you behind at this rate.'

'Honestly, the exercise is doing me the world of good,' Cole said hurriedly. His stomach rumbled again.

'Want to rest for a minute?'

'No, I just want to eat. I'm really hungry.'

'Hungry and weak as a kitten, I expect. And there's me forcing you halfway to a sprint. It's fine, there's no rush.'

Cole tried not to let his frustration show as Derkin stopped to massage his joints. He stared glumly at Newharvest, peering down into the crevices that scarred the ground. Most were only a few feet deep. Rainwater pooled at the bottom, bubbling due to the underground gases that rose beneath the town. One or two cracks were deeper and held nothing but impenetrable darkness below.

A stray dog suddenly dashed past Cole and kicked up a

shower of mud, which splattered all over his face. He wiped it away angrily.

'Why are there cracks everywhere?'

'They say... the Blight was formed... when the Black Lord's body fell from the heavens,' Derkin replied, sucking in air.

Cole realized he had picked up speed and that Derkin was struggling to keep up. He felt suddenly embarrassed at the shame on the little man's face. It couldn't be easy getting around on those horribly bowed legs. He slowed down, feigning exhaustion himself in an effort to salvage the corpse-carver's pride. 'The gods don't die easily,' he said wearily. 'And they really hate their corpses being harvested.'

'Ah, so you know about magic-mining?'

'A little,' Cole replied glumly. He remembered the Swell – the resting place of Malantis, Lord of the Deep. The terrifying moment his ship had been swallowed up by that accursed stretch of the Broken Sea would haunt him forever.

They resumed their journey and eventually reached a great crowd that had gathered before a raised platform in the centre of town. Cole could make out a man tied to a stake in the middle of the platform. He seemed to have a sneer glued to his face, and it took Cole a moment to realize someone had sliced a big chunk out of the right side of his mouth. The resulting scar had given him a permanent lopsided grin.

There was a ripple of movement behind the captive. Cole's eyes widened as he recognized the three pale figures lurking behind the stake. The robes of their order were unmistakable. 'The White Lady's handmaidens,' he said darkly.

Derkin nodded. 'The Trinity.'

One of the handmaidens drifted to the edge of the platform and addressed the townsfolk. 'This man has been sentenced to death. Let his fate serve as a warning to all present. Obey the laws laid down by our mistress or suffer the consequences.'

'Fucking raper,' shouted a woman in the crowd to answering jeers.

The handmaiden turned to her sisters. 'Proceed.'

Together the Trinity pounced on Mockface and he disappeared behind a whirlwind of white robes. Slender arms seemed to blur together. Seconds later the handmaidens parted, leaving a flapping torso that fountained blood down onto the rain-swept platform.

Mockface hadn't even had time to scream.

One of the handmaidens held up the man's head, winning cheers from the crowd. The handmaiden tossed the head from the platform and it landed in a puddle with a loud splash. The arms and legs followed to further cheers. One arm flopped down just in front of Cole, who was grateful he had nothing in his stomach to puke up. Derkin limped past him with surprising speed, then knelt down and began chopping away with his cleaver. A moment later he held up a bloody finger with a ring still attached. 'Silver,' he said, with a whistle of satisfaction. 'Ma will like this.'

Cole stared in horror. 'What did he do to deserve that?'

Derkin placed the finger inside his coat. 'Goldie, Corvac's girl, she accused Mockface of forcing himself on her. You don't get on Corvac's bad side. He's the leader of the Mad Dogs. They run the mining operation.'

'They could have hanged him or something! Anything but *that*.'

The White Lady's handmaidens descended the platform and ghosted over to them, bright blood flecking their perfect ivory faces. They seemed not the slightest bit discomfited by the fact they had brutally dismembered a man with their bare hands but moments ago.

'You were to dispose of this one,' uttered one of the handmaidens. It was difficult to tell if it was a statement or a question.

'He woke up before I went to work on him,' answered the corpse-carver diffidently. 'He has some experience mining magic. Could be a real asset out in the Blight.'

The handmaiden drifted right up to Cole and placed a gore-covered hand on his cheek. He tried not to flinch away. 'There is something unusual about you,' she said. 'You bear the mark of death... and yet you are not of the Unborn. Who are you?'

'No one important,' he replied quickly, hoping Derkin kept his mouth shut. He had no idea what the pale woman meant by the *Unborn*, but he was beginning to think it wise to keep his true identity quiet. The White Lady had ordered him killed, after all.

'Tomorrow you will accompany the others to the Horn,' said the pale woman. 'You will finish each day so sore you cannot stand. Your muscles will scream for mercy, but none shall be forthcoming.'

'Try to escape and you will suffer the same fate as that one,' added a second handmaiden, gesturing at Mockface's sneering head. A pack of strays had begun to sniff around it. 'There will be no release for you. No release except for death.'

Derkin tapped the edge of his cleaver. 'Don't worry,' he said brightly. 'I won't let you become a shambler. Bessie will take care of that.'

'Thanks,' Cole mumbled. He was beginning to wonder how things could possibly get any worse.

They stopped outside of a tavern in the east side of town. A painted sign displayed 'The Black Lord's Re-Spite' in crude letters above a bad illustration of a horned figure quaffing a tankard of ale. Cole glared at it, finding little humour in the bad pun. 'Will I be staying here? It's not as bad as I expected,' he conceded.

Derkin cleared his throat. 'Actually, the dosshouse is over there.' He pointed to a huge building opposite the tavern. The windows were boarded up tight, the roof drooped, and the entire structure looked ready to collapse at any moment.

'At least it's dry.' Cole splashed over to the door, eager to get out of the rain and eat something, anything. He gave the door a shove and it creaked open on loose hinges, revealing a common room illuminated by a handful of glowing spheres hanging from the ceiling. The place stank of damp and old sweat. A handful of rough-faced men lounged around playing cards. A few shot Cole baleful stares.

'Those are glow-globes,' Derkin said, gesturing up at the spheres. 'The Trinity create them from raw magic mined from the Blight. It's too dangerous to hang torches in these buildings – something catches fire and the whole town could spark like kindling after a spell of dry weather.'

They crossed the common room. At the far end was a wooden stairwell. Derkin stopped there for a moment, grimacing and rubbing at his joints again. 'Let me tell you the shape of things in Newharvest,' he said, giving his fingers a good crack. 'The Trinity rule here, assisted by Captain Priam's Whitecloaks. After that there are three groups. The Freefolk, including the Mad Dogs, can come and go as we please. The Indebted are stuck here until they've paid off whatever sentence landed them on one of the convict ships. And then there's the new crowd, the Condemned – like you – doomed to die in the pits for whatever terrible crime you committed in Dorminia.'

'This is bullshit! I haven't committed any crime.'

Derkin scratched at a spot on the end of his nose. 'Well, it's not for me judge...'

'Why are you looking at me like that?'

'The two men on the ship that got into a fight with you. I heard they had to be scrubbed off the planks they were in so many pieces. I know you were upset about getting stabbed and all. But it seems to me you might have anger issues.'

'This is all wrong,' Cole said furiously. 'I didn't kill anyone on the ship. I wasn't even conscious until an hour ago. And it was the Darkson that stabbed me.'

'Who?'

'The Darkson. The White Lady's master assassin. I had a hunch something wasn't right with him.'

Derkin stiffened suddenly. 'That's a weird thing to say.' Without another word he turned his deformed back on Cole and began to climb down the stairwell.

Cole followed behind, confused at what he had done to upset the strange little man. They emerged from the stairwell into what could best be described as a well-kept sewer. The walls were naked stone and at least an inch of filthy water sloshed around on the floor. Cole thought he saw tiny shapes darting around at the edges of the light provided by the glow-globes above.

'These are the Condemned dormitories,' said Derkin, rather brusquely. 'Follow me and I'll find you a bed.'

They splashed through the water that flooded the halls. Beds lined both walls, dozens of them, little more than rotting wooden frames filled with sacks of straw and topped by dirty blankets.

The worst of Dorminia's convicted criminals stared at Cole and Derkin as they passed. They were a group of men for whom the term 'ragtag' conveyed a certain charm they didn't deserve: a rogue's gallery of thieves, ruthless killers and the simply deranged. Most of the prisoners lounged dejectedly on their beds. Some paced back and forth, faces twisted in anger. A few seemed on the verge of committing murder. At least one already had, judging from the body sprawling face down in the water.

Derkin saw the corpse and shook his head ruefully. 'They've only been here a day and already they're killing each other. Looks like you and me aren't taking the night off after all, old girl.' He gave his cleaver an affectionate pat.

At the end of the hall a single bed lay unclaimed.

'This one's free,' Derkin said. His annoyance seemed to have passed. 'You aren't looking well.'

Cole reached up to his face. His skin felt cold to the touch. 'Do you have a mirror?'

'What's that?'

'You mean you don't know— Never mind. Pass me Bessie.'

Derkin hesitated before handing him the huge cleaver. It was twice the size of Magebane and at least three times the weight. Cole angled the blade under the light of the glow-globe above and examined his reflection in the steel.

'Shit.' His face was gaunt, almost cadaverous. He hadn't noticed how thin he was until now. Even more shocking was his skin, which was far paler than he remembered, almost the same ghostly pallor as the White Lady's handmaidens. To add to his woes, there were thick streaks of grey in his black hair.

'I'll bring you some food,' said Derkin softly. 'The quartermaster is a friend of my ma. I'll wrangle something out of him.' The little man reached out and patted Cole on the arm sympathetically. 'Try to stay positive. Things will look better in the morning.'

Cole handed over Bessie and watched numbly as Derkin hobbled off back down the hall. He thought of Sasha. How had she reacted when she had learned that Garrett and the other Shards had been murdered? She must think *him* dead too. He was trapped in this hellish town with no way to contact her, and if he tried to escape he would be hunted down and killed. Once he would have secretly revelled in this kind of predicament, regarded it as yet another way to prove himself, to show the world what a hero he was.

He sat down on the end of his bed and put his head in his hands. He had been a fool back then. The truth was that he was no braver or smarter or more talented than anyone else. He was no hero. He was just Davarus Cole, a common bastard.

A moment later he heard someone approaching. He looked up expecting to see that Derkin had returned. Instead he found a hairy ape of a man sitting naked on the bed opposite. The man was clearly a halfwit and was trying unsuccessfully to balance a miner's cap on his flaccid manhood. It kept slipping off and splashing down onto the floor. He caught Cole watching him and his heavy brow furrowed in anger. 'Don't look at me,' he moaned.

Cole heaved a big sigh. He was sick with hunger, but he decided not to wait for Derkin. He wanted sleep to carry him to oblivion. He grabbed hold of the blanket, intending to bundle himself into bed and forget about the world and its injustices for a short while at least.

Instead he paused, blanket in hand, and stared down in disbelief at the mattress. It was covered in fresh shit.

Cole hurled the blanket down on the wet floor, and then in fury he turned and aimed a kick at the oak trunk at the bottom of the bed. He hit it harder than he intended and heard his foot crack.

'Hurr hurr!' The halfwit laughed uproariously as Cole hopped around in agony. The big oaf was like a child witnessing the performance of a street mime for the first time.

Rage surged inside Cole, terrifying in its intensity. He wished he had Magebane to hand: he would have driven it right into the halfwit's face just to shut him up. He looked around, searching for something, anything, to use as a weapon. He was so furious he could hardly see straight—

Caw.

It was the bird from his dreams again. Calm washed over him like a cooling tide quenching hot sand. He glanced down at his foot. The pain was gone.

Some instinct compelled his gaze down the hall and he caught sight of a tall, ragged figure in a black coat watching him, though a moment later he realized there was a red cloth wrapped around the man's face and he couldn't possibly see a thing...

'Who—' Cole began, but then he stopped in confusion. He blinked a few times, wondering if his eyes were playing tricks on him.

The man had disappeared.

Thirty-one Years Ago

'**Y**OU READY FOR this?' Orgrim hefted his great warhammer and stared into the mist. The early-morning air was utterly still, not a sound to be heard except for the soft gurgle of the Icemelt. Even the birds in the trees had fallen silent. A sign that demons were near.

Kayne took a deep breath. He had waited five years for this moment. Each morning he would rise just before the sun, climb the battlements of Watcher's Keep to stare out at the colossal Devil's Spine mountains far in the distance, dreaming of the day he would join his brothers at the Borderland. And now that day was here.

'I'm ready,' he replied, though his heart was beating fast and his hand felt slippery on the hilt of his longsword. He raised his shield and glanced at Taran beside him. The Greenman seemed just as nervous as he was. Maybe more.

'Remember your training,' Orgrim said. 'Demonkin are weak and stupid, but they strike fear into a man's heart like the rest of their kind. Master that fear – or better yet, turn it into a weapon. And watch out for their claws.'

'I saw a Lakeman die of demon-rot,' Taran said. 'He turned black. Lost his fingers and then his arms. Nasty way to go.'

'Sounds like it,' Kayne muttered.

'Give me a warg or a troll. Even a giant. Demons, they can't be reasoned with. They got no mercy. They ain't natural.'

Kayne remembered a young voice screaming his name, and

his grip tightened on his longsword. 'Natural or not, they die like anything else,' he growled.

Orgrim gave him a look he knew well. 'Keep your temper in check, Kayne. A true Warden requires more than just skill, he also needs discipline.'

Kayne nodded and forced himself to relax. Orgrim had saved his life more than once. He had spoken up for him before the King, and then again back at the Keep, when old Kalgar had judged Kayne too reckless for the Borderland. He had even put himself forward to accompany Kayne on his Initiation. He reckoned he owed it to the big Easterman not to let him down.

'Let's move,' Orgrim grunted. He set off into the mist, Kayne and Taran falling in just behind him. This close to the river the ground was soft underfoot and their boots sank deep with every step. At one point the mud almost swallowed Kayne's left foot and he nearly tweaked his knee – the same knee the Shaman had fixed outside the Great Lodge all those years ago. Red Ear had paid the blood price for that. Kayne swore then that he would pass the Initiation, for his dead friend as well as for Orgrim.

But most of all, he would pass it for Dannard.

The ground slowly rose as they made their way deeper into the Borderland, sticking close to the river. Here and there a few patches of snow remained from the long winter just gone, but the Icemelt had thawed and the sun quickly burned away the mist that still clung to the hills. Eventually they crested a low rise and Orgrim raised a hand, calling a silent halt. 'There,' he whispered gruffly, pointing down.

Kayne's eyes narrowed. Scattered across the bottom of the depression were the butchered remains of a herd of mountain goats. The grass was slick with their blood, still steaming in the chill morning air.

'They haven't touched the meat,' Orgrim growled. 'Demons don't eat.'

Standing in the middle of the carnage were the demonkin: a half-dozen hairless creatures the size of large children. Gore dribbled from razor-sharp claws at the end of long arms containing one too many joints. The faces of the demonkin were blunt and shapeless masses, featureless save for two empty pits for eyes and an oversized mouth bristling with teeth.

Despite their savage appearance, the most disturbing thing about the demons was how still they were. They were motionless, as unmoving as a stone. Apart from killing, demons had no purpose. No reason to exist at all.

'Demonkin are blind,' Orgrim whispered. 'We'll sneak up on them.'

Kayne and Taran nodded. The Code forbade attacking another man from behind, but ambushing demons was fair game. Borun would be waiting for them further down the river, on the edge of the Borderland. His spirit eagle had already scouted out the area and confirmed that no other demons lurked nearby.

'I'll take the second on the left,' Kayne said. Orgrim nodded and raised his mighty hammer.

'Taran, you take the far left. I'll handle the others.' Orgrim crouched low and set off down the hill, using the cover provided by the occasional tree to close on his targets.

Taran clutched his spear tighter and Kayne thought he saw the man's hands tremble. He gave the Greenman a nod, and then he sprinted off after Orgrim.

The demonkin were facing away from the Highlanders. As Kayne got closer to his target, he felt the terror begin to worm its way into his heart. Demon fear was a base response to the unnatural, an intense feeling of dread that could paralyse the bravest man or turn him into a gibbering wreck.

Kayne himself had experienced that crippling fear once before.

The demon had caught up with them outside town. Kayne's father had given his life to buy him and Dannard time to escape.

For a moment they thought they might make it out of Riverdale alive, but then that awful shriek had frozen Dannard to the spot. Kayne's own response had been to keep running. To keep on running and not look back, even as Dannard managed to scream his name, begging him to help.

His younger brother had worshipped him, and Kayne had left him to die.

He closed on the demonkin, cleared the remaining distance in a mighty leap and cleaved the fiend's head in half. Foul ichor sprayed over his face but he paid it no mind. He dashed straight past the toppling body, blurring gaze narrowing on the two demonkin fifty yards ahead. Without warning their heads twisted a full half-circle to regard him. The eyeless scrutiny lasted but a moment and then the demonkin burst into life, pivoting around and lurching towards him with startling speed.

Kayne didn't hesitate. He smashed one fiend in the face with his shield, knocked it back a few feet. He thrust his sword through the leathery flesh of the other, driving it deep into the demonkin's chest. It flailed at him with taloned hands but he got his shield up just in time, heard wood split as the claws shredded it like parchment. He tossed the ruined shield aside, severed one probing arm with a mighty slash and then beheaded the fiend with the reverse stroke.

He got his longsword back up just as the last of the demons pounced at him. The blade became tangled in its arms and they went into a clinch, Kayne desperately jerking his head from side to side to avoid those snapping jaws.

There was a flicker of movement behind the demon and then its skull exploded in a shower of gore. Kayne thrust the body aside to see Orgrim standing there, pulverized demon brain flecking the steel head of his mighty hammer.

'The hell you doing, Kayne?' the big Easterman bellowed at him. 'That bastard almost had you. That weren't part of the plan.'

105

Kayne lowered his sword, panting hard. The anger was still there, simmering. He tasted demon blood in his mouth and spat it out in disgust. Before he could reply, Taran's terrified cry snatched his attention. The young Warden was on his knees, a demonkin bearing down on him, his spear hanging out of its back.

Kayne found himself running before he could think. He reached the demon just as Taran's shield was torn from his hands. He grasped the haft of the spear and drove it deeper into the fiend, giving it a vicious twist.

'Scream,' he whispered in cold fury.

The demon made no sound. He forced the spear right through the fiend until the sharp metal head burst through its chest in a splatter of black gore. It twitched and went limp, but Kayne wasn't done. He hurled the body to the ground.

'Scream, you bastard!' he hissed. 'Scream like Dannard screamed.' He stabbed the corpse in the head and chest, filling it with holes, heedless of the blood spraying over his legs. He slammed the point of the spear through the fiend's lolling mouth, pushed it up through its brain, and then levered it with vicious force, trying to tear the head right off.

'It's dead, Kayne.'

He looked up. Orgrim and Taran were watching him in astonishment. 'Dead,' he said numbly. He blinked away tears. He hadn't realized he'd been crying.

Borun suddenly appeared over the rise, his spirit eagle soaring far above him. The rangy young spirit-scout took in the carnage with wide eyes.

'What're you doing here?' Orgrim barked. 'You're inside the Borderland. This ain't no place for a boy.'

'I thought you were in trouble,' Borun protested.

'You're supposed to keep well away from the fighting. You're a spirit-scout, not a Warden. You're not even a man yet.'

'I'm almost fourteen.'

Despite everything, Kayne couldn't help but smile. He liked Borun. The boy reminded him of Dannard.

Orgrim shook his head ruefully. 'Come on,' he said. 'Let's get back. The citadel awaits its newest Warden. Though I'll leave out the part where he ignored my orders and sprinted off like a madman.'

Kayne hesitated. He'd lost it completely, he knew. Could have got them all killed. 'I let you down. I don't reckon I'm fit to be a Warden.'

'No man can be certain how he'll react when he's nose to nose with a demon,' Orgrim replied levelly. 'We used to send boys out into the Borderland. Kids no older than Borun. They all cracked. It takes a man who knows his mind to stand before a fiend and not shit his pants. You killed three demons and saved Taran's life.'

Taran stared at the corpses of the demonkin. They were already beginning to dissolve into puddles of black ooze. 'I owe you, brother.'

Kayne shrugged. 'You'd have done the same for me.'

They climbed back up the hill and headed west, back towards Watcher's Keep, the great stronghold that guarded the East Reaching against the worst of what the Devil's Spine spat out. On the way they stopped by the side of the Icemelt. Kayne was washing demon blood from his face when Borun crouched down beside him. The spirit-scout gazed wistfully across the river. 'I'll be a Warden one day. Just like you.'

'Then you'd best prepare for years of shit food and a bed as hard as an anvil.' Kayne grinned suddenly, remembering how he would tease Dannard when their mam was alive. 'Better put some muscle on those scrawny arms too.'

'I'm stronger than I look!'

'Ha! I reckon there's more meat on that girl you like.'

Borun threw himself on Kayne, who was unbalanced from leaning over the river. The two of them tumbled in with an almighty splash. It was so cold they could hardly breathe, especially with them both laughing so hard. They wrestled and dunked each other under the water, just as he and Dannard had done when they were children. It didn't dull the anger that burned inside him, the terrible rage that could ignite at a moment's notice. But, for that afternoon at least, he could forget about everything and enjoy a friendship he thought would last forever.

Into the Swamp

'**B**RICK'S DOING MY head in.'

Kayne looked up as the Wolf stalked over. Even Jerek's disgruntled scowl was a welcome distraction from the bitter memories that had been tossing around his skull for the last few hours. 'What now?'

Jerek spat and gestured towards the rough shrubbery where Brick had gone to take a piss. 'Boy keeps going on about his uncle like the man's some kind of hero. Got a mind to tell him this Glaston's a yellow-bellied shit and be done with it.'

Kayne raised a bushy eyebrow. 'You mean you haven't done that already?'

Jerek kicked at a patch of dirt and frowned. 'Boy idolizes his uncle. Ain't that bad for a bandit's get, got a decent head on his shoulders.'

Kayne raised a hand to his mouth, half faking a yawn to hide his surprise. The list of folk Jerek liked or at least actively tolerated could be counted on one hand with fingers to spare. 'He ain't that bad' was about as ringing an endorsement as any man ever got from the Wolf.

Grunt ambled over and grunted. Kayne nodded in response and mumbled a perfunctory 'all right', not knowing what else to say. Grunt had been travelling alongside them for days now, but it was hard to make conversation with a mute and they had settled into a routine of a polite greeting followed by a long, uncomfortable silence. Jerek in particular was comically awkward around the big greenskin. He and Grunt reminded Kayne of two big mountain bears that had sized each other up and quietly decided to keep their distance.

As Grunt approached, the Wolf sniffed pointedly and strode off to survey the narrow rise they were camped on one more time. Kayne had to admit that Grunt didn't exactly smell fresh, but then he doubted any of them did just then.

'How's your sack?' he asked, not knowing what else to say. Grunt looked momentarily aghast before understanding dawned in his amber eyes. He nodded as if to say *everything's in order, thanks for asking.*

The sack in question was tied to Jerek's mount. Grunt had made that concession on the second day, when it was either that or be left behind. The sack must have weighed at least a hundred pounds, yet the mute had somehow kept pace with the horses' slow trot for a good score of miles before flagging. In the end Brick had convinced Grunt that they weren't going to ride off and leave him behind. Kayne was still curious about the sack's contents, but he had given his word that no one would mess with it and that was that.

They'd had no more trouble with hill-men or bandits or anything else except for an angry badger whose sett Grunt had accidentally disturbed. Despite his savage appearance it was clear the warrior was not at home in the wilderness. Brick had put an arrow through the animal from fifty yards and Jerek had skinned the beast and roasted it over a fire. Truth be told it had tasted like shit, but game was scarce and a man had to make do. They'd half expected Grunt to tear into the meat raw, maybe slobber everywhere for good measure, but the mute's snout had practically curled in distaste as he chewed.

'We're almost out of the Badlands,' Kayne said. 'Mal-Torrad next. The underground cities ain't nothing but ruins now. There's things living there that are best avoided, but they don't bother you so long as you stick to the road.'

Grunt's eyes went wide. He opened his mouth and moaned,

clearly distraught at something he'd just heard. Kayne glanced over to the bushes where Brick was taking his sweet time. 'Not sure I understand you,' he began sheepishly. He was fumbling for something else to say when Jerek's sudden reappearance spared him further embarrassment.

'Two-score riders,' the Wolf snarled. 'Coming from the south and east. An hour away, could be less.'

Kayne hurried over to the shrubs and yelled for Brick. There was no response, so he shouted again.

Brick finally emerged from the bushes, looking flustered as he tugged on his trousers. 'What?' he said reproachfully. 'I can't go when you keep yelling.'

'Got us a host of bandits heading towards us,' Kayne said. 'Think your uncle betrayed us to Asander and sent word that we're here?'

Brick shook his head. 'He'd never do that. My uncle hates Asander. They must have found our tracks and followed us north.'

Grunt was watching them with a bewildered expression. Kayne looked from the big mute to the sack tied to Jerek's stallion and gave the green-skinned warrior an apologetic shrug. 'We've only got two horses. I figure now might be a good time to part ways, friend.'

Grunt lifted his monstrous club thoughtfully. Kayne readied himself in case the mute decided to make a play for one of the mounts, but the big stranger just nodded and ambled over to Jerek's horse to begin untying his sack.

'Wait.'

They turned to Brick. He looked mighty nervous all of a sudden. 'I know somewhere we can hide,' he said slowly, as if unsure whether what he was suggesting might in fact be worse than a band of murderous horsemen riding towards them. 'There's an old tower in the swampland near the coast. It's only a few miles west of here. Bandits won't venture near it.'

'I'm guessing there's a "but" coming here,' said Kayne.

'They say a wizard lives there. A necromancer.'

'Ah.'

Jerek snorted. Kayne swatted at a fly that had pitched on his face. All things considered, Brick's revelation wasn't the worst he'd been expecting. 'A necromancer, you say? Ran into a few of those back in the day. The Shaman never had any truck with those that mess with the dead. What d'you reckon, Wolf?'

Jerek shrugged. 'I ain't fussed. We've dealt with wizards before.'

Kayne nodded. 'Right, that settles it. We ride for this tower. Worst comes to the worst, we can hole up there and try to hold them off. Their horses won't be no use to them in a swamp.'

Brick's freckled face went pale. 'But the dead walk the swamp!'

'Fuck the dead,' Jerek spat. 'We got forty man after us. Easier to dodge a stroller than a storm of arrows.'

'Ain't that the truth,' Kayne muttered. He walked over to Grunt. 'You can ride double with me. Or you can take your chances and continue north on your own. The bandits might let you be. Course, they might not.'

The big mute made a hand signal to Brick, who responded with a gesture of his own. 'He thinks the swamp is the better bet,' the red-headed youngster said. 'But he really hates wizards.'

Kayne grinned and slapped Grunt on the back. 'You and me both.'

Grunt gestured at Brick again, a more complex series of movements the old Highlander could barely track.

Brick's lips pursed in concentration. 'He says you mentioned some ruins.'

'You mean Mal-Torrad?'

'Yes. He says that last time he was there...' Brick's brow furrowed in puzzlement and he repeated the hand signs. Grunt nodded, a profound look of despair on his face.

'What about Mal-Torrad?' Kayne asked again.

'He says the Mal-Torrad that he remembers wasn't in ruins.'

*

They rode hard and fast. It wasn't far to the coast but Kayne's mare was sweating and shaking by the time they reached the outskirts of the swamp. Riding at a mad gallop with a big green savage clinging to him wasn't Kayne's idea of a good time, not with the recent farce of their flight from Farrowgate still fresh in his mind. To make matters worse, even at the breakneck pace Jerek set the bandits were closing fast.

'Place looks like a right shithole,' the Wolf grunted as Kayne's horse drew level with his. Both animals were breathing hard.

'Do you think they'll follow us into the swamp?' Brick asked. He looked terrified, though it wasn't clear if that was due to the bandits, the threat of undead horrors lurking in the swamp or just sharing a horse with Jerek.

Kayne shrugged. 'Only one way to find out.'

The ground grew soggier as they proceeded deeper into the wetland. Soft mud quickly disappeared beneath stagnant water that stank worse than the streets of Dorminia on a hot day. The vegetation grew thicker, monstrous willows casting baleful shadows over the group in the light of the dying sun. Mangroves dipped their spiderlike roots into the rising water, forming a treacherous web that threatened to snare their unhappy horses. When the swamp reached knee height and thick patches of reeds began to block their way, they finally dismounted in order to clear a path. Buzzing insects swarmed around them. Every rustle of movement from the swamp had them glancing around nervously. All except for Jerek, who seemed preoccupied with the state of the boots he'd purchased back in Ashfall.

'Twenty silver down the shitter,' the Wolf declared bitterly. 'Leather will be ruined now. Best pair of boots I had in years, these.'

'I'll buy you a new pair,' Kayne said wearily. Something had bitten him on the ear; it was itching and starting to burn. The water rippled nearby and a cold reptilian head bobbed up for a moment before vanishing. 'There's snakes in this water. Hope they ain't poisonous.'

'There are giant snakes that can swallow a man whole down in the Sun Lands,' Brick said, not particularly helpfully, if Kayne was being honest. 'My uncle told me about them.'

'Your uncle spouts a lot of shit,' Jerek growled.

Brick's face went bright red but he said nothing.

Jerek muttered something and swung an axe viciously at the thicket of reeds clawing at him. A good handful sprang right back up and slapped him across his bald head. Face twisting in rage, he proceeded to stamp them all into the swamp, raising a hell of a racket.

'What's wrong with him?' Brick whispered as Jerek splashed around, uttering curses raw enough to make a sailor blush.

Kayne frowned. 'The Wolf sometimes lets his anger get the better of him. You get used to it.'

'Motherfucking swamp.' Jerek tore a handful of reeds out of the water with his bare hands and flung them away. Even his stallion shied back in the face of his rage.

'I know it was you that spared me,' Brick said quietly as they watched the Wolf take out his frustrations on the swamp. 'He would have killed me.'

'If Jerek really wanted you dead, you'd be dead. There ain't much me or anyone else could do about it.'

Suddenly, Grunt moaned and pointed a thick green finger at a cluster of trees up ahead. A large band of ragged figures had appeared in the distance. The shadows cast by the trees overhead obscured their faces, but their lurching walk was unmistakable.

'Shit,' Kayne muttered. 'Strollers. Dozens of 'em.'

'Strollers?' Brick repeated, dread in his voice.

'The walking dead, lad.'

Kayne released his horse's reins and reached over his shoulder to draw his greatsword. Grunt raised his club. His cat eyes seemed to burn orange beneath his brutish brow.

'Getting sick of this shit,' Jerek rasped, though if anything he looked fairly pleased at this latest development. He'd failed to

114

get the better of the reeds and seemed eager to get stuck into a less stubborn foe.

Kayne placed a comforting hand on Brick's shoulder, noting the way the boy's bow trembled in his grip. 'Strollers can't be stopped by arrows. Not unless one takes 'em right through the brain. I figure the poor light makes that a tough ask, even for you.'

'What should I do?' Brick asked, voice shaking slightly.

'Stay behind me and make sure the horses don't bolt. You ready, Grunt?'

The big mute bared his tusks in reply. The gesture would've looked mighty impressive, except just then the water rippled ominously right in front of him and he jumped back, almost dropping his club.

Another handful of corpses emerged from the swamp around them. Worm-eaten eyes stared hatefully from bloated faces the colour of old vomit, rancid water dripping down decomposing bodies teeming with parasites. Despite the fact they had them surrounded the strollers seemed strangely hesitant to attack. Never one to pass up an advantage, Kayne kicked out at the corpse of a middle-aged woman just in front of him. Her left breast had half rotted away, giving her a lopsided appearance. The corpse went down with a splash, taking another stroller with it.

Grunt swung his huge club, a mighty sweep that snapped bones and lifted two of the corpses clean out of the swamp. Jerek was a whirlwind of steel, axes cleaving rotting limbs from bodies.

'Watch out for the teeth!' Kayne warned as a stroller lunged at Grunt, too close for the mute to bring his huge weapon to bear. The greenskin turned as the corpse reached towards him, bit down suddenly with his own tusks and ripped half the stroller's head clean off. That won a grim nod from Jerek, though Grunt himself looked as if he wanted to heave, utter disgust on his bestial face.

Kayne sliced the head from a stroller. Then he spun and cut another in half at the waist, black blood spraying all over his leathers. He looked around for more of the creatures but they were all accounted for, bloated torsos and flopping limbs making an unholy soup of the swamp around them. The approaching horde slowed its advance.

'Something's wrong,' said Brick. 'They're not attacking. Maybe we should hold off—'

Jerek's axe glittered through the air and split the head of the stroller at the front of the nearby group. Together he and Grunt charged forward and hurled themselves into the corpses.

There was another splash behind Kayne. He turned to stare into the mouldy face of a boy around Brick's age. This newest stroller wore a black tunic that was still in good repair. To Kayne's surprise, the corpse opened its mouth and spoke.

'Enough of this.'

Kayne stared at the creature. The deep, cultured voice that had just sprung from that broken-toothed pit of a mouth didn't belong to any dead child. The words seemed to come from far away, as if they had travelled through a long tunnel before spilling from the stroller's rotting maw. 'You can talk?' Kayne asked uncertainly.

'This corpse is but a conduit for my words. I am Nazala, the master of this swamp.'

'The necromancer,' Brick whispered.

Kayne's eyes narrowed. 'What do you want with us?'

The corpse gestured towards Jerek and Grunt, who looked to be having a hell of a time brutalizing the unresisting corpses. 'My tower is not far from here. I offer safety from those that mean you harm. But first you must cease destroying my minions!'

Kayne hesitated. He'd learned the hard way that wizards weren't to be trusted. But they had forty bandits hot on their heels and he reckoned the swamp held enough of the dead to drag them all to a watery grave if this necromancer willed it so. Better to take a helping hand when it was offered, even if the hand in question was decidedly slimy and missing half its fingers.

'Hang on.' He waded across to Jerek and Grunt. The green-skin twisted around, a severed arm hanging from his mouth. He relaxed when he saw Kayne and let the arm drop with a splash, something like shame in his amber eyes.

'Don't worry about it,' the old Highlander said. 'I've done worse when my blood's up. Turns out the strollers want to help us. Could be why they're not slavering after our flesh like the dead usually do. You hear me, Wolf?'

Jerek had one of the corpses in a headlock and was punching it repeatedly in the nose. 'Yeah.'

Kayne waited patiently for a moment. 'You can probably let go, then.'

'Huh.' Jerek released his grip on the stroller, half the corpse's face now smeared over his knuckles. 'That's for my boots,' he spat.

They splashed back to where Brick waited with the horses and the necromancer's undead mouthpiece. The boy had done an admirable job of keeping their mounts calm despite the fear in his green eyes. The youngster had some steel in him, Kayne thought. It was easy to forget how terrified he himself had been the first time he had come face to face with a stroller.

If a corpse could look peeved, this one managed it. Nazala's voice sounded unmistakably cheesed off. 'You destroyed twenty of my minions.'

'Sorry. We got carried away.'

The necromancer was silent for a time and Kayne feared he might be reconsidering his earlier offer. But eventually the corpse raised a putrid hand and gestured towards the horde. 'My minions will intercept your pursuers. I hope the Bandit King's men are not so nonchalant in the face of death.'

Kayne shrugged. 'Death's face ain't the ugliest I've seen. It's the living you need to worry about, in my experience.'

Another slight pause. This time there was a note of melancholy in the hollow voice. 'Night will soon arrive and with it horrors beyond even my authority to command. My grandson will show you to my tower.'

Kayne glanced at Jerek, who only scowled down at his boots. Grunt seemed preoccupied with checking that his sack was in order. Brick stared wide-eyed at the talking corpse before turning to Kayne.

'Did he just call this thing his *grandson*?'

It turned out the necromancer's tower was in fact an ancient keep set atop a hill, surrounded by ruins that appeared to have once housed living quarters before they flooded. Here and there debris poked up above brackish water. The roof had collapsed around most of the perimeter, but there was a section of building to the right of the decaying gatehouse that seemed mostly intact. Their cadaverous guide slowed as they passed through the crumbling archway. 'The stables are still serviceable. You may leave your horses within.'

Kayne peered into the stable building. The thick walls were green with algae and the smell was awful, but several enclosures contained livestock and there was fresh horse feed in a sack in one of the stalls.

Brick secured their mounts. Grunt was reluctant to leave his mysterious burden behind, and after a brief exchange with the red-haired youngster he decided he would remain with the horses. Their guide led them out of the stables and up the overgrown path that curved up the hill. The tower loomed ominously above them, reminding Kayne of the great citadel that dominated Watcher's Keep. 'Seems a bit out of place in the Badlands,' he observed as they neared the entrance.

'This castle was once an Andarran outpost,' Nazala's mouthpiece explained. 'The lord of the castle had it constructed to keep watch on the Yahan, and to pursue relations with the underfolk of Mal-Torrad to the north. During the Godswar the sea rose and flooded the coast. All here perished.'

They reached the huge iron doors. They were free of rust, and Kayne wondered if the necromancer had placed some magic on them to guard against the depredations of the swamp. Without warning the doors creaked slowly open – and out stepped Nazala.

'Not one of you bastards,' Jerek muttered.

The black-skinned southerner staring back at them raised an eyebrow. 'Don't mind him, he just don't like wizards,' Kayne said hurriedly. He was about to ask what a Sunlander was doing this far north when he heard Brick gasp behind him.

'You… I've seen your face before…' The young bandit's voice trailed off; his brow creased in confusion.

Now that it was no longer projected through the decaying throat of a corpse, Nazala's voice was welcoming, pleasant even. 'Ah. You've met my twin, Shara.'

'The Seer is your twin?'

'Only by way of blood. Everything else we once shared is as dead as the bodies that litter this swamp. Tell me, child. What did she say?'

'She said I was a catalyst. That I would bring blood and fire to the north. I was only four years old, I don't remember much. My uncle stole me away soon after.'

Kayne didn't like the sudden hunger in the wizard's blood-shot eyes as the southerner stared at Brick. 'Why are you helping us?' the old warrior demanded.

'The four of you… interest me. Two Highlanders, far from home yet casting shadows long enough to stretch to the Trine. A green-skinned humanoid the nature of which even I am unfamiliar with. And this child of prophecy.'

'I'm not a child,' said Brick.

Nazala ignored that. 'I have had dinner prepared within. Join me and we shall discuss how we might be to able help one another.' The necromancer turned, black robes trailing behind him, and strolled back inside the keep.

Kayne hesitated. He was hungry and tired and if the wizard spoke true the bandits giving chase wouldn't be bothering them again in a hurry. But trusting a necromancer seemed akin to putting your chin on an executioner's block and expecting him to give you a nice head massage. He was still deliberating when Jerek barged past him.

'You coming?' the Wolf rasped. 'Reckon I might be able to salvage these boots if we can find a fire.'

'Your boots will be the death of me,' Kayne muttered. But he nodded at Brick, and together they entered the necromancer's tower.

The Iron Man

'**D**EAD.'

Sir Meredith stifled a sigh. Bagha had a penchant for stating the obvious that never ceased to irritate him. Almost as much as that ridiculous bear-skull headdress he wore. It was as if the stupid brute was trying to mock him, parading his buffoonery like one of the clowns from the travelling circuses that passed through the kingdom of Tarbonne in early autumn.

'Kingswood is just ahead,' he said impatiently.

He stepped over the corpse, disturbing a buzzard that had been enjoying a leisurely dinner. By the look of it the wolf had only been dead a short while. With all the recent fighting around Heartstone, carrion birds had grown as ubiquitous as the bad food and toothless women his compatriots seemed to relish in equal measure.

'Looks like it was demonkin what did for it,' Ryder said, pointing to the deep gouges in the wolf's hindquarters. Ryder was the oldest of the three men, tall and rake-thin and with a long face that reminded Meredith of the coyotes that haunted the Badlands. To further add to the effect, he was also missing the top half of his right ear.

'*That* did for it,' Meredith replied, unable to stop himself. 'Not *what* did for it.'

'What's your point?

'Correct grammar, Ryder. We're Kingsmen, not cock-waving savages. We should treat our words with the same care we place in our martial prowess.'

'I ain't got no martial prowess,' Bagha rumbled. 'That's what my wife used to tell me. Before I chopped her head off.'

Meredith shot the enormous warrior a hateful glare. 'If I didn't know better I might suspect you were mocking me.'

'Huh?'

Sir Meredith spread his gauntleted hands. 'I don't ask that you recite Balcaz or comport yourself with the dignity of the great warrior-bards of the Garden City. That would clearly be a bridge too far. But, *damn it*, you could at least not confuse simple words. And the occasional bath wouldn't go amiss either! Standards in this accursed backwater are even worse than I had feared.'

Ryder snorted up a mouthful of phlegm and spat it out. He smiled nastily, revealing sharp yellow teeth. 'What're you even doing here, iron man? You went south over twenty years past. Why come back?'

Meredith grimaced and stared off into the distance. That was a subject he had been pondering a great deal of late. 'I fail to see how it's any of your business. But if you must know, I was the victim of a tragic misunderstanding. There are men that want to kill me. Powerful men.'

'So you fled back north?' Ryder gave a barking laugh that grated on Meredith's nerves like a spear point shoved down his earhole. 'The Sword Lord himself, turning tail and scarpering home like a scolded dog.'

Sir Meredith felt the blood rush to his face. 'It was a tactical withdrawal, you bloody cretin!' he roared. It took all his considerable strength of character not to draw his sabre and challenge the man to a duel right there and then. Ryder might be a dead eye with a bow, but Sir Meredith had learned the art of swordsmanship at the hands of the Old Masters in Carhein. He was no simple barbarian like his countrymen.

He was a *knight*.

Ryder yawned and scratched his neck. If he had taken offence at Meredith's insult, it didn't show on his stubbly face. 'Getting late in the day. Let's finish our business here.'

They resumed their journey, following the road east from Heartstone and heading deeper into the King's Reaching. Just behind them Lake Dragur gleamed in the afternoon sun. The road would continue for hundreds of miles, through the Lake Reaching and then the East Reaching until finally it terminated at Watcher's Keep. At this very moment Orgrim Foehammer and his entourage would be making the journey in the opposite direction. The chieftain of the East Reaching had been summoned along with his counterparts from the other undeclared Reachings. The one exception was the Green Reaching, whose stated neutrality Krazka had yet to address. The forthcoming meeting between the four chieftains could well decide the fate of the High Fangs.

Another hour passed before the trio came within sight of Kingswood, a small village on the side of a hill with a shallow brook gurgling just below. Shranree had provided Krazka with the names of every known sorceress in the King's Reaching. Those who had not yet travelled to the capital and presented themselves to Shranree, such as the two that were reported to dwell in this small settlement, were to be escorted back to Heartstone forthwith. Either they agreed to join the King's circle or they would be feeding the worms before the day was out.

The Kingsmen halted just before the village. Sir Meredith was grateful for the respite; he was sweating heavily beneath his armour, which these days felt a little too tight around the stomach. Standing around guarding the King wasn't doing much for his waistline, which was why he had volunteered for this undertaking in the first place.

'Want me to scout the area?' Ryder asked. He had good eyes, the Lakeman. All the more galling when one considered he was at least ten years Meredith's senior and carried not an ounce of fat on his lean frame.

'No,' replied Meredith. 'If they try to escape, or offer any resistance, we'll put the village to the torch.'

He hoped it wouldn't come to that. He had witnessed enough

smouldering flesh when he and Wulgreth had burned the corpses of the Black Reaching sorceresses on the hill outside Heartstone. The disappointment on Wulgreth's face as he had watched the corpses burn might have been a curious thing to many, but Sir Meredith had known the truth of it. He had always been able to read a man. It had been obvious in the Northman's ravenous, bloodshot eyes; he had been imagining all the pleasure he could have had with the bodies of those freshly killed women.

'Degenerate bastard,' he swore bitterly. The foulness of the human spirit never ceased to repulse him.

'Who're you talking to?' Bagha rumbled.

'No one,' Sir Meredith snapped. 'Men of intellect often have cause to curse when contemplating the iniquities of the world.'

Bagha turned to Ryder. 'You got any idea what he's talking about?'

The rangy old Lakeman shook his head. 'Not a clue.'

'Pah!' Sir Meredith drew his sabre. It slid from the scabbard with a satisfying hiss. 'If the pair of you are done revelling in your ignorance, it is time we took care of the King's business.'

They climbed the hill and made their way past the short wooden fence that surrounded the village. Kingswood was little different to the other small settlements that dotted the King's Reaching. The buildings were constructed from timber cut from the adjacent woodland, and they lined a dirt path running from one end of the village to the other. An ancient well stood in the centre, the stone overgrown with weeds and beginning to crumble. A boy and a girl played nearby, chasing a chicken that had escaped from its coop, while a dog sunned itself on a rock. It eyed the three men warily as they approached the children. Sir Meredith had always hated dogs: the damned animals seemed to dislike him on sight.

The children stopped chasing the chicken and stared up wide-eyed as Meredith clanked towards them. Bagha loomed on his left, while Ryder slunk along to his right.

'Is that a bear skull?' the girl asked, after a moment of silence.

She pointed a grubby finger at the monstrous helmet Bagha wore.

'Yeah. I killed it. A big brown bear up in the Pinewood.'

'What's your name?'

'Bagha.'

'You're funny! What about these old men? Are they your friends? They look mean.'

Sir Meredith bristled with righteous indignation. Old man? He was barely forty! 'Mind your tongue, girl,' he barked. 'You don't speak unless you're spoken to. We're looking for two women. Leyanne and Minerva. You will tell us where they can be found.'

The children looked at each other. 'We don't know,' said the boy.

He could tell by the child's eyes that he was lying. Back when he had fought under the Rag King's banner, Sir Meredith had won a small fortune at card games in the taverns and gambling halls on the roads between the Shattered Realms. He could call a bluff twenty feet away.

'Lies!' he said sternly. 'Don't treat me like a fool.'

A door opened and a well-muscled man stormed out. He wore a woodcutter's axe at his belt. 'What's going on? Who are you?'

Ryder drew his long hunting knife and made a show of picking his teeth with the tip. While Meredith appreciated Ryder's intent to intimidate the fellow, he couldn't resist a grimace at the sight. The Lakeman's dental hygiene was frankly deplorable.

'The sorceresses,' Ryder said. 'Where are they?'

The woodcutter frowned. 'They live just over there, in the big cabin. Don't go causing no trouble, you hear? Leyanne and Minerva are two of the sweetest women a village could wish for. Besides – you don't wanna make a sorceress angry.'

Sir Meredith sneered at that. His sabre had tasted the blood of no fewer than four sorceresses atop the hill twelve days past.

He grunted at Bagha and Ryder and the three of them barged past the woodcutter, who disappeared back inside his hut, ushering the children before him.

The cabin in question was bigger than Kingswood's other buildings – closer in size to the houses one might find in the poorer districts of Carhein. Meredith gave the door a shove and found it locked. He rapped on it with his iron gauntlets, leaving small dents in the wood.

Bagha unharnessed his huge war mace, four feet of solid steel. 'I'll break the fucker down,' he growled.

Sir Meredith raised his eyes towards the heavens. Fortunately, the door creaked open before the brute beside him could indulge his latest bestial impulse. A full-figured woman in a green gown stared back at him. Behind her, another woman was sitting at a table in front of what looked suspiciously like a book. She got to her feet immediately.

'Which one of you is Leyanne?' Meredith demanded.

'I am,' said the larger woman in the green gown.

'In that case, I must assume you are Minerva.' Meredith stared at the willowy woman standing by the table. She was dark-haired and fine-boned. Quite unusual in a Highlander woman. He cleared his throat. 'The two of you will accompany us back to Heartstone. There can be no more hiding. The King expects every sorceress to do her duty and defend the capital from our enemies.'

'We want no part in this conflict,' Leyanne said.

'You don't have a choice in the matter. The King's instructions were clear. Join his circle or face execution for treason.'

'You can't threaten us!'

Ryder suddenly grabbed hold of Leyanne's hair and pulled her face close to his, so close she must have had a faceful of his rancid breath. He gave her a wicked grin. 'That weren't no threat. Do what you're told or I'll have you squealing like a pig.'

In response, the sorceress raised her hands and frantically whispered words of arcane power. Meredith felt the abyssium ring on his finger begin to pulse and grow warm as it absorbed whatever hostile magic was being directed at the three Kingsmen.

A moment later Leyanne's hands dropped to her sides, eyes widening in shock as she realized her magic had failed her. 'How—'

Bagha clubbed her over the head with his mace. The woman dropped like a stone.

'*Anne!*' Minerva screamed. She began to move to the fallen woman, but Meredith blocked her path and guided her firmly back to the chair. 'Don't,' he said, as her lips began forming words of power. 'Your magic is useless against us.'

She didn't obey him at first. In a fit of pique he backhanded her across the face, bloodying her lips. He grabbed her chin and forced her to meet his gaze. He immediately regretted striking her. She was a pretty one, and hitting a woman was conduct unbecoming a true knight such as he.

Sir Meredith pointed behind him at Bagha and Ryder. 'Listen to me,' he whispered urgently. 'Those two men are dangerous. The big one haunted the roads of the Lake Reaching for years, robbing and murdering. I'm led to understand he would dismember the bodies of his victims, sometimes wearing their heads for weeks at a time. The grey-haired fellow is the lone survivor of a notorious gang that burned villages and killed children in their sleep. Our new king values skill at arms more than he does moral fortitude, and so he pardoned them both in return for their service. But make no mistake. If you refuse us, they will kill you.'

Minerva's breath quickened and her face went pale with fear. Sir Meredith placed a gauntleted hand on her shoulder. 'I'm not like them,' he said. 'I take no pleasure in killing.' He pointed at the book on the table. 'I see you like to read.'

The sorceress gave a distracted nod. Her gaze seemed fixed on the prone form of Leyanne.

'Then you are a rarity here. What are you reading at the moment?'

'A book my mother left me. Just some stories about knights. Why… why isn't she moving?'

At the mention of knights, Meredith's heart surged in his chest. 'Milady!' he exclaimed in delight. 'I *am* a knight! A knight of Tarbonne! I was forced to return to this land due to dire circumstance, with little recourse but to take up the kind of employment that best fits my skills. But not my character, I assure you.'

'Leyanne? Leyanne! You… you killed her…' If Minerva had heard his words she gave no indication. That disappointed Sir Meredith, but he wouldn't give up so easily. At long last, he had found the one. He turned to Bagha and Ryder.

'Take this woman's sister outside.'

The two Kingsmen dragged Leyanne across the floor and out of the door, leaving behind a thin trail of blood. Minerva must have seen it, for she screamed again.

'Hush. Hush now.' Sir Meredith smiled down at the pretty sorceress. She couldn't have known it, but the spirits had blessed her this day. He would save her; whisk her away from this place.

And in return, she would fix him.

Slowly he went down to one knee. 'Minerva. From the moment we met, I felt something between us. Let me take you away from here. I realize this may seem precipitate, but I've always believed a man must be guided by his heart as well as his head.'

Minerva stared at him. 'What?'

'Marry me.'

A moment of silence followed, and then the sorceress began to laugh. It wasn't the right kind of laughter, it sounded wrong. 'Marry you? My Leyanne is dead.'

'Nonsense. A splash of cold water and your sister will be fine.'

'She's not my sister!' Minerva's voice was a despairing moan.

Meredith frowned. Whatever did the woman mean?

'Marry you…' Minerva repeated incredulously. 'I don't even know your name.'

128

He gave her his best smile. 'Sir Meredith, my lady. Did I mention I am a knight?'

'Meredith? That's a girl's name.' Minerva laughed again, hysterical laughter, a high-pitched shriek that seemed to stab him right through the heart.

Something broke again.

He stumbled out of the cabin, trying to wipe the blood off his hands but instead smearing it over his breastplate. It was everywhere, all over his face, on his boots. Some had even managed to soak his undertunic.

Bagha and Ryder were waiting for him just outside. Leyanne's body sprawled at their feet.

Bagha shifted guiltily. 'I hit her too hard.'

'The other one?' Ryder asked.

Meredith shook his head.

They made their way out of the village in silence. Fifty yards from the cabin the dog began to bark at them, darting and biting at Sir Meredith's feet as if it wanted to tear his boots off. He gave it a hard kick and the dog yelped and quickly went still. He picked up the twitching animal and dropped it down the well, where it made a small splash.

Half a mile from Kingswood, a group of men led by the woodcutter chased them down.

'Butchers,' he spat. 'You killed those poor women. What you did to Minerva… you're sick.'

Sir Meredith turned away. 'Go home,' he said.

'You murdered them! They were good women. Never did no one any harm.'

'I believe what you mean to say is that they never did *anyone* any harm.'

'Fuck you!' The woodcutter raised his axe. The half-dozen men behind him followed his lead, clutching cudgels and axes and makeshift daggers.

Sir Meredith killed three of the men before Bagha and Ryder

had even readied their weapons, driving his sabre through the woodcutter's heart himself. Then he let Bagha cut off their heads, which they brought back to the village and placed along the fence posts while the survivors peered out from doorways, sobbing or cowering in terror.

Before they left Meredith had a change of heart. The Kingsmen decided to torch the place after all.

Just a Girl

SASHA'S HEAD FELT as though someone had used it as an anvil.

She rubbed at her temples and, not looking where she was going, she stumbled and almost fell into a passing merchant, a narrow-faced fellow who smelled faintly of garlic and perfume. He glowered at her and muttered something to the attendant hurrying along behind him. She caught a few words: 'clumsy' and 'bitch' muttered in a lilting Tarbonnese accent. She swallowed an angry retort and resisted the urge to slam an open palm into his face. Kicking up a fuss in the market would only invite more delays. She was already late; Ambryl would be growing suspicious.

Not for the first time that morning, Sasha cursed herself for succumbing to that insidious voice in her skull.

She had thought she had it under control after the incident with the moon dust she'd pilfered from the harbourmaster's office back in Dorminia. They'd been halfway across Deadman's Channel when a powerful gust of wind had ripped away her cloak and upended the pouch hidden within, coating both the deck and the swarthy captain in the silvery powder. Ambryl's threat to toss her overboard had forced a promise from her she had kept for the best part of a fortnight.

But yesterday evening the all-devouring need had returned with a vengeance. With the bag of *hashka* gone she was down to the green pills she'd discovered in Cole's apartment. They were a poor substitute for the moon dust; it had taken half the pills to get a decent buzz. An early-morning trip to the market had seemed like the perfect excuse to clear her head and avoid an inquisition from her older sister.

The white marble streets sparkled beneath Sasha's booted feet as she made her unsteady way between aisles of perfectly ordered booths. Stalls paraded a range of wares from every corner of the continent: merchants had crossed the sun-kissed sands of the deep south and braved the wild Unclaimed Lands to the east to bring their goods to the City of Towers. She saw traders from places as distant as Shamaath. The Shattered Realms in particular were well represented: there were crates filled with olives and blood-red cherries from Djanka; fine wines from Tarbonne; rows of brass cutlery from Espanda; even a few expertly crafted suits of armour from Grantz, superior to anything forged in the Trine. There were no weapons – the White Lady forbade the trade of such items in her city.

Sasha grimaced as a merchant from the Unclaimed Lands loudly extolled the merits of his patented miracle elixir three feet from her ear. She turned away, only to find herself staring into the face of a Whitecloak.

'Everything in order, lady?' The guard's tone didn't drip with the hostility Sasha would expect from one of Dorminia's Crimson Watch. In fact, the Whitecloaks seemed to possess none of the belligerence of their counterparts across the Broken Sea.

'Yes, officer,' she replied. The remaining pills were stashed safely back at the inn in which they were staying, the Lonely Siren, and in any case she had done nothing to warrant a search.

'That man,' the guard said, nodding at the Tarbonnese merchant now bartering loudly with an Ishari silk trader. 'Did he harass you in any way?'

Sasha stared at the guard in confusion. 'What?'

'I saw him put his hands on you.'

She shook her head and reached up to flick her long brown

hair from her eyes. It was beginning to annoy her. 'I stumbled into him. It was my fault, I wasn't looking where I was going.'

'Are you certain?' The Whitecloak's jaw clenched slightly. 'Being unfamiliar with our customs is no excuse. You press charges and that bastard will lose a finger or two. The White Lady takes a dim view of those that go around molesting women.'

Sasha flinched at the mention of severed fingers. Sudden visions of Three-Finger's scabrous face melting in the fire of the burning warehouse exploded in her mind like an errant fire-bomb. 'He didn't molest me,' she said quickly. 'Besides, we're in a market. Things happen. It's no big deal.'

She didn't add that Thelassa's Grand Market was positively timid compared with the Bazaar in Dorminia. There, customers and merchants alike pressed together so tightly no one could be certain whose hand was on what. And as long as said hands weren't clutching three inches of steel, no one much cared. On a few occasions a Watchman himself had seen fit to cop a good feel of her. She hadn't complained. It was just how the world was.

'In that case I'll take no further action. Good morning to you.' The guard nodded and walked off, his spotless cloak falling neatly behind him.

Sasha stared in the direction of the palace and massaged her throbbing temples. The Whitecloaks were seemingly unflappable and, she'd discovered to her annoyance, apparently incorruptible. Despite threats of impending disaster and attempts at bribery, not one of the guards on duty at the palace had allowed the sisters inside to speak with the city's fabled Magelord. After their third attempt in as many days, Sasha and Ambryl had been forced to admit defeat and plan an alternative approach. A week of bad-tempered bickering had followed with no progress. Sasha was just about ready to take the next ship back to Dorminia. The whole scheme seemed preposterous anyhow.

Turning up on the doorstep of the most powerful wizard in the land, clutching a scrap of tattooed flesh and bringing tales of imminent destruction at the hands of beings that haven't been seen in two thousand years, if indeed they ever existed at all... No wonder you sent us to do your dirty work, Halfmage.

There had been something different about the wizard, she had to admit. An unexpected gravitas that had convinced her, against her better judgement, to trust him. But it was obvious now that it had all been a crock of shit, a fanciful story put together by a man who in all likelihood wasn't quite sane. The most surprising thing of all was that Ambryl had bought it, too.

Sasha exited the Grand Market and began the long walk back to the inn, taking the main avenue that led west towards the harbour. The sun rode high overhead, bathing the city in a brilliant glow. Slender towers reached towards the heavens on both sides of the street. Delicate spires cast colossal shadows, dappling the white marble and giving the city an eldritch quality, like a vision from a dream or drug-induced hallucination. Thelassa was as beautiful as Dorminia was ugly, a delicate jewel perched on the east coast of the Broken Sea.

Yet there was something disquieting about this place. The longer she remained, the more uncomfortable she felt. Maybe it was just paranoia. The last time she quit the moon dust she had hidden inside her room for days, convinced a shadowy figure was stalking her. Cole had blundered into her apartment looking to borrow some money and she had almost knifed him in the gut. It was funny now, looking back. Or at least it would be, if Cole were still around.

A flood of memories consumed her then, and she walked the streets oblivious to the crowd that was gathering on the side of the road. It wasn't until the sound of cheering reached her ears and a line of men appeared in the wide, tree-lined artery leading from the palace that she realized a parade was approaching.

'What's going on?' she asked an old woman fussing with a small boy, likely her grandson. He kept fidgeting and staring at others in the crowd. To Sasha's mind he was just doing what any other child would do, but his guardian seemed to be growing increasingly frustrated by his behaviour.

'The Sumnians are leaving,' the woman replied. 'Going home to the Sun Lands. The White Lady wants the city back to normal for the Seeding.'

'The Seeding?'

The woman gave her a peculiar look. It seemed almost... *wistful*. 'The Seeding Festival. The Mistress herself will walk these very streets and bless those she deems worthy. Lucas, stand still! It's rude to stare! You don't want the pale women to see you gawking.'

The child dropped his eyes and stared at the ground. Glancing around, Sasha saw girls playing and laughing while the boys were as quiet as mice as they timidly watched the advancing soldiers. Scattered among the gathering crowd, the White Lady's handmaidens stood motionless in their virginal white robes.

Sasha hesitated. Ambryl would be growing suspicious at her absence. She ought to hurry back, but she felt an obligation to stay and witness the departing army's farewell.

She found a place next to the old woman and waited. The boy dared glance up at her, earning him a painful cuff around the back of the head from his grandmother. Sasha frowned at that before her attention returned to the avenue.

The Sumnians marched twenty abreast. Striding along at the very front of the procession was General Zahn: eight feet tall and resplendent in his ornate golden armour, like some mythical being out of the Age of Legend. The general raised his monstrous spear and won an answering cheer from the crowd. His company followed after him, forty ranks of dark-skinned warriors grinning and waving at the onlookers.

D'rak's company were next. They had suffered the heaviest losses in the fighting, and only a few hundred men formed up behind the flamboyant general with his exotic curved swords.

Sasha met his eyes for a moment and the sudden smile on his face reminded her of Cole. He had that same boyish enthusiasm.

She wiped a tear from her cheek, hoping no one had seen her moment of weakness. Cole was the most infuriating person she had ever known. There were times she would have happily throttled him, moments when his foolishness and sense of entitlement had driven her to distraction. He had alienated most of the other Shards with his behaviour. She remembered pleading with her mentor, promising Garrett that one day Cole would repay the faith the old merchant had shown in him.

And he had. Despite his bravado, beneath it all Cole was exactly what he had always claimed to be. He was a hero. Not a coward and a junkie like her. A hero.

And now he was gone.

The parade was almost past. Zolta's company was the last to march by, a full one thousand men. The Fat General had suffered not a single loss in the conflict. He waddled along at the front of his company, as wide as he was tall, the many-coloured silks he wore dripping with sweat. Behind Zolta, soldiers pushed carts piled high with loot plundered from the Noble Quarter in Dorminia – their reward for their dubious role in the liberation of the Grey City.

The sight angered Sasha. It was Dorminia's wealth they were stealing away to the south. Riches that could have been used to help the poor and the starving. She was about to turn and cut through a side street when one particular southerner caught her attention. Whereas the other men wore leather vests and marched in formation, this one cloaked himself in a black robe and walked alone at the rear of the company.

'You!' she shouted. 'I know you! You're the Darkson!'

The cowled head turned towards her, but the man did not slow.

'It's me! Sasha! I need to speak with you! It's about Davarus Cole, the boy you trained. He hasn't been seen since the night… since Salazar died.'

Since the night he killed Salazar, she had been about say. But it wouldn't be smart to blurt out the truth. Not with the White Lady's handmaidens beginning to take notice and Thelassa's immortal mistress clearly wanting the facts of Salazar's demise covered up.

The man who called himself the Darkson hesitated. Beneath that hood she knew there was a surprisingly distinguished face. However, all she could see now were his eyes. They seemed to give her a guilty look before flicking away. The assassin increased his stride, losing himself in the men just ahead of him.

'Wait!' She began walking to keep pace with the soldiers, weaving around onlookers in the crowd, struggling to catch a glimpse of the Shamaathan. 'You know something about his disappearance! What is it?'

Sumnian faces turned to stare at her. Some laughed while others gestured obscenities. She ignored them, crossed the avenue and began pushing her way through the soldiers until she finally caught sight of the Darkson again.

Only a few more steps...

There was the sensation of air brushing against her cheek and then one of the White Lady's handmaidens suddenly blocked the way. 'Go no further,' the pale woman ordered in her monotone voice.

Sasha stared boldly back. She knew the handmaiden could tear her apart in an instant if she chose, but the blackness was rising, despair devouring her fear and driving her onwards. 'I need to speak with that man.'

'You may not. This is your final warning.'

Her teeth ground together. She stared daggers at the pale woman. She wished she were Brodar Kayne or Jerek the Wolf, so that she might cleave the thing apart. She wished she were a wizard like Brianna or the Halfmage, so that she might obliterate it in a burst of magic. But she wasn't any of those things.

She was just a girl.

*

137

Lyressa looked up from cleaning glasses as Sasha stumbled through the door of the Lonely Siren. The proprietress of the inn was a kindly woman heavy with child. Sasha felt a moment of guilt as she elbowed past her towards the stairs, but it quickly shrivelled and died. Nothing mattered, not the words that spilled from Lyressa's mouth, words that barely registered, or the woman's angry expression. The only thing that mattered was that all-consuming need.

She took the creaking steps two at a time. They were wooden; the entire building was constructed from timber rather than the white marble for which Thelassa was famous. The Siren was the cheapest inn the sisters had been able to find, located in seemingly the only part of the city that smelled like a big city ought to.

Just then Sasha couldn't have cared less if the whole place had reeked of shit. She barged into her room, shielded her eyes against the blinding light of the sun that filtered through the window and hurried across to her bed. She thrust a hand beneath the pillow, searching frantically for the drugs hidden there, the key to the oblivion she craved.

There was a whisper of movement behind her. She felt something break on the back of her head.

And then she was on her back, staring up at the rafters, dancing lights exploding in her vision. A roar began, somewhere far away. It grew louder, until her skull was raging hot fire and a sudden, wet throbbing threatened to burst it apart like a rotten fruit.

'Is *this* what you're looking for?' Ambryl loomed into view above her. Her sister dangled the bag of green pills in one hand. In the other she held the remnants of the vase she'd just broken over Sasha's head. She allowed the shards to shower down to the floor, and then she crushed them beneath a booted foot, grinding them deep into the throw rug that covered the empty space in the middle of the room.

'You hit me,' Sasha whispered. She blinked furiously, trying to stop the world from spinning.

'Yes.' Ambryl knelt down and grabbed a fistful of Sasha's hair. 'You promised you would get yourself clean, sister. Swore that you possessed no more narcotics. And yet look what I found hidden in your bed.' She gave the bag a shake.

'How... how did you know about them?'

'You are aware that I served Lord Salazar. That I was an Augmentor for several years. You have no idea of the things I did to protect the city during that time, little sister. I learned to read a lie in a person's eyes before it left their tongue... often just *before* the tongue left their mouth. I have maimed and killed and tortured. And I regret nothing, because whoring oneself on the streets gives one a unique perspective on necessity. It is for that reason that I assign to you no blame for your role in Dorminia's fall. You did what you had to do. But I will warn you one last time: don't ever lie to me.'

Sasha winced as Ambryl released her grip on her hair. Her sister's hand came away red with blood. 'I'm bleeding,' Sasha said numbly.

'It's only a flesh wound. Ask yourself, sister. What would you have done if instead of me lurking in the shadows just then, it had been a man? A man, waiting to force himself on you.'

Sasha didn't reply. She was beginning to feel faint.

Ambryl stashed the drugs on her person and turned to leave the room. 'I will dispose of these pills and send Lyressa to clean up this mess. I hope this lesson was worth the cost of that broken vase. We have little enough coin as it is.'

'Wait,' Sasha said weakly. Her sister paused near the door. 'A woman at the market told me about a festival called the Seeding. The White Lady herself will walk the streets. This could be our chance.'

'Our chance,' Ambryl echoed.

'To deliver the Halfmage's message.' Sasha didn't know why she felt so calm. She ought to be furious, aghast that her own sister had just broken a pot over her head. Instead she felt empty.

'To hell with the Halfmage.'

'But you said you believed his story!'

'Oh, I do. He was telling the truth. Or at least what he believed to be the truth.'

'Then what—'

'I didn't come here to deliver a message to the Magelord of this city.' Ambryl turned to stare back at Sasha, and the expression on her sister's face was more terrifying than the dead stare of the White Lady's handmaidens. 'I came here to kill her.'

Unbroken

DAVARUS COLE BLINKED away sweat and attempted to swallow. His throat felt drier than the dust that coated him from head to toe. The pickaxe was heavy in his hands and rubbed painfully against the sores on his palms. He took a shuddering breath and tried to focus on the sheer rock face in front of him. The stone was black and pitted all over, as if some disease in the earth were slowly eating it away.

He craned his neck and stared longingly up at the blue sky peering down through the fissure. The walls were thirty feet high. There was no way out of the pit, not until sundown when the operation would halt for the day and the Mad Dogs would haul the miners out.

It was hard to be certain of the time, but Cole guessed it would be another hour before work ceased and they could all head back to Newharvest. The Indebted and Condemned would each be handed a warm meal and a handful of copper coins; chump change they could spend as they saw fit, though each man was required to return to the dosshouse shortly after the curfew bell or face dire consequences.

Cole had spent his meagre earnings on fresh bandages and salve from the town physician. Though his stomach wound appeared to be healing, it still leaked foul pus when he pushed himself too hard. It was bothering him now.

'Urgh,' he said.

'Easy, Ghost. Don't let the Mad Dogs see you struggling.

Those bastards will cut your throat and call for the corpse-carver before you're done twitching.'

Smiler flashed a grin as if there was something terribly amusing about the prospect. He had the most perfect set of teeth Cole had ever seen, a mouthful of pearly whites that fitted the rest of his face about as well as a sweet cherry chart served on a bed of horse shit.

'I need water,' Cole croaked. The other miners had taken to calling him Ghost, and that was very much what he felt like. Closer to dead than alive. Every day he grew paler and weaker. His hair was more grey than black, now.

'I'm all out,' Smiler said. He gave his waterskin a shake to demonstrate. 'You could ask the retard. Thought the two of you were close.'

Cole frowned and turned to the third man in the pit. Dull Ed was chipping away at the rock with relentless enthusiasm, his face screwed up in concentration as if the act of repeatedly banging a hammer against a wall was a delicate task that required absolute focus. Ed might be lacking in brains but he never seemed to grow tired of the arduous and mind-numbing work.

Cole stared at the waterskin hanging from the big man's waist and licked his parched lips. 'May... may I have some of your water?'

The halfwit looked up and his mouth sagged open in confusion. 'Whuh?'

'Your water, Ed. May I have some?'

Ed looked down at his waterskin. His broad face slipped into a sly grin, and Cole sighed, immediately regretting asking the man for a favour. The Condemned transported from the Obelisk's dungeons were for the most part the kind of men a three-copper whore would cross the street to avoid. Smiler's eyes held something dark, something even the brightness of his smile couldn't disguise; Smokes would mutter constantly about his desire to set fire to anyone within his immediate vicinity; Shank had already lived up to his name, proudly boasting of gutting the poor sod Derkin had found face down in the dormitory on the day Cole had awakened from his fever. Dull Ed, however, was different. There was no malice about him, only an endless appetite for juvenile pranks and an unsettling habit of crawling naked under Cole's blanket in the middle of night, whispering fearfully about monsters hiding under his bed. At first Cole had tried kicking him out, but the halfwit had caused a scene and woken half the dorm and in the end Cole had let him stay. If nothing else, Ed's lumbering body next to him halved the likelihood of getting stabbed by Shank in the middle of the night.

'Please, Ed. Just pass me the skin. I'm thirsty.'

The halfwit smiled. 'Here,' the big simpleton rumbled. He held out the waterskin.

Cole reached across to take the proffered skin. He felt a sudden burst of charitable feeling towards the big fellow. 'You know, Ed, I don't care what the others say about you. As far as I'm concerned, you're all right—' He recoiled as a splash of water struck him right in the eye.

'Hurr hurr!'

'Cut that out!' Cole rasped. Despite his outrage he ran his tongue greedily over his lips, lapping up every last drop of water running down his face.

Oblivious to Cole's anger, Ed gave the waterskin another shake. He wore a huge grin, clearly delighted by the trick he'd just pulled. 'Hurr hurr!' he boomed again.

Cole grabbed the waterskin before the halfwit could waste any more of the water. He attempted to wrest it off him, but though Dull Ed had the mind of a child his body was six and a half feet of solid muscle beneath a layer of flab. The two of them lurched around the pit, locked in an ungainly dance, Ed's laughter loud enough to wake the dead – which in the Blight was a very real risk.

'Ghost!' Smiler's warning caused Cole to look up. Staring down into the pit were a handful of scowling faces.

'Ed, stop! The Mad Dogs are watching us,' Cole whispered urgently.

The big man paid him no mind. With another roaring laugh, Ed grabbed him around the wrists and then swung him around, spinning Cole like a doll.

The world seemed to blur. The black walls surrounding him became one long, dark tunnel, Ed's beaming face at the centre. Cole suddenly recalled his nightmare aboard the ship, floating in an endless void, the yawning maw of a sentient skull-planet waiting to swallow him up—

The vision was interrupted as Smiler inadvertently took one of Cole's boots right in the face, stumbling back to bump painfully into the side of the pit.

Finally the momentum slowed as Ed decided he had had enough fun for the moment. Big chest heaving, the halfwit set Cole down and proceeded to stagger unsteadily around the pit, a huge smile plastered to his face.

'The *fuck* is going on down there?' bellowed a familiar voice from above. Leather harnesses were lowered into the pit. 'Get up here! If I have to tell you again, my men will fill you full of quarrels and I'll send for the corpse-carver to bring you up in pieces.'

'Good job, shits-for-brains.' Smiler spat. He had a nasty cut on his face and might have been talking to Cole as much as to Ed. He flashed his teeth, but it was less a beaming smile of happiness and more the snarl of an angry dog about to rip someone's throat out. 'You've got us into trouble now.'

Cole heaved a weary sigh and grabbed a harness. He couldn't understand why this kind of thing kept happening to him.

One at a time each of the three men was pulled from the shaft. Cole had to squint against the sudden fury of the red sun overhead as he was dragged out and dumped onto the hard ground. The wasteland that was the Blight stretched out in every direction: tortured black earth where little grew, in

144

places torn open and weeping noxious fumes. The few trees that had managed to put down roots in the area were twisted and sickly things, corrupted by the presence of the dead colossus lying broken beneath the earth.

To the west, Newharvest sprawled like a cancerous growth. Just outside town was the dark outline of the gigantic metal silos in which the magic ore gathered by the miners was deposited at the end of each day.

'Look at me, bitch.'

Cole tore his gaze from the Blight and towards the even more uninviting sight of Corvac.

The leader of the Mad Dogs and overseer of Newharvest's mining operation was a wiry little man. What he lacked in size, Corvac made up for with a mean streak a mile wide. That and the kind of demented overconfidence only the unquestioning loyalty of fifty armed thugs could impart.

'You deaf, bitch? Want me to clean out your ears with my sword?'

Cole shook his head. Ed was still struggling with the straps of his harness, and one of the Mad Dogs helped him out of the device none too gently. 'Dumb bastard,' the man muttered. A dozen other Mad Dogs quickly encircled the three miners. They were hard-faced fellows, armed with crossbows and short swords.

Behind Corvac and his Mad Dogs rose the Horn. It towered over them, a monstrous projection of some unearthly black material that seemed to drink in the fading sunlight. From what Cole remembered from Garrett's history lessons, the body of Tyrannus was said to have exploded when it fell from the heavens and struck earth, the pieces of the dead god scattering to eventually form the Blight. Below the Horn rested the Black Lord's severed head. Its vile presence enriched the surrounding bedrock with more concentrated magic than anywhere else in the Trine. But it also made the immediate area incredibly dangerous.

Corvac was looking Cole up and down now, his thin lips curling as though he were examining a particularly foul-smelling turd. 'They call you the Ghost. They say you killed two prisoners aboard the ship that brought you here.'

Cole said nothing. Better to keep silent, in his experience. He had a nasty habit of talking himself into trouble.

'You ought to be putting in the shift of three men to make up for the two you murdered,' Corvac continued. 'You ought to be working your *gods-damned* arse to the bone.'

The Mad Dog leader swaggered forward and thrust out his chest until he was nose to nose with Cole, who wasn't a tall man but nonetheless had a good few inches on Corvac. 'Instead I see you fooling around with the big retard there like it ain't my nuts you're busting. Like it ain't right and proper that murderers and rapists and other scum should pay their debts to society. Let me ask you something.'

'Yes?' Cole hazarded.

'Do I look like a cunt?'

Cole licked his lips. 'Uh... no?'

'Then why are you trying to fuck me? No one fucks Corvac!' The Mad Dog's voice became a shriek and he sprayed spittle all over Cole's face. He spun and strolled over to Smiler. 'You. Are you trying to fuck me?'

'Me?' Smiler flashed a puzzled grin. The wrong move.

Corvac lashed out with the hilt of his sword, smashing Smiler right in the face. Blood and broken teeth exploded from the Condemned's mouth, and Smiler dropped like a stone. 'You piece of shit,' Corvac whispered hoarsely. 'Giving me that queer smile like you're picturing your dick in my mouth. I told you. No one fucks Corvac! The three of you will pay for your part in this fractious!'

'Fracas,' Dull Ed uttered. He hadn't said a word up until then.

Corvac turned to the halfwit. 'What did you just say?' he asked, voice a deadly murmur.

'Fracas,' Ed repeated solemnly. 'You spoke it wrong.'

146

Corvac was across to him in an instant, his knee driving into Ed's stomach, sword hilt bludgeoning the big dullard over the skull. Ed hit the dirt and then began to sob like a child.

'You're calling *me* stupid? These men hang on every word I say! You're a cretin who can't even tie his own bootlaces!' Corvac aimed a vicious kick at Ed's head, leaving a scarlet imprint of his boot on the halfwit's face.

Something stirred inside Cole. 'Stop hurting him,' he said in a dry rasp.

The Mad Dog's eyes narrowed to slits.

'It was my fault,' Cole added quickly, scarcely able to believe what he was saying. 'I'm responsible. If you have to punish anyone, it should be me.'

He didn't know why he had spoken up. All he knew was that he couldn't watch Ed get kicked to death. It wasn't the halfwit's fault he had the mind of a child.

Corvac made an exaggerated show of pointing at Cole with his short sword and turned to his men. 'Take a look at this one, lads! Seems we got a genuine hero on our hands!'

'I'm no hero,' Cole muttered.

'You're a fucking idiot is what you are!' Corvac sprang at him, the point of his sword aimed straight at Cole's chest.

A year ago it would have struck home. It was a nice move, a deftly executed killing stroke. He might be a bully but it turned out Corvac knew how to use a sword. Yet he was no Brodar Kayne. Davarus Cole had been trained by the Darkson, the most infamous assassin in the south, a master in the arts of unarmed combat.

He waited until the sword was a foot from his chest and then suddenly he pivoted at the waist, turning so that the steel tip skewered empty air where his body had been but a moment before. Quick as a snake, he grabbed hold of Corvac's sword arm as the man's momentum carried him past. A twist and a tug later and he was standing before the Mad Dog leader, Corvac's own short sword now gripped firmly in his pale and callused hands.

'You sneaky little *bitch*!' Corvac snarled, red-faced with anger or embarrassment or quite possibly both. 'Men! Kill him!'

Cole watched the crossbows being raised, listened to blades whispering from sheaths. There was a certain dignity in this, he reflected. He would die a good death, sword in hand. Then he saw Derkin watching him with a sad expression, and his calm faltered at the sight of Bessie in the hunchback's hands. Dignified or not, he didn't relish the prospect of that huge cleaver going to work on his corpse. All thoughts of a defiant last stand abandoned, he squeezed his eyes shut and waited for the end.

'Stand down. All of you!'

Cole dared open one eye a crack.

A handful of Whitecloaks were approaching, led by Captain Priam. For the most part the town's garrison did not venture outside Newharvest, leaving the running of the mining operation to the Mad Dogs. Whatever his reasons for being here, Captain Priam's shaved head was the most welcome sight Cole had seen in days.

'What's going on?' Priam demanded. He had a soft voice, almost feminine, but it carried well and contained a quiet strength. He reminded Cole of Captain Kramer, the skipper of the *Redemption* – the ship that had taken him on the ill-fated voyage to the Swell.

Kramer was also the first man Davarus Cole had ever killed.

'Rebellion!' Corvac barked in response to Priam's question. 'These Condemned must die!'

Captain Priam shook his head and gestured towards the north. 'There's been an incident at the Fist. The earth shifted and a dozen men were crushed. We cannot afford to lose anyone else.'

'Shit.' Corvac spat and turned away.

*

Cole leaned back in the chair and stared glumly down at the table. It was a rickety thing, covered in scratches and with a wobbly leg on either side. Smiler and Ed sat opposite Cole. The former nursed a swollen jaw, while the latter was wrapped in bandages and carried more bruises than the rotten apples unscrupulous fruit merchants occasionally sold in Dorminia's Bazaar for ten a copper. That Ed had been able to walk back to town unaided was testament to the halfwit's unexpected tenacity. He had taken a heck of a beating, and Cole considered himself a good judge in such matters, having been on the receiving end of a fair few in his time.

Across the table from the three men, an old Condemned named Whistler shook his shaggy grey head and gave a throaty chuckle. 'You're a rare one, Ghost. Thought I'd seen it all, but to hear how you plucked Corvac's sword from his hand and turned it against him... Sounds to me like one of them tales the young women like to read about. Of heroes and suchlike. All that shite.'

'It was just a trick I learned,' Cole said irritably. Why did everyone insist on thinking of him as a hero? He was a bastard and a whoreson. 'You know what I've learned?'

'Yeah?' obliged Whistler.

'That true heroes don't exist. The world sucks the goodness out of everyone sooner or later.'

'That's a cynical point of view.'

'Well, it's true! I used to be an optimist. People were drawn to me because of it. Drawn to my charisma. I even had a henchman. His name was Three-Finger and he was a good sort. But just like me, the grim reality of life got to him eventually. Turned him into a bitter husk of a man.'

'A sorry tale and no mistake.'

'It's just how I feel. I don't even have money for a beer.'

Neither he nor Smiler nor Ed had been handed any coin at day's end. Corvac wasn't the type to let go of a grudge easily.

Cole's stomach growled again. The evening meals seemed

portioned to leave the miners just the right side of famished. He was hungry, broke and had made an enemy of one of the most powerful figures in Newharvest.

'I wish I could help,' Whistler said. 'But I'm out of coin too. I could really use a warm beer and a cold woman.'

Cole frowned. 'Don't you mean a *cold* beer and a *warm* woman?'

'Yeah. That's what I meant.' Whistler shifted uncomfortably.

Smiler sucked on his remaining teeth for a moment before speaking. His mouth was all swollen and he looked as though he had swallowed a handful of stones. 'Whithler... didn't you uthe to work down at the morgue? I'm thure I remember your fathe. How'd you end up in the Obelithkth dungeonth?'

'It don't matter,' Whistler snapped. They sat in silence for a time, lost in their thoughts. Except possibly Ed, who just looked lost. Cole glanced up when he heard footsteps approaching.

'You must be the one they call the Ghost.'

The speaker was a burly man with green eyes. Behind him loomed two equally large men.

'Yes,' Cole answered wearily. He knew he had taken a risk coming to the Re-Spite, what with the Mad Dogs all riled up about the incident with Corvac. He was quickly reaching the point where he no longer cared.

'They call me Floater. Mind if I buy you a beer? That prick Corvac's been tormenting us for months. It's about time someone stood up to him.'

Cole breathed a relieved sigh and beckoned them to sit. Floater took a seat while the other two men went to order drinks. 'Only a few more weeks till I'm outta this hellhole,' Floater said. 'Does me good to know Corvac got a taste of his own medicine before I left. I'm looking forward to telling my children about it once I'm back in the City of Towers.'

'You're Thelassan?' asked Whistler.

'Yeah. Second shipment. I got six months for slapping a shop-keep after she tried to swindle me. Most of the Indebted from the first shipment are home already. Those that survived the Blight, that is. Lost a couple of pals at the Fist just today.'

Floater's friends returned with a tray piled with tankards. The big Thelassan handed one to Cole, who stared down at the murky liquid within. He gave it an experimental sip and winced. It tasted like the cheap pisswater they served in Dorminia's scummiest dives.

'I'd go slow with this stuff,' warned Floater. 'It's stronger than you think.'

'I can handle myself,' Cole replied, a little defensively. It was true, his drinking prowess had been near legendary among the regulars of Dorminia's taverns. He smiled, remembering all the times he had had to drag his friends from the dives lining Copper Street, so drunk they could barely stand. Sometimes he'd been the one who couldn't walk out. He would wake up in a gutter somewhere, his friends having disappeared after he'd squandered his allowance buying them all drinks. That didn't seem right somehow. Not now that he thought about it.

He frowned and brought the tankard up to his lips, then downed the beer in one long gulp. It tasted like bilge water but there was no denying the warm glow it left.

'It's funny,' Floater was saying. 'Working the Blight's hell. But I tell you, I've felt more... *alive* here than I ever did back in the City of Towers.'

Floater's friends nodded their agreement. The man's observations didn't make much sense to Cole, but as long as the Thelassans were supplying the drinks he wasn't going to argue.

'So then, Ghost,' Floater said, passing him another beer. 'How'd you learn to dodge a sword? And why are you so damned pale? If I didn't know better I'd think you one of the Mistress's handmaidens. Except they're all female.'

Cole took a long sip of his beer and stared into the depths of the murky liquid. 'I've seen a few things in my time. Done some stuff you probably wouldn't believe. I even considered myself a hero, once. Then I was betrayed. I took a dagger in the stomach.

I think it was coated in some kind of poison. That's why I'm so pale.'

Floater nodded at Ed. 'Sounds pretty heroic, the way you stepped in to rescue your friend there.'

Cole shrugged and drained the rest of his beer. There was a pleasant glow in his chest now. 'Garrett always said you have to protect those weaker than you.'

'Garrett?'

'My mentor. He was murdered.'

'Tough break.'

Cole nodded and grabbed another tankard. He took a long gulp, draining it faster than he intended and accidentally spilling some over his lap. 'The Blight won't break me,' he said suddenly.

'What's that, Ghost?'

'I said the Blight won't break me. I'm going to escape. I'm going to find Sasha.'

'Thatha?' Smiler repeated, creating a moment of confusion around the table as the others tried to work out what the hell he had just said. 'Who ith thhe?'

'She...' Cole searched for the words. When they'd last parted Sasha had told him he was an asshole. Told him that Garrett would be ashamed of him. She'd been angry, probably on her time of the month if Cole was any judge of women. She hadn't meant what she'd said to him. Had she?

'Sasha is the reason I won't die in this place,' he rallied, impressing even himself. He emptied his tankard and set it down on the table, a little unsteadily.

'You're Condemned,' Floater told him gently. 'You're stuck here for life. There's no way out.'

'No way out,' Cole repeated, slurring the words slightly. 'Who says there's no way out?' He thought of all the times he had endured against the odds. *The Swell. The Obelisk. The Darkson's betrayal. I survived them all. They have no idea who I am!* Well, it was time they learned.

He surged to his feet and snatched up Whistler's beer.

'Hey, that's mine!' the old man protested, but Cole ignored him. He drained the beer in a single gulp and flung the empty tankard across the table. It landed with a loud clatter, getting the attention of half the tavern. Just as Cole had planned.

'My name is Davarus Cole,' he hollered. 'I've been tested at every turn. Suffered adversity you can't even begin to understand. But I'm still standing. You would as well attempt to break mountains with your bare hands as break me! You would as well try to shackle a raging storm! Know this: Davarus Cole… *will not be caged!*'

'Twat,' someone muttered at a nearby table.

Cole swayed slightly. 'I'm going for a piss,' he announced dramatically, still lost in the moment. The glow-globes overhead seemed to pulse as he staggered towards the door. The floor heaved beneath him. Annoyed faces stared at him and he stared right back, unafraid. He felt almost like his old self again, and it felt good.

Just before he reached the door, it opened and a small group of women sauntered in. There were no female miners in Newharvest, only a handful of Freewomen looking to make some easy coin before they returned to the City of Towers. Many were the wives of Mad Dogs, though none were wedded to Whitecloaks; apparently Thelassa's city guard did not take wives. In any case, these particular women did not look like the marrying sort.

'Excuse me,' Cole slurred, making to walk around the women. As he moved past, the wavy-haired blonde at the front of the group placed a hand on his arm.

'Fancy a good time, darling?' she drawled, giving him a wicked grin. Her breath was warm on his ear and Cole felt himself respond. It had been long time since he had felt the soft touch of a woman. He stared at her, noting the revealing cut of her clothing, and a suspicion began to take hold.

'Are you a whore?' he asked loudly.

The woman's smile remained fixed on her face even as her eyes hardened. 'We don't use that word around here. I'm whatever you want me to be. A silver will buy you ten minutes with one of my ladies.'

'I only need two,' Cole said, thinking he might borrow a few coppers off someone. 'Do you offer discounts?'

The whore's eyes flashed in anger. 'No.'

The sound of chairs scraping backwards filled the room as men rose and began fishing around in their pockets, counting their coins out onto the tables. Cole glanced at his own table with bleary eyes. Floater and his two friends had wandered over to the bar. Smiler was asleep, wide-open mouth revealing the sorry mess Corvac had made of his once perfect teeth. Whistler just looked angry, though Cole couldn't think why.

One by one the whores paired off with punters and departed into one of the rooms at the back. No one approached the blonde. Cole thought that odd seeing as she possessed the most obvious assets, though if he were being honest none of the women were exactly great lookers.

'Excuse me,' he said, reaching out to guide the woman gently out of his path, but she chose that exact moment to turn and say something to another hooker and his hand accidentally brushed against her breasts.

The blonde slapped his hand away angrily. 'You pay first, you fucking animal!' she snapped. The sudden change in her demeanour shocked Cole even through his drunken haze. 'Give me a silver and I'll tug you off. That's all you're getting. I ain't no piece of meat.'

'I don't have any money,' Cole said. 'I just want to go for a piss.'

The woman's face twisted in rage. 'You've already tasted the goods,' she hissed. 'Now you pay. Or I'll see you get what Mockface got!'

'Hang on, that's not fair!' Cole glanced over at his table again seeking support. Whistler seemed about to say something, but then he looked down at the tankard Cole had hurled to the floor and frowned.

'No one fucks Corvac,' Ed said suddenly.

'You're damn right they don't!' the blonde spat. She pointed a quivering finger at Cole, pressing it right up into his nose. 'And no one fucks me without paying!'

'Just get out of the way,' Cole said, angry himself now. He thrust her aside and stormed towards the door. He turned back just before leaving, petty irritation getting the better of him. 'Pay you?' he said sarcastically. 'You should pay *me*.'

Cole felt a little guilty when he saw the shocked outrage on the woman's face, but it had been a long day. He had the girl of his dreams waiting for him back in Dorminia. Even if he had possessed the coin, he would be damned if he'd disrespect himself or Sasha by paying for such an average-looking hooker.

The night air was pleasantly fresh after the stifling heat of the tavern. He made his stumbling way around the side of the Black Lord's Re-Spite until he found a spot illuminated by the light from the building opposite. Then he tugged out his cock and began to relieve himself with a satisfied sigh.

He found himself thinking of the mysterious blind stranger who had appeared to him at the dosshouse. He wondered if it might have been a hallucination, some lingering effect of the poison that had knocked him unconscious for the best part of a month and sapped the colour from his skin. He still wasn't sure how he had survived. Every now and then he thought he could hear a crow cawing, but it was always just on the edge of hearing, too faint for him to be sure.

'There he is!'

The triumphant shriek came from behind him. Cole spun, inadvertently spraying piss over the trio of men who were charging right for him. Fumbling with his breeches, he barely had time to thrust his manhood away before they were upon him. One of them punched him in the head; another kicked his legs away. He fell against the wall of the tavern. A boot slammed into his chest, pinning him down.

'Ghost!' Corvac spat.

'You know this little shit?' It was the blonde from the tavern.

'You bet I do. Ain't that right, bitch? First you embarrass me in front of my men. Then you disrespect my woman. What, she ain't good enough for you? My Goldie's not fit for the mighty Ghost? Or maybe you're just scared you can't satisfy her?'

'Tiny dick,' Goldie sneered. 'He's got a tiny dick. I saw it just now. He ain't no real man. Not like you, baby.'

Cole's heart was hammering in his chest. Between the punch one of Corvac's lackeys had just landed on him and the alcohol coursing through his veins, he was too dizzy to think straight.

'Are we going to execute him like we did Mockface?' Goldie asked hopefully.

Corvac shook his head. 'That'd be too easy. This is personal.' He gestured at his thugs. 'Turn him around. Pin his arms. I'm gonna show this bitch what a real man is.'

Cole flailed desperately as Corvac's goons grabbed his elbows. They were bigger than him and stronger than him. He couldn't escape their iron grip. He felt his breeches being pulled down and suddenly bile rose in his stomach. He heard Corvac positioning himself behind him.

'You don't fuck Corvac,' the Mad Dog leader whispered. 'Corvac fucks you.'

Cole waited, eyes squeezed tightly shut, trying not to sob. He wouldn't give them the satisfaction.

He waited. Waited some more. For that awful moment.

'Fuck. It's happened again. *Fuck*. Useless piece of—'

'I can help, baby, just let me just warm you up—'

'Get away from it, you dirty whore! Gaz, pass me that cudgel you keep on your belt. The old pick handle.'

'This? Shit, boss, I don't want it shoved up—'

'I don't care give a fuck what you want! Bitch needs to learn his place. Now gag him. I don't want his screams drawing attention. We've only got a quarter-bell until curfew.'

As it turned out, it was considerably shorter than a quarter-bell. Barely more than a few minutes, in fact. But for Davarus Cole it seemed to last an eternity.

The Better Place

'**D**OES... DOES IT *hurt?*'
Her mother shook her head but couldn't disguise a slight intake of breath as Yllandris gently wiped the blood from her brow with a wet rag. Her skin had already begun to swell. Soon she would bear a vicious bruise that nothing would be able to conceal. The other townswomen would gossip, muttering that perhaps she had done something to deserve it, that she must have disappointed her husband somehow. Yllandris had overheard them once when her mother had sent her to buy fish at the market. They saw only her father's firm jaw, the reputation he had brought back with him from the West Reaching.

They didn't see the blackness that had festered within him since he had returned from the war. The drink-fuelled rage that had her cowering in her room while her mother bore the brunt of his demons.

'It's only a bruise. You should go to bed. In case your father comes back.'

'I wish he'd died at Red Valley.'

Yllandris caught the slap before it reached her cheek. Somehow that made it worse. 'Don't,' her mother whispered. 'Don't speak like that.'

Her mother's hand felt small and weak in her own. Yllandris stared down at the broken earthenware scattered across the floor with eyes suddenly wet with tears. 'I'm sorry,' she said.

Her mother hesitated; then she wrapped her arms around

her and pulled her close. 'It's not your fault, sweetheart. None of this is your fault.'

'I'll find a way to help us,' Yllandris whispered. 'I'm almost a woman now. I'll find somewhere for us both to live, so he can't hurt you any more. Just wait and see.'

Her mother smiled at her and took her chin gently in her hands. 'I don't doubt it. You're strong and beautiful and clever. Whatever happens, I will never regret marrying your father. Because without him I wouldn't have you.'

'I'll make you proud,' Yllandris said. She hugged her mother close: close enough to hear her heart beating.

'You already have, child,' her mother replied, running trembling fingers through her hair.

Yllandris opened her eyes. Early-morning sunlight seeped through the cracks in the roof far above, illuminating motes of dust dancing golden between thick wooden beams. For a moment she was hopelessly disorientated. She felt someone tugging on her hair and twisted her neck, half expecting to see her mother smiling down at her.

Instead she stared up into the sweaty face of a young boy. He blinked at her uncertainly. 'Rinny said to wake you,' he mumbled. He fiddled with her hair a moment longer, then wiped his nose with a grubby hand and stifled a big yawn.

Yllandris sat up and looked around, slowly familiarizing herself with her surroundings. She was curled up on the floor of the Foundry, in one of the many storage rooms off the central forge chamber. The heat was stifling: her shawl was covered in sweat and the dry skin on her cheek bothered her more than usual.

She remembered waking in the early hours of the morning, feeling terrified and alone. She thought she had heard a mysterious bang coming from the direction of the Great Lodge – a sound like a clap of thunder. Still half-asleep, she had walked the short distance from her hut to the welcoming glow of the

Foundry and settled down among the town's orphans. Several of the children were watching her now, wide-eyed and sleepy-faced.

'Rinny?' Yllandris repeated slowly.

The boy nodded. 'She's with Yorn and a stranger with weird eyes. The iron man is here too!'

The iron man? Yllandris rose unsteadily. She felt uneasy, and a moment later she realized it was the absence of noise that unsettled her. For weeks the Foundry had reverberated with the pounding of hammers on anvils and the screeching of bellows. Now the roar of the furnace was the only sound she could hear through the thick stone walls.

She brushed herself down and then made her way towards the source of the heat, heedless of the sweat that trickled down her face and made a damp mop of her black hair. As recently as two months ago the thought of facing the world in such a state would have horrified her. Since then she had seen the face of true horror and it had chased away such petty vanities. They belonged to a different woman now.

She slowed as she approached the pair of huge furnaces that dominated the forge chamber. They still burned bright, but elsewhere anvils lay unused, hammers and tongs haphazardly left atop them. The blacksmiths had apparently downed tools and vacated the Foundry in a hurry. All except old Braxus, who had been tasked with overseeing the endless production of new weapons the King had ordered. He sagged before the leftmost furnace, looking exhausted.

To either side of the blacksmith were Yorn, and the Northman with the bloodshot eyes whose face seemed familiar. The third Kingsman, the armoured warrior who had helped murder the Black Reaching sorceresses, was facing Braxus and appeared to be remonstrating with him. Corinn waited timidly nearby.

'Yllandris,' Yorn grunted when he saw her. 'The Shaman's forces are marching on Heartstone. Your sisters are gathering at the north gate.'

Yllandris's mouth was suddenly dry. 'Did Shranree send you to fetch me?'

Yorn shook his head and gestured at Corinn. 'The girl told me you were here. Figured I'd better let you know.' The expression on his face might have been one of pity.

'Thank you,' Yllandris stammered. There was no telling what Shranree would do if she were late this time. She took a deep breath to calm her nerves. *Shranree doesn't matter. Nothing matters now. I've made my choice. Soon it will be over.* She hoped she had the courage to follow through with her plan.

The Kingsman in the plate armour raised a gauntleted hand to wipe sweat from his brow, then folded his arms and scowled at Braxus. The movement was accompanied by a faint clanking sound.

The iron man, Yllandris realized. She had never seen anyone covered in so much steel. He was encased from head to toe.

'You see this sword?' The Kingsman drew his blade and held it up before him. 'This was forged by Dranthe, the finest steel smith in Tarbonne. I won it from one of the Old Masters in the Circle ten years past. With this weapon I have fought a dozen wars throughout the Shattered Realms. With this weapon I have killed a hundred men.' The warrior tapped the blade and turned it slightly, showing off the perfect edge in the red light of the furnace behind him. 'This sword can cleave through the strongest armour. The balance is so exquisite that I could place it tip down on that anvil there and it would not topple. This is art, created by an artist.' He sheathed his weapon and turned to retrieve something from the table beside him.

'This', he said, holding up two halves of a broken longsword, 'is shit. Shat out by a man with not the slightest concern for the warriors expected to carry it into battle. Tell me, blacksmith, what happens when a man attempts to parry steel with excrement?'

'Excrement?' Braxus repeated, his heavy brow creased in confusion.

The Kingsman sighed. '*Shit*, Braxus. Excrement means shit. But permit me to answer my own question. The man with shit in his hands dies. I know this because no fewer than seventeen of the town's defenders have perished as a result of the flawed steel foisted upon them by you.' He flung the broken sword away. The shattered blade and hilt struck the ground with an angry clatter.

'It's not our fault,' Braxus said, waving a meaty hand at the pile of swords stacked in the corner of the forge. 'We don't have time to temper them properly. We're doing the best we can.'

'Perhaps you should find men to assist you. Men instead of children.'

'They've got nowhere else to stay,' Braxus protested. 'The orphans help out with a few errands; we give them something to eat and a place to sleep. There ain't no harm in it. We're doing them a kindness.'

The Kingsman gestured at Corinn. There was bitter amusement in his heavy-lidded eyes. 'Old men and their kindnesses... I know how that goes. There aren't many lies a man won't tell himself to excuse the dark corners of his soul.'

Braxus's face flushed crimson and he took a step towards the Kingsman. He was past sixty, but his neck was as thick as an ox's and his arms rippled with muscle from a lifetime spent hammering iron. 'What's your meaning?'

The Kingsman sneered and his gaze settled on Yllandris. 'It's not hard to understand why you like them so young, Braxus. Just look at this one. Only twenty years on her and she's already fit for pasture. In Tarbonne, a wife who allowed herself to go to seed so quickly would find her marriage annulled. You should be ashamed, woman.'

Yllandris felt like she had been punched in the gut. She reached up to her face, self-consciously trying to cover the angry red patch on her cheek. The familiar trembling began in her arms.

'Do you have what the King requested?' The speaker was the Kingsman with the bloodshot eyes. His voice was soft, velvet-like, and he wore a golden key on a chain around his neck.

162

Yllandris focused on his face, trying to remember where she knew him from. Anything to take her mind off the shakes.

Wulgreth, she realized. *The Northman who went missing months ago, during the march to Frosthold. He was lost. Presumed dead. How did he survive? Why is he here?*

Braxus turned to the Kingsman and handed him a tiny piece of metal. It was smooth and rounded, like the barrel of the strange device Wulgreth had given Krazka on the hill outside Heartstone. Wulgreth examined it for a moment with his strange bloodshot eyes, and then he stashed it in a bag at his belt.

Yorn cleared his throat. 'We're done here. Braxus, grab a sword. We'll need every able-bodied man in Heartstone at the gates once the Shaman arrives. Meredith—'

'That's *Sir* Meredith, you bloody savage! I was knighted by the Rag King himself!'

Yorn's teeth ground together as he struggled to keep his calm. 'We ain't in the Lowlands now. We answer to only one king and that's the Butcher King. The man we're sworn to protect.'

Sir Meredith grimaced. 'You need not remind me.' He turned on his heel and stormed out of the Foundry.

Yllandris watched his noisy exit. She shifted from leg to leg in an effort to stop the shakes taking hold.

'What's his problem?' Braxus demanded.

Yorn spat. 'He spent too much time down south. Got some queer ideas in his head. Good with a sword though.'

The three men departed, leaving Yllandris alone with Corinn and a few orphans who had dared poke their heads into the chamber. 'Are you okay?' Corinn asked gently, her face filled with compassion. Yllandris felt suddenly ashamed of her weakness.

'Yes,' she lied. She wasn't okay, she wanted to break down and cry, but she needed to be at the north gate before Shranree noticed she was missing or her plan would be in ruins.

A small hand took hold of hers. She looked down to see the boy who had woken her moments ago. He stared up at her shyly.

'I don't like the iron man. Or the Northman. They have ugly eyes. Not like you: you're pretty and kind. And you took my friends away to the better place. I wanna go there too. Can I?'

Yllandris swallowed a sob and ran from the Foundry.

Twenty-six Years Ago

'**I** CAN SMELL it. Like flesh boiled too long in the pot.'

Moshka's wizened face twisted in disgust. Blink demons were among the rarest of their kind, highly cunning and able to evade even the most determined pursuers. The fiend had led them on a chase through half of the High Fangs, from the deep valleys of the East Reaching to the great meres of the neighbouring Lake Reaching and then south to here, the Green Reaching.

This time, Brodar Kayne would not allow the demon to escape.

The three men spurred their horses forward. Spring in the Green Reaching was a sight to behold. Gently rolling hills and emerald grass stretched out as far as the eye could see, dotted by small farms that kept the Heartland region supplied with food when the harsh winter months turned it into a white wasteland. The Greenmen were often derided as a soft people, handier with a plough than a sword, but the fact was that without them the Treaty that had held for the last few hundred years would never have endured. Even the meekest of men would march on their neighbours when starvation loomed.

They galloped past fields of maize, low fences surrounding rows of vegetables that would eventfully find their way to tables in Heartstone and Yarrow, even as far north as Lister in the Black Reaching. Nervous faces watched them as they rode by. Wardens rarely had reason to venture so far west. When they did, it could mean only bad news.

Moshka drew his horse in alongside Kayne's. The *veronyi* had left his home in the mountains to accompany them on this hunt. Witch doctors were said to possess strange powers and insights beyond the ken of even the Shaman. Not magic like the sorceresses possessed, or the spark of power that saw young males transcend and take beast form when they came of age – no, the wise men of the high places, the *veronyi*, possessed an affinity with the spirits of the land itself.

'He's near,' Moshka hissed.

Kayne frowned. They weren't far from Beregund. If the demon reached the capital before they caught up with it, there was no telling what kind of carnage it would wreak. The warriors of the Green Reaching had no real experience fighting fiends. It was the duty of Kayne and his brothers to ensure that none made it through the Borderland.

'Borun,' he shouted. 'We're getting close.'

His friend turned in his saddle. 'You ever fought a blink demon, Kayne?'

'No, not fought. But I reckon I know about 'em better than most.' His hands gripped the reins tighter and his teeth clenched together. He remembered Dannard's scream. It still haunted his dreams, even after all these years.

They rode hard until they came to a small farmstead next to a field set aside for pasture. Kayne noticed immediately that something was very wrong. The field was covered in wool, great clumps of it, as if the sheep that grazed the land had somehow shrugged off their coats and fled. As the men drew nearer, Kayne saw that the wool was still attached to the skin of the animals, which had been stripped right off the bone. There was no sign of the carcasses.

Just then a terrible whining noise cut through the nicker of the horses. It came from over by the pen near the farmhouse. Kayne turned, and his gorge rose at the sight that greeted him.

It was a shepherd's dog – or at least what remained of the animal. The hind legs had been torn off at the knees and the snout was horribly mangled, one eye hanging from its socket and the other rolling in mindless terror. The dog was attempting to drag itself away from the pen, desperate to escape whatever was inside the enclosure. Its mind hadn't caught up to the fact it should be dead.

The three men slid from their mounts. Moshka hobbled over to the dog and knelt down. The old man whispered a few soothing words and placed his hands around the animal's throat. It stopped whimpering and a moment later went still. The *veronyi* released his grip and lowered the dead animal gently to the grass. Then he stood and brushed off his tattered old robes, the bone bangles around his wrists clinking out an eerie tune in the afternoon sun. 'The demon is in the pen.'

Kayne nodded and drew his sword.

'We'll take its head back to the Keep,' Borun growled. 'Give it to old Kalgar as a retirement gift. Maybe Orgrim will mount it in the Commander's chambers when he moves in.' The Warden-in-training hefted his great battleaxe and gave it an experimental swing. He had shot up like a weed in the last year or two. He was as tall as Kayne and already stronger than many warriors ten years his senior.

'You're not a Warden yet. Leave this to me.'

Borun snorted. 'Six years as a spirit-scout counts for nothing? I'm a match for any man at Watcher's Keep save you, Kayne. Let me help kill this bastard.'

'I said no, brother.'

Borun's face flushed with anger. 'Then why bring me along? I guided you here. You telling me I have to stand and watch while you go it alone? Or is that what you want? "The great Brodar Kayne. First Warden to kill a blink demon single-handed in fifty years." That what this is about? Your reputation?'

'I ain't doing it by myself, Borun. I've got Moshka.'

The farmhouse door creaked open and a female face peeked out. Kayne caught a glimpse of extraordinary steel-coloured eyes, wide with terror. He brought a finger to lips, motioning at the girl to go back inside. 'Guard that door,' he told Borun. 'Worst comes to the worst, you buy whoever's inside time to escape.'

The young Warden-in-training still didn't look pleased, but he turned and walked over to the farmhouse, positioning himself in front of the doorway.

'Moshka. I reckon it's time,' Kayne said.

The *veronyi* threw back his head and began to chant words Kayne didn't recognize. The old man's eyes rolled up to expose the whites beneath. The straggly grey hair that fell around his bald crown floated up of its own accord, forming a wispy circle around his skull.

A moment later, the ground beneath the pen began to tremble. Soon the earth shook as if struck by the fist of some angry god below. Kayne felt the first wave of demon fear assail him but it was a familiar sensation now, robbed of the raw power that had threatened to break his resolve during his first few years in the Borderland.

The sheep pen shook violently. Somewhere within, the demon howled, a sound that cut through the passing of years to stir the embers of memory to life.

Kayne was back in Riverdale, hearing his brother's screams, tears spilling down his face yet too terrified to go back and help. He'd always been the big brother, the one Dannard would turn to when the other boys in the village had bullied him for being too soft, too shy. They'd left him alone once Dannard's older brother had a word with them. Brodar Kayne had killed a man when he was eight years old. He wasn't scared of anything.

At least that's what they had thought, in the naivety of youth. As it turned out, Dannard's big brother had shit himself and hidden in a ditch and sobbed himself raw the night the blink demon ravaged Riverdale.

The fiend howled again. Kayne embraced the terror as he had been taught on the training yards of Watcher's Keep, turned it into cold fury and made of it a shield. He stalked towards the enclosure, longsword raised. He couldn't change the past... but he could claim vengeance for Dannard and his father and the rest of the village.

There was a ripple ahead of him, like hot air shimmering on a summer morning after a storm. An instant later the blink demon appeared, melting out of nothingness as if an invisible curtain had just been pulled aside.

It looked like a Highland cat, save that its fur was dark purple and it was a good deal more slender. A single eye stared out above a feline snout. The demon's mouth suddenly yawned open, revealing serrated teeth that were surely too long to fit inside its maw. Blink demons were even less a part of the world than others of their kind, and they ignored the natural laws that bound man and beast alike.

The demon's tongue slowly unrolled from its mouth, the sides as sharp as a steel blade, capable of sawing through bone and sinew. Bloody drool dripped from its fangs.

'Moshka, now!' Kayne roared. In response, the *veronyi* made a fist.

The earth rose beneath the demon in an explosion of dirt. Giant fingers of mud and stone closed around the fiend, holding it tight. Demons could shrug off steel and in most cases magic with little effort, but the wise men of the high places, the druids or witch doctors or whatever name a man chose to call them, they relied not on magic but on the spirits of land and sky and sea to do their bidding. Moshka would pay a price for their help later, but for now the demon was trapped.

Kayne charged at the fiend and brought his longsword flashing down to connect with the demon's skull as it thrashed around. The blow failed to break bone, so he tried again and this time was rewarded with a sharp crack. Black blood bubbled around the hole in the thing's skull, but it took another few seconds of hacking before the head fell apart and the creature stilled.

Without warning the enormous fist disappeared back into the earth, dragging the slain demon down into the ground.

When the dust finally settled, all that remained was a giant mound of dirt.

Kayne glanced back at Moshka, who looked as though he was about to collapse from exhaustion. The ancient *veronyi* had done the Wardens a great service by agreeing to accompany them this far west; at his age the druid's body might not survive whatever price the spirits claimed.

'Kayne! The pen!' It was Borun's voice, filled with alarm.

He looked towards the enclosure. Something was emerging. Something dark and feline and covered in blood. Another blink demon.

It padded out of the pen, its single eye fixed on Moshka. It paused for second, and then that great orb snapped shut.

An instant later the demon was halfway to the old man.

Kayne shouted a warning and Moshka looked up. The demon blinked again and then it was right opposite him, razor tongue probing outward to rend the druid. Moshka's robes fell apart, shredded like wheat, but somehow the man inside them had disappeared. The tattered cloth drifted away, leaving the demon to probe the earth with its tongue, searching around for its prey. It made a horrible hacking sound and began to spew up an entire sheep, skinless and half-digested.

Borun seized the moment and sprinted towards the fiend, axe raised high. 'No!' Kayne yelled, but it was too late to stop him. The trainee Warden began to falter as the demon fear assailed him. Finally he stumbled to his knees, the axe tumbling from his shaking hands and a sob escaping his lips. It was a matter of seconds before the blink demon noticed him.

Kayne searched around wildly. There was an abandoned shepherd's crook on the grass close by. He scooped up the tool and focused on the demon, trying to calculate the distance between them. He guessed there were maybe forty yards. How far could a blink demon travel in a single jump? He reckoned thirty, based on the speed with which the fiend had closed on Moshka.

He shuffled backwards, measuring the steps, and once he reached what he thought was the right spot he hollered at the fiend, trying to get its attention. For a moment its gaze settled on Borun, and Kayne's heart sank. Then the fiend's head rotated in his direction. That solitary eye fixed on him. And then closed.

The demon reappeared right where he thought it would.

Kayne tensed. *Wait for the eye… Wait for the eye…*

His left hand held the crook in the air, the hook pointing slightly downwards. In his right he clutched his sword.

The eye closed again. Kayne took two steps back.

And then he sprang forward, the hook sweeping down, just as the demon's head melted out of the air in front of him. He caught it around the neck, gave the crook a sharp tug to force the head down. With his other hand, he drove his blade right through that staring eye.

'That's for Dannard,' he said grimly as the fiend convulsed, spraying blood all over him.

Kayne wiped the gore off his blade and walked over to Borun. The young warrior had risen shakily to his feet and was staring at the ground, eyes filled with shame.

'Brother.' Kayne placed a hand on Borun's shoulder. 'You got closer than most could have without the proper training. First time I met a blink demon I shat myself. Next time you'll be ready.'

There was a sound from behind them – a soft wheezing noise. It was Moshka. The *veronyi* was as naked as the day he was born, saggy grey flesh hanging off bones that almost seemed to poke through his skin. He looked even frailer than usual, so brittle he might break at the lightest touch. He tried to open his mouth to speak but only a soft rattle emerged. A thin trail of drool dribbled down his chin.

Kayne removed his cloak and placed it over the old man's shoulders, wrapping it tight to preserve his decency. 'Borun, go fetch the owner of that farmhouse. Tell 'em to bring a clean set of clothes.'

Minutes later a trio of women followed Borun out of the farmhouse, the youngest carrying breeches and a woollen tunic. All three looked horrified at the carnage strewn across the field. After a moment of stunned silence the eldest spoke. 'My name is Lellana,' she said. 'We fled indoors when we heard the howling. You... you are Wardens?'

'Aye, that we are. I'm sorry we didn't get here quick enough to save your flock.'

The woman shook her head. 'Rather the sheep than my sister or cousin. Father would like to invite you for dinner. He is sorry he could not come himself, he is sick and confined to his bed.'

The youngest, little more than a girl, held the clothes out for Moshka. When the old man did not move, Kayne took them from her hands instead. He met her eyes briefly and was struck by their beauty. They were silvery grey, like the surface of a lake in the early-morning sunlight. She glanced down shyly and her expression grew concerned.

'You're hurt,' she said, pointing at his leg. He was bleeding just above the shin, where the demon's tongue must have caught him. 'I can bind that for you,' she added timidly.

'It's just a scratch,' he said, though now she had mentioned it the cut was beginning to sting something fierce.

The third woman cleared her throat a little noisily. 'Lellana and I will show you inside and fix up your wounds. May, you should start clearing up this mess. The smell will attract wolves if we're not careful.'

The youngest nodded. Then she noticed the body of the dog and let out an anguished cry. She dashed over to the dead animal and wrapped her arms around it, tears streaming down her face. 'Ruffles,' she sobbed.

'It's just a dog,' said the slightly older girl. 'You're embarrassing us. You're sixteen, May, no longer a child.'

'Mother brought Ruffles home when he was a pup. He's one of the only things I have to remember her by.'

Kayne hesitated. Then he walked over to the girl and the

lifeless animal she held in her arms. 'I had a dog when I was a boy,' he ventured slowly. 'I was fond of him. Missed him when he was gone.' He felt stupid as he spoke the words, certain that whatever he said would only make things worse. He'd always been awkward with women.

But the girl looked up at him, and her tears stopped. Again he was struck by her beauty.

'Tell you what,' he said. 'Why don't we all go inside and eat. Say hello to your father. Then I'll help you clear the fields, and together the two of us can bury Ruffles.' He reached down. The girl took hold of his hand. Her skin felt soft in his palm. 'What's your name?' he asked, as he helped her to her feet.

'My sister and cousin call me May,' she replied shyly. 'But my real name is Mhaira.'

Blood Magic

BRODAR KAYNE TOOK another sip from the wine glass and stared into the flames which lit the grand hall of the necromancer's tower. The fire sent shadows dancing across the ancient tapestries on the walls. Long-dead Kings of Andarr stared out with severe expressions that were almost a match for the frown on Jerek's face.

The Wolf hadn't shifted from the fireplace or uttered so much as a word since they were seated. It seemed as far as Jerek was concerned, being invited to dinner by a necromancer and waited on by a host of grinning skeletons wasn't worth commenting on. Not when he had the fate of his boots to worry about. Every few minutes he would swap which of the boots he held before the fire, slowly drying his precious footwear with the same care a mother might show her newborn infant.

'More wine?' Nazala queried. The southerner raised a hand and beckoned to his minions. Kayne heard the rattling of bone behind him and then a skeletal arm leaned over his shoulder, clutching a bottle of red that was probably worth a small fortune. The old warrior was sorely tempted; the wine tasted sweet and fruity, and it was the first time anything save water had passed his lips in many a week. Still, he reckoned whatever business this wizard wanted to discuss was best looked at with a clear head. And in any case, Brick seemed intent on drinking enough wine for the two of them. Kayne frowned as the boy emptied yet another glass. His face was flushed, freckled cheeks threatening to turn the same colour as his hair.

'I'll pass,' Kayne grunted. Nazala gestured and the fleshless arm withdrew.

The necromancer sat back in his chair and crossed his hands over his lap. The flowing black robes he wore fell like a shroud to gather on the wood-panelled floor below the big darkwood table. 'Twenty-six years,' the southerner mused. 'And you speak of this woman with the warmth of a man newly wedded.'

'She's the only woman I ever loved,' Kayne replied. 'Didn't know I could love like that till I met her. We were married the following year. Can't say I ever saw that coming. But I don't reckon I'd change a thing.'

'Then you have simply not lived long enough. I once loved my twin Shara with the whole of my being. Now? I would bury her alive! Savour her every scream before I filled her mouth with dirt and left her for the worms to feast upon.'

Brick piped up, sounding a little the worse for wear. 'You must really hate her. I never had a brother or sister but I can't imagine hating them like you do.'

Nazala gave a melancholy sigh. It was difficult to place the man's age. Though the southerner had fewer lines on his face than Kayne, his eyes told a very different story. They were tired and bloodshot and filled with the weariness of one who's seen too much evil in the world. Seen, and maybe done.

'Love and hate are two sides of the same coin. You must understand, child, we shared everything, Shara and I – until the moment she betrayed me and my heart died in my chest. After centuries of unconditional love I felt as empty as a grave. Hatred is all I have left.'

Kayne raised an eyebrow. 'I might've misheard, but did you just say *centuries*?'

Nazala nodded. 'My twin and I were born in the Shining City far to the south. That was almost four hundred years ago, when the magical storms unleashed during the Godswar still ravaged these northern lands.'

Kayne blinked, hardly believing what he was hearing. The

necromancer's claim seemed unlikely, but the expression on his face suggested he was deadly serious. 'How'd the two of you cheat death for so long? I thought only the Magelords lived forever.'

'Not just the two of us,' Nazala replied, almost absent-mindedly, remembering events long ago. 'We were eight in total. Each of us excelled in one of the eight schools of magic – or at least the eight schools that are common knowledge. Our master introduced us to the hidden ninth school. The forbidden school, of power evoked through pain and sacrifice.'

'Can't say I like the sound of that,' Kayne said warily.

'It was fear of the ninth school that brought the Congregation's wrath down upon those with the gift,' Nazala continued. 'Of those in the Alliance who would eventually become Magelords, only our master foreswore the oath to never again practise blood magic. We travelled the continent, we Bloodsworn, doing his bidding. And in return he rewarded us with the knowledge we craved.' The wizard shook his head and gripped the sides of his chair. 'We did bad things, my twin and I. Terrible things. For power. For life everlasting.'

'Why'd she betray you?'

Nazala's eyes narrowed. 'One day I told Shara that I could no longer serve our master. I could murder no more innocents at his behest. I assumed she would stand with me. After all, we had chosen this dark path precisely so that we could be together for eternity.' The wizard's voice dropped to an angry whisper. 'The following night she tried to kill me in my sleep. I survived and fled here.'

Kayne glanced across the table at Brick. The youngster's eyes were looking decidedly glassy. 'Why a swamp? Seems to me a powerful wizard could set up home wherever he chose.'

'The Pattern is weak here. The barriers between life and death, between reality and the places where demons dwell, are thin. My twin's magic is greater than my own – but here in the swamp, surrounded by the dead, my necromancy keeps me safe. Both from Shara, and my one-time master's other... apprentices.'

'You ain't told me who this mysterious master is.'

Nazala shifted uneasily. 'He has gone by many names. Here in the north he uses his true identity. Or at least the persona he chooses to present as his true identity. Marius.'

Kayne's brow furrowed. He'd heard that name before. 'Marius is dead, last I heard. Drowned with his city by the Tyrant of Dorminia. I doubt even a Magelord could survive a billion tons of water dropped on his head.'

Much to Kayne's surprise, Nazala's slender black hands twitched nervously. There he sat, a powerful and immortal necromancer, suddenly anxious at the mere mention of a dead man. 'I served Marius for centuries,' said the southerner. 'If I learned anything during that time, it is that he operates outside the comprehension of mere mortals. Perhaps even other Magelords. Where Marius is concerned, one should never presume anything.' Nazala rubbed his hands together as if cleansing himself of unpleasant thoughts. 'Enough of such matters. I wish to discuss how we might be of service to one another. You wish to return to the High Fangs, no? With my assistance you can be back in the mountains within a few days.'

Jerek shifted slightly where he sat drying his boots by the fire. He didn't turn, but the way his head rose a fraction betrayed a sudden interest.

Brick waved an arm in Kayne's direction, accidentally knocking over his glass in his enthusiasm. He was clearly half-drunk. 'You can go home to Mhaira,' he said, a big grin on his face.

Mhaira. He thought of her smile, the way she could lift his mood just by walking into the room. 'Don't get me wrong, I'm mighty grateful,' he said slowly. 'But I can't help wondering what you might want in return.'

The necromancer's gaze settled on Brick. 'My accursed twin believes this boy is a bringer of prophecy. A marker in the Pattern, if you will. Destined to shape events to come.'

Kayne began to feel a sense of unease. It was an instinct that had served him well over the years.

'You will bring fire and blood back to the north,' Nazala continued. 'That is what she told you, is it not, child?'

'I'm not a child!' Brick answered, sounding awfully like one.

The veins threading the necromancer's eyes seemed to turn a brighter shade of red. 'You possess power. Destiny runs in you. In your blood. Such potential can be... harnessed.'

A dark foreboding wormed its way into Kayne's heart. 'What are you saying?'

Nazala climbed to his feet. Despite the heat of the fire, a sudden chill seemed to wash through the chamber. The necromancer approached Brick, studying the boy as a man might eye an appetizing dessert. 'The power I shall draw from this child's sacrifice will bring Shara to ruin.'

Kayne leaped to his feet, reaching for his greatsword.

'Your steel is useless,' the necromancer said coldly. 'No earthly metal has been able to harm me for over two hundred years. The ironguard spell cost me the lives of several cousins.' He gestured at the skeletons positioned around the chamber.

'These skeletons were your *family*?' Kayne said in horror.

'Blood magic demands that a wizard gives up everything they hold dear. We sacrificed them all over the years. Our cousins. Our aunts and uncles. Eventually even our children. The corpse that guided you to this tower was once my grandson. He was a favourite of mine. But I required his sacrifice to heal myself after Shara's attempt on my life, and so I killed him. I grieved for many years.'

'You're not having the boy!' Kayne snarled.

'Why doom yourself for the sake of a bandit's whelp?' Nazala asked. 'He is nothing to you. And what of your own son? You told me he was in danger. Would you abandon him to an uncertain fate while you throw your life away here? I have no quarrel with you, Sword of the North. I will infuse your horses with magic to speed your passage and you and your friend can go home. Back to your family.'

Brick's face had gone white with terror. 'Don't leave me!'

Kayne closed his eyes. What was the life of a bandit's off-spring against everything he still held dear? Against the son and wife who were waiting for him in the north?

'You and your uncle tried to murder us, lad.'

'But… we had a deal…' Brick's voice cracked.

'Kayne.' It was Jerek. The Wolf was out of his chair. He bent down and tugged his boots back on his feet. 'Let's go,' he said.

'Listen to your friend. He understands the value of pragmatism.' Nazala placed a slender finger on Brick's forehead. 'Calm, child,' he whispered. 'The agony will be intense, I fear, but it will not last so long.'

Kayne's fists clenched. *What was the life of a bandit's offspring against everything he still held dear?*

It was everything.

He reached for his sword again, but just then Jerek met his gaze, face a grim mask, and shook his head. The Wolf rose slowly and brought his fists up from his sides.

He clutched a dagger in each hand; the daggers he kept hidden in his boots. They were glowing red-hot.

Jerek flung them at the necromancer, first the left dagger and then the right, a blur of motion. The steel blades sank deep into Nazala's flesh. But they drew no blood, and for a second or two seemed to cause him no distress. The wizard merely stared at them in amusement. He hadn't been lying about his immunity to steel.

The heat, though, was a different matter entirely.

Nazala suddenly screamed and scrabbled wildly at the hilts protruding from his chest as the stench of burning flesh filled Kayne's nostrils. He searched for a weapon that might possibly be of use against the necromancer. There was nothing, not unless he wanted to bludgeon the wizard to death with a chair.

Bone clanked behind him. Kayne spun and caught the skeleton's grasping arm an instant before it closed around his throat. He twisted viciously and felt the arm snap off in his hand. The broken end was jagged and sharp.

It would serve.

Without a second's hesitation Brodar Kayne leaped across the table and plunged the makeshift dagger down. Down through Nazala's neck, tearing through flesh and muscle. Blood immediately welled up around the horrific wound. The necromancer's hands fell away from the dagger hilts in his chest and he reached up, flapping pathetically at the bone lodged in his throat.

Kayne stared down at the wizard, meeting the necromancer's shocked expression with eyes the colour of a clear sky on a winter morning. He gave the bone a twist; Nazala slobbered fresh blood over his arm. 'You don't harm your own,' he growled between clenched teeth. 'And you don't... hurt... children.'

The necromancer gasped one final time and then went limp. There was a cacophony of noise behind Kayne as Nazala's servants fell apart in a shower of falling bone. A skull rolled across the floor and bumped into his foot. He kicked it away just as Jerek came to stand beside him. The Wolf was wearing gloves, but the sheer heat of the fire had burned through the leather while he was heating his daggers. His palms were red and blistered and would likely scar. Once more Kayne found himself overcome with guilt.

Brick rose unsteadily to his feet and stumbled over. He stared down at Nazala's corpse, and somehow he went even paler. 'What about Mhaira?' he asked in a trembling voice.

'What about her?' Kayne asked.

'You could have gone home to her. Instead you... you saved me.'

Kayne placed a hand on Brick's shoulder. 'There weren't ever a choice involved. You'd know that if you'd met Mhaira. She'd never have forgiven me.'

Brick nodded. 'Thank you. I—' He stopped mid-sentence. Then he turned, bent over, and promptly vomited up the contents of his stomach.

Jerek heaved a weary sigh. 'Fuck it,' he grumbled. 'I'm gonna round up a few of these bottles, take them back to the stables. At least that green bastard can hold his drink.'

They found Grunt fast asleep in a bed of hay, his muscular arms wrapped tightly around his mysterious sack. Jerek decided to wake him by pouring half a bottle of wine over his snout, which almost resulted in one of the horses getting injured as the greenskin flailed around in sudden surprise. The mute was a good deal more appreciative when he learned they'd brought wine back with them. He even showed Jerek how to make a salve from swamp mud and plant roots, which the Wolf applied to the burns on his hands.

A few hours later the companions left the swamp, heading north towards the Purple Hills.

Assimilating

THE WOMAN WAS barely recognizable. Both her legs had been caught in the fire, which had melted away the flesh and exposed blackened bone and sinew.

Eremul the Halfmage felt a brief of moment of empathy for the corpse before deciding his sympathies were better spent on the living.

Soon this morgue will be positively bursting with the emaciated remains of the starved. Assuming the city doesn't burn down before then.

The latest victim of Melissan's fanatics had been a clerk on her way home from the council building near the centre of the city – one of Lorganna's employees. She had been crossing the street when a firebomb exploded right in front of her. It was the fourth such attack in the past two weeks. Another warehouse had burned down near the Hook; a shoemaker and his family had been cooked alive in the west end of the city when their home was set aflame; a tavern had gone down in a raging inferno, though most of the patrons were unharmed; and, most worrying of all from where Eremul was sitting, a firebomb had turned a ship floating in the harbour into a burned-out wreck. There seemed to be no pattern to the attacks, no sign of a clear strategy to support his theory that the Fade were somehow directing the rebels.

The Halfmage turned to the second body he'd requested be removed from the wooden boxes that filled the niches cut into the walls of the chamber. Each housed a corpse that would be taken to a private cemetery if the deceased had been a person of means, or to the great public graveyard off Crook Street if they had not.

The mutilated body that lay on the cold slab would not be granted the dignity of a burial. The Collectors would take the corpse to the furnace below the morgue, where it would be incinerated. Criminals weren't afforded the privilege of taking up valuable space in the ground.

'They weren't kind to him,' said the mortician, Marston, from where he was lurking behind the Halfmage. 'I've rarely seen a corpse so badly mutilated. Though there was one young lady the Collectors brought in last week that seemed to be rotting from the inside out, if you can believe that. Made a hell of a stench, I can tell you.'

Eremul nodded absent-mindedly, not really paying attention. His gaze was fixed on the corpse before him. He knew a thing or two about torture: the time he'd spent in the Obelisk's dungeons was a memory that still kept him awake at night. Even he was shocked at the abuse that had been heaped upon this man. The toes and fingers had been removed, one eye had been gouged out, and terrible scars covered the torso where a hot iron had been pressed against his flesh.

The Halfmage winced when he saw the jagged wound between the corpse's legs. A bloodstained scrap of flesh was all that remained of the fanatic's manhood. No one could accuse the Council of not utilizing every technique available to them in their efforts to extract information from the rebels, but so far none of the fanatics had surrendered information that might lead to Melissan's capture.

He turned to Marston. 'Would you be so kind as to turn him over, so that I may examine his back?'

The mortician ran a hand through the greying tufts of hair springing haphazardly from his balding pate. 'You know you shouldn't be here. You don't have the authority.'

'This is the last time. You have my word.' Clearly news of his dismissal from the Council had got around. Timerus really did bear a grudge against him, the slimy Ishari bastard.

Marston puffed out his cheeks. 'Only because it's you, Halfmage. You understand I need to keep my nose clean. Especially after the, ahem, debacle with my assistant.'

Eremul raised an eyebrow. 'Debacle?'

'It's probably best if you don't ask.'

The mortician moved to the slab and placed his gloved hands on the corpse. He was a heavy-set man, strong despite his advancing years. Hefting corpses around was hard work, Eremul supposed. As a young man he'd never enjoyed physical labour and had avoided it where possible. That was something he had come to regret after his legs were taken from him. But in recent weeks he had observed his arms growing thicker and stronger from pushing his chair around the city: a development he found strangely pleasing.

The fanatic's back was crisscrossed with lash wounds. The torturer had evidently taken a whip to him before moving onto subtler methods. Eremul scanned the cold flesh, looking for the tattoo, that peculiar script which all the other fanatics whose corpses he had examined displayed on some part of their body.

There it was: a tiny flourish of black ink just below the small of the back. Eremul traced it with a finger, following the shape. Something about it felt... odd.

'Ahem.' Marston cleared his throat nosily. 'Did I mention the trouble I had with my assistant? You understand I'm not here to judge, but I feel I have to inform you of a certain moral responsibility—'

'Be quiet.'

The Halfmage evoked a trickle of magic and held it at the tip of his index finger. Very slowly he brought it down towards the tattoo...

Which began to move, twisting beneath the skin, the strange black script writhing to get away from the probing digit. The

Halfmage raised an eyebrow. Could it be that this tattoo was *alive*?

Eremul reached deeper, summoned forth more magic. He channelled it against the twisting ink until the skin began to ripple. It was as if the script itself were an insect, desperate to burrow out of the corpse and escape—

He caught a glimpse of something tiny and black and spider-like scuttling away. It disappeared into the shadows at the edges of the chamber and then was gone.

'Oh *shit*,' he said.

Lorganna,

I made a disturbing discovery while at the morgue earlier this afternoon. The tattoos on Melissan's fanatics appear to be sentient beings – a kind of parasite that lives under the skin of the host and is inert until exposed directly to magic. Unfortunately, in the process of ascertaining this information, this particular subject escaped. It would be advantageous if you could arrange for me to have access to one of the rebels imprisoned in the Oblong dungeons, so that I may investigate further. As always, absolute discretion is apropos to our relationship.

E.

He set the quill down. A moment later he picked it back up and carefully blotted out 'apropos', replacing it with 'essential'. The word hadn't quite fitted and, besides, whilst he enjoyed the opportunity to practise his penmanship, one didn't want to sound pretentious.

The Halfmage carefully rolled the parchment and sealed it with wax, then sat back in his chair. He winced at the various niggles that assaulted him. His arse throbbed, his lower back ached, and his writing hand had begun to cramp. He would have liked to take a short nap, but he needed to be at Artifice Street in a couple of hours. After careful consideration he had reluctantly concluded that it might be a good idea to wash away the stench of death before his soiree with Monique.

She is curious, that's all. The woman has no romantic interest in you. Don't make a fool of yourself.

He thought back to the romantic liaisons he had enjoyed during the course of his thirty-five years of life. There had been the stolen kiss with the neighbour's daughter when he was a child – he'd been heartbroken when her family had moved away. Shortly after that, the Great Plague had claimed his parents and he'd been moved to the boy's orphanage in Orchard Street. As was the case for most of the boys, his hand had been his only source of relief during his first few years at the institution.

He recalled with vague horror his fourteenth birthday. His friends had taken him to a brothel and paid for a whore for him. He had been halfway aroused before the sour stench of the woman's breath robbed him of any desire to consummate the deed. After a long moment of awkwardness the hooker had settled on tugging him off, a decidedly unsatisfactory experience he had done his best to portray as a revelation akin to the Creator's First Decree to his friends later that night.

A year later he had discovered his latent magical ability and the Obelisk had summoned him for trials. Somehow he had impressed enough to earn an apprenticeship. Most of his instruction in the wizardly arts had come from old Poskarus, who had little time for relationships and even less time for women, and so even his teenage years were decidedly lean when it came to the pleasures of the flesh.

After the city-wide mageocide known as the Culling and the loss of his legs, any lingering desire for intimacy he may have possessed withered and died. Hatred became the only companion he needed; vengeance the singular passion that stirred his bitter heart.

Eremul smiled ruefully. It felt strange, sliding into something approaching normality. Doing what *other* people did. Almost as if he were an imposter. He wasn't sure this was what he wanted, and yet he was curiously reluctant to disappoint Monique. Despite the fact the trek to Artifice Street would be exhausting and he would rather spend the evening with a good book and Tyro on his lap.

Where are you, boy? He hadn't seen the scruffy little mongrel in a while. He wheeled his chair around the depository and eventually found Tyro curled up in the corner, apparently asleep.

The Halfmage selected a clean robe and laid it out on his bed. Then he wheeled himself to the washroom. It was always a trial to bathe, a complicated process it had taken many attempts to get right. He crawled into the chair Isaac had designed for him, and then positioned himself above the drainage hole that fed directly into the sewers beneath the harbour. He yanked on a rope connected to a simple pulley system and the bucket suspended just above his head upended, showering him with cold water. Once he had finished scrubbing himself clean, he unhooked the bucket and placed it near the door to be refilled for the next time.

Eremul returned to his room and spent a couple of minutes pulling on the robes. He was worried they might appear ostentatious, but then he cursed himself for a fool.

Fussing over my appearance is akin to a leper worrying if his breath is fresh. Any woman that loves me will do so for my other qualities. Whatever they may be.

Now that he thought about it, perhaps this 'date' wasn't such a good idea after all. Still, he had a letter that needed to be delivered. He'd be damned if he'd gone to the considerable effort of taking a bath only to hand a grubby urchin a piece of parchment.

He applied a dash of perfume, feeling like an utter cretin. Then he returned to his study to retrieve the letter, casting a quick glance to where Tyro lay to see if he was awake.

Blood-red orbs stared back at him, as sinister as infanticide.

He jolted back in his chair. 'T-Tyro?' he gasped, his heart hammering in his chest.

The dog padded over and sniffed around his robes, then looked up at him with adoring brown eyes. Eremul reached down a trembling hand. Tyro licked his fingers with his warm, wet tongue and made a whining sound, begging for food. Just as he always did.

'Tyro... what's happening to me, boy?'

I really ought to have had that sleep this afternoon.

Though he was certain the sinister vision was a result of tiredness and pre-date nerves and maybe a lingering paranoia from Isaac's betrayal, the Halfmage still found himself shaking a little as he left the depository.

'Deliver this to the Grand Council building. I want it to go directly to the Office of Civic Relations. If anyone asks, you never saw me.'

The boy nodded. He was wafer-thin, so underfed that a strong wind might blow him away, or so it seemed. 'One silver sceptre,' the orphan mumbled.

'A whole silver?' Eremul shook his head in mock outrage. 'That's daylight robbery! But it seems I have little choice. Be sure to give your friends some food as well, you understand me?'

He tossed the coin at the kid, who pocketed it and ran off. In truth, with prices rising at an alarming rate, a silver would not buy much beyond a couple of loaves of bread. With each passing day more of the city's poor seemed to be begging on street corners or rooting through piles of refuse looking for something to eat. There was a sense of desperation in the air: an increasingly volatile mix of hopelessness and fury that threatened to ignite at any moment. Only the dubious promise of the Pioneer's Deal was postponing a city-wide uprising.

And with the notable exception of Lorganna, it seemed no one on the Grand Council gave a rat's ass.

The new Civic Relations Minister had contacted Eremul three days after he had been banished from the Council Chamber. In her letter she had expressed a desire to help his investigations into a possible connection between the rebels and the Fade. Though their correspondence did not strictly break any laws, the fact Eremul was *persona non grata* with Dorminia's Grand Regent made the situation delicate. Eremul suspected it was only his hero status keeping him out of the Obelisk's dungeons.

He pushed his chair through Artifice Street, noting the absence of customers in the more expensive shops. The new taxes the White Lady had imposed were sucking the city dry.

The faces change, but the fist stays the same. Always squeezing. Crushing the life from the poor. Grinding them down while their labour feeds the insatiable appetites of the lucky few.

Eremul realized he himself fell into the latter category, at least in a broader sense. He felt guilty at having agreed to meet Monique in one of the city's more expensive taverns. The Rose and Sceptre was a large building situated between a jeweller's and a locksmith. Monique was waiting for him when he arrived. She was dressed as before in a long black skirt and tight top. Her glossy hair fell perfectly to the nape of her neck. Her lips and the base of her eyes were painted violet, accentuating her flawless skin.

The squeak of his chair's wheels on the wooden floor drew the attention of just about everyone else sitting in the tavern, much to his annoyance. Monique smiled when she saw him, and that helped soothe his irritation.

'You look dashing,' she greeted him, her voice carrying the sensual quality that had kept his imagination so busy over the past couple of weeks.

The Halfmage glanced down at his sweaty robes, at the bottom hem hanging limply over the stumps of his legs. 'You may wish to get those glasses checked.'

Monique laughed. He tried to remember the last time he had made a woman laugh, but drew a blank.

'The custom in Tarbonne is for the man to choose wine before dinner is ordered.'

'I thought I recognized that accent,' he said, eager to impress. 'Tarbonne. Once the brightest jewel of the Nine Kingdoms – as they once were known.'

Monique adjusted her glasses. 'Not so bright now, it is true. They are beset by war. Bands of mercenaries travel the Shattered Realms, fighting for any false lord with gold to spare. I fled north to escape it all.'

'You fled here, of all places? I suppose the grass is always greener from afar. How long have you been in the city?'

'Two years. Did you wish to order wine?'

Shit. Idiot. He'd forgotten about the wine. 'You choose,' he offered gallantly. 'I'll pay.'

'You don't think I can afford it?'

'Er...' *Shit! I've done it now!*

Monique smiled, a wry twist of the mouth that made him feel all kinds of things. 'I'm just playing, silly!'

'Ah.' Eremul wiped the sweat from his brow and gurned a smile. 'Sorry. It's been a busy day and I haven't been sleeping well recently.'

'We all need our beauty sleep, yes?'

'People like me don't get beauty sleep.'

The server arrived and Monique ordered a bottle of white. 'The best wine in Tarbonne,' she said happily. 'Produced in the capital itself. Men have died to protect the vineyards of Carhein.'

'Men have died for less than that here.'

Monique looked embarrassed, almost as if she had said something wrong. Eremul cursed himself again.

Why can't I talk to women? What the hell is wrong with me? Quick, make conversation. Something that won't make you look like either an arsehole or a complete fuckwit.

'I have a dog,' he said. *Shit!*

'Really? I like animals!'

'You do?'

'Yes. Especially horses. I'm riding to Westrock soon, for the flower show. Maybe you would like to come with me?'

'I... ah...' *I can't sit a bloody horse*, he thought bitterly, but what he said was, 'I would love to.'

'Excellent! Shall we eat? All this talk is making me hungry.'

They were about to order when there was a sudden commotion near the door. A man and a woman stumbled in, two children trailing behind. The four of them looked half-starved. The children stared longingly at the plates of food, eyes fevered with desperation.

'Please!' the father pleaded. 'We need food. Anything! Just the scraps if you can spare them. I beg you.'

'If you have no coin to spend then get out!' The server stormed over and shook his fist right in the man's face.

'But my children are dying! Please—'

'Get out. Out, you rat bastard! Take your ugly wife and kids with you. Now, before I call the Watch!'

Trembling, dragging his sobbing wife with him, the man left the tavern. The children followed behind them like lost souls.

The server walked back to where Eremul and Monique were seated and shook his head ruefully. 'My apologies. Some people think the world owes them a living. They don't seem to realize we're all in this together.' He flicked some imaginary dirt from his gold-embroidered jacket in distaste. 'Now, what can I get you?'

'Soup,' Eremul said flatly.

The server's mouth twisted in disapproval. 'And you, madam?'

'Soup,' said Monique. 'The cheapest you have.'

The server stormed off, muttering under his breath about rat bastards, and Eremul made a mental note to check his soup when it arrived for anything untoward. He doubted the man would dare spit into the victuals of the city's sole surviving wizard – but if he did, unpleasantness was certain to follow.

Fortunately for all concerned, their soup when it arrived appeared free of bodily fluids. They finished their bowls and decided to go for a walk, or in Eremul's case a trundle. Deep in

191

conversation, they accidentally bumped into the family that had been begging in the Rose and Sceptre earlier. The children were staring dully into space while their parents scavenged spoiled food from stinking piles of refuse at the side of the road.

The Halfmage reached into his robes. He withdrew the golden spire with which he had intended to treat both Monique and himself to a three-course meal and gave it to the disbelieving father. He also handed him stern instructions to take the Pioneer's Deal once he and his family had filled their bellies.

The sun eventually fell, and Eremul prepared to say goodbye to Monique. He'd made peace with the fact the date was an unmitigated disaster.

I tried, he thought pathetically. *At least I tried*.

But before she left, Monique kissed him on the cheek and wished him a good night, saying she was very much looking forward to seeing him again.

Scars of War

THE HORN SOUNDED across Heartstone. Yllandris quickened her pace, hurrying down dirt roads riven with cracks in the heat of high summer. Dust flew up from her boots, making her sneeze. Warriors jostled her on their way to the Great Lodge. As Yllandris hurried past the huge structure, she glimpsed the King pacing back and forth while the town's defenders assembled in the great clearing. The Six stood guard nearby.

The streets had long ago emptied of women and children; the town's non-combatants had taken shelter in their homes. If it came to it, the womenfolk had demonstrated in the past that they would take up arms and fight just as viciously as the men. It just wasn't clear which side they would fight *for*.

'Sister!'

A woman's voice hailed Yllandris as she passed the bakery old Mother Marta had run for years. Marta might be as fat as a hut but she was a kindly woman who would often hand out free pastries to the town's foundlings.

Yllandris turned her head and saw Rana hurrying towards her. Rana owned the apothecary shop just opposite the bakery. She was a senior member of Heartstone's circle, a middle-aged woman of stern countenance whose wares were said to be inferior to Walda's on the opposite side of town, despite the fact the other woman possessed not a magical bone in her body.

'Walk with me,' Rana said. It was more an order than a suggestion. Yllandris had never been popular among her peers, and

Shranree's open hostility had done little to discourage a similar attitude from the other sorceresses.

They continued together to the north gate, walking in silence. The horn sounded again, another call to arms. A stream of warriors filed down the road, many of them the wrong side of forty and wearing forlorn looks that suggested they thought they wouldn't live out the day. The news had spread. The Shaman was coming to reclaim his domain, and this time there would be no Herald to oppose him.

Shortly after seizing control of Heartstone, Krazka had made an example of the greybeards who refused to accept him as their new king. The two sorceresses held their noses as they passed the gallows that had been erected in the centre of town. After weeks of exposure to the predations of insects and hungry carrion birds the corpses had been all but stripped bare, and the stench wasn't as bad as Yllandris had feared. Still, a glance at the remains of intestines hanging down over half-eaten genitalia was almost enough to trigger another shaking fit.

In an unexpected moment of empathy, Rana hooked an arm under Yllandris's and guided her down a side street in order to avoid the worst of the gruesome spectacle. 'Things will get better,' the woman said, though her voice lacked conviction. 'Shranree believes our people are on the verge of greatness.'

'Greatness?' Yllandris echoed, trying to sound respectful, to keep the incredulity out of her voice.

'Our new king will lead us to the prize that was always meant for us. Even in this Age of Ruin, the Lowlands are a veritable paradise. No Highlander need ever starve again once we claim them as our own.'

'The King cavorts with demons! *Demons*, Rana – the threat our menfolk have for centuries died keeping us safe from. And now they are here, outside our very walls.'

Rana looked troubled. 'The Lowlands are vast. Vast, and filled with fools who have grown soft and lazy. Let them suffer as we have suffered. We are blessed – our men peerless in battle, our women wise and strong in the gift of magic. We will find our true place in the world. A place we *deserve*. The demons are a means to an end. The King himself says so.'

Yllandris listened in silence. A few months ago Rana's arguments would have made a kind of sense. She had been willing to do anything in order to get what she felt was owed her. Manipulate anyone. Betray anyone.

Now she said, 'The King sacrifices children to the Herald.'

Rana flinched at that and said nothing more.

Beyond the gallows, they passed a crater in the ground the size of a tavern, left behind after the Shaman's titanic struggle with the Herald had flattened a dozen buildings. The Magelord and the huge winged demon had clashed in the skies just outside the city, plummeting to earth in a maelstrom of raking claws and knotted muscle, the Shaman a blur of bronze beneath the gigantic midnight bulk of the Herald. At first it seemed the Shaman might be the stronger of the two, flinging the demon around like a man might toss a blanket. But then he had begun to falter. The demon's talons left terrible furrows in his flesh, bloody wounds that would have killed a mortal. It had taken a last-minute charge by the Brethren to drag the Shaman away to safety. Many Transcended had died in the retreat, torn apart by the winged terror as they guarded their master with their lives.

If Krazka's flurry of executions after snatching power quieted talk of resistance, the Herald's ruthless display of efficacy had silenced it completely.

Shranree was waiting for them at the north gate. Half the great King's circle was already there with her. She looked mildly disappointed when Yllandris joined them, but she recovered quickly.

'For once you are on time. Could it be the recent lesson I delivered has finally sunk in? I pray it is so.' Shranree's voice was sickly sweet, as false as a whore's affections. 'Take up your position. Now we wait.'

Yllandris curtsied and did her best to appear deferential. *Give her no reason no doubt you. Act like a chastened child.*

She is too arrogant to suspect anything. Her hand trembled suddenly and she willed herself to be calm. Fear was only uncertainty about the unknown, after all. There was no uncertainty about one very particular aspect of her plan.

Whatever happened during the next few hours, she would not live to see tomorrow.

It was midday when the Shaman finally arrived at the gates. The Brethren led the vanguard of his great army, a chaotic menagerie of beasts undyingly loyal to their master. Natural enemies ambled side by side: monstrous bears shoulder to shoulder with lean grey wolves, mountain cats padding alongside great white elk to form deadly ranks of antler and tooth and claw. Despite their savage appearance, the Brethren moved with a purpose and unity that set them apart from natural beasts.

Once the Brethren had been men gifted with the spark of magic. At some point in their lives a yearning had arisen in them to transcend, to become one with a host animal. After they had found a suitable candidate they underwent the Shaman's ritual and merged their mind with the body of their host. Many of the Brethren served to help defend the Borderland. While few in number, they were immune to demon fear. Without their support the army laying siege to the King's Reaching for the last month would never have made it to Heartstone's walls.

Behind the Brethren came Carn Bloodfist's host. The Bloodfist's army numbered over ten thousand – twice what Heartstone had mustered. Soon the army of the Black Reaching would arrive to bolster the Shaman's forces further. Mace's change of heart was a significant blow to Krazka's plans. It remained to be seen how the Butcher King would deal with that setback. For now, he had more immediate concerns. The warriors of the West Reaching eventually halted a safe distance away, marshalling outside the range of the King's circle and whatever magic they might try to bring to bear.

Another great horn blast split the air to mark the arrival of

Krazka and his entourage. They approached up the wide dirt avenue that led from the centre of town, and the massed ranks of Heartstone's defenders parted for them. The King strode along confidently, his white cloak billowing behind him.

The Butcher King reached the north gate and gestured to one of the Six – the big brute with the ridiculous bear skull atop his head. Despite his size Yllandris did not judge him the most frightening of the men that guarded the King. Sir Meredith, the ironclad warrior: he made her skin crawl. The lean warrior with the bow looked as though he would peel a man alive for the sport of it. As for the strange Northman with the bloodshot eyes, Wulgreth, there was something not quite right about that one. Yorn looked distinctly out of place among such company.

'Open the gate,' Krazka commanded. The huge bear-skulled warrior moved to obey, single-handedly lifting the beam that sealed the gates and dropping it to the hard earth with a loud thud. An eagle soared overhead, emboldened by the absence of the Herald. No chance it was mere coincidence; it must have been one of the Brethren, or else a spirit animal spying for the Shaman's forces. Krazka could have ordered his sorceresses to blast it out of sight, but instead he made an elaborate show of tidying his cloak and adjusting his sword belt. With a nod to his Kingsmen, who fell in behind him, Krazka pushed open the gate and strolled out to meet the opposing army.

Yllandris's heart hammered in her chest. She hadn't been privy to the exact details of Krazka's plan. She doubted any of the sorceresses had, even Shranree. All she knew was that when the King went out to challenge the Shaman, she and her sisters would follow. Then they would wait, and would do nothing. Not until the signal.

The Brethren snarled and stamped as Krazka approached, but they did not attack. The King halted a stone's throw from the bestial horde and raised a gloved hand. 'I would speak with the Shaman,' he thundered. 'Let's see if old potato face is brave enough to settle this man to man. Just him and me. No one else needs to die.'

Yllandris was impressed despite herself. Much as she hated the child-sacrificing maniac, she was forced to admit that Krazka possessed balls of steel.

There was a brief moment of chaos among the Brethren. A moment later they parted and out stormed the Magelord, a study in wrathful fury made flesh.

Even with the ugly scars still raw on his skin – the legacy of his battle with the Herald – the Shaman cut an imposing figure. As always he was naked from the waist up, corded muscles bulging from every inch of his prodigious torso. Glacial blue eyes full of cold fury stared out from the Magelord's blunt face.

'Charlatan,' he boomed, his voice like a great iceberg shifting in the Frozen Sea beyond the Blue Reaching. 'You dare take the place of the rightful king! You dare bargain with demons, allowing them to pass unhindered into my domain! You dare defy *me*!'

'Charlatan?' Krazka spat. 'That's rich coming from you. The Herald told me some things, see. You ain't one of us. You never were. You came here from the Lowlands, fleeing like a wounded dog after your woman was burned alive. You stole magic from the heavens and used it to make yourself a god. Well, you ain't no god.'

The Shaman bared his teeth. 'I make no claim to godhood. But the strong rule the weak. That is how it has always been. I keep this land safe from what lies below the Spine.'

'What lies below the Spine is *opportunity*. You'd have us sit here in this little corner of the north, worshipping your sweaty arse while the winters get harsher and food grows scarce. That's what Beregund was about, wasn't it? I killed for you there, and in the North Reaching. They broke the Treaty, so you had them razed them to the ground. I got no problem with that.'

Krazka took a single step forward and in one lightning movement drew his abyssium sword. The grey metal seemed to *throb*, as though it hungered to taste the flesh of the immortal. 'What I got a problem with are hypocrites. You're too much of a coward to risk war with your peers in the Lowlands, that's the truth. Aye, you might be a wolf compared to men who ain't tasted the bounty of the gods. But the weakest of wolves, they're still the runts of the pack.'

The Shaman clenched his great fists, and his voice thundered with terrible rage. 'Enough talk, worm! I accept your challenge. Samaya, reveal yourself.'

The air stirred near the Magelord. One by one the sorceresses that had been lurking behind the Shaman under a spell of invisibility melted into view. Yllandris gasped softly, glanced at Shranree and saw her twitch in surprise.

The leader of the West Reaching circle, Samaya, was as willowy as Shranree was rotund. 'I await your command,' she said demurely, though her eyes revealed her discomfort at this turn of events, as if carefully laid plans had been unexpectedly altered.

'Allow none to interfere in this duel,' the Shaman's voice boomed. 'We fight according to the Code. Let the winner take what they will. The loser will receive only death.'

The two sets of sorceresses formed a ring around the Magelord and the King, each woman facing her counterpart across the circle. The Brethren waited a hundred yards back, the army of the West Reaching a half-mile beyond that. Yllandris glanced behind her and saw the town's defenders massed just inside the walls. There was no appetite for battle on the faces of the town's veterans, nor the reinforcements from the Lake Reaching.

Yllandris could feel her heart thumping in her chest. Her sisters seemed just as nervous. Rana had gone an unhealthy shade of white; Esther had chewed her nails to the quick; even Shranree wore a fresh sheen of sweat on her face.

The Six seemed much more relaxed. They stood just outside the circle of women, weapons sheathed and hands on their belts.

Sir Meredith looked almost scornful, his heavy-lidded eyes filled with contempt, as if the face-off about to take place was a personal affront to his dignity.

Yllandris paid no more notice to the iron man. With a grunt the Shaman launched himself at Krazka, intending to crush the imposter beneath his mighty fists.

The Butcher King danced out of the way at the last instant, leaving the hulking Magelord clutching at thin air.

'Huh.' The Shaman braced himself and then suddenly he hurtled up into the sky, plummeting back down a moment later to strike the earth in the exact spot Krazka had been standing but a second before. The King rolled to his feet with the grace of a cat, responded with a dazzling combination of strikes that would surely have overwhelmed all but the very best swordsmen.

The Shaman caught the blade between his palms.

Immediately the scars on the Magelord's chest began to open up. His muscles visibly sagged and lost their definition, his ageless face began to wrinkle.

With a grunt, the Shaman tugged the sword free of Krazka's grasp and tossed it aside. 'Abyssium,' the Magelord growled. 'Demonsteel. You think me a fool?' The weeping scars on his body began to smoke, knitting themselves back together. His face shifted and regained its youthfulness, his torso sculpting itself back into the image of perfection once again.

Krazka scrabbled backwards. 'Now!' he roared.

Yllandris felt Shranree's sudden probing as the leader of the King's circle reached for the magic of her sisters, demanding they surrender it. The sorceresses did as she commanded, pouring their collective strength into the dumpy little woman with her hands held aloft to the heavens.

Yllandris summoned her own power and felt the familiar tingling thrill of magic as it raced through her veins. She opened herself up to Shranree, surrendered as much of the magic as she dared. But she held something back, a tiny thread she refused to yield.

Shrieking, rapturous with the magical maelstrom raging within her, Shranree finally evoked the great spell she and the King had been planning all along. She pointed a finger at the Magelord. The Shaman jolted and then suddenly froze, paralysed by the enormous energies pouring from the leader of the King's circle.

By the time the circle's counterparts from the West Reaching realized something was amiss, the Six were already among them. Swords and axes bit into flesh in great explosive gushes of red spray. The West Reaching sorceresses attempted to unleash their own magic to defend themselves – but they could only stare in horror as their spells fizzled and died, consumed by the abyssium rings the Kingsmen wore beneath their gloves.

The faster among the Brethren were already halfway to the carnage when a dozen blink demons suddenly manifested right in their path. The fiends had been hiding in the tunnels Krazka had ordered excavated just north of town. The ten feet of earth that separated their ambush spot from the surface was no obstacle to them, no barrier to beings for whom the laws of the world were as mutable as clay.

Krazka retrieved his sword and stalked towards the immobile Magelord. 'Took me twenty years to get to this point,' the one-eyed King mused. 'Not bad for a whore's get left to die in a cesspool. You got no idea what it takes to climb up out of that pit and reach for the stars. Maybe once upon a time you did. But you forgot.'

Krazka raised his demonsteel blade, lining up the razor edge for a killing blow. 'There ain't no rules, see. No Code. There's only the strength of a man's desires and the things he's willing to do to see 'em fulfilled. Me, I want the world... and there's nothing I won't do, no man, woman or child I won't kill, to get it.'

... no man, woman or child I won't kill, to get it...

Yllandris found her courage at last.

She seized the tiny thread of magic she had kept hidden from Shranree. The woman's face was rigid in concentration, the vein in her forehead throbbing, sweat pouring down her cheeks. Even with the combined sorcery of the circle, it took every bit of Shranree's focus to keep the Shaman under her spell. She hadn't considered the potential for treachery. She was too arrogant to believe anyone would dare.

Circle magic was unique to the sorceresses of the High Fangs. Whilst the circle leader could draw upon the power of her sisters, it also required trust, for where a member of the circle could give, she could also take. In practice such a thing was almost unheard of. A sorceress who dared hijack a circle's power from its leader faced execution on the spot.

Yllandris, however, had made peace with death.

She opened herself wide, like a flower spreading itself before the sun, and seized the magic, draining it from Shranree. The woman's eyes widened and her focus faltered, and a second later she screamed in outrage.

Krazka's sword flashed down—

—and missed, as the Shaman found himself suddenly free of his invisible chains. He lashed out at the false King, a blur too fast for the eyes to follow, and though Krazka somehow moved to evade the full devastating force of the blow the punch glanced off the side of his face, lifting him up off the ground.

Yllandris heaved a ragged sigh and allowed the stolen magic to dissipate harmlessly away. It was over. She ignored the confused shouts from her sisters; she blocked out Shranree's shrieking curses. The woman would realize what had happened soon enough – but by then it would be too late.

She watched as the Shaman moved to finish off the fallen King. Krazka was on the dirt, his face a ruined mess. He appeared to be fumbling for something in his cloak, but there was nothing that could possibly help him against this relentless immortal, nothing that could harm this half-god—

Bang.

The sound was like a thunderclap, so loud it left her ears ringing and drove her to her knees.

The Shaman looked down at his chest and his blunt face creased in puzzlement. There was a small hole just below his left nipple. In the silence following the explosion, the pitter-patter of his blood striking the grass could be heard.

Opposite the Magelord, thick smoke wreathing his disfigured face, Krazka clutched the strange cylindrical device Yllandris had first glimpsed on the hill west of town.

Suddenly the Shaman staggered. He began to change shape, sprouting feathers, desperately seeking the raven form that would allow him to escape. Half-shifted, he leaped into the air and zigzagged through the sky, crimson droplets raining down on the Brethren and blink demons locked in their desperate struggle below. He made it a few hundred yards and then faltered before tumbling out of the sky.

Somehow, Krazka climbed back to his feet. He lurched over to the sorceresses like a drunkard, sword in one hand, gently smoking metal cylinder in the other. Yllandris flinched as she saw the horrific damage that had been done to his face. Krazka's cheek was shattered and his right ear hung off the side of his head.

The King thrust the tip of his sword right up against Shranree's throat. 'What... the... fuck?' he growled, red spittle flecking the edges of his mouth.

Shranree pointed a quivering finger at Yllandris. Her voice was a screech. 'It was that duplicitous whore! She broke the circle!'

Yllandris thought she had reconciled herself to dying, but as the King's dead eye settled on her she felt that familiar twitching begin in her legs and arms. Krazka stashed the metal device inside his cloak and staggered over to her, looking as if he might topple over at any moment. With most of the right side of his face torn off he looked more sinister than ever, as grotesque as any demon from the Devil's Spine. She flinched as he placed an arm around her shoulders.

Just ahead of them the Six had finally finished massacring the West Reaching sorceresses. Butchered and broken bodies littered the ground, small piles of tangled limbs and blood-matted hair. Krazka whistled and the Kingsmen moved to join him, their weapons dripping scarlet beads, soaked from the black work they had just undertaken.

Yorn met Yllandris's eyes. The shame on his face would have made her cry if she weren't so terrified.

Krazka pointed to the north, where the Brethren and blink demons were a whirlwind of tooth and claw and deadly serrated tongue. 'Rain fire down on them,' he ordered Shranree. 'I want to watch them burn.'

'My king… what about the Shaman? If he returns—'

'The Shaman's done. He's got a piece of abyssium stuck inside him. Braxus knows his craft.'

'What will you do with her?' There could be no doubt as to whom Shranree's 'her' referred.

Krazka removed his arm from Yllandris's shoulders. 'Call me soft, but I've always had a weakness for a pretty woman.'

She dared to hope then. Maybe the King intended to keep her as a concubine. The thought sickened her, but at least she wouldn't have to die. Anything was better than death.

She never saw Krazka's hand move. All she saw was the glitter of steel in the corner of her eye. Then she was on her knees, reaching up to her face out of pure instinct, feeling her hands flood with the warmth of her own blood. So much blood. A moment later the pain hit her like a hammer.

'Lucky for me you ain't so pretty now,' Krazka whispered, though she hardly heard him above the sound of her own screams.

Twenty-five Years Ago

HIS HANDS WERE sweating despite the light snow that swirled down from the sky to settle on his face and beard. His breath came in short gasps. He'd been a Warden for six years, faced down demons and giants, the worst of what the Devil's Spine had to offer – but he'd never been as nervous as he was just then. He stared at the ground and tried to calm his beating heart. This was it. There was no escape.

'She's beautiful,' said Taran beside him. His voice was an awed whisper.

Finally he looked up. Like the last of the snow in the sun's firstborn rays, all his fears melted away.

Beneath the fur cloak thrown around her shoulders to ward off the winter chill, Mhaira wore a blue gown that reached down to her ankles. Her sister and her cousin had braided her long brown hair. She looked like a princess rather than a simple shepherd's daughter. He stared at her, mesmerized by her beauty. He was the luckiest man in the world.

Borun walked beside Mhaira, his arm locked with hers. Just behind trailed Lellana and Natalya. Both women looked thoroughly miserable, though the former at least appeared to be making an effort to disguise the fact. As she drew closer Kayne saw that Mhaira's eyes were wet with tears. She smiled at him, the astonishing smile that could light up an entire room, but there was pain there. A pain she couldn't disguise.

Ashamed for his earlier nerves, he wanted nothing more than

to go to Mhaira and take her in his arms. She seemed to read his intentions and gave a slight shake of her head, the hurt in her brilliant grey eyes eclipsed by a sudden and profound love for him.

'I, hmm, believe we are almost ready.'

Rastagar adjusted his robes and fiddled with the wreath hanging around his thin neck. The *veronyi* was surprisingly spry for a man of his advanced years, though he seemed to have something permanently lodged in his craw. He cleared his throat noisily before continuing. 'Spirit Father, step forward.'

Borun went to stand before Rastagar, returning Kayne's grin with one of his own. The new Warden was every inch a man now. Though the beard he was growing was a sorry-looking thing, the rest of him had filled out dramatically in the last year. He was broader in the shoulder even than Kayne, stronger than any man at Watcher's Keep save the Commander himself and only Kayne regularly got the better of Borun when they practised on the training courts – the very courts they were now standing upon.

Rastagar reached into the bag at his waist and withdrew a pinch of dirt. He rubbed it into his palms, working the soil deep into his many wrinkles. 'Spirits of the earth,' he intoned, loud enough for all gathered to hear, 'I entreat you, bear witness to the joining here today of Brodar Kayne and Mhaira, daughter of Magnar, who sadly passed from us yesterday morning. May you nurture his soul so that it may be reborn and returned to us anew. In his place, Borun of Karsus has volunteered to stand as Spirit Father. He will be the stone that fortifies this couple in times of hardship, the bedrock that helps support the weight of years when they seem too heavy to bear. May he forever hold true.' The *veronyi* reached out and placed a hand on Borun's forehead, marking a line with the dirt on his finger. When he was finished the *veronyi* nodded in satisfaction. Borun stepped back, and Kayne and Mhaira stepped forward.

Kayne stole a glance at his bride. Mhaira was crying freely now, tears streaming down her cheeks. The determination he saw in those eyes, the strength she must have possessed to go through with the ceremony after her father had perished on the journey, both humbled Brodar Kayne and filled him with wonder.

The *veronyi* turned to the brazier that crackled behind him. 'Spirits of flame,' he intoned. 'I beseech you, keep the love between this couple burning bright through the years to come. May the warmth in their hearts never fade, and the fires of their passion gift us with children to make our land strong.'

Rastagar placed his hands in the brazier longer than any man ought to. When he finally withdrew them, he carried a tiny flame in each of his palms. 'You will each grasp one of my hands,' he instructed. Mhaira had been nervous about this part of the ceremony, afraid she would get burned even though the other women had assured her that the spirits would not let that happen. Her father's death had robbed her of that fear, and she clasped the *veronyi*'s left hand without hesitation. Kayne took hold of the druid's right hand. He felt a fleeting moment of intense heat before it faded and was replaced by a pleasant warmth that spread through his body.

Rastagar turned to the table beside him and carefully lifted the two cups placed there. 'Spirits of the sea,' he droned, 'I implore you, nourish this couple. Wash away any doubts that yet remain. Drink!' Rastagar handed each of them a cup. Kayne lifted his and swallowed the salty water within. It tasted unpleasant, but tradition demanded that the water used in the joining ceremony should be true seawater, drawn from the Frozen Sea itself. The spirits clearly approved of the practice, since no one who took part in the ritual ever got sick from the briny fluid.

The *veronyi* retrieved the cups and placed them back on the table. Then he removed the wreath from around his neck. The wreath was created from the branches of the great evergreens that grew throughout the northern Reachings, coloured with pale blue violets that matched Mhaira's dress perfectly. 'We are nearly done,' the old man whispered. 'Take the wreath. Hold it between you. High in the air, where all can see.'

Together Kayne and Mhaira took the wreath and turned to face the gathering. It was the moment Kayne had most been dreading. He'd never been comfortable with crowds.

He stared out across the packed court at the folk assembled there. Most of the faces he recognized. There was the High Commander, Orgrim Foehammer himself. Old Master Harlan, who despite his gruffness was the most beloved instructor at the citadel. Renno the Quartermaster; the blacksmith Braxus, whom Kayne had come to befriend in recent years; and dozens of Wardens and Wardens-in-training besides. There were men he had fought alongside, men who had saved his life and men whose lives he had saved, all of them united in their duty to guard the Borderland against the threat from the Devil's Spine.

There were a fair number of women, also. The training yard was sprinkled with the wives of Wardens who like Kayne had chosen to marry. Most of the womenfolk lived in Eastmeet or in one of the small settlements on the outskirts of the capital. Life on the eastern frontier could be lonely and sometimes perilous, but it was a life Mhaira had chosen so that they could be together. Kayne was a Warden, sworn to protect this land. For the next four years, at least.

He glanced at her then, standing beside him, and he was filled with pride. Pride in her bravery. Pride in her faith in him, in her devotion in following him here.

Pride that this was the woman carrying his child.

Rastagar cleared his throat. 'Finally I call upon the spirits of the sky. I beg you, watch over this couple as they join their lives to become one. Just as the twigs that form this wreath grow strong in union, so too will their souls entwine and endure the greatest hardships together. I offer this wreath to them now, so that they may remember the words spoken here this day.'

The *veronyi* leaned forward and placed a withered hand on each of their shoulders. 'You may now exchange rings.'

Kayne went first, placing the golden band he'd bought from an Eastmeet jeweller on the fourth finger of Mhaira's left hand.

Her eyes widened when she saw it, and he wondered if he had made a poor choice. However, when she turned back from Lellana and presented him with a silver band, he realized with dismay that the look on her face had been shame. 'Father didn't have much money,' she said, tears bright on her cheeks. 'When he got ill the three of us struggled to run the farm by ourselves. I'm sorry—'

Kayne placed a finger gently on her lips, shushing her. 'I love you,' he said simply. 'And I don't reckon there's a ring or jewel in all the world that's as pretty as your eyes. If anyone ought to apologize it's me, for subjecting 'em to this ugly mug of mine for the rest of our days.'

He pulled her close then, not caring a damn about the watching crowd. Wrapped his arms around her as if he would never let her go.

'The joining is complete,' Rastagar announced to an eruption of cheers. 'I now pronounce you, hmm, husband and wife.'

Lellana and Natalya came to congratulate them. The latter's face was as sour as curdled milk. 'I hope your lives are happy and filled with joy,' she said, her voice unmistakably bitter. 'After all, Uncle Magnar gave his own life to try and be here.'

'Cousin!' Lellana shot Natalya a warning look. 'It was his choice. We all knew the risk this time of year. He would have been proud of you, little sister.'

Mhaira embraced Lellana as Kayne nodded his thanks. Braxus came forward and gave him a handshake of such ferocity it might have caused serious damage to a smaller man. 'Welcome to the bliss that is married life, lad. Best advice I can offer is never go to sleep angry after an argument.'

'Aye? So resentment don't build up?'

'Who said anything about resentment? A man needs his breakfast served in the morning.' Braxus chuckled at his joke. A moment later his face became sombre, and he held out the wrapped bundle he'd been carrying under one huge arm. 'I wanted to give you this. Forged it some years past. Had the bright idea that one day I'd hand it down to my son. But, well, children ain't happened yet and I figure me and Sal aren't getting any younger. Shame, as I've always liked the little 'uns. Anyway, it's yours now.'

Kayne pulled the cloth from the bundle. It was a sword – a big two-handed monster of a weapon. He gave it an experimental swing. 'Brax... I can't accept this. It's a work of art.'

The blacksmith waved away his protests. 'There ain't no man better suited to it.' Without another word Braxus turned and strolled off, leaving Kayne standing there clutching three and a half feet of steel.

'Looks like we've both come a long way,' rumbled Orgrim Foehammer from behind him. The new High Commander of Watcher's Keep clapped him on the shoulder with a meaty hand. 'I remember us rolling around on the banks of the Icemelt years ago. We never did find Skarn's gang.'

'Likely as not they turned on each other in the end.'

'Perhaps.' Orgrim placed his hands on his belt and stared out eastwards, towards the Borderland. 'Four more years, Kayne,' he said, after a moment of silence had passed between them. 'Then you got a choice to make.'

Kayne nodded. 'I reckon it's already made.'

Orgrim nodded and then bid him farewell. Borun wandered over, a big grin on his face. 'Well, that's done it. Who's gonna go whoring with me now?'

'What're you talking about? I never went whoring with you!'

'Aye, true. No wonder you're so bloody good with a sword, Kayne. You've had more practice swinging your weapon than any man I know. Let's see if you can keep up now you've got a woman doing it for you.'

'Cheeky bastard!' Kayne had to chuckle at the sheer nerve of his young friend. Mhaira had finished speaking with Braxus's wife Sal and was about to make her way over to them. He lowered his voice. 'I wanted to thank you,' he told Borun. 'For stepping in at the last minute. For volunteering to stand as Spirit Father.'

210

Borun shrugged. 'You'd have done the same for me. Not that I'd ever be stupid enough to wed. Brothers forever, aye?'

Kayne nodded, and the two men bumped their fists together. 'Brothers forever.'

Mhaira joined him and the two spent the next while in each other's arms. Kayne placed a gentle hand on his new wife's stomach. 'We'll name him Magnar,' he whispered. 'If he's a boy. After your da.'

Mhaira hugged him tighter and he knew that had been the right thing to say. He stroked her hair, thanking the spirits for bringing this woman into his life. As he stood there with his arms wrapped around her, he became strangely aware of the sensation he was being watched. He looked up to see a large raven perched on the edge of the tallest tower, staring down at him.

The bird screeched once and then took to the wing, soaring west in the direction of Heartstone.

Choice and Consequence

*B*ROTHERS FOREVER.

Brodar Kayne poked the dying embers of the campfire and cracked his knuckles, easing the stiffness from his fingers. His joints had been bothering him worse than ever since they'd left the swamp. The pervasive sense of decay in that place seemed to have somehow wormed its way into his own aching body, making him feel even more beaten-up than usual. He stared up at the stars, thinking of Mhaira. Of the night they'd spent together after their joining.

It was funny how the years took their toll on a man. On his health, slowly robbing him of his youthful notions of immortality until he was glad just to be able to get up in the morning. On the hopes he'd once had; ambitions that had fallen by the wayside; dreams that would give a man purpose one minute and feel as empty as the night sky the next.

Yet for all that time stole, there was that handful of moments during a lifetime that would remain etched in the memory. It was those moments that defined you, Kayne reckoned. The choices made. The friends won and lost. The decision to do the right thing or the easy thing, and it was impossible to tell which of the two a man would choose until the time came. Even a man he had once called brother.

There was a rustle of movement behind him and Brick crept over to sit beside the fire. The boy had been awfully quiet since the necromancer's tower. Kayne passed over a bowl of the rabbit stew they'd cooked up for supper. 'We'll ford the River of Swords tomorrow,' he said. 'Once we're through the Purple Hills, you're free to go.'

'Uh-huh.' Brick seemed less excited by the prospect than he had a week or two ago.

'No sign of your uncle. Where d'you reckon he's got to?'

The boy spoke around mouthfuls of food. 'Maybe he's hiding from the Bandit King's men. Do you think they found our trail?'

Kayne shrugged. 'More than likely. Something tells me we ain't seen the last of them, at any rate.'

Brick finished his bowl and set it down on the grass. He stared into the guttering flames, and when he spoke again his voice sounded very small. 'Why did you save me back at the swamp?'

'We had a deal. You're our guide.'

'I'm not stupid! You don't need me. You never needed me. Jerek could guide you through the Badlands blindfolded. That necromancer might have killed you!'

'He might've. But he didn't.' Kayne reached down and rubbed his aching knees. 'I weren't so different to you once upon a time, lad. Someone gave me a chance, and I took it. Figured I owed you the same.'

'And Jerek?'

'What about him?'

'He risked his life for me. I thought he hated me. I thought he hated everyone. He's always threatening people.'

Kayne rubbed a hand ruefully over his bristly chin. He needed a good shave. 'What a man says and what a man does are two separate things,' he said slowly. 'A person can present as many different faces as there are folk to believe in 'em, but you never learn the truth of their character till they're put to the test.'

Brick's brow creased in confusion. 'I don't understand.'

'Words don't mean nothing. Being agreeable ain't the same as being *true*. When it comes right down to it, it's a man's deeds that define who he is.'

Brick nodded slowly.

'You're a good kid, Brick. Never do anything your heart knows is wrong just because someone told you to. Not even your uncle Glaston.'

'He's not a bad man, you know,' Brick said quietly. 'He rescued me from Asander and the Seer. He raised me as his own. All the showiness, it's just an act. He needs his followers to believe he's smarter than they are.'

Kayne remembered Skarn and the things that bastard would do to impress or intimidate the rest of his gang. Skarn would never have rescued a child. More likely the opposite. Maybe this Glaston wasn't as bad as he thought. 'You ask me,' he said slowly, 'any man who raises another's as his own can't be that bad a sort.'

That seemed to lift Brick's spirits, but before he could reply the sound of clashing steel rang out across the camp. Kayne leaped to his feet, fearing they were under attack, but when he turned it was to see Jerek and Grunt facing off. The Wolf had his twin axes in his hands, while the big greenskin clutched a pair of swords they'd found in Nazala's tower.

Kayne was about to ask the pair why they were fighting – though as far as the Wolf was concerned, a reason was generally an optional extra – when Grunt bared his tusks in a grin. Jerek simply nodded, the tiniest of movements that for him passed as a towering act of respect. 'Not bad. Where'd you learn to fight?'

Grunt made a series of gestures and then formed a dome shape with his hands.

'He was a gladiator,' Brick translated. 'He fought in the great arenas far to the east. Then a... princess? No, a wizard took him away. He woke up in a box, in a big city. But he thinks something's wrong. The world's not the same as he remembers.'

Kayne breathed a sigh of relief. He wouldn't like to bet on a winner if the pair ever came to blows for real. 'Aye,' he said wryly. 'It never is.'

The River of Swords wound down from the Purple Hills all the way west to the Broken Sea, cutting a jagged line across the northern reaches of the Badlands that was passable only at a few scattered points along its great length. Though the river rarely ran deeper than the height of three men, the currents were often strong enough to pull even the most determined swimmer beneath its churning waters.

The ford they were currently inspecting lay many miles west of the spot Kayne and Jerek had crossed into the Badlands earlier that year. The ford was narrow, perhaps two hundred feet across. Kayne saw something dark in the shallows and reached in. He brought out a length of rusted steel, so corroded it felt as though it would break apart in his hands under the slightest pressure.

'How long do you reckon this has been there?' he asked Brick.

The boy shrugged. 'It's hard to tell. The horse tribes fought many wars over this land. According to Yahan beliefs, whichever tribe held the hills beyond the river were blessed by the gods.'

Kayne tossed the remains of the ancient sword back in the water. 'Seems to me that if the horselords had spent less time killing each other and more time getting along, they might've eventually conquered the southern lands.'

Jerek stared across the water and spat. 'Reckon you could say the same about the High Fangs.'

They dismounted and secured their horses, fastening their packs as well as Grunt's mysterious sack tightly to their mounts. The big mute led the way, wading out into the swift-moving water, which quickly rose until it reached his waist. The horses were less than happy, snorting and squealing and pulling back on their reins, but between the four of them the companions managed to stop the animals getting themselves drowned.

Near the middle of the ford, Brick slipped and went under. Only a quick reaction by Jerek saved his life, the Wolf reaching in and pulling the boy up before he was swept away by the current. The young bandit opened his mouth to stammer his thanks but Jerek simply turned away. 'Watch what you're doing,' the Wolf growled.

When they were almost across the river, less than thirty feet from shore, Glaston rode into view.

The moustachioed bandit must have been hiding behind the thicket of trees lining the bank. He sat astride his showy white stallion, fancy sword hilt sticking out from his hip and flamboyant ponytail swaying behind him. He held his gloved hands out before him, palms open to show that he carried no weapon. 'Peace!' he called. 'I wish only to talk.'

'Uncle!' Despite his near drowning, Brick's face lit up. Jerek muttered a torrent of curses.

'Got any friends hiding behind those trees?' Kayne called out, keeping his voice level.

'I'm alone.'

'Get off your horse. Slowly. And keep your hands where I can see them.'

Glaston did as he was asked, sliding effortlessly from his saddle. He locked his hands behind his ponytail and then went to his knees, a gesture that struck Kayne as perhaps a trifle dramatic.

Brick splashed his way out of the river, almost tripping as the others waded through the shallows. The boy threw his arms around his uncle, who patted him fondly on the head.

'Calm, Wolf,' Kayne whispered. Jerek's face was like thunder, his teeth grinding together as if he were chewing rocks.

'You tried to kill us,' Kayne said pointedly, once they joined Glaston and his nephew on dry land.

The bandit inclined his head. 'For that I can only apologize. My men were near starved and our situation had grown desperate. Things got rather... out of hand. I was thinking only of their welfare, and that of Brick here.'

'Prick,' Jerek rasped.

Kayne crossed his arms, trying to appear forbidding despite being soaked to the bone. In truth, he couldn't really blame Glaston. You did what you had to in order to survive. 'Why are you here?'

'I bring dire warning.'

'Let's hear it, then. If it's a good one we might just let you ride away.'

'Allow me to start at the beginning. I had been trailing you for weeks, as you were doubtless aware. When I saw my nephew was in no immediate danger I decided to keep a safe distance and bide my time. Then a sizeable band of Asander's men showed up and you fled to the swamp.'

'Go on.'

'I watched an army of corpses chase Asander's men from the swamp. They regrouped to the east, and I managed to get close enough to eavesdrop on their conversation. They're planning to ambush you in the hills ahead.'

Kayne's eyes narrowed. 'Why ride all this way just to warn us?'

Glaston placed a gloved hand on his nephew's shoulder. 'Whatever our grievances, I could not allow Brick to ride into danger.'

A moment of silence passed, and then Kayne grunted. He'd have done the same in the circumstances. 'We need to pass those hills,' he said. 'We ain't got a choice. Not if we want to make it to Mal-Torrad.'

The bandit leader smiled, revealing perfect white teeth. 'I know of another route through. I can show you the path, with Asander's men none the wiser. Consider it my apology for attempting to rob you.'

'Bullshit,' Jerek spat. 'You're lying.'

'I have no reason to lie, friend. I only wish to see my nephew safely returned to me.'

Brick turned to Kayne, his green eyes shining with excitement.

'Let my uncle come with us! He knows these hills better than anyone alive.'

Glaston raised an eyebrow. 'You rather seem to be enjoying the company of these men.'

'We had a deal, Uncle. You always taught me to keep my word.'

Kayne cleared his throat. 'You're free to go, Brick. I reckon you've lived up to your end of the bargain already.'

To his surprise, Brick looked disappointed. 'But I wanted to help,' the boy said. He reminded Kayne of Magnar just then, and the old warrior's objections died in his throat when he saw the hopeful expression in those emerald eyes. He glanced at Grunt, who shrugged, and then at Jerek, who seemed on the verge of exploding.

'All right, lad. You and your uncle can guide us through the hills. But after that we go our separate ways.'

'For fuck's sake, Kayne.' The Wolf shook his head in disgust and spat in the river. Brick, though, wore a big grin.

'There were skeletons,' Brick was telling his uncle. The two of them were riding double on Glaston's horse up in front. 'Skeletons that moved!'

Glaston listened to his nephew in silence. Occasionally he would stroke his moustache. Kayne followed behind, Jerek just to his right, Grunt to his left.

Hills rose all around them, blanketed by purple flowers. Glaston twisted in his saddle and gestured at the colourful view.

'The dahlia flower,' the bandit said. 'The Yahan cultivated them. They believed the stems would drink the blood of the fallen, and that the flowers would house the souls of the dead until the Great Wheel turned and they were reborn anew. They were a primitive people, the horselords. Rather like your friend there. What exactly... *is* he?'

'Grunt?' Kayne replied. 'Dunno. Never thought to ask. Don't see as it's important.'

'Not important? You could be travelling with a monster.'

The big greenskin made a gesture with a finger you didn't need to know hand language to understand.

Kayne thought about pointing out the fact that Grunt had never tried to kill him, but in the end he decided to let it pass for Brick's sake. 'How'd you know all this stuff? The names of flowers, facts about the horse tribes and such.'

'My father taught me to read, just as I taught Brick. I have acquired many books over the years. There is nothing more valuable than the written word.'

'Brick said you got noble blood in your veins. That your ancestors were Andarran princes.'

Glaston slumped slightly in his saddle. 'That's right.' He seemed a good deal more subdued than during their last encounter, but then Kayne figured getting your followers killed and fleeing like a coward would rob anyone of a certain amount of bravado.

They squeezed along a narrow gulley winding down between two hills, and soon they emerged into a steep basin. Fast-rising slopes surrounded them all on sides, drowning in towering dahlia flowers dense enough to conceal a small army. The perfect spot for an ambush, in fact.

Jerek immediately brought his horse to a halt. 'I fucking knew it,' he growled.

The flowers shifted and then began to part. Bandits slunk out of the foliage, bows raised and arrows targeted at the small group below. Glaston suddenly spun his white stallion around, positioning his nephew between himself and the Highlanders.

'Uncle?' Brick said, panic rising in his voice. 'What's going on?'

'Shush. Say nothing.'

The bandits kept on coming, a host of them, ready to launch a storm of arrows at a moment's notice. From this distance, the bandits couldn't miss.

'Shit,' Kayne said. He met Glaston's eyes and saw the truth there. The man had set them up.

'Well, well. If it's not the two goat-fuckers that killed half my band this winter just past.'

Kayne squinted. His eyesight was bad and getting worse, but he didn't need to strain hard to recognize the identity of the speaker. There weren't many bandits wide enough for two men. 'Fivebellies.'

'You remember me!' The corpulent bandit placed a hand over his huge stomach and gave it an affectionate pat. 'Twenty-seven of my men are dead thanks to you. I should have listened to my stomach; it never lies. The pair of you turned the roads near Emmering into a bloodbath.'

'Never start something you can't finish.'

Fivebellies smiled nastily. 'Oh, I plan to finish it right enough. But first we're taking you to meet the Bandit King. My cousin's got something special planned for you.'

Glaston shifted on his horse and ran a finger nervously over his moustache. 'I delivered them as promised. Where's my reward?'

Brick flung his arms back, whacking his uncle in the face. The youngster threw himself from the horse and scrambled to his feet. 'You said you would lead them to safety,' he screamed. 'You lied!'

'I had no choice in the matter!' Glaston exclaimed. He dabbed at his nose, where Brick's elbow had drawn blood. 'I'm done with this life, boy. I spent years convincing Raff and Slater and the rest to join us. Now they're all dead and we're back to square one.' The bandit yanked off his gloves and hurled them to the grass. 'I'm too old for this,' he said wearily. 'We're never going to beat Asander. Better to let bygones be bygones and take the gold. We'll settle somewhere in the Unclaimed Lands. You can find yourself a girl.'

'But I promised them! You taught me never to break my word!'

Glaston sighed. 'Things change, Brick.' He turned to Fivebellies. 'As we agreed? Twenty gold and you let my nephew and me leave in peace.'

Fivebellies nodded. 'Sawyer, give the man what he's owed.'

Kayne watched what happened next with a bone-deep weariness, a familiar sickness in his stomach. The bandit named Sawyer raised his bow and fired an arrow that hit Glaston in the shoulder, knocking him from his stallion. Glaston tried to rise, but a second arrow thudded into his back, knocking him face down in the mud. Still he struggled to his knees, began to crawl towards Brick, who tried to run to him.

Kayne saw the danger. He grabbed hold of the boy, dragging him back kicking and screaming. 'Easy, lad,' he whispered. 'Easy. It's too late now.'

Fivebellies heaved a big sigh. Then he ambled over to Glaston and drew his scimitar. 'Seems I have to do everything myself,' he grumbled. He reached down, jerked Glaston's head back, and ran the edge of his blade across the man's throat.

The blood seemed to pour out endlessly. It sprayed all over the grass, over Fivebellies' face, even over Glaston's white stallion, which snorted and danced away, crimson spots flecking its alabaster hide.

Brick went limp in Kayne's grasp and began to sob.

Fivebellies let Glaston's body fall to the ground. 'The rest of you drop your weapons. That means you, whatever the hell you are.'

Grunt bared his tusks and looked like he was about to charge. Kayne caught his gaze, shaking his head desperately. The greenskin hesitated. Eventually he placed his swords on the grass, his amber eyes narrowed in fury. One of the bandits came over to inspect his sack.

'Looks like some kind of giant egg,' he said, sounding puzzled.

'Just get it secured,' Fivebellies replied. 'We'll see what the Seer makes of it. What you staring at, scarface?'

Jerek was glaring a hole in the fat bandit.

'Let it go, Wolf,' Kayne hissed.

'I said, what are you staring at?' Fivebellies glanced over his shoulder just to be sure there was still an army behind him.

'Fuck if I know,' Jerek rasped. 'But if I had to guess, I'd say a bloated sack of shit that'll be a corpse soon enough.'

Fivebellies' face went a bright shade of crimson. 'Asander said to bring you back alive,' he snarled. 'But he didn't say in what condition.' He lashed out hard with the pommel of his scimitar.

Jerek made no effort to block the blow, taking the full force of it right on the chin. A second later he grinned and spat a glob of blood right in the bandit's face.

'Hard man, are you?' Fivebellies roared, wiping crimson drool from his face. 'We'll see about that. Sawyer, shoot him in the leg. I want to hear him scream.'

Kayne's hands twitched. He was a moment away from drawing steel, consequences be damned. Then he looked down and saw Brick silently weeping and the desire to go down fighting drained away. If this turned into a bloodbath, Fivebellies might well decide to add Brick to the pile of corpses. He couldn't be responsible for that.

The bandit named Sawyer nocked another arrow. Time seemed to stand still as he pulled back the bowstring. And then released.

Jerek didn't even flinch. The Wolf looked down at the arrow sticking out of his leg with an expression that might've been carved from granite. He reached down, grabbed the shaft between his fists and then snapped it off, tossing the broken end away as if it were a stone he'd just dislodged from his boot.

Fivebellies' mouth opened and closed, his jowls wobbling as he struggled for words. Finally, he turned to the men on the hill behind him. 'Bind their wrists and ankles,' he spluttered. 'Don't be gentle.' He turned back to the captives, and though his beady eyes held the kind of dull malice Kayne had seen a hundred times before on a hundred different faces, his next words nonetheless sent a chill through the old warrior's blood.

'The Bandit King's gonna have himself a nice big bonfire.'

Rock Bottom

D AVARUS COLE DROPPED the blue-veined rock into the cart. It landed with a clink that should have been satisfying. It should have been, but it wasn't. Nothing seemed to matter any more.

'Ghost? You all right?'

He flinched as if someone had struck him, but it was just Smiler delivering his day's yield. The man flashed a gap-toothed grin beneath a thick layer of dust and grime.

'Fine,' Cole answered dully. The sun was already sinking below the horizon; the nights were coming in earlier now. Autumn was on the way.

'You want to go for a drink this evening? You've been keeping to yourself an awful lot lately.'

Cole shook his head.

Smiler leaned in close. 'I thought you were going to escape?' he whispered. 'You hardly say a word any more. What happened to the man who faced down Corvac? The man who was determined to get home to his girl?'

'He's gone,' Cole said quietly.

'Gone?'

'That's right. There's nothing left for me now but this place.' He spread his hands towards the tortured landscape. The Horn rose tall and ominous, looming over fissures in the black earth from which the miners were currently being hauled up by the Mad Dogs.

Corvac sauntered over, and Cole flinched back. The Mad Dog leader peered into the cart and gave an approving grunt. 'Not a bad day's work. You keep this up, I might decide you deserve an allowance again.'

The overseer suddenly shoved himself up against Cole until they were chest-to-chest. Corvac's crazy eyes glared up at him, his thin mouth twisting into a sneer. 'Course, you try to fuck me again and you know what will happen. Don't you, bitch?' He slapped the handle of the pick he held in one hand slowly against the palm of the other.

Cole swallowed. 'Yes,' he whispered.

'Good. Now get back to town. I don't want to see your pasty face again until tomorrow. You got me?'

'Yes.'

Corvac reached up and patted Cole's cheek, then went to join his men. He said something to the other Mad Dogs and pointed at Cole, prompting an eruption of laughter.

'What was that about?' asked Smiler.

'Nothing.' Cole turned his back on his friend. Shoulders hunched, he began the long walk back to Newharvest alone.

The dosshouse was half-deserted when he arrived. He entered the common room and collected his evening meal from the cook, then descended the stairs and stepped quietly through the dormitory, not wanting to draw attention to himself. He found his bed at the end of the hall, sat down and kicked off his boots. He shovelled the warm stew into his mouth, hardly bothering to chew the food – it was too much effort; all he wanted was to collapse into bed. Despite his utter exhaustion, he hadn't been able to sleep much recently. The nightmares were keeping him awake.

He was halfway through the bowl when a shadow fell across the bed. He looked up to see Shank staring down at him. He had something shiny in his hand. A knife stolen from the kitchens.

'Give me your food,' Shank said in a soft voice. He had some peculiar mannerisms and a funny way of walking that could lead men to underestimate him. That was a dangerous mistake – as one of the miners had already discovered.

Cole shook his head. 'No, it's mine.'

The glow-globe on the ceiling above illuminated Shank in a sinister light. Outside, the great cloud that had begun to gather as Cole walked back to Newharvest decided to shed its weight. The first patters of rain struck the roof.

'Goldie says Corvac made you his bitch.' Shank tittered and checked behind him, like a naughty child who'd discovered a secret he wasn't supposed to know. 'She says he's going to break you.'

Cole's heart sank. 'Why won't he leave me alone? I do what he tells me. What more does he want?'

Shank giggled. 'Goldie won't let him forget what you did to her.'

'I didn't do anything.'

'That's not what she said.' Shank shook his head, disgust plain on his face. 'I'm not claiming to be an angel. I've murdered men. Skinned them alive, in fact. But I've never disrespected a woman like you disrespected Goldie. You don't treat a lady like that.'

Cole stared up into Shank's judgemental glare. After all he had suffered, the things done to him that night outside the tavern, this stone-cold killer was going to admonish *him*?

The glow-globe on the ceiling seemed to burn brighter. The beating of the rain on the roof outside turned into a roar. As if oil had been poured on a fire, rage flared inside Cole, sudden and terrible, just as on the night he'd first arrived in Newharvest and discovered someone had soiled his bed. He could feel the intense anger throbbing through his veins and it took all his willpower not to charge Shank there and then. 'You're an idiot,' he spat. 'Leave me alone.'

Shank kicked the bowl out of Cole's hands. The contents splattered all over Cole's face and his miner's outfit and even the bed. The stew in that bowl had been the only food he would receive until morning. It would have been kinder had Shank simply pissed in his face.

Overcome with fury, Cole threw himself at Shank, trying to knock the other man to the ground. But the last couple of months had seen his strength waste away, and lost in rage he forgot all the lessons the Darkson had taught him. Shank managed to keep his balance and drove a knee into Cole's nutsack, stunning him. The wiry knifeman forced him to the floor, twisting the blade to rest it against his neck.

'You stupid shit.' Shank's breath was hot and sour. 'You're Corvac's bitch, else I'd murder you like I did that other sod. But I can still have some fun.' Shank's arm slid down his body, the knife gleaming in the light of the glow-globe. Their tussle had put some distance between them and the globe overhead, and as they moved away from its baleful light Cole found that his anger was almost instantly replaced by desperate terror.

'No!' he begged. 'Please no! I'll give you my food, all of it, tomorrow and every day until you say otherwise. Don't hurt me.' There had been a time when he would never have begged so pathetically, but that part of him had died the night Corvac and his gang had ambushed him outside the tavern.

Shank smirked and pressed the knife closer. 'Goldie was right. You really are a tiny dick. At least you won't miss it much.'

'You stop that!' The ponderous voice boomed out across the dormitory. Suddenly Ed was there, dragging Shank back, tossing him across the room as if he weighed nothing. The halfwit's brow was furrowed in anger and he waved an admonishing finger in Shank's face. 'You mustn't hurt my friends.'

Shank snarled and leaped at Ed, driving his knife into the big halfwit again and again. Ed didn't react. He just stood there with a confused expression as the steel entered and left him, splashes of blood flicking from the plunging blade. Eventually several men rushed forward to restrain the crazed knifeman, but by then it was too late.

Ed looked down at the gory mess Shank had made of his chest. 'Oh,' he said. Then he collapsed.

'Ghost?'

He tried to open his eyes. The world was a blur, and he felt so very heavy. He attempted to hack up some saliva to wet his throat, but there was nothing left. His mouth was as dry as old bone.

'Man down,' shouted another voice from far above. There was a brief pause. 'It's Corvac's bitch.'

A face materialized a few inches from his nose. The smile on that face triggered a memory, which swirled out of the fog of his befuddled mind.

A piano.

The smile reminded him of a piano, black and white keys arranged side by side. Garrett had owned a piano. His mentor had purchased it in Shadowport and transported it across the Broken Sea to his estate in Dorminia. It was the envy of everyone who saw it. Sasha had learned to play a few arrangements, haunting in their beauty. Cole himself had never been able to master the instrument. Sasha had always been smarter than him.

'Ghost!' repeated the first voice. 'Stay awake! If you drift off, you might not wake up again.'

He felt himself being lifted, and then he was floating through the air. What had the piano man called him? Ghost?

He was a ghost, soaring up on ethereal wings to fly away to a better place. But if he were a ghost, that must mean he was dead. It didn't seem so bad, he reflected. In fact, it was rather peaceful.

Thud.

He struck the ground with a painful jolt. Something was torn from his shoulders, and rough hands prodded him.

'Boy's all skin and bone. It's a wonder he lasted as long as he did. You think he's done?'

Footsteps approached, crunching over hard stone. 'He's done. Throw him in the shambler pit.'

He knew that voice, and the man it belonged to.

Corvac.

Memory flooded back. He'd collapsed in the pit. The pick had slipped from his hands as exhaustion finally got the better of him.

Corvac's words twisted around in his brain, unfolding like a sheet of parchment and burning their meaning into his brain like fire.

Throw him in the shambler pit.

Overseeing the miners could be dull work, and so the Mad Dogs had created their own perverse form of entertainment. The shambler pit, where dead workers were tossed and left to rot until the Blight brought them back, devoid of everything that had once made them human.

Cole struggled desperately as he was dragged along the blackened wasteland towards the ditch, but his efforts were feeble. He heard a few muttered protests from the Mad Dogs, the more decent among them voicing their objections to Corvac. Still, none dared step in to stop what was happening.

They reached the edge of the pit. Corvac placed a booted foot on Cole's chest and for a moment the Mad Dog leader seemed almost apologetic. 'This is for disrespecting my woman,' he said. 'No one fucks Goldie. Not without paying. She told me to tell you that.'

And with that, Corvac shoved him over the side of the pit.

The walls weren't quite sheer, and Cole bounced off them on the way down to the bottom, breaking at least two ribs. Despite the terrible pain, he lifted his head with a colossal effort and took in his surroundings.

The pit was about thirty feet across and roughly circular. Near the middle of the pit the bodies of two dead miners sprawled on the ground. As Cole watched in agonized horror, the corpses began to twitch. The heads of the dead miners slowly turned on their rotting necks, rotating around to stare at him with mucus-glazed eyes. In a terrifying succession of moans and cracking limbs, the corpses climbed slowly to their feet.

When he was younger Cole had imagined that when he eventually died it would be in a blaze of glory. He often daydreamed of his heroic last stand, enemies piling onto him from all sides and bearing him down only for him to rise up again, half a dozen swords sticking out of his body, roaring his defiance.

He never for a moment imagined he would die starved and broken at the bottom of a pit, chewed apart by slavering corpses.

The shamblers shuffled closer, rotting flesh sloughing off their bodies, mouths opening and closing shut with a horrific clicking noise.

Cole tried to block out the world as the Darkson had taught him. To slip away to a place of utter tranquillity. The *snap* of the shamblers' jaws made it impossible to focus and lose himself. He opened his mouth to roar his defiance, but all that emerged was a pathetic squawk.

He closed his eyes again. He was done. *I'm sorry, Sasha*, he thought. *I failed you.*

There was a whisper of movement above him, a slight rustle of air as something passed overhead.

'Caw.'

He opened his eyes. A crow was fixing him with its beady stare. 'Cole,' it said.

'You... I know you. You're the bird from my dreams.'

Command them. The voice thundered inside his skull. *Command them to halt and they will yield to you.*

'How?' Cole tried to move but it was no good, he had no strength left. 'How are you talking to me?'

There is no time to explain. Summon forth the power that is within you, child. Bend them to your will. Do it now.

And suddenly the crow was gone, beating wings lifting it up out of the pit and into the steel sky.

The shamblers were almost upon him. The snapping jaws inched down, broken teeth inches from his face, so close now that he could smell the creatures' breath, a rotten stench that made him gag. What had the crow said? *Bend them to your will.*

He summoned all his courage, all his willpower. 'Stop,' he rasped.

And the corpses froze.

'The fuck is this? Come on, you raggedy bastards! Bite his face off!' Corvac's frustrated scream bellowed from the edge of the pit.

Cole stared at the putrid heads just above him. The malevolence in their eyes, the infernal force that animated the corpses, seemed to have faded.

It was me. I told them to stop... and they obeyed me.

He laughed suddenly, a manic outpouring of pain and grief and relief. He was still laughing when a maggot wriggled from the eyelid of the nearest shambler and tumbled down into his mouth.

'Back!' he ordered, choking down bile. The corpses withdrew.

'I don't believe this... Now even the dead are trying to fuck me!' Corvac was incandescent with rage. 'Burn them! Burn those whore-spawned dead fucks!'

A handful of Mad Dogs clambered down into the pit carrying torches and swords. The shamblers lurched towards them, but they were quickly set aflame as torches were thrust at their feet. Soon they were smouldering on the ground.

Corvac stormed over to Cole and drew his sword. 'I don't know how you did it, but you've embarrassed me for the last time, you little prick.'

'Lower your weapon.'

It was Captain Priam. The Whitecloaks had arrived and were climbing down into the pit, Derkin trailing after them. 'What did I tell you?' Priam called sternly to Corvac. 'We can afford no more losses until the new shipment arrives. This Condemned is still drawing breath.'

Derkin attempted to descend the pit but slipped halfway down, thudding painfully to the bottom. He climbed to his feet and hobbled over to Cole. 'Come on. Let's get you out of here.'

'You went to fetch Priam?' screamed Corvac. 'You twisted little shit!' He looked like he wanted to run the hunchback through – but with the Whitecloaks around, he dared not make a move.

'I couldn't let you torture him any more,' Derkin said fiercely. 'It's not right.' The corpse-carver placed a comforting hand on Cole's brow. 'You can stay with me until you've recovered. Ma will look after you.'

'Thank you,' Cole gasped. A moment later darkness claimed him.

The Seeding

'WELL, WHAT ABOUT *this* one?'

Ambryl examined the mask with a furrowed brow. 'This one' was of reptilian design, with a long snout and over-sized teeth painted around the breathing hole.

'Are you high again, sister? I would rather the rat mask we saw in the last shop than this... monstrosity.'

Sasha sighed. For someone who claimed to have no interest in fashion, Ambryl was taking her sweet time choosing a costume for the festival. First it had been the dress, an adventure that had taken the best part of the morning before she settled on a green frock costing almost double what they'd budgeted for. Then they had needed to look for shoes, a fiasco that had severely tested Sasha's resolve to kick her drug habit once and for all. Sixteen days on and somehow she was still hanging in there, despite the cravings that kept her awake at night and occasionally reduced her to a trembling, emotional mess.

Ambryl scowled at the masks. There were all manner of designs on display, most inspired by creatures real or imagined. Some resembled cats, other wolves or exotic birds. One mask depicted a bizarre tentacled monster that reminded Sasha of the magical abomination she'd destroyed months back. The exploding quarrel had been Isaac's invention, a device he claimed could revolutionize warfare if produced in sufficient numbers. Sasha thought she might have been able to replicate the weapon, but if Isaac was indeed what the Halfmage had claimed the best thing she could do was to forget that it had ever existed. The world needed no more weapons capable of such devastation.

'How much for this one?' Ambryl asked the shop owner, a small, timid-looking woman of middling years.

'Twenty silver,' the shopkeep said. 'But for you, fifteen.'

'Five,' Ambryl replied coldly.

'Fourteen.'

'Five.'

'That's not how we conduct business in the City of Towers,' the shopkeep said, mild admonishment in her voice.

Ambryl's hazel eyes narrowed dangerously. Sasha took a quick step forward and positioned herself in front of her older sister. 'Thank you for your time but we'll shop elsewhere.'

They left Masquerade and decided to make their way back to the first shop they'd visited. The marble streets were teeming with people. The Seeding Festival seemed to have energized the typically subdued Thelassans – Sasha saw eager smiles and eyes bright with anticipation, from the women perhaps more than the men.

'You have to stop doing that,' she remonstrated with Ambryl as they walked. 'This isn't Dorminia and you're not an Augmentor any longer. You can't just bully people.'

Her sister sneered. 'These Thelassans are soft. Have you seen the way the men lower their eyes as we pass? We are wolves among lambs here.'

'We're *guests*,' Sasha replied. 'We're going to speak with the White Lady and bring warning of the Fade, that's all. Then we're going back to Dorminia.'

Ambryl's gaze narrowed again. Sasha could think of no one that teetered on the edge of fury as often as her sister, except perhaps for Brodar Kayne's friend the Wolf. Jerek's outbursts usually stopped at a torrent of curses and possibly the odd death threat. Ambryl's anger, on the other hand, was like a steel blade in a velvet glove: sudden, unexpected, and usually murderous in intent. Sasha still had the bump on her head to prove it.

'I came here to deliver vengeance,' Ambryl hissed. 'The life of the White Lady for that of Lord Salazar.'

Sasha stopped dead in the street. A passing woman gave them a curious glance; she must have noted their expressions for she quickly looked away and hurried off. 'We discussed this, Ambryl—'

'I told you not to call me that.'

'Fine, Cyreena. Look, you *cannot* approach the mistress of this city with malice in your heart. She's a Magelord, one of the most powerful wizards who ever walked the land. Even Salazar never challenged her openly. You'll get us both killed if you try to confront her.'

Ambryl's mouth twisted and she flicked blonde hair out of her face. 'You know, I believe I preferred you when you were drugged out of your skull. Let's hurry and find these accursed masks. Your insatiable appetite for shopping has delayed us quite long enough.'

Ambryl strolled off, leaving Sasha standing there, mouth hanging open in shocked outrage. She closed it with a frown and lengthened her stride to catch up with her sister.

They returned to Liza's Costumes and inspected the masks there a second time. Sasha found a fox mask that cost only two silvers, and after another quarter-bell of dithering Ambryl finally picked out a mask that seemed to please her. It resembled a woman with serpentine features. 'What's this mask supposed to be?' Ambryl asked the shop owner.

'That is a succubus,' the woman replied. 'A creature of legend. It was said to tempt men with promises of carnal pleasure, only to later steal their souls.'

A smile played around Ambryl's mouth. 'I'll take it,' she said.

Glittering stars crowded the night sky above Palace Avenue, as if even they were drawn to the spectacle playing out below. The streets heaved with men and women, the men wearing smart trousers and jackets, or at least expensive shirts, the women sporting gowns of all shapes and colours. Everyone wore a mask, even if only over the top half of his or her face. All who attended the Seeding Festival had to conceal their identities or else face scorn from the other revellers.

Sasha adjusted her fox mask and nodded at Ambryl and they began working their way through the crowd towards the palace. At some point during the evening the White Lady herself would greet her subjects. They wanted to be as close as possible to the palace gates to boost their chances of getting an audience with the Magelord when she eventually emerged.

Music played from somewhere in the city. A violinist plucked out a tune that started slowly but gathered momentum, drawing folk together to dance. The strange Thelassan docility slowly disappeared as other instruments joined the violin, creating an orchestra that seemed to echo all around them.

Sasha dodged around a couple locked in each other's arms. He wore a mask in the shape of a dog, she a hunting bird of some kind. A bear-faced gentleman approached Ambryl for a dance, but her sister pointedly turned her head away and shouldered right past him.

The smell of perfume tickled Sasha's nose, not now numbed from moon dust as so often before, and a small group of Whitecloaks appeared and began handing out glasses of wine. Sasha took one. It tasted good, as fine a wine as any Garrett had acquired during his many business expeditions.

'There are too many people!' Ambryl grumbled. Her sister had a point; there must have been thousands of Thelassans lining the great avenue leading to the palace. Curiously, there were no children, and hardly any women who looked to be beyond their child-bearing years. Sasha recalled the wistful look on the face of the grandmother back at the market.

'Let's get closer,' she shouted in order to be heard above the swelling music. She had no idea where it was coming from.

There wasn't an instrument in the world that could create music loud enough to travel the length of the avenue. It was as though the music sprang from the marble beneath their very feet.

Another Whitecloak approached, a handsome fellow clutching a silver tray in his hands. The White Lady's soldiers did not wear masks: theirs were the only faces not concealed. The guard smiled at the sisters and offered them another drink from the tray. Sasha reached out a hand but Ambryl slapped her arm away. Her sister's hazel eyes narrowed behind the succubus mask. 'Keep your wits about you! What wits that aren't addled, at any rate.'

Sasha repositioned her mask and poked her tongue out at Ambryl in irritation. A couple strolled past her, a tall man and a long-legged woman wearing a scandalously short dress revealing her calves. Sasha turned to stare at the pair as they sauntered by. Someone laughed to her right, and she glimpsed another couple kissing. The woman gasped softly as her partner ran his hands down her sides, and ever lower—

Sasha quickly looked away, only to discover that Ambryl had disappeared.

Shit.

The music was growing louder and more intense. The crowd seemed to be drawing closer together. A woman bumped into her, apparently by intent, and she felt something pushed into her hands. She looked down and her breath caught in her throat.

It was a thimble. Filled with moon dust. Filled with *hashka*.

Her hands started to tremble. She glanced wildly around, saw others were furtively and not-so-furtively raising their hands to their noses, snorting the silver powder being passed around. She hesitated, the thimble halfway to her own nose.

She'd promised Ambryl she would give up the drugs. But it was one thing to stay clean when you had no money and no way to feed your habit. It was quite another to have temptation handed to you literally on a plate.

Sasha brought the thimble up to her nostril and snorted it all, taking the entire hit in one go.

And it felt good. So damned *good*.

Something brushed against her ass. She twisted around and slapped the man's groping hands away, then gave him a shove that sent him stumbling back into a small group of revellers who were now in various states of undress. She felt warm breath on her ear and then a woman's fingers brushed through her long brown hair, another hand running down her thigh—

'Get off me!' she shouted. Heart racing, she barged her way through the naked and half-naked bodies that were intertwining on the marble streets beneath her. Sighs and gasps of pleasure and that relentless music filled her ears. She focused on the palace just ahead, her breathing coming in short, sharp gasps.

'Sister!' It was Ambryl. Her sister was hastening towards her. She had that look in her eye, the one Sasha had come to fear. Her succubus mask was slightly askew and there was fresh blood under her fingernails. She stepped over a couple who were rutting on the ground like a pair of dogs in heat.

'What's going on?' Sasha whispered. Ambryl shook her head and aimed a kick at the man at her feet. It caught him in the face just as he was getting into a rhythm, much to his partner's disappointment.

Sasha looked around in shock. The streets were a forest of naked bodies locked in various carnal acts. All but a few revellers seemed lost in a state of utter abandonment.

All of a sudden the music died. Sasha felt Ambryl grab her arm, and her sister pointed towards the palace.

The White Lady was among them.

She was exquisite, a creature of unearthly beauty. She wore a gown of near transparent white silk that revealed a perfect figure beneath. Her platinum hair seemed to sparkle in the starlight overhead, falling around a face the perfection of which words could not adequately describe. Most remarkable of all were the Magelord's eyes: a brilliant violet that made Sasha's breath catch in her throat. Cole had described his audience with the White Lady with all his usual dramatic flair, and as usual Sasha had taken it with a large pinch of salt. She saw now that even Cole's description had not done the Magelord justice. This was a goddess made flesh.

Behind the White Lady drifted her handmaidens, flawless compared to most but plain and vacant beside their divine mistress. They followed her as she glided down the avenue, the Magelord's lambent gaze drinking in the vast orgy that throbbed on the marble streets with approval. Finally her eyes settled on the sisters, and Sasha found herself struggling to breathe.

'You two,' she said in a singsong voice. 'The Seeding calls and yet you refuse its lure. Who are you?'

Sasha tried to speak but couldn't force out a single word. She stood there stupidly, but Ambryl was not so overcome. Her sister took a bold step towards the White Lady. 'I am Cyreena. This is Sasha, my sister. We bring you warning from Dorminia. From a certain Eremul the Halfmage.'

The White Lady's purple eyes did not blink. 'I know of him.'

'He has found evidence that suggests an ancient race known as the Fade are returning to these lands. Already they are sowing discord on the streets of Dorminia through human proxies. I present this evidence to you on his behalf.'

Sasha watched numbly as Ambryl approached the Magelord. Her sister reached into the small bag hanging from her shoulder and withdrew the jar with the tattooed flesh preserved in salt. She broke the seal and held the container out to the White Lady. 'The fanatics all bear this same tattoo. The Halfmage believes it is written in the language of the Fade. He hoped you may be able to translate it.'

The White Lady took the jar and reached a delicate hand inside, seemingly unconcerned by the gruesome nature of its contents. She withdrew the preserved scrap of flesh, examining it with her violet eyes. The slight curiosity on her face was quickly replaced by irritation and Sasha felt her chest tighten in sudden terror.

'I see no tattoo. This is nothing but a scrap of decomposing flesh. You dare come to my city to present me with *this*?'

'What?' Ambryl's eyes narrowed in confusion. 'But there *was* script there! I saw it myself. It was written in black ink.'

The White Lady raised the grisly evidence. 'Nothing.' She tossed the scrap away and then waved a finger in the air. Suddenly, Ambryl's bag was torn from her grasp. It floated across to the Magelord, who began to casually inspect the contents. She paused for a moment – and then from the bag she withdrew a gleaming dagger.

Sasha's heart threatened to burst from her chest.

'Was this meant for me?' the Magelord asked softly. 'Do not lie to me, child. I can read the truth in your eyes.'

Somehow, Ambryl's face remained a mask. 'You killed my master. He gave me everything, and you had him murdered.'

'Who was this master you speak of?'

'Salazar.'

'I see.' The White Lady's gaze turned to Sasha. 'Your sister does not share your sentiments. The two of you were close once – yet now you are as different as ice and fire. What happened to create such a rift between sisters?'

'Men,' Ambryl hissed. 'Rebels opposed to Salazar. They murdered our parents. They... *broke* us.'

The White Lady's purple eyes locked on Ambryl's. 'Men cannot break us, child. We are stronger than they. I would tell you many things if you would join me inside the palace.'

Ambryl hesitated. There was no fear in her eyes, only curiosity. Finally she nodded and turned to Sasha. 'I'll see you later, sister.'

Sasha slipped through the Siren's door, trying not to make any noise. She need not have worried. Lyressa was still awake and was sitting at a table with her husband Willard.

'Hello, dear,' the proprietress said. 'We couldn't sleep. The baby is kicking.' She smiled at her husband. Willard returned the smile, his kindly face filled with adoration. 'Did you enjoy the festival?' Lyressa asked.

'I'm not sure.' Sasha blinked uncomfortably. The light from the brazier by the door seemed too bright and was hurting her eyes. 'I'm sorry to be rude, but I really must get some sleep. Goodnight to you both.'

She hurried up the stairs to the room she shared with Ambryl. She opened the door, pulled it shut behind her and then flung herself on her bed, staring up at the ceiling. She was still buzzing from the *hashka* hit. The events of the past few hours swirled around in her head, a whirlwind of confusing thoughts, feelings and emotions. She was worried about Ambryl, but she knew her sister could take care of herself. Besides, the White Lady didn't appear to bear her any ill will.

She thought of all those people coming together, the relentless music driving them into each other's arms. All those naked forms writhing together, the intoxicating perfume making her feel lightheaded. It had been frightening but, she had to admit, exciting too.

She was restless and bothered. Her body was still tingling with excitement and nervous energy and the *hashka* kick that hadn't quite faded. Slowly her hands inched downwards, brushing over her stomach and her thighs. Finally she touched herself, gasping at how wet she was. She felt so very lonely. Her hand began to move, gaining momentum, just like the music at the palace. Seeking release, seeking something—

There was a sudden scream from downstairs, followed by the crash of furniture breaking.

Sasha jumped up from the bed, racing out of the room and down the stairs.

Willard was on the floor, blood running down his face. The table he had been sitting at was overturned and one of the chairs was broken.

There was no sign of his wife.

'They came for her,' he sobbed. The anguish in his eyes stopped Sasha in her tracks. 'They came for Lyressa and our baby.'

Always a Choice

'START BY ROUNDING *up a few foundlings. They're no use to me, but they'll serve.'*

'What do you mean?' asked Yllandris, though deep down she knew.

'Been a while since the Herald last killed. It needs to feed.'

Krazka's words crawled round and round her skull as she wandered through the streets of Heartstone. The panic had begun to die down now; the townsfolk were beginning to come to terms with the fact that King Magnar had been overthrown by the chieftain of the Lake Reaching. Perhaps they assumed the Shaman would soon return, and everything would go back to the way it was.

For Yllandris, nothing could ever go back to the way it had been. Not after she'd seen what that butcher had done to Magnar. Not after he had given her the order she was on her way to carry out. She could have refused him, but she was a coward. Not a brilliant schemer and a prodigy as she had believed herself to be.

A coward.

She felt the shakes starting in her legs and quickened her pace, trying to walk them off. Then she remembered her objective and slowed to a shuffle. She considered collapsing right there on the soggy earth, surrendering to the fit that threatened to take hold. The temperature was plummeting with the onset of evening, and a night under the stars might well find her body cold and lifeless come the morning. But if she failed to carry out Krazka's orders, Magnar would pay the price.

And besides. She was a coward.

The old abandoned mill was just ahead. The building had long ago fallen into ruin. The roof was rotting and filled with holes, but it provided rough cover for the town's foundlings when there was nowhere else available. Yllandris herself had spent several nights between the sagging walls of the mill as a child. But for the arrival of her magic after her first moon's blood she might have ended up like so many other orphans: dead from starvation or disease or the elements, or forced to become someone's concubine or wife. Those without family did what they had to in order to survive. The High Fangs were a harsh country.

Yllandris pushed open the mould-ravaged door of the building and raised a hand to her mouth as the stench of waste hit her nostrils. Not just waste; there was sickness in the air, too. A dozen small faces turned to stare at her – fewer than she had expected.

'Who are you?' asked a young girl sitting in a bed of filthy straw. Her hair was matted with dirt and her clothes were little more than rags. An older boy moved to stand beside her, a protective brother watching out for his younger sister. Yllandris would have liked a brother or sister. Maybe if her father had had a son he wouldn't have drowned himself in drink; maybe her mother would still be alive.

'My name is Yllandris,' she replied. 'I...' She choked on the words she was about to say.

'What's wrong? Are you crying?' The young girl tried to get to her feet but was too weak. Yllandris saw then just how emaciated she was; another victim of the wasting sickness: the disease that had taken so many of Yllandris's friends when she was a girl. Judging from the smell and the visible condition of the children huddled around the mill, at least half would not live much longer than a year. The other children must have sensed *the danger and found somewhere else to stay before they too got sick.*

'I'm fine,' Yllandris said. She bit her lip so hard she tasted blood. 'I'm a sorceress. Sorceresses don't cry.'

The girl's brother spoke. 'You're a sorceress? Prove it!'

Another boy coughed nearby, a hacking sound that told of some illness in his lungs.

Yllandris held out a trembling hand, palm facing up. She drew upon her power, evoked a small flame that danced back and forth across her fingertips before it fizzled out. In another time and place, the gasps from the watching children might have made her smile.

'Show me some more! I want to see more magic!' cried one of the foundlings. Another clapped happily.

'Not right now. There... there's a magic show about to start outside the Great Lodge,' Yllandris lied, hating herself. 'But there's only room for three more children.'

'I wanna go! Me! Me!' A chorus of voices piped up, broken by a few racking coughs. Yllandris wanted to scream, to tell the children that it was a lie, to order them to flee town and not look back. But that too would be a death sentence – they would freeze out in the wilds.

She stared around the room with desolate eyes. The young girl's condition was the most hopeless, followed by the boy with the cough. Who else? Did it even matter?

'Let me take my sister,' the boy said. He met Yllandris's teary gaze, and she could read what he was thinking in the sadness behind his eyes: She's going to die. I know she is. Let her see the magic show before she's taken from me. Give her that much. Please.

Yllandris tried not to sob.

In the end, she selected the young girl and her brother, and the boy with the cough. They accompanied her to the Great Lodge, Yllandris carrying the girl in her arms. She was shockingly light.

There she put on a magic show for them all. Though the two sorceresses didn't really get along, Rana volunteered to help Yllandris. Together they produced a spectacle that had the three children laughing with glee.

Towards the end of the show, Yllandris cast a spell to put the orphans into a deep magical slumber – one from which they would never awaken. Shortly after, the Herald arrived and whisked them away. That was the last time they were ever seen alive.

Later, Yllandris learned that the girl's name had been Jinna. Her brother's name was Roddy, and the boy with the cough had been called Zak.

She said a prayer for them every night. And whenever she slept, their faces haunted her nightmares until she awoke, screaming.

Her eyes shot open. She screamed.

Or at least she tried to scream; her throat was so raw from crying and thirst that she made only a choking sound. As always when she woke, she reached up and brushed her fingers against the wound on her face. It was sticky and wet and felt warm to the touch. It throbbed constantly, a dull ache that occasionally intensified into a stabbing pain. When that happened, she would huddle helplessly against the side of the wicker cage and sob until the agony eased. The wound resisted her efforts to magically heal it; it had been inflicted with demonsteel, and though the Shaman had been able to knit the wounds Krazka had inflicted on him back together, she was no Magelord. She would carry that terrible scar for the rest of her life.

Please let it end. I want to die. Please let me die.

She shifted slightly, attempting to stretch her legs in the little space the cage allowed. The movement caused the effluence that had collected in the prison to squelch beneath her. The soft bed of shit and other waste kept her warm during the coldest parts of the night. Kept her alive, though she prayed for an end to her misery.

Perhaps when winter came the cold might finally claim her. But it was only the start of autumn. The promise of a quick death was still months away, if indeed the Butcher King would even allow such a thing. He might decide to have her moved from this open cesspit and placed elsewhere.

The thought of spending the rest of her life in a cage made Yllandris want to tear out her hair and scratch out her eyes. Two weeks in this nightmarish prison, and already she was going mad.

She heard Magnar shift in the cage opposite. He had been imprisoned for two months. Somehow he seemed to have retained his sanity, though of late they rarely talked. There was little to say to each other.

Magnar spoke then, his voice a rasp. 'Yllandris.'

'Yes?' she answered, her own voice weak and despairing.

'I never told you that I'm sorry.'

Yllandris turned to face him. She could see the wounds Krazka had inflicted on his naked torso; the jagged scars where his nipples had been sliced off; the stumps of fingers that had been cut from his hands. Magnar's muscles were beginning to waste away and his handsome face had grown gaunt. The remarkable grey eyes she had found so enchanting had lost much of their lustre.

Like her, Magnar was covered in waste. The shit and piss that occasionally rained down to cover them had horrified her at first, but now she had become numb to it. Unlike the terrible wound on her face, dirt was nothing water couldn't wash away.

'You're sorry?' she repeated, suddenly confused.

He nodded. His dark hair had been recently chopped off, leaving stubble that barely covered the bumpy, scabbed mess Krazka had made of his scalp. The Butcher King beat him terribly at least once a week.

'I grabbed your hair and hurt you. Just before the Herald attacked Heartstone. You'd angered me.'

Yllandris tried to recall that night. She and Magnar had been in bed together, resting after their lovemaking. She had unwisely brought up the day he watched his mother burn on the Shaman's pyre.

'I swore never to lay hands on a woman,' Magnar continued. 'I broke that promise.'

Yllandris remembered her own father's treatment of her mother. He had beaten her bloody more times than she could count. Before the final time, when he had gone too far and no broken apology or promise to change could ever bring her back.

'I forgive you,' she whispered.

Magnar was silent a while before next he spoke. 'You asked me how I could allow my own mother to be consumed by fire. The answer is that I couldn't. My mother's alive, Yllandris.'

Despite everything that had happened, Magnar's words still managed to shock her. 'How?' she gasped.

'The Shaman needed to make an example. My father had betrayed him. The chieftains already resented me for my youth, and because of my father's actions I had become the son of a traitor. The only way to appear strong was to appear ruthless. The Shaman wished to teach my father a lesson and to reinforce my own position with my chieftains. I had no choice but to agree. My aunt was guilty of inciting rebellion. No one deserves to perish in flames, but I had no choice.'

'I saw your mother burn.'

'The Shaman used magic to change my aunt's appearance to match that of my mother. It was my aunt who burned.'

'Why are you telling me this?'

'You must have wondered what kind of monster could sacrifice his own mother. I wanted you to know that I am not that monster. I never wished to be king. I thought I could perhaps use my influence to do some good, to show my father that I was worthy of his name. I just wanted make him proud. Can you understand that?'

Yllandris stared at the man in the cage opposite her. The pain in his eyes threatened to choke her, and she knew then that she truly loved him. Before she had merely loved the King. Now, she realized, she loved Magnar Kayne.

'Yes,' she replied, her voice threatening to break. 'I understand.'

'I'll make you proud,' Yllandris said. She hugged her mother close: close enough to hear her heart beating.

'You already have, child,' her mother replied, running trembling fingers through her hair.

Would her mother be proud of her now?

There was movement above, at the edge of the cesspit. For a moment she feared another bucket of sewage was about to be emptied over them, but a rickety rope ladder was lowered and then Yorn climbed down into the pit. The Kingsman had a pack thrown over his broad shoulders. Their provisions. They were fed every other day, just enough to keep them alive.

'Here,' the big warrior grunted, reaching into the bag and pulling out a loaf of old bread and a fresh skin of water.

Yllandris stared at Yorn. His bearded face was troubled; his dark eyes looked as though they were wrestling with some impossible decision. He was a decent man, she knew. This couldn't have been easy for him. 'The King wants me to fetch some foundlings,' he blurted out, much to her shock. He was the taciturn sort. It was unlike him to show such emotion. 'The Herald spoke words in his head. It needs another sacrifice before it can summon more demons from the Spine.'

At Yorn's words, Yllandris went cold. In her mind's eye the faces of Jinna and Roddy and Zak stared at her accusingly. 'No...' she whispered. 'You can't...'

Yorn's teeth were grinding together. 'The hell did I end up doing this sort of shit?' he roared suddenly. 'I just wanted to be a Kingsman! Like my uncle!'

'Don't do it, Yorn. Please,' Yllandris begged.

'I ain't got no choice. If I don't, someone else will. The iron man, or Wulgreth, or that bastard Ryder.'

'Yorn... there's always a choice.' It was Magnar.

The Kingsman turned to stare at the deposed king. 'Those were your father's words. He told you what happened at Red Valley?'

'Yes. He told me. He told me that you were true, Yorn. I made you captain of the guard because of your actions that day. Because my father respected you.'

The big warrior frowned and stared off into the distance. Remembering events long ago, no doubt. Yllandris knew only a little of what had happened at Red Valley. Her own father had come back from that place a changed man.

Yorn seemed to make a decision then. He unsheathed his broadsword. 'Screw this,' he muttered. 'This ain't right. None of this is right. I'm getting you out of there.' He began hacking at Yllandris's cage.

'Someone will hear you!' Yllandris whispered.

'The King's locked in council with the chieftains,' Yorn grunted, his breath coming in hard gasps. 'Reckon we've got a few hours to get you out of here.'

'Get me out?'

'The west gate. I should be able to convince the guards to let you pass. Shit, almost got it...'

With a mighty swing of his broadsword, Yorn finally broke through the cage. He sheathed his blade and then grabbed hold of the slashed bars, pulling on them with all his impressive strength. They began to creak and then split. With a final, enormous grunt, he tore away a large section of the prison. It came free in his hands with a loud *crack*. Yorn tossed aside the broken wicker, then reached down a scraped and bleeding hand and helped Yllandris to her feet.

'Now you,' Yorn puffed, turning to Magnar's cage.

'I'm staying.'

Yllandris wobbled and almost fell. After a fortnight caged in that awful prison, her legs felt like they belonged to someone else. 'But we can free you—'

'No. Every second you waste here puts you in danger.'

'Magnar—'

'I'm weak, Yllandris. I wouldn't make it far. And when Krazka discovers I'm gone, he will send half the town out searching for me. Go now. Save yourself.'

She met his eyes, those beautiful pools of iron grey she had spent many a moment gazing into as they lay together on his bed in the Great Lodge. They'd talked of having children once. She remembered that night, every last detail.

'I won't leave the foundlings behind,' she said suddenly.

Yorn grunted and shook his head. 'They'll only slow us down. We can make it to the Greenwild if we hurry. The Lowlands are beyond the forest. Even Krazka won't follow us there.'

'I won't let that bastard hurt a single one of those children,' she said, an edge of steel in her voice she had never known she possessed. 'We leave with the orphans. Or I'll kill as many of Krazka's men as I can before they cut me down.'

'Go with her, Yorn,' Magnar whispered. 'You're a Kingsman. As your rightful king, I command you to see them to safety. Please.'

Yorn hesitated. Finally, he nodded.

Yllandris met Magnar's eyes one last time. 'I love you,' she said. And for the first time in her life, she meant it.

They climbed out of the cesspit, Yllandris's arms screaming with the effort of scrambling up the rope ladder. Then they hurried to the Foundry. The streets were almost empty – it was still early, and if anyone thought it odd to see a sorceress covered in shit trailing after a grim-faced Kingsman, they did not mention the fact.

Yllandris waited outside the great building, lurking in the shadows while Yorn went inside to fetch the children. The big warrior was herding them out of the door, the blond-haired Corinn at the front of the group, just as Braxus arrived.

Yllandris tensed, readying herself for whatever she must do to silence the old blacksmith. But he merely stared at her. His eyes widened slightly when he saw the wound on her face. He turned to Yorn.

'Gonna be a nice day, by the looks of it.'

'Aye,' replied Yorn.

'Good day to take the little 'uns for a walk, I reckon.'

'Aye.'

Braxus raised a meaty hand to his mouth and stifled a yawn. 'If anyone asks, they were gone when I arrived.'

'Thank you,' said Yllandris. The old blacksmith merely nodded. Then he glanced up at the rising sun and went inside the Foundry.

Yorn led the way towards the west gate. Yllandris pulled her soiled shawl up to hide her face as they neared the exit.

'How did you get that terrible wound?' whispered Corinn beside her. The fifty children they'd gathered at the Foundry trailed along behind. Most of them were still sleepy. A few looked excited at the prospect of going on an adventure, such as Milo – the boy who had roused her in the Foundry the day all hope had died.

'That doesn't matter now,' Yllandris replied. 'We need to get as far away from Heartstone as possible. You're the oldest child. I'm going to need your help. Can you do that? Can you help me?'

Corinn listened. When Yllandris had finished speaking she nodded, her expression focused and determined.

The guards on the gate recognized Yorn as he approached. While they eyed the children suspiciously, they knew better than to challenge a Kingsman. They opened the gates, closing them behind the group afterwards.

There was still a slight chill in the morning air as they passed the pit where the dead had been piled and left to rot. Yllandris waved at the others to continue while she descended to look for the bones of the foundlings that had been sacrificed to the Herald. She gathered them up and placed them carefully into a sack, which she slung over her shoulder. They would be her burden to bear and hers alone. The children watched curiously,

251

all except Corinn too young to make the connection between the bones in the pit and the recent disappearance of their three friends. Yllandris had told them they had gone to a better place. The lie still made her want to curl up and die.

As they turned south towards the Green Reaching, which lay so many miles distant, Yllandris glanced at Heartstone one final time. Like many sorceresses, she possessed a very faint gift for foresight.

Just then her gift was telling her she would never see Magnar or the capital again.

Changing Times

S IR MEREDITH'S BACK was killing him. The four men sitting at the King's table in the Grand Throne Chamber had been locked in discussions for hours.

And by 'locked in discussions', the knight thought sourly, what he really meant was the ignorant posturing of feral dogs barking at one another. The art of civil discourse was lost on his countrymen.

He didn't say as much, of course. He was paid to guard the King, not offer his insights into the uncouth politics of this damnable country.

Things had been so very different back in the Lowlands. After he had helped the Rag King win back his throne Sir Meredith had accompanied his liege lord on many a diplomatic mission throughout the Shattered Realms. The unpleasantness with the Duke certainly couldn't be blamed on Sir Meredith – and yet because of that series of unfortunate events he found himself back in the High Fangs, standing guard over a one-eyed loon while his armour chafed him raw and his lower back sent throbs of agony racing up his spine.

The words shot out before he could stop them. 'A pox upon the whoresons responsible for this debacle!'

'What was that, iron man? You say somethin'?' grunted the warrior beside him. Red Rayne's nose was half-ruined by the endless *jhaeld* he snorted. A terrible habit, Meredith reflected – the sign of a man lacking both self-control and confidence in his own prowess. He himself had never felt the desire to partake of the resin of the infamous fireplant. A knight such as Sir Meredith triumphed through superior swordsmanship and a cool head, not berserker savagery brought on by mind-altering substances.

He was relieved to see that none of the other men around the table had heard his latest outburst. 'I was merely clearing my throat,' he told his counterpart testily. It was difficult to keep his feelings locked inside sometimes. Hard to stomach the injustices he had suffered without giving voice to his frustrations.

He gazed around the chamber one more time. His eyes narrowed as they swept over the rustic accoutrements that decorated the hall. Stuffed heads of primitive beasts, ancient swords and shields, helms of decorated heroes... all the trappings of a people stuck in a benighted existence. He doubted his kinsmen would know real culture if they were given a guided tour of the Royal Museum of Carhein by the Grand Curator himself. It galled Sir Meredith. In fact, it infuriated him.

'Bloody barbarians!' he blurted out.

The King's eye swivelled to regard him. 'Something the matter?' he grated. The right side of his face was a sight to behold, a mass of terrible bruises and disfigured flesh. Even the efforts of his sorceresses hadn't been able to fix the damage.

'No,' Meredith replied. Though he made an effort not to let the scorn show in his voice, he refused to add the honorific Shranree and the others used when addressing this barbarian king. Oh, Krazka paid well for his services, in gold as well as in other things promised to him, and Sir Meredith had to concede that the usurper knew how to use a sword. But when it came to the heart of the matter, he was just another bloody barbarian.

Even if he *had* cut down that fool Vard with such astonishing speed. Even if he *had* demonstrated impeccable swordsmanship against the Shaman: swordsmanship to rival that of a knight.

'Where's Yorn?' Krazka barked, interrupting those troubling thoughts.

Where *was* that big, stinking bastard? Meredith looked questioningly at Rayne, who merely shrugged and wiped his nose with the back of his hand. On the opposite side of the king, Bagha and Ryder stared at each other dumbly.

Krazka spread his hands in a gesture of wounded incredulity. 'See, this is what's wrong with the world. You give a man something he's always dreamed of, a position of honour that any Highlander worth his salt would die for, and he decides to knock off when it suits him. I'm starting to regret murdering his predecessor.'

'He went to feed the prisoners,' Wulgreth said from over where he stood guarding the entrance to the chamber. 'He should have been back hours ago.'

'What prisoners?' growled Orgrim Foehammer.

The largest of the four men seated around the table – though still some way smaller than Bagha looming nearby – Orgrim Foehammer was the only man present whose name Sir Meredith had already been familiar with before his return to the High Fangs. For many years the High Commander of Watcher's Keep, Orgrim had grown fat since assuming the mantle of chieftain. Still, he cut an impressive figure. For an old man.

'You'll see soon enough, Foehammer,' the King replied. He slid gracefully from his throne at the head of the table. 'It's time to choose,' he said, walking slowly around the circumference of the table. 'You're either with me or you're against me. I ain't one for half-measures.'

Sir Meredith shifted slightly. About bloody time, he thought. He could hardly wait to remove his damned armour.

'I'll send word of my decision when I've discussed it with my sons,' growled Hrothgar. The chieftain of the Blue Reaching stroked his grey-blond beard and scowled. He had travelled far to be at this gathering – all the way from the desolate tundra on the edge of the frozen sea.

'And you?' Krazka asked Narm Blacktooth. The Deep Reaching was key to the King's plans, Meredith knew. If Krazka could win Narm's support, he would have a powerful ally positioned directly between the King's Reaching and the now-hostile Black Reaching.

The Blacktooth spat out a mouthful of the foul substance he was fond of chewing, the root of some plant native to his Reaching that left his teeth as black as tar. The vile stuff hit the table and splattered over the wooden surface. Sir Meredith bristled with anger. Any man who had dared showed such disrespect at the Rag King's court would have lost his teeth and most probably his life. Meredith would have seen to it himself.

'If this war drags on much longer my people will starve come the winter. You don't leave me much choice.'

Krazka nodded, and for a moment he seemed lost in whatever glorious future he was seeing in his mind's eye. 'When we march on the Lowlands, Blacktooth, you won't ever need worry about bellies going empty again. There'll be food enough for every Highlander.'

Narm got to his feet. 'Who said I'm marching anywhere? Naw, I'm thinking the Shaman will retake Heartstone. No man crosses a godkiller. Not even you, Butcher King. May as well throw my sword in with him and Carn Bloodfist and help speed things along.'

The King's face darkened. 'Maybe you ain't heard, but the Shaman's dying.'

'So you say. Don't reckon it's that easy to kill an immortal. I heard what happened to Mehmon and his town when they thought they could defy the Shaman's will. Can't say I fancy burning on a pyre when this all goes tits-up.'

Krazka's lone eye bored into the chieftain of the Deep Reaching with an intensity that seemed almost otherworldly. 'You're making a mistake, Blacktooth.'

Narm turned his back on the King and walked away.

'Where d'you think you're going?' Krazka's voice was a deadly whisper.

Narm Blacktooth paused halfway to the door. 'The Code forbids a man to attack a guest in his own home. Even kings don't break that rule.'

'That so?' said the Butcher King. 'Well, the times are changin'. Wulgreth, stop that weasel-faced cunt!'

At that, all hell broke loose.

Hrothgar surged to his feet, roaring in protest. Sir Meredith and Red Rayne moved to restrain him while Wulgreth closed on Narm Blacktooth, levelling his deadly spear at the chieftain.

'You treacherous fuck!' Narm snarled. 'I brought a hundred men and three sorceresses with me from the capital. When I don't return to camp this night, they'll send word to Underfort. You kill me and the armies of the Deep Reaching will boil out of the valleys seeking bloody vengeance!'

'Nobody's gonna send word,' Krazka said. He glanced behind him. 'Shranree, tell your sisters to begin razing Blacktooth's camp to the ground. I want every man and woman reduced to ashes. No survivors. No one left alive to tell a tale.'

The air shimmered behind the King and suddenly Shranree melted out of the air. Her face was coated with sweat from the effort of maintaining her cloak of invisibility. 'They're already in position, my king.'

Sir Meredith met the sorceress's eyes, and a moment later he felt himself go hard beneath his armour. The woman was larger than his tastes usually veered towards, but she was a competent conversationalist and her preferences in the bedroom had come as an unexpected surprise. It was because of her appetites that he had put his back out the night just past.

'They'll find out eventually!' Narm was screaming now. 'You won't be able to keep your crimes a secret forever!'

'Who said anything about forever?' Krazka replied evenly. 'I just need to keep 'em quiet until the Herald's opened the hidden ways beneath the Spine. Shouldn't be long now, not once I've sent a bunch of innocent souls his way.' He nodded at Wulgreth, and the Northman drove his spear through Narm Blacktooth's stomach, giving it a vicious twist. The chieftain of the Deep Reaching sank to his knees, black drool dribbling down his chin.

'Foehammer!' cried Hrothgar. 'We can't let this stand! This is a violation of the Code!'

Orgrim Foehammer couldn't meet his counterpart's gaze. 'The Code's a thing for a different age,' he said quietly.

Krazka stalked over to Hrothgar. 'Orgrim's a man who knows how to move with the times. Why drown fighting against the tide when you can ride with it?'

'You've thrown in with this... this lunatic?' Hrothgar's face was disbelieving.

The Foehammer's shoulders slumped. 'The demons grew too many. I couldn't sit by as Watcher's Keep fell. I couldn't see my people overrun, be torn apart and defiled in ways you couldn't imagine.' Orgrim's voice was heavy with despair. 'I had no choice, Hrothgar. Do you understand me? Imagine if it was your sons staring into the face of a demon horde.'

'Speaking of sons,' Krazka cut in smoothly. 'How'd they find the trip here, Hrothgar? I hope they're enjoying the sights of Turthing.'

Hrothgar flinched as if struck. 'How'd you know I left them up in Turthing?'

'I'm paying someone in your entourage. Loyalty ain't what it used to be.'

'If you've harmed them... you... you fucking—'

'They ain't been harmed. Yet. But here's the situation as I see it. You're gonna head back to the Blue Reaching and start marshalling your forces. For every five hundred warriors you send, I'll let one of your boys go. If a month passes without any reinforcements arriving... Well, I'll still send a son back, 'cept this time he'll be in a box. And more than likely in pieces. Depends on the size of the box, I guess.'

Hrothgar looked as though he had aged ten years in a single minute. 'The Code... my honour...'

'Aye, you're old school. Just like Orgrim here, until he saw sense. Like I said, the times are changing. And just to prove I'm serious, I got something to show you.'

Sir Meredith's nose wrinkled with distaste as he held the torch out over the cesspit. If his peers at the royal palace could see him now, why, they would soil their own robes laughing. Once he had been the Sword Lord, a champion of the Circle and First Knight of the King. Now he was aide-de-camp to a mad barbarian who was currently scrabbling around in a literal shithole. How the mighty had fallen.

'May this accursed country and everyone in it *drown* in shit!' he swore, unable to stop himself.

'Reckon you could hold that torch still and shut the fuck up?' the King shouted up at him from the pit.

Sir Meredith stiffened. If any other man had dared address him in that tone, he would have challenged them to a duel instantly. He had killed men for less back in Tarbonne. Yet somehow he managed to keep silent. An admirable feat of self-control, he told himself. He wasn't *afraid* of the one-eyed barbarian King. Fear had absolutely nothing to do with it.

'She's gone!' roared Krazka. 'That bitch is gone! Get down here! All of you.'

The Kingsmen climbed down into the pit. Sir Meredith came last, cursing and blustering with every step, his armour feeling as though it weighed as much as a horse. He reached the bottom and felt his boots squelch on something unpleasant. He winced, and then he brought his torch up and looked around.

A moment later he saw the broken cage. Shattered pieces of wicker floated in pools of stinking piss and muddy faeces. It would have taken a strong man indeed to have hacked apart the prison and freed its occupant. Sir Meredith met Krazka's gaze, and even the human effluence surrounding them was a pleasant sight compared with the fury burning in that lone orb.

'*Yorn*,' rasped the King.

He stomped through Heartstone, his armour clanking angrily with every step. A flash of magic lit the night sky to the west; the King's circle were still laying waste to the Blacktooth's camp. Shranree's passions would run hot tonight, but Sir Meredith cared not for that. The acrid stench of burning flesh overpowered even the stink of the shit that clung to his boots, but he paid it no mind.

Behind him, Rayne and Ryder hurried to keep up. 'Why're you so pissed off, iron man?' Rayne asked. 'A sorceress and a bunch of kids fleeing town is nothing to get so worked up about.'

'None of your bloody business!' Sir Meredith snapped. The guards on the western gate had told them what had happened. He probably hadn't needed to kill them afterwards, but their negligence in allowing Heartstone's foundlings to flee uncontested was simply intolerable, and Sir Meredith was in no mood to be lenient.

They reached the Foundry. Judging by the red glow emanating from within, it appeared at least one of the furnaces still burned. Sir Meredith kicked open the door and stormed in.

It was deserted save for the old greybeard Braxus. The burly blacksmith had his back to them and didn't turn as their booted feet echoed through the chamber. Instead he leaned over the anvil beside the furnace and continued to hammer away at whatever he was working on. The molten metal in the open forge cast an eerie orange glow over the scene.

'Braxus.' Meredith halted ten feet behind the blacksmith, who for a moment did not respond. Finally he seemed to nod, and then he very carefully placed his hammer down on the anvil before turning.

'I guessed I'd be seeing you here.'

'You know why we've come?'

'I reckon so.'

Sir Meredith drew his sabre. 'Then you also know what's about to happen. Why did you do it, old man? Why let them go?'

Braxus's brow furrowed as if he didn't understand the question.

'Was it the sorceress? Did she cast some kind of spell on you? It won't change your fate, but it might at least excuse your actions. Your betrayal. It might save your *honour.*'

'Honour?' Braxus laughed, a deep, booming sound that reverberated through the chamber. 'They call you the iron man. I know a thing or two about iron myself. Worked it for forty years. The thing to remember about iron is that no matter how long you spend beating it, shaping into something worthy, if the ore ain't any good it'll always break. You can't disguise bad iron, no matter how hard you try. Same thing applies to a man's character. You might act like some kind of knight or lord or whatever they call them in the Lowlands, wearing your shiny armour as if you're better than everyone else. But inside you're rotten.'

Sir Meredith's eyes narrowed. 'Tell me where Yorn and the sorceress are taking the foundlings.'

Braxus shrugged his heavy shoulders. 'Damned if I know. But if I did, I don't reckon I'd be telling you.'

The Sword Lord took a couple of steps towards the blacksmith. 'When we catch up with them I shall execute the traitor Yorn myself. No doubt my colleagues here will take advantage of the situation to rape the sorceress. One can hardly hold that against them – it is after all part of their base nature. Now, what happens to the children is still for me to decide. With every obstinate word that tumbles out of your mouth, I fear my heart grows harder.'

'They're kids, you crazy bastard. They're innocent.'

'There is no innocence. Not in this world.'

The old blacksmith stared at Sir Meredith, meeting his gaze, as if searching for something. 'You're not rotten,' he said at last, as if some truth had just been confirmed. 'You're broken.'

You're broken.

The words opened the black pit inside him and all the ugliness of his soul surged out, screaming.

He brought his sabre flashing around just as Braxus reached for the hammer resting on the anvil. The blacksmith was still a strong man, but he had slowed in old age, if indeed he had ever been fast. Sir Meredith cut his arm off at the elbow before the hammer was even halfway raised. Braxus stared dumbly as the severed limb flopped to the ground, the hammer tumbling from his fingers to strike the floor with a bang. Meredith sheathed his sabre, then grabbed Braxus around his thick neck. He spun the blacksmith around and forced his head down, down into the molten iron.

Red Rayne looked away, and even Ryder's face paled a little. Braxus himself didn't make a sound. He only shuddered, and a moment later his body went limp.

Sir Meredith hardly noticed. He was remembering hands running down his trousers. Pulling them off while he panicked, not knowing what was happening. Not knowing until he was much older, and by then it had been much too late.

He had tried to flee the memories. He had left the High Fangs and journeyed south, thinking he could be reborn in a distant land where no one knew his face or the things that had been done to him. For a time it had worked. He became someone else.

But eventually the inescapable truth caught up with him. It was there in the mocking smiles of the courtiers. It was there in the faces of the women he knew fucked him out of pity. It was there in the dark desires that had arisen within him of late, desires that had ultimately played some part in the duke declaring war over the ugly matter of his grandson. Meredith bitterly regretted not disposing of the boy's body.

He dragged Braxus's corpse away from the furnace. The blacksmith's head had melted away from his shoulders, leaving only part of his jaw. The knight let the body flop to the ground and turned to the other Kingsmen.

'Krazka needs those orphans returned to Heartstone. He's promised them to the Herald. We'll chase them to the ends of the earth if we must.'

To fail in his quest wasn't an option. After all, he too wanted what had been promised to him.

Twenty-four Years Ago

BRODAR KAYNE DREW his cloak tighter and bent his head into the breeze. It sent his hair dancing around his shoulders as he leaned forward on his mare and listened to the howling of the wind through the nearby hills and the sound of the horse's hooves striking the road that led back to Watcher's Keep. There'd been a bitter chill in the air the last few days. Winter was coming again.

Had it been almost a year already? He was going to miss the first anniversary of his joining, he realized unhappily. He wanted to turn around, to tug on the reins and gallop straight back to Mhaira and his newborn son. Duty called him back to the Keep before he'd barely got to know his beautiful little boy.

He saw Magnar's face in his mind's eye again. The babe had Mhaira's eyes, sure enough, but he reckoned his son had been lumbered with his father's nose. The more he takes after his mother the better, he thought wryly.

He tried to stay positive. Only three more years in the Borderland and he'd be free to return to Mhaira, this time for good. He would be a proper husband and father. Use his pension to build a house somewhere on the outskirts of Eastmeet. He wasn't much of a carpenter, but he reckoned there was no small number of men who'd volunteer to lend a hand.

Kayne's reputation had spread far beyond Watcher's Keep. Ever since he'd slain the two blink demons a couple of years back, more youngsters than ever were turning up at the great citadel, hoping to imitate the Warden with the bright blue eyes and the sword that never faltered. Over the last seven years Brodar Kayne had killed more demonkin that he could count, dire wolves and trolls by the dozen. Even a giant that had wandered down from the Spine the autumn just past.

There was a certain satisfaction in his skills being acknowledged, he had to admit. Before stepping down to be replaced by the Foehammer, Kalgar had told Kayne that though he might be wild and reckless, he trained harder than any other Warden. It was that relentless anger which had driven Kayne to be the best. He reckoned he'd mastered that fury now he was a father, or at least he hoped he had.

He was still thinking of Magnar, of the moment he'd first cradled his son in his arms, when his horse screamed and bucked wildly beneath him. He caught a glimpse of a feathered shaft sticking out of the animal's flank a moment before he was thrown to the ground with bone-jarring force. The mare bolted, leaving him flat on his arse and staring up at the late-afternoon sky.

Another arrow struck the mud a hand's breadth from his head. He rolled and leaped to his feet, ignoring the explosion of pain in his back. Pain was just the body's way of telling a man he needed to focus. Now that his burning anger had dulled, Kayne found ice-cold clarity easy to come by. So easy that Taran and the others had started to question if he had ice in his veins.

With fire and ice the strongest swords are forged. Braxus had told him that once. He sometimes wondered if his friend had missed his true calling as a bard. He had a way with words, did Brax, when he chose to use them.

Kayne drew his longsword, feeling naked without his shield. It was strapped to the back of his mount and the horse was probably halfway to Watcher's Keep by now. He looked around without seeing his attackers, though a quick glance at the arrow sticking out of the ground suggested they were hiding in the hills some ways over to his left. Sure enough, a voice suddenly called out from that direction.

'Been a while, angel eyes.'

He'd been wondering why outlaws would attack a Warden, and a well-known one at that. Not any more. Like a dormant volcano stirring to life, the old rage began to burn. 'Skarn.'

'I knew you'd remember me! What did I tell you, Ryder? I told you he'd remember me!'

'Should I shoot him?'

'In a moment. So, angel eyes. We heard the stories while we was down in Glistig a few months back. Hard to believe it was the same coward who bailed on us all those years ago, but the description seemed to match. They say you're a hero now.'

Kayne tried to keep his voice calm, though his blood was like molten metal in his veins. 'Come out where I can see you.'

'I don't think so. How are you enjoying fatherhood? Heard you got a wife and son over in the village near here. Thought the boys and me might go pay them a visit after we're done with you.'

His heart seemed to freeze in his chest. 'You go near them, you're a dead man. You and everyone with you.'

'That's the spirit! Could have done with that attitude back when we was cutting a bloody swathe through the Green Reaching. Instead you fled with that limp-dick Red Nose or whatever the fuck his name was. Lost half the band soon after. Men are like horses – once one breaks, they all start running off.'

'What do you want?' Kayne asked, mouth so dry his voice was little more than a rasp. He glanced around, searching for anything he could use to his advantage, praying that the archer wouldn't take that as a sign to start shooting at him again. Out of the corner of his eye he saw a building.

'What do I want? I want you *dead*, angel eyes. And after that, I want your wife dead. Your babe, too.'

The world seemed to go red. He wanted to scream his outrage, to charge at Skarn and tear the murdering bastard's face off with his bare teeth. But he knew that meant certain death. No, he had to be ice. Not fire, but ice.

'You'll have to catch me first!' he roared. He turned and made a break for the building.

The spirits must have been looking out for him just then, as two more arrows missed him, one practically shaving the side of his neck. He reached the door of the house and flung himself inside. Three pairs of eyes stared at him, a father and a mother and their daughter. They were sitting at a table having their evening meal.

'What the hell—' the man started to say, but Kayne cut him short.

'I ain't got time to explain,' he said quickly, slamming the door shut behind him. 'I got a notorious band of outlaws hot on my heels. Help me barricade the door and shutters.'

After a moment's hesitation the family rushed to assist him. They turned the table over and shoved it against the door, then locked the shutters and began piling the barrels that were stacked near the hallway against them. 'Is there another exit?' Kayne demanded.

The father, a mead-maker judging by the barrels, gave a nervous nod of his bald head. 'There's a trapdoor in the back that leads to a cellar. A ladder exits to a orchard just behind the house.'

There was a bang on the door. 'I know he's in there,' Skarn shouted from outside. 'Open up or you'll soon learn why they call me the Scourge.'

'Keep 'em distracted,' Kayne barked. He darted out of the room and down the short hallway until he found the trapdoor. He grabbed hold of the iron ring and heaved it open, then leaped down into the cellar. Dozens of barrels lined the walls. Kayne sprinted past them towards the ladder at the far end. He scaled it, thrust open the wooden hatch above and dragged himself out. Big straw beehives filled the orchard. Kayne could hear a faint buzzing from within, but at that moment his attention was focused on the five men crowded around the door of the house. They'd yet to notice him.

He crept around the outside of the orchard, moving from tree to tree just as he had during his Initiation test all those years ago. One of the outlaws had a torch and was trying to set fire to the building.

Kayne watched the men for a moment, calculating the odds. He picked up a nearby rock and tossed it over the heads of the gang. He didn't hear it clatter back to earth, but it must have alerted the men as Skarn and a young, thin-faced fellow with a bow moved away to investigate. That left three men, one of whom was preoccupied with burning the house down. It had already caught fire; thick smoke curled away from the front of the house, reducing the visibility. Improving the odds just that little bit more.

Kayne seized his chance.

He reached the men an instant before they noticed him. He thrust his sword through the chest of one, then yanked it free and opened another from neck to waist. The third rushed him, rusty short sword levelled at his face. Kayne dodged to avoid the clumsy thrust and chopped down, taking his attacker's hand off. He was about to finish the shrieking outlaw when an arrow zipped past his cheek. Kayne grabbed hold of the wounded brigand and spun him around.

'Fire at me again and this one gets it,' he yelled, using the man as a shield. Without a moment's hesitation, the narrow-faced archer nocked another arrow and fired. Kayne's hostage screamed as the arrow hit him right in the stomach.

'Sod this,' Kayne muttered.

He charged forward, using the brigand as a battering ram now. Another arrow thudded into his meat shield, and then Kayne was upon the archer. He thrust the dying man aside as the outlaw fumbled for his sword. Kayne slashed down with his own blade, but just then something hit him in the side. His long-sword went wide, taking off half the archer's ear rather than cleaving his skull as he'd intended.

He became aware of a sudden, sharp pain and glanced down

to see a bloody dagger emerging from his leather hauberk. The steel had gone in deep. Kayne, forcing himself to remain calm, looked up into the deceptively bland face of Skarn.

'Didn't see me lurking in the shadows, angel eyes?' the outlaw leader hissed. 'Seems you forgot how to fight dirty.'

Skarn's long-bladed scalpel, that terrible weapon with which he'd done such wicked things all those years ago, glinted red in the light of the flames above them. There wasn't room for Kayne to bring his sword to bear, no room to do much of anything except move his head. So he butted Skarn in the face.

The outlaw was stunned only for a second, but Kayne was on him faster than that. He drove his sword through the man's stomach and gave it a vicious twist, gutting the bastard just as Skarn had gutted that poor woman the night Kayne and Red Ear split from the gang.

Kayne released the hilt of his sword and kicked the squealing outlaw to the ground. Then he threw himself on the man, punching him in the face again and again. He felt bone crack beneath his knuckles, felt his own hands crack. He didn't care.

'You threaten my family? You threaten my son? My little boy? Die, you fucker! Die!' Kayne snarled and raved, oblivious to everyone and everything except the loathsome face beneath his bloodied fists. He didn't stop, not even after Skarn the Scourge had passed from the world. It was the intense heat that eventually caused him to pause and look up.

The whole house was ablaze, flames eating the timber like a hungry wolf devouring a deer. Kayne suddenly remembered there was a family inside.

Shit.

The entire front half of the building was a raging inferno. Even if the door hadn't been blocked from the inside, the fire made it completely impassable. Unmindful of his injured hands and the blood running freely from the wound in his side, Kayne raced back to the orchard. He slid down the ladder into the cellar, coughing and spluttering as smoke filled his lungs. He ran on regardless, clambering out of the trapdoor and staring around wildly for any sign of the family.

The main room was a raging firestorm, too hot to approach. Burning timber had fallen from the ceiling and blocked the exit from the room, which was thick with black smoke. The girl was trapped under the pile of smouldering timber and lay unmoving. Kayne saw the other bodies then and knew that they were all dead, the parents fallen victim to the noxious smoke while they were trying in vain to free their daughter from the wreckage.

He collapsed to his knees, hot tears rolling down his soot-stained face. The superheated air burned his lungs but he didn't care. An entire family had died because of him. They might have fled down into the cellar. Instead they'd stayed and tried to distract Skarn like he'd ordered them to, and now they were all dead. Because of him.

Unexpectedly he heard a muffled cry for help. He wiped his eyes and looked up; he saw another door further down the hallway, one he hadn't noticed before. The door was slowly being consumed by fast-moving fire. The cry sounded again, fainter this time.

There was someone trapped in the room beyond the door.

'Hold on,' Kayne tried to shout, but it came out as a tortured rasp. He tried to charge at the door, but the heat drove him back. In desperation he picked up a nearby barrel and hurled it with all his strength. The barrel struck the door, and it exploded in a shower of shattered wood and sizzling mead.

A moment later the room's occupant crawled through the empty doorway.

The youngster was terribly burned, his face a red and blistered mess and his ruined clothes smouldering gently on his body. Kayne grit his teeth and inched towards the boy, closing his mind to the terrible pain. He grabbed hold of the lad, lifted him across his broad shoulders.

'Hold still,' he gasped, choking on smoke and tasting blood in his mouth. 'We'll get you out of here.'

He carried the youngster down the cellar and up through the orchard and away from the burning house. He would never understand how he managed it. Not with a handful of busted knuckles and a dagger wound in his side. He was certain they would die on the road to Watcher's Keep.

But somehow neither of them had died. It would become a habit in later years.

The Seer

'O N YOUR FEET, greybeard.'

Kayne gasped as the rope was pulled tighter around his throat, dragging him up from the ground. He clambered to his feet, his muscles protesting every inch of the way. He'd lost track of the days they'd spent trussed up and tied to horseback. Every scar and old ache he'd collected over the years seemed to hurt all at once.

His captor finally let the rope go slack and Kayne moved his head from side to side, trying to work the stiffness out of his neck. The others were also being pulled roughly to their feet. The Wolf's face was pale behind his burn scars and he clearly favoured his right leg. The arrowhead was still lodged in the left. If it wasn't treated soon chances were he would lose the limb.

All around them was a forest of tents. There must have been hundreds. The majority were tiny bivouacs made of leather or goat hair, but there were a handful of larger tents as well, stitched together from colourful fabrics stolen from the Free Cities of the Unclaimed Lands or plundered from travelling merchants.

Far to the west, rising above even the tallest tents and bathed in the light of the dying sun, Kayne could see the Purple Hills. The four of them had been brought east. Deep into the Badlands, into the very heart of Asander's domain.

As they moved through the great camp, men scowled up at them from crackling campfires before returning to sharpening their weapons. Women huddled in groups and pointed before turning back to their gossip. Children peered out over the tops of barrels or from behind tent flaps. Most of the faces staring back at Kayne were filthy and decidedly underfed. The Badlands held little enough game to support small bands of skilled hunters, never mind a sprawling tent town housing thousands.

Starvation didn't seem an immediate concern for the bastard clutching the end of the rope tied around Kayne's neck. Fivebellies was surprisingly fit for a man his size, setting a brisk pace that his saddle-stiff and injured captives struggled to match. Kayne tested the bonds around his wrists for the hundredth time, finding no joy. Fivebellies' men had seized their weapons, including the greatsword Braxus had forged for him all those years ago. Attempting an escape would be suicide.

As they were marched deeper into the camp, one of the bandits led away the horses they'd purchased back in Ashfall. They were sorry creatures compared with the animals their captors rode. Kayne saw a team of horses that would fetch a king's ransom in the Trine grazing a stretch of grassland between clusters of tents. He wondered briefly why the bandits hadn't given up raiding and simply established a trade agreement with the Free Cities. He reckoned it would've made life a hell of a lot easier for everyone.

Suddenly Jerek stumbled, his wounded leg buckling. Fivebellies glared and then turned to the bandit beside him. 'Hand me your whip,' he rumbled. He took the riding crop from his subordinate and began to lash the Wolf with it, driving the leather deep into Jerek's unprotected arms and neck, leaving deep red welts. 'You like that, scarface?' he taunted. 'Not so tough now, huh? Know what we do with horses that've gone lame? We slit their throats, then chop them up and boil the remains. No sense wasting good horseflesh. Maybe we'll do the same to you.'

'They ought to boil your corpse,' Jerek spat back. 'You'd feed the entire north for a year. Fat prick.'

Fivebellies' cheeks reddened. 'We'll see how clever you are when I cut out your tongue, scarface. After your meeting with the King I want you alone. Just you and me.'

'Go fuck yourself.'

That earned the Wolf a fresh beating. Kayne struggled against his bonds again, but his hands were secured tight behind him. Grunt's face was glum, utter despair in his yellow eyes. Brick was as pale as a ghost. The boy flinched every time the leather snapped against Jerek's exposed flesh.

'I ought to apologize,' Kayne murmured to Brick. 'I got us into this.'

Brick's mouth quivered. 'I'm the one who should be sorry,' he said in a voice filled with pain. 'My uncle betrayed us.'

'Not your fault, lad. Some point in our lives, we all hold faith with someone we shouldn't.' He remembered his encounter with Borun down in the Trine months past. He looked at the Wolf, whose muscular arms were a mass of scarlet welts. This was what his friends got for trusting in his leadership.

Fivebellies finally decided he'd beaten Jerek enough for one day. The corpulent bandit handed back his subordinate's horse-whip and patted his stomach. 'Whipping a man always makes me hungry,' he complained. 'Come on, move your arses, before I bloody starve to death.'

The captives stumbled forward. Somehow Jerek remained on his feet, though the way he was staggering and lurching a casual onlooker might've easily mistaken him for one of the strollers back at the swamp. Seeing the look in the Wolf's eyes, Kayne didn't fancy being in Fivebellies' shoes if the grim Highlander ever got free of his bonds.

Soon they were led to a giant pavilion that dwarfed the other tents. Most of Fivebellies' men broke away from the group at that point. The dozen that remained levelled their bows at the four prisoners, their expressions suggesting they would open fire if they so much as farted without permission. Fivebellies chose that moment to unleash a mighty belch. Then he gestured to the vast pavilion with a meaty hand. 'The King awaits us,' he declared. He gave Kayne's rope a tug and the old warrior was forced to scramble behind the bandit as he waddled through the entrance flap.

The torches affixed to poles around the circular structure gave off little light, and it took a moment for Kayne's eyes to adjust to the gloom. He wasn't greatly surprised to see the trove of plundered goods that filled nearly every inch of available space. Crates overflowing with fine fabrics were stacked alongside bookcases filled with ancient tomes worth their weight in gold coins. Expensive tapestries had been carelessly rolled up and tossed amongst the jumble of silverware. Plates and chalices, knives and forks and jewellery boxes stuffed with valuables were all piled haphazardly. Kayne didn't have much of a merchant's eye, but he reckoned there must be tens of thousands of spires' worth of treasure stuffed under the pavilion's dome.

On the far side of the pavilion, illuminated by the light of two braziers positioned either side of the high-backed wooden dining chair serving as his throne, towered Asander the Bandit King.

He was an extremely tall man – a good few inches taller even than Kayne, despite the fact his shoulders were stooped a little with age. He wore a deep blue doublet over his thin frame. No doubt it had once belonged to some rich merchant down in the Trine, but it didn't look out of place on the Bandit King. Kayne had been around powerful sorts much of his life and he recognized when someone had what folk might call a presence. This Asander had it in spades.

The Bandit King was staring down at a table, stroking his long grey moustache and examining what appeared to be a map. As Fivebellies led the captives forward, he looked up and fixed them with a stare that spoke of a mind as sharp as steel.

'Cousin,' Asander said in a clear voice belying his advancing years. 'Shara told me to expect your return.'

A shadow unfolded from the darkness behind the throne. As it drifted nearer, the light of the braziers revealed the soft curves of a woman wearing tight-fitting silks as dark as her features. Kayne had seen a similar face before; the resemblance was striking. Shara the Seer was every inch her brother's sister.

'I serve you as ever, my king,' she said in a voice like velvet. She drifted closer and placed a hand on Brick's brow. The dusky scent of her perfume made Kayne's nose tingle. 'My divinations informed me of the death of my twin. They also intimated that a prophecy I foretold years ago would shortly be fulfilled. This young man is the catalyst I spoke of. The boy who will bring blood and fire to the north.'

'He's but a child,' Asander said. 'Are you certain?'

'The future is never certain. The Pattern can be discerned by those with the talent for divination, but the view it affords is hazy, liable to be misread by the careless eye.'

Asander nodded and turned to Fivebellies. 'What of these others? Why have you brought them here?'

'This is Brodar Kayne and Jerek the Wolf, my king – the Highlanders that slaughtered half my band last year. This big green savage was with 'em too. He don't talk. Someone cut out his tongue.'

'Where did you find them?'

'Well now, there's a funny story. Glaston himself approached us. Offered us a deal. He led them right into our trap.'

'I trust you gave him a suitable reward.'

Fivebellies' broad face split into a nasty grin and he ran a thick thumb across his throat.

'You bastard!' Brick cried. 'That was my uncle!' He made to charge at Fivebellies, but the bandit who had hold of his leash gave it a vicious tug and he was jerked back, choking and spluttering, unable to breathe.

Asander stepped away from the table and raised a hand. Kayne saw that the King was missing his left foot and in its place was a wooden peg. 'Enough. Let the boy breathe.'

The bandit let the rope go slack and Brick gulped in air, his face near as red as his hair. Kayne forced himself to relax.

Another second and he'd have thrown himself at Brick's tormentor, consequences be damned.

Fivebellies must have noticed his intent. 'Those two are spirited bastards,' the fat bandit said, glowering at Kayne and Jerek. 'I'd kill 'em quickly if I were you, my king.'

'Your advice is duly noted, cousin.'

A heavy silence followed. 'What happened to your leg?' Kayne asked. Fivebellies growled at his impudence, but the King raised a hand to forestall his cousin's wrath. He didn't appear perturbed by the question. If anything, he looked faintly pleased.

'When I was a boy I fell from my horse, breaking every bone in my foot. My family left me behind to die. I would have perished were it not for Shara.' His eyes went to the Seer and lingered there, a look that Kayne well recognized. This self-proclaimed King was hopelessly smitten with his foreign adviser. 'She came to me, told me she had divined a glorious future for us. But if I wished to live to see it, I would first need to cut off my foot.'

'That which has no value must be sacrificed,' Shara said softly.

Asander nodded. 'With Shara's guidance I learned to read, and to influence men's hearts through words and ideas instead of brute strength. The disparate gangs of the Badlands began to rally to me. In time, all bent their knee.'

'My uncle never did,' Brick said, though he sounded weary. Too weary for a boy of his years.

Asander chuckled. 'Your uncle was among the first to swear allegiance. But he absconded when Shara read your destiny in the flames. Glaston thought himself clever, but he could never accept the lessons Shara taught me.'

'He was not ready to sacrifice,' echoed Shara.

'Nazala told me all about you and your sacrifices,' Kayne growled. 'Right piece of work, your brother. Can't imagine what it took for him to say enough was enough and walk away from you. Far as I can see, there ain't no crime worse than murdering your own family.'

Shara smiled. 'I would show you something.'

Kayne stared out across the shadowy lake. Every so often the dark liquid would bubble and pop, as if there were hidden energies at work beneath the surface.

'What am I supposed to be looking at?' he asked warily.

Shara turned to the bandit beside her. The man's bow had been fixed on Kayne from the moment they had left the pavilion. 'You see that floating object there?' She pointed to an unidentifiable mass twenty feet from shore. 'Go. Retrieve it for me.'

The bandit didn't seem best pleased by the order. 'What if I get stuck?'

'You won't. The tar is thicker nearer the centre of the lake. This close to the shore it is little more than water.'

'What about him? The King's orders—'

'Get in. *Now.*' For a second the Seer's eyes seemed to burn red, as though the gates of hell had been thrust wide open. The bandit paled slightly. Then he carefully laid down his bow and waded out into the lake.

'Place it on the ground,' Shara commanded, once the man returned with the dripping thing. The bandit did as he was told, but as he lowered it he seemed to realize what it was and leaped back with a startled yelp.

Kayne stared at the grotesque prize. It was a horse's head. Most of the flesh and muscle were missing and it was covered in the sticky black substance of the lake, but the shape was unmistakably equine. A few yellow teeth poked out of the mouth where the tar hadn't quite reached.

He turned back to the lake. Even in the fading light, he began to see that what he first thought were pieces of rock were in fact body parts, and not just horse – he fancied he saw the head of a woman bobbing along not six feet from where they were standing. 'The hell happened here?' he whispered.

'The lake you see before you is a new addition to the land, at least as far as these things are measured. Before it flooded, this site was once a neutral meeting ground for the Yahan tribes. Every two years the horselords would gather from all over the north to trade. They would number in the tens of thousands.'

A terrible understanding began to dawn in Kayne. 'Go on,' he said.

'Centuries ago my brother and I came to dwell among the Yahan people. Despite their savagery the horselords proved welcoming. Perhaps it was our skin that led them to trust us. We were not like the pale folk of the south, with whom they had skirmished for countless years. We learned much of their culture, even came to enjoy their way of life as we grew old among them. Eventually we became aware of time's relentless march. We began to realize the truth of our mortality.'

'Aye,' Kayne said quietly. 'I know how that feels.'

Shara reached into the lake of tar and to Kayne's horror plucked out the severed head as it bobbed past. The seer held it up and regarded it curiously. While the eyes had long ago rotted away, there was enough left of the face to tell that it had once belonged to a young woman.

'We recalled our master's instruction in the practice of blood magic. With a large enough sacrifice, even immortality could be bought. And so we waited for the tribes to gather here. Together with another of our master's students, Wolgred, we fractured the earth below the basin. Black death gushed forth to swallow the horselords. Those that tried to flee, we forced back. Men, women and children – all died, their remains preserved here in this lake. In the course of a few days the Yahan were rendered near extinct.'

Shara tossed the head back into the lake, where it landed with a splash and then sank slowly from sight. Kayne stared at the woman, wondering how such an agreeable face could conceal such evil.

Their escort must have been wondering the same thing. He pointed his bow at the Seer, an arrow nocked and ready to fire.

'You're a monster,' the man whispered. 'You murdered an entire people.'

Shara raised a hand and the bandit jerked suddenly as if struck. 'Yes,' she said smoothly. 'And I would do it again. In truth, I felt more regret over the loss of the horses. At least they might have served a purpose. The Yahan were an unremarkable people. Their disappearance was no great loss.' The Seer pointed at the lake. 'You are not fit to serve. Drown yourself.'

Without a word of protest, the bandit walked into the lake.

He moved in an unnatural lurching motion, as if invisible strings steered his body. Kayne reckoned that was exactly what was happening. The Seer's eyes burned red as she worked her foul magic and he considered charging her, but his hands were still tied and there was no telling what kind of magical protection the woman possessed. It would go ill for the others back at the tent if he chucked his life away here.

The bandit soon disappeared in the lake of tar. Shara turned back to Kayne and shrugged her shoulders. 'Don't feel bad for him. His fate was sealed the moment I chose him to escort us here.'

'You're a cold bitch,' Kayne spat back.

Shara merely smiled. 'I did not bring you here just to show you this. I received a vision last night. One I have not yet revealed to anyone else. In my vision I saw four men. Three were kings. The fourth man carried a sword.'

'What's that got to do with me?'

'I understand you were named Sword of the North, Brodar Kayne. A warrior without peer. A killer without mercy.'

Kayne flinched. 'That was a long time ago.'

'It was *you* in my vision, Brodar Kayne. You stood before the Bandit King. You knelt before the Butcher King. And you sent the Broken King to his death.'

As he listened to the Seer's words, a shiver passed through Kayne. 'Who were these kings?' he demanded. 'You see their faces?'

'The Bandit King is obviously Asander. As for the other two, who can say? I know only that you will be instrumental in events to come. Asander intends to burn you alive, but the Pattern wills what the Pattern wills. You must be allowed to follow your road to its conclusion.'

It took a moment for Shara's words to sink in. 'You're letting me go?'

'In a manner. You will conveniently escape.'

'I will? What about Asander?'

Shara examined her nails. 'The King knows only what I require him to know. He is a useful tool but a tool nonetheless. I imagine he will send men after you. You should hurry north.'

'What about my friends?'

'They were not part of my vision.'

'I ain't going anywhere without them.'

Shara raised an eyebrow. 'You speak as if you do not fear death.'

'One of the upsides of getting old. The knowledge that death's always right around the corner. Ain't no point fearing it.'

A ghost of a smile played around Shara's mouth. 'Your friends are worth nothing to me. If they escape too, why, it is no great loss.'

'What about Brick? You said he was a child of prophecy. That he'd bring back the true rulers of the north.'

Shara waved a dismissive hand. 'Oh, he already has. I found the egg amongst your possessions. You have no idea what it is, do you? The true masters of the north will indeed return – and they will serve *me*.'

'Nazala seemed certain Brick was important.'

'My twin understood little about the subtleties of divination. The fool is better off a corpse. He was always most comfortable around the dead.'

'Sounds like we're done here.'

'Not quite.' Shara reached behind her and her silks suddenly fell away, leaving her standing stark naked before him. 'It is a

281

rare thing to encounter great men. A thing one must cherish while one can, for the threads of your lives are often cut short. I offer myself as thanks for ending my brother's wretched existence. Ride me, Sword of the North.'

Kayne stared at Shara's perfect figure, at her ample bosom and smooth skin and bright red lips.

Then he turned away and spat. 'I'm a married man,' he said. 'And even if I weren't, I'd sooner drown myself in that lake than lie with you.'

'I could force you,' Shara whispered. 'Seize control of your body like I did that fool I sent to his death.'

Kayne's eyes narrowed. He met Shara's gaze, stared back unflinching. 'Maybe you could. But I promise you this. One day I would find you, and no amount of blood magic or sacrificing innocents would save you from what I would do to you.'

Shara was silent for a moment. 'Very well, Sword of the North,' she hissed eventually. 'Let us return to the King.' She reached down to collect her clothing. 'I hope the Pattern never wills it that we meet again.'

God-touched

'ARGH.'

'Oh, you poor thing, it's leaking again. Let me fetch some ointment for that.'

Cole watched Derkin's ma shuffle away and lowered his head to the bundle of old rags that passed for his pillow with a pitiful groan. He reached down to his stomach hesitantly, fearing what he would find. Right on cue, his fingers brushed against the wet stickiness and he recoiled in horror.

He was dying, that was the truth. Somehow his stomach wound had opened when he'd been tossed in the shambler pit. As if the broken ribs and cracked skull he'd suffered weren't enough. As if the things Corvac had done to him that night outside the tavern hadn't already left him broken, body and soul.

He listened to the sound of rain beating against the tin roof of the little hovel and he thought of all the misfortune that had befallen him over the last year. His whole world had been shattered, everything he believed in revealed to be lies. The fire that once burned so brightly within him was gone forever. The world was a cold and empty place.

A misshapen shadow crawled across the wall in the light of the single candle illuminating the tiny room, and Derkin hobbled through the door.

'Ma's just getting her stuff ready,' he said. His bulging eyes took in the sorry state of his guest. 'I'm not letting you leave here until you're feeling better.'

'I won't ever get better. I'm done, Derkin.'

'Now, don't say that. My ma will get you back on your feet. She used to treat the sick back when... before we left Thelassa.'

Cole raised his head a fraction to stare up at the corpse-carver. 'Why did you come here? This place is hell.'

Derkin looked away. 'I'm not supposed to talk about it.'

Cole sighed and his head sagged back down onto the make-shift pillow. His friend would chat for hours about all manner of things, but there were certain topics that made him clam up instantly. Such as his past in the City of Towers.

He glanced down at his wound again. The ripe smell of the yellowy pus oozing out of his stomach almost made him gag. 'This is the Darkson's fault,' he spat with a venom he had never known he possessed. 'This is all his fault. That treacherous bastard.'

Cole could hear Derkin's ma pottering around in the next room, taking her sweet time getting the ointment prepared. The shack only had three rooms, and Derkin had surrendered his own room for Cole's use. The hunchback gave him every meagre comfort he could manage, a kindness for which Cole tried his best to appear grateful.

'Try not to dwell on the past,' Derkin said gently. 'I know you're feeling down right now. At least your fever seems to be breaking.'

Since the Whitecloaks had rescued him from the pit, terrible headaches and strange nightmares had tormented Cole. Surreal visions of skull-faced deities plagued his dreams night after night, leaving him drenched in sweat, his heart hammering wildly. He thought back to the talking crow and the shamblers that had somehow obeyed his commands. They too must have been part of his fevered hallucinations. How could they possibly be real?

He glanced down at his hands. They were paler than ever, the flesh as maggoty white as the handmaidens'. Whatever the true nature of the poison coursing through his veins, it was close to killing him.

'Derkin...' Cole whispered. It was time.

The corpse-carver moved an awkward step closer. Perhaps it was his imagination, but even with the drumming of the downpour outside Cole could hear the hunchback's heart beating in his chest. The relentless pulse reminded him of Garrett's timepiece. That seemed like a lifetime ago now.

'Yes?' Derkin asked.

Cole closed his eyes. 'I want to end this.'

Derkin didn't reply straight away. In the sudden silence Cole thought he could make out his friend's mother's heart beating from the other room. *More hallucinations*, he thought bitterly. Whilst he'd always possessed a keen ear, there was no way any man could make out a heart beating through a wall, even one near as thin as parchment.

'Derkin?' Cole said again, still with his eyes tightly closed. 'Did you hear me? I said I want to die. I don't want to suffer any more.'

The slap rattled his jaw and left his face stinging. Cole's eyes shot open and he stared at Derkin in shocked outrage. 'Ow! What was that for?'

'You listen here,' Derkin demanded angrily, rubbing his deformed fingers. By the looks of it the slap had hurt him as much as it had Cole. 'I know you've suffered some terrible things recently. I heard what Corvac did to you.'

Cole stared up at the ceiling and didn't reply, blinking desperately, hoping Derkin would think the sudden tears in his eyes were down to the slap he'd just given him.

A misshapen hand settled on his arm and gave it a comforting squeeze. 'Don't let them break you,' his friend whispered. 'You're stronger than they are.'

'I'm not strong,' Cole replied hoarsely. 'I'm a nobody. A common bastard.'

Derkin shook his head. 'That doesn't matter now. It's not what you're born as that's important. It's what you become.'

'You don't understand.'

'Don't I?' Derkin said quietly. 'Look at me. I was born a freak. My ma and I were sent to live with all the other undesirables. There's a whole city beneath Thelassa, a city no one ever sees except criminals and the deformed. The Mistress doesn't want people like me ruining her perfect paradise.'

Cole thought back to his lessons with the Darkson in the ruins beneath Thelassa. 'Sanctuary?' he whispered. 'You mean there are people living in those ruins?'

Derkin nodded gravely. 'People and other things. The Abandoned. They're like men, but... they're not all there.'

'That's why you came to Newharvest, isn't it?' Cole said slowly. 'To escape the ruins. Even this place is better than where you came from.'

'Yes. At least here I'm worth something. I have a livelihood, a home of my own. I can look after my ma.'

Cole stared at the hunchback and was overcome with sympathy. How hard must Derkin's life be with his curved spine and twisted fingers and eyes that seemed to stare off in opposite directions? He himself had enjoyed an easy time of it growing up in Dorminia, he realized. If he'd ever wanted for anything, he'd merely had to ask. The Grey City was a hard place for most, but the truth was that he had been privileged. Maybe he ought to have been more grateful for the blessings he'd enjoyed. Looking back, he had at times been selfish and self-centred. Most of the time, if he was honest.

His rare moment of introspection was interrupted by the sudden and strange sensation something was amiss. It took him a moment to realize what it was. He could hear a second heartbeat coming from the next room: a second heartbeat besides that of Derkin's mother.

'Derkin,' Cole whispered urgently, dread rising in him. 'You'd better check on your ma.'

The hunchback's brow creased in confusion, but he nonetheless hobbled over to the door and poked his head into the other room.

'Hello, runt. Corvac sends his regards.'

Cole's blood froze. It was Shank, the Condemned who'd stabbed Ed and left him fighting for his life.

Derkin's outraged cry cut through the sound of the storm raging outside. There was the crash of furniture breaking, and then silence.

'You *bit* me, you little swine!' came Shank's voice, shrill with disgust. 'What kind of man bites another? You might've given me some sort of disease! Well, you can just lie there and watch while I skin your ma alive. After that I'll deal with your friend in the room over there.'

Cole searched around frantically, desperate for a way to escape. There was a shutter on the wall above his head, which Derkin and his mother occasionally opened to let in fresh air. It was closed due to the awful weather battering Newharvest, but if he could just struggle to his feet...

The world swam as he tried to rise. He staggered, knocked over the piss bucket next to the bed and felt warm liquid soaking his trousers. He didn't care about that, he was too terrified the clatter would alert Shank.

He released the latch on the shutters and flung them wide open. Windswept rain immediately gusted in to sprinkle his face. The window was just wide enough to crawl through. He took a shuddering breath and prepared to climb out.

Derkin's sobs tore his attention away from the opening. He looked from the doorway to the window and back. The old Cole wouldn't have hesitated; he'd have stormed into the room and confronted the deranged knife-wielding maniac without a second's thought.

He wasn't that man any more and besides, he didn't have a weapon. There was nothing he could use against Shank. Not unless he fancied wielding a piss-stained bucket. Full of self-loathing, he readied himself to climb out of the window.

There was a sudden flapping sound from outside, and a dark shadow fell across the room. Cole jumped back in shock. Beady eyes stared at him from the window, black feathers dripping wet from the storm.

'*You*,' Cole whispered.

The crow had landed on the window ledge. It was clutching something in its claws, something bright and sharp and with a large ruby in the hilt—

'Magebane,' Cole gasped.

The crow released the dagger and the weapon clattered to the floor. 'Caw,' the crow said. Not cried, but *said*.

Cole reached down with shaking hands. The last time he'd seen his magical dagger was the night he had slid its cold length inside Salazar's withered old body. As his hand closed around the jewelled hilt, a soft blue glow sprang up around the blade.

'Please,' begged Derkin from the other room. 'Don't hurt her. That's my ma.'

The crow leaped down to the floor and regarded Cole with a frighteningly intelligent gaze. Cole looked at the bird and then out of the window. He could seek refuge with the Whitecloaks. Shank would be arrested, Corvac too if Cole could prove the Mad Dog leader had freed the knifeman. He hesitated again.

Davarus Cole was no hero. But neither was he a coward. He wouldn't abandon his friends.

Gritting his teeth, he turned and stumbled towards the doorway.

Derkin was curled up on the floor, a big gash on his head. A broken chair lay nearby. Shank was leaning over Derkin's mother, a fistful of her hair in one hand. A trickle of blood ran down the side of her face where the knifeman had made a small cut in her scalp.

'Ghost,' the maniac drawled when he saw Cole standing in the doorway. 'I was planning to save you for last. Corvac promised to pardon me for stabbing that big retard if I brought your head back to him.'

'Let her go,' Cole said, trying not to let his weakness show. His hands were trembling and his heart was racing and he felt as though he might collapse at any moment. He raised the glowing dagger in his shaking palm.

Shank whirled Derkin's mother around, positioning himself behind her. He placed the edge of his own knife against her neck. 'You come any closer and I'll slit her throat. Is that... magic? The Trinity will tear you apart when they learn you've stolen it from them!' The knifeman shook his head in self-righteous indignation. 'I might have butchered men and women like hogs but I've never *stolen* from anyone. You're nothing but a dirty thief. You know something? People like you make me physically sick.'

Cole stared at Shank. At the bastard who'd threatened to cut off his balls, who'd made a ruin of poor Ed's chest. Who was even now threatening to slit the throat of a helpless old woman.

Something snapped.

'Shank,' he said flatly, all his fear forgotten.

'What?'

'Fuck off.'

He had only a few inches to aim for, the top of Shank's forehead poking out just above his hostage's bun of white hair. It was a tiny target, a difficult ask even back in his glory days, but a cold certainty seemed to guide his hand as he flicked Magebane around and launched it at the deranged knifeman.

The spinning blade nicked the old woman's hair on its way to burying itself in Shank's skull. He stood there dumbly for a moment, the ruby hilt sticking out of his head and quivering almost comically. Then he collapsed stone dead.

Cole stared at Shank's corpse. 'I killed him,' he said incredulously.

Derkin's ma seemed more confused than afraid. 'I thought it mighty strange, him being outside in this weather. That'll teach me to open the door to strangers.'

Cole shook himself from his stupor. He rushed over to the old woman and examined her cut. 'You're bleeding.'

She waved a wrinkled hand at him. 'Oh, it's nothing, dearie.

I'll be fine. Babykins!' she cried suddenly. 'You're hurt! My baby's hurt!'

'Ma, don't call me that in front of my friend,' Derkin said desperately, rising panic in his voice as he tried to climb back to his feet. His mother bustled over to help him up, fussing over him, heedless of her own wound.

Cole bent down to retrieve Magebane. Shank's expression was accusatory, his eyes wide with shock in the moment of his death. Cole gripped the dagger's handle, preparing to wrench the blade free. As his fingers closed around the hilt a sudden surge of strength washed through him and he gasped. He felt *alive* – more vital than he had for many weeks.

He stared down at his hands. Even as he watched, the colour began to return to his skin, ghostly pale flesh slowly turning a healthy pink. He felt a pulling sensation and looked down. His stomach wound was somehow knitting back together.

'Ghost!' Derkin exclaimed, having finally regained his feet and assured his ma he wasn't in any immediate danger of keeling over dead. 'You look ten years younger.'

Cole reached up and touched his head. His hair felt thicker and less brittle. The deep exhaustion that had settled into his bones had all but disappeared. 'What's happening to me?' he said, bewildered.

'You just fed upon that man's soul,' said a measured voice, as hard as iron. Standing in the doorway was a tall man wearing a tattered black overcoat. He had a red cloth tied around his eyes.

'Now then, how did you get in here?' Derkin's ma exclaimed. Staring at the man, though, Cole knew the answer immediately.

'You're the crow,' he whispered. 'You saved my life in the shambler pit. You spoke to me. In my head. Are you... are you some kind of wizard?'

The stranger cocked his head, a movement that struck Cole as distinctly birdlike. 'I've been watching over you since Dorminia, Davarus Cole. Since I found you propped against a building, your life bleeding out. I was on the ship that brought you to this place. I saved you from the men who were trying to rob you.'

'It was you that killed them,' Cole said, putting the pieces together in his head. 'You killed them and took Magebane.'

'Yes. *To keep it safe*. The weapon you hold is an anomaly. Forged of an alloy of abyssium, the demonsteel that drinks magic, and yet is somehow itself enchanted with great power. A most potent tool.'

'Salazar made it for my father, who passed it down to me. I don't want it. It's an evil weapon.'

'There are no evil weapons,' the wizard replied. 'Only evil men who wield them. I knew Salazar, many centuries ago. He was one of the few I considered my equal in the age before the fall of the gods. My memories are grains of sand scattered by the winds, but this I remember.'

'You're a Magelord?' Cole exclaimed, shocked.

'A Magelord?' The man laughed, a harsh sound absent of humour. 'I played no part in the Godswar. Immortality is a burden I need not suffer.'

'The gods perished centuries ago! If you're not a Magelord... how are you still alive?'

'For five hundred years my soul survived housed in the undying body of my familiar,' the wizard explained. 'Every minute I walk the earth in my true form brings me closer to death. I am not immortal. I merely choose *when* to spend the time remaining to me.'

'What are you doing here? What... what do you want?'

The wizard in the tattered coat shrugged. 'What every man wants. The truth. I want to know who I am.'

'You mean you don't know?'

'If I did I would not require your help! Long ago, the White Lady stole my memories. Stripped my mind bare of everything except my name: *Thanates*. I remember little, but this I know.'

'Why would she do that to you?'

'I do not recall. But I intend to find out.'

Cole glanced at Derkin and his mother, aware that neither had spoken in a while. There was something odd about them; their eyes were fixed in place, locked on the tall figure with the cloth around his eyes.

'You put a spell on them,' Cole said accusingly.

'Yes,' agreed the wizard who called himself Thanates. 'They will not remember I was here. Now, listen to me. There is no time for questions. Retrieve your dagger.'

Cole bent down and wrenched Magebane free from Shank's skull. The curved blade came free with a soft pop and a spatter of blood. Despite the wizard's warning not to ask questions, Cole couldn't stop himself. 'You said I fed on Shank's soul. I was dying, but now I feel stronger than ever. What's happening to me?'

'The stolen divinity Salazar possessed. It would seem your dagger can absorb more than just magic.'

'I don't understand.'

'The two of you shared a link through Magebane. When he died, the dagger transferred a part of his soul to you. Like Salazar, you are now god-touched – a custodian of the Reaver's divine essence. Death itself resides in you. Feed it and you will grow stronger. Resist... and it will feed on *you*.'

'God-touched,' Cole whispered. He stared down at his hands.

'Do nothing to draw attention to your powers! And keep away from the glow-globes that illuminate the town. The magic mined from the Black Lord's corpse is tainted. The Blight itself spreads madness, but the glow-globes exacerbate its effects.'

That brought a dozen new questions to Cole's lips, but before he could speak Thanates raised a gloved hand and his next words caused them to die in his throat. 'The White Lady will soon have this town razed and all within massacred. We have but one chance to avert disaster. Listen carefully and I will tell you what must be done...'

Shadowport

S ASHA LEANED OVER the rail again and heaved. She hated sea travel. The motion of a ship beneath her feet made her feel nauseous at the best of times, and standing on the deck of *The Lady's Luck*, staring down at the mass of bloated corpses rotting in the waters of Dusk Bay, was decidedly not the best of times.

The ship had departed Thelassa's harbour yesterday afternoon. A monstrous crowd had gathered to watch them leave. The White Lady herself, the city's beloved ruler, was to lead a rescue mission to the flooded remains of Shadowport, searching for survivors. Which would have been a noble gesture – three months ago.

Sasha wiped sour vomit from her chin and tried not to let her cynicism show on her face. She recalled the dead bodies that had washed up in Dorminia's harbour in the weeks following Salazar's greatest crime. There'd been little chance of anyone surviving a billion tons of water dropped on the city. No chance at all they could have clung on this long, even if they'd somehow survived the initial catastrophic magical assault.

Ambryl's voice drifted over her shoulder. 'Something troubling you, sister? Perhaps you should seek refuge below deck if the sight of death unsettles you so.'

'It's not the sight of death that unsettles me, it's this endless rocking.'

And the moon dust I snorted this morning, she thought, but she didn't add that last part. She still felt guilty about the jewellery she'd stolen from the Siren. Willard had been passed out drunk in the common room and the opportunity was too good to resist. The silver necklace and bracelet had fetched a good handful of gold between them and hunting down a dealer had been laughably easy. It seemed that in Thelassa, narcotics changed hands as readily as coin.

There was still no sign of Willard's wife Lyressa, who had been taken the night of the festival. Sasha felt awful about taking advantage of the woman's absence, but that taste of *hashka* during the Seeding had awoken all her old needs. She was a mess.

Ambryl was watching the approaching coastline with pursed lips. 'I begin to see how foolish I was,' she said bitterly. 'Salazar was no god. He was a *tyrant*. And like all men when they do not get what they want, he lashed out. How many bodies churn beneath the waters here, sister? Thousands? Tens of thousands? Innocent victims of one man's greed and wounded pride.'

Behind Ambryl, the all-female crew busied themselves as they neared land. The White Lady's handmaidens were motionless statues, while the Magelord herself stood near the prow, staring at the ruins of the city up ahead. If the watery graveyard they were passing through bothered her, it didn't show in her enchanting purple eyes.

'What did you talk about at the palace?' Sasha asked her sister. The adulation on Ambryl's face as she gazed at the White Lady troubled her. Just like the crowd that gathered to cheer them on their way, Ambryl seemed to worship the immortal wizard. Almost as if she were a goddess.

From would-be assassin to devoted follower in the space of a week. The turnaround in Ambryl's attitude was frightening.

'We spoke of many things, sister. Of the injustices we both have suffered. Before the fall of the gods, the Mistress was the high priestess of the Mother.'

'So it's "the Mistress" now?'

Ambryl shot her a look. 'It was a *man* that made her turn her back on the church and the Congregation and join the Alliance.

She was the greatest wizard of her age and might have reconciled the church with the mageocracy. But he poisoned her heart. It was he we must thank for leading us to this Age of Ruin.'

Sasha crossed her arms and stared out over the railing. Not so long ago Dusk Bay would have been heaving with trading vessels and fishing boats. Only a year past a fleet of warships had sailed forth from Shadowport to engage in a naval war with Dorminia over the Celestial Isles.

Now the bay was a desolate wasteland. She hadn't spotted even a single fish amongst the wreckage of the city. As far as Sasha could see, it was only a matter of time before the cartographers scribbled out Dusk Bay and replaced it with Dead Bay.

'Lyressa still hasn't returned,' she whispered so that only Ambryl could hear. 'According to Willard, the White Lady's handmaidens took her. He won't say why.'

Ambryl shrugged and took a bite out of an apple she had rustled up from somewhere. 'We won't need to put up with his moping around for much longer. I serve the White Lady now, sister. Soon I will be part of the governing council.'

Sasha stared at Ambryl in shock. 'We agreed we were going back to Dorminia after we delivered the Halfmage's message!'

'Pah. Dorminia holds nothing for us now.'

'It's our home.'

'No, it *was* our home. A different "us". Where men break, women bend and adapt. This is my chance to show the sole remaining Magelord in the Trine that I can serve her as I once served Salazar.'

Sasha was about to argue when the captain of *The Lady's Luck* cried out a warning. There was a horrible grinding noise from below, followed by the sound of cracking wood. The ship heeled perilously to port before righting itself with a gigantic splash that soaked the sisters to the bone.

The White Lady glided over to the helm of the ship and placed her perfect hands on her slender waist. 'Captain, what is the meaning of this?' she demanded. Her voice was like birdsong on a warm spring morning, but there was an undercurrent of menace, a storm gathering on the horizon.

'We hit some ruins,' said the ship's captain. She was a proud woman of middling years, but in the face of the White Lady's displeasure she sagged with shame, like an ageing hound whose bowels had betrayed it at an inopportune moment and exposed its frailty to its master.

'Are we in any imminent danger of capsizing?' the Magelord asked softly.

'No, mistress. The harbour is just ahead. We will dock there and I will assess the damage.'

'Very well.' The White Lady glided over to Ambryl and Sasha, who swallowed drily, suddenly afraid. For all her other-worldly beauty, there was something deeply unsettling about this woman.

'The two of you will join the party that will accompany me to shore. I am curious what secrets these ruins may yet reveal about the ruler of this city. Marius was ever an enigma to me. I wish to see with my own eyes whether the warning you delivered has merit.'

'Warning?' Ambryl echoed, clearly surprised her mistress would bring up the topic. 'You refer to the Halfmage's message?'

The White Lady nodded. Her platinum hair fell perfectly around her exquisite face, but there was a flicker of... *concern?*... in her extraordinary violet eyes. 'My sources in Dorminia support your view that this "Halfmage" is a paranoid man given to unlikely claims. Still, prior to its destruction there were certain aspects of Shadowport's recent successes that troubled me. As does one other matter.'

'Mistress?'

'The first of the ships sent to the Celestial Isles were due back last week. They have yet to return.'

If Dusk Bay brought with it gruesome yet predictable sights, the deluged streets of Shadowport were a nightmare of smaller details that drove home the true extent of the horrors inflicted on the city.

Sasha stepped gingerly around a murky pool in the middle of the street and stared at the dead couple floating in the water. The two of them were entwined, a tangle of rotting limbs and soft grey flesh sloughing off bone. From the looks of it, they'd spent their last few seconds locked in each other's arms.

One of the man's legs poked out of the water at an odd angle, an old break that hadn't healed properly. Nearby, an iron pan floated among the detritus of devastated houses. Flattened buildings stretched out as far as the eye could see, an endless patchwork of levelled walls surrounded by rubble and sprawling pools of stinking saltwater that had yet to dry in the months following the colossal wave which had torn through Shadowport. What was once the largest and most prosperous city in the Trine was now a watery graveyard. The ghosts of the fifty thousand who had perished would remain forever ignorant of what had befallen them.

The White Lady halted as they passed the dead couple, forcing the rest of the group to stop. The chosen crew members of *The Lady's Luck* looked around in confusion. The rest of the crew were back repairing the ship. The damage to the hull was less severe than feared, and the captain had seemed confident the ship could be made seaworthy within a few hours. However, the White Lady had 'suggested' the iron-haired captain accompany the expedition and leave the supervision of the work to her first mate. The woman had paled at that, and it seemed to Sasha that something unspoken had passed between the Magelord and the skipper. A threat, maybe. Or perhaps a verdict.

'Great magic was worked here,' the White Lady said as she examined the street. 'Not Salazar's cataclysmic evocation, but magic of a different nature. A binding spell.'

'Another wizard present in the city at the time of the disaster, perhaps,' said a handmaiden in a deadpan voice. 'Shadowport welcomed those with the gift.'

The White Lady's eyes narrowed. 'A spell such as the one worked here is beyond most. Even Brianna could not achieve such a feat.'

Sasha remembered Brianna's last stand outside the gates of Dorminia, blood running from her eyes as she was torn apart by the sheer force of Salazar's magical assault. She had liked and admired Brianna.

The urge to pull out the *hashka* stashed inside her cloak suddenly threatened to overwhelm her. Her palms began to sweat, the blackness that was always lurking inside her skull threatening to swallow her up.

'Sister,' said Ambryl beside her. 'Do not let it master you. You've done well to stick to your promise.'

The hint of something like warmth in her sister's tone shocked her enough to jolt her back from the precipice. *I broke my promise*, she wanted to yell. *I always break my promises.*

The expeditionary group continued through the drowned streets of Shadowport. As evening began to fall a cloud of insects rose from the ruins, a buzzing horde that covered the sisters and the crew of *The Lady's Luck* in red bites but left not a single mark on the White Lady or her handmaidens. It was as if they were invisible to the swarming bugs. Sasha glimpsed corpses crawling with black beetles. At one point she watched as a huge centipede scuttled from the nose of a teenage boy, and she tasted bile in the back of her throat.

They followed the wide avenue leading from the harbour for another hour before finally they reached the remains of the Palace of a Thousand Pleasures. The residence of the Magelord Marius had once been surrounded by a great garden, a botanical wonder hosting trees and flowers gathered from every corner of the continent. Now it was a swamp of decomposing vegetation swarming with insects.

'And so we come to the heart of the pestilence that infests this city,' the White Lady announced. She whispered a few words and suddenly the air shimmered. Moments later a raging windstorm sprang up around the group, a shielding sphere that moved as they moved, as if they were at the very eye of the storm. The wind generated by the sphere buffeted Sasha, sending her hair dancing around her head and keeping the biting insects at bay. 'Stay close to me,' the White Lady commanded.

They picked their way over fallen masonry towards the palace building. The White Lady's handmaidens hopped from stone to stone with terrifying agility, avoiding the swampy ground. Their mistress floated a foot above the dirty water, as serene as a goddess, utterly unfazed by the mire Sasha and the others were forced to wade through. They were soaked and covered in filth, but the Magelord refused to slow and they had to hurry to avoid falling outside her magical protection. Once they passed the gardens, the White Lady waved a desultory hand and the sphere dissipated.

Soon they reached the wreckage of the interior. Even with the destruction wrought by Salazar's magic, it was easy to observe the former splendour of the Palace of a Thousand Pleasures. Golden statuary lay upended. Delicately constructed furniture was shattered beyond repair. Fabulously expensive carpets had been utterly ruined by seawater. A few rooms had survived and were structurally sound, though the contents were invariably spoiled. Sasha was fortunate enough to have grown up in Garrett's estate in Dorminia, but even the trappings her foster father had enjoyed were a peasant's lot in comparison with the luxuries she witnessed in those chambers.

Beyond the remains of the throne room, a set of stone steps led down into the palace dungeons. The White Lady paused on the very top step and stared down into the blackness below. 'Marius was a man of many appetites,' she said. 'One might view his city from afar and conclude that he embraced an enlightened attitude, but that would be a mistake. At the heart of every man is a beast, no matter the clothes he dons or the words he utters or the ideals he professes to hold. Let us now peer beneath the mask of this particular beast.'

The White Lady descended the steps, her handmaidens trailing her. Sasha and Ambryl brought up the rear, together with the crew of the *Luck*. Though the dungeons had flooded along with the rest of the palace, an outlet somewhere below had allowed the water to escape, leaving only a few shallow puddles and an incessant drip that accompanied the party ever deeper. Blackness soon swallowed them until the White Lady uttered a word and floating globes of light blinked into existence, illuminating the way. Soon an iron door bled into view on the left side of the passage. Upon finding it locked, the Magelord beckoned and her three handmaidens tore it clean off its hinges, forcing it with a brute strength not even the strongest men could hope to match. Not for the first time Sasha wondered about these pale women. She had heard them referred to in hushed whispers as the 'Unborn', and that had done little to assuage her unease.

The White Lady stepped through the door into darkness. A moment later her conjured lights danced their way into the room, shedding light on a large and richly decorated cell. Sasha followed, and her gaze lingered on the furnishings for only a moment before finding the naked and emaciated corpses chained to the walls at the rear of the cell.

The dead prisoners were all women, and they were all young. Brutal metal implements rested on a rack nearby, and no few of them had seen use, judging by the obscene wounds the women bore. The floating lights revealed the prisoners to be of assorted ethnicity. There were a pair of pale Highlander women; a red-headed girl of Andarran heritage; a petite dark-haired girl from Tarbonne or possibly Espanda in the Shattered Realms to the south; and even a black-skinned Sumnian.

'Marius's sex slaves,' the White Lady proclaimed. 'It appears he collected them with the same passion with which he collected exotic flora for his gardens. They died here, chained up like dogs.'

Sasha had to turn away before she vomited again.

They continued through the dungeons, passing similar

chambers filled with mutilated corpses, the work of a truly deranged mind. 'How could anyone do this?' Sasha whispered.

The look Ambryl gave her seemed almost triumphant.

At the very rear of the dungeons, a long and narrow corridor led to a single iron door painted a dull red colour. The White Lady turned to the captain of *The Lady's Luck*. 'You go first,' she commanded.

The grey-haired captain swallowed and raised a hand in salute. Alone she proceeded down the corridor. She was a third of the way along when a hidden compartment on the left wall suddenly swung open and there was a flicker of steel as a blade trap was sprung. Then the woman was on the floor, clutching what little remained of her legs, hot blood spraying everywhere.

The White Lady nodded in satisfaction. 'The magical wards once guarding this passage are no more. Even so, whatever lies in the room beyond must be of great value. To employ such crude mechanical traps is an assault on good taste.'

She gestured and her handmaidens sprang into action, the three of them racing down the corridor in a blur. More traps were triggered, all of them evaded by the pale women and their lightning reflexes. A concealed pit opened in the floor and the handmaidens seemed to shift direction in mid-air, running *along* the walls to land safely on the other side. Finally they reached the door and turned to wait for their mistress.

'Come,' the White Lady said. She glided down the corridor, stepping neatly around her maimed captain, skirting the edge of the pit where a thin ledge provided just enough room to cross. Sasha and the others followed, though two of the crew stayed behind to help their stricken skipper. There was little they could do except gather up the shredded remains of her legs and try to stem the bleeding.

'Why didn't she help her?' Sasha whispered to Ambryl. Her sister only shrugged in reply.

They joined the White Lady and her handmaidens in the room beyond the corridor. As the floating lights darted into the room, Sasha readied herself for whatever gruesome sight awaited her.

But it was only a pair of naked skeletons. They were sitting in upright positions, thick straps and chains securing them tightly to their seats. Whoever the skeletons once were, they had been dead a long time.

On closer inspection Sasha saw that both skeletons were oddly shaped: they would be extremely tall were they to stand. Their bones were incredibly long and thin and delicate – almost inhuman.

The White Lady stared at the skeletons for a long moment before turning to her handmaidens. 'Remove the chains and secure the remains. We return to the ship immediately.' It seemed absurd, but Sasha thought she glimpsed something like disquiet on the Magelord's face.

As they were leaving the room, one of the crew approached them in the passage and pointed a trembling finger at her whimpering captain. 'Mistress,' she said in a shaky voice. 'She needs healing. Please.'

The White Lady glanced at the stricken woman sprawled in a spreading pool of blood. 'I have no place for the foolish or the careless. Tell my erstwhile captain that *The Lady's Luck* no longer favours her.'

'She will die, mistress.'

In response, the Magelord merely nodded. 'I trust she will. I have no place for the foolish and the careless. Nor do I have any place for cripples.'

Sasha hid in her tiny cabin aboard *The Lady's Luck* and brought her finger up to her nose. She inhaled long and hard, feeling the sweet powder fill her world. Soon it would carry her away to a better place – just as the first available ship out of Thelassa's harbour would carry her back to Dorminia, once she had collected her belongings from the Siren.

The White Lady's callousness had left her shaking. For weeks she had suspected something was seriously wrong in the City of

302

Towers. Her sense of unease had only increased following the Seeding and the strange events that had taken place that night. The odd behaviour of the Thelassans, Lyressa's disappearance... even her sister's rapid conversion to the cult-like worship of the city's ruler. It was as if Thelassa was under some kind of spell. She remembered the Magelord's words back at the Palace of a Thousand Pleasures.

Let us now peer beneath the mask of this particular beast.

Marius had indeed been a sadist, but Sasha was beginning to wonder if the White Lady was any better. Now all she needed to do was convince her sister of the Magelord's true nature.

Lost in the thrill of the hit, she didn't hear the door creak open. Didn't realize the object of her thoughts was standing in the cabin behind her until she felt Ambryl's nails digging painfully into her shoulder.

'You lying whore.'

Sasha twisted around, spraying moon dust everywhere. 'A-Ambryl! Wait, I'm sorry—'

'Not here. When we return to the City of Towers, dear sister, you and I are going to have words.'

'I'm going home.'

'What did you just say?'

'I'm going home. Back to Dorminia.'

Ambryl's hard eyes narrowed dangerously. 'We already discussed this. There is nothing for us there.'

'There is nothing for *you* there, Ambryl.'

'My name is *Cyreena*, damn you. Why return to the Grey City, sister? We have no family. No friends. No reason to care about that place at all.'

'Cole might still be alive—'

'Oh, not this absurdity again. I met this boy once, this Davarus Cole. He was a braggart, a charlatan, and a fool. His disappearance was a blessing.'

Sasha stared at her sister in disbelief. 'You never told me! Why didn't you tell me?'

'Why should I?' Ambryl demanded. 'You need to start moving on, sister. Moving on from the past.' Her voice softened a little. 'Now that we're in the White Lady's favour, no one will ever harm us again.'

'The White Lady's a monster.'

'She's everything we could ever dream to be, you stupid girl! Caught between a wolf to the north and a wolf in sheep's clothing to the south, two males with their armies and their bluster and their perversions – and yet she won.'

'I don't care about winning. I only care about surviving.'

Ambryl grabbed hold of Sasha's chin and twisted her head painfully. 'All I've ever wanted is to protect you,' she said softly. 'I'll lock you in a cell if I must – until the demons release their hold and the sister I know is returned to me.' And with those words, her sister turned and stormed out of the cabin.

Sasha slumped back against the wall and buried her head in her hands, letting the *hashka* spill to the floor.

Reflections

'WAKE UP. WE have to go.'

Yllandris opened eyes as heavy as sin and stared up at Yorn's bearded jaw. How long had she been sleeping? An hour?

Time had lost all meaning now. She was beyond exhausted, fever-sick from the wound on her face that refused to heal, her shoulders chafing from the sad burden she carried. The pain didn't matter any more. She just had to keep moving.

Somehow she climbed to her feet, though they were so numb she could hardly feel them. She knew the foundlings had it worse; their legs were only half as long her hers. A few children wouldn't stop crying because of their blisters. Though it broke her heart to watch them suffer, they couldn't afford to slow their pace. Not until they reached the Greenwild.

She stumbled through the shallow valley in which they'd called an all too-brief halt and surveyed the sleeping children spread out across the autumn grass. Most had simply collapsed in the spot they'd been standing, falling into a deep sleep as soon as their small bodies had touched the ground. She hesitated, overcome with guilt by what she was about do. It couldn't be helped.

She clapped loudly, moving from child to child. Some stirred and managed to rise, rubbing at tired young eyes. Others were oblivious to her efforts, so overcome with exhaustion they could have slept through a thunderstorm.

Fortunately, Corinn rose to lend a hand. The girl's hair was a dirty mess and her blue eyes had lost a little of their lustre, but she cared for the other children with the dedication of an older sister. Yllandris had been like that, once. Before the day she'd crawled out of bed to find her father sobbing over her mother's battered body. Before she'd forced herself to become as cold as the winter snow in order to survive.

Corinn made a brief circuit of the campsite, rousing children and offering soothing words. Yorn busied himself portioning out the provisions they'd foraged. The Green Reaching remained neutral in the civil war that had engulfed the rest of the Heartlands, and even the Butcher King understood that the breadbasket of the High Fangs was too important to embroil in the conflict, but it was dangerous to seek refuge so close to the King's Reaching. Krazka would find them eventually. And if not he, the Herald when it eventually returned. There could be no sanctuary, not until they were out of the High Fangs.

'Why aren't they pursuing us?' Yllandris had asked Yorn, the third day after they'd fled Heartstone. The taciturn warrior had merely shrugged. Whomever Krazka had sent to hunt them down, they appeared content to bide their time.

They were leaving it late. The Greenwild was only a few miles ahead now. Even the best trackers would quickly lose their quarry in the labyrinthine depths of that vast and preternatural forest. For the first time since they'd set out from the capital, Yllandris began to hope they might make it to safety.

But that hope was quickly dashed. An hour after breaking camp, they were cresting a hill when Yorn spotted a small group approaching from the north. 'Looks like half a dozen,' the big warrior rumbled. 'They're on foot.'

Yllandris shielded her eyes and scanned the horizon. Her vision had deteriorated since Krazka had sliced her face open, but she could see the group Yorn referred to. While they were too distant to make out exact details, one of the figures glittered silver in the bright afternoon sun and it took only a moment before a terrifying realization dawned.

It's the iron man. It has to be him.

Yllandris turned to Yorn. 'Sir Meredith is with them,' she said. Yorn gave a grim nod of his shaggy head. 'He… he has an abyssium ring. My magic won't work on him. They'll chase us down.' She blinked away tears. She'd known this was a foolish plan. She'd known it all along.

The orphans were watching her curiously, all except Corinn, whose pretty eyes were filled with fear.

'I just wanted to save them,' Yllandris whispered. She heard a soft clacking noise and realized she was shaking so badly that the bones in the sack were knocking together.

'Go.'

Yorn spoke the word slowly and deliberately. His eyes were locked on the approaching group, utter determination carved onto his craggy face. 'I'll delay them as much as I can.'

Yllandris took a deep breath and tried to calm her trembling body. 'You can't fight that many.'

Yorn drew his broadsword, and his gaze narrowed as if he were seeing events long ago. 'Rayne ain't the only Kingsman that survived Red Valley. I was there too. I killed a lot of men that day. I'm not going down without taking a few of them with me. Take the children and flee. Don't look back.'

Yllandris reached out, placed a trembling hand on Yorn's broad shoulder. 'Thank you,' she said. 'For everything.'

The big warrior merely nodded. Then he busied himself untying the wooden shield strapped to his back.

Yllandris turned to the orphans. 'Quickly, children. We must make it to the Greenwild before nightfall.'

Sir Meredith raised the visor of his iron helmet and wiped sweat from his nose. He turned to Rayne beside him. The fool's beard was coated in red powder, and every so often his face would twitch as if someone had just poked him in the arse with a spear. It was simply too much to abide.

'Do you have no honour?' he said accusingly.

Rayne watched the burly figure of Yorn approach. His eyes looked suspiciously moist. 'Honour?' the Westerman repeated quietly. 'I've forgotten what this is.'

'Honour is not indulging your sordid addiction to *jhaeld* while you are supposed to be performing the King's duty!'

'And the farmers we killed? Where was the honour in that?' Rayne shook his head, knuckles white on the hilts of the twin scimitars at his belt. Having seen the weapons in action, Meredith was forced to concede that Red Rayne's epithet was apt. A *jhaeld*-addicted cretin he may be, but the man knew how to fight.

'Those were the King's orders,' he lied. In actual fact, they were his idea. 'The executions sent a much-needed warning to this land of sheep-buggerers. I learned the value of fear from the Rag King. Terror can be more effective than an army in quelling potential rebellion.'

Ryder flashed a yellow smile and ran a hand over his grey stubble. Despite being the wrong side of fifty, the lean tracker seemed to possess more stamina than any of the younger men who had set out from Heartstone in pursuit of the traitor Yorn and the stolen foundlings. 'Reminds me of the good old days, all this killing folk to send a message,' he said. 'Time was when the whole of the Green Reaching feared the Scourge and our little gang.'

Sir Meredith grimaced at the man's stale stench. Ryder was nothing but a base killer, a contemptible companion for a knight such as he. It was frankly insulting that he was expected to tolerate the man's company on this quest. 'The Scourge?' he spat contemptuously. 'Your lack of imagination is equalled only by your absence of hygiene, dogface.'

'It was Skarn what came up with it, not me,' Ryder replied easily. 'And my name ain't dogface.'

He was a hard one to ruffle, this Ryder, thought Sir Meredith. Like all men lacking pride and honour. Like all men possessing natures that barely rose above the feral beasts of the wild. 'Little more than a dog in truth,' he blurted, the words bursting out before he could stop them.

Ryder's eyes narrowed. 'What was that, Sword Lord?'

Sir Meredith waved a dismissive hand. 'Never you mind! Now, shut your mouth and spare my nostrils your rancid breath. The turncoat approaches.'

The three Kingsmen and their retinue readied their weapons as Yorn made his slow and deliberate way towards them. The treacherous bastard was badly outnumbered, not to mention outmatched, but Sir Meredith couldn't deny a slight thrill at the romance of it all. A lone man, striding out to meet certain death – it reminded him of the tales his mother used to read to him. Her stories of knights and chivalry had been his escape, a world he would retreat to when his grandfather chose to pay him a visit in the middle of the night. Meredith's biggest regret was that the old degenerate's heart had given out before he was old enough to exact his revenge.

'Should I shoot him?' Ryder murmured. Sir Meredith hadn't seen him retrieve an arrow from his quiver. He was a fast draw. A dead eye, too, judging from the way he'd put an arrow in the back of that farmer's daughter from sixty yards.

'No,' snapped Meredith. His hand went to the pommel of the sabre at his belt. 'I shall offer him a duel.'

'Careful, iron man. Yorn fought at Red Valley. Killed almost as many men as the Sword of the North.' Red Rayne's head slumped as if the memory shamed him somehow. Ryder too winced at something Rayne said. As he lowered his bow he rubbed at the stub of his missing ear.

The Sword of the North. Sir Meredith kept on hearing that name. The father of the deposed King had been a famed warrior, some kind of legendary figure of whom his countrymen still spoke in awed tones.

Sir Meredith sneered. It was all so bloody provincial. Every man who knew one end of a sword from the other carried some kind of reputation in the High Fangs. It was yet another symptom of cultural ignorance, this celebration of mediocrity. He himself had met true legends down in the Lowlands; he had studied under them, fought against them in the Circle. They were towering colossi compared with the stick men the Highland people held in such laughable esteem. 'Reputations mean nothing to a true knight,' he proclaimed. 'Witness.'

He advanced boldly. As he closed on Yorn a whiff of the man's stench reached his nostrils, and behind his visor Meredith's mouth curled in disgust. This coward and his sorcerous accomplice must have driven the children hard to keep ahead of justice. No doubt it had been days since last they bathed, though in Yorn's case it could well be months or even years. Their pathetic attempt to flee was an exercise in futility. Sir Meredith and the others would have caught them sooner had they not seized the opportunity to instil some fear into these sheep-herding recalcitrants. When the chastened men of the Green Reaching eventually came slinking over to Krazka's side like a scolded dog, perhaps *then* the one-eyed barbarian 'King' would give his knight the recognition he deserved.

Yorn and Sir Meredith halted a short distance from each other. The turncoat raised his shield and gestured beyond Sir Meredith with his broadsword. 'I want to speak to Rayne.'

'A traitor doesn't make demands of his superiors.'

'I'm no traitor.'

Sir Meredith drew his sabre then. He stared at the big warrior, with his filthy beard and unkempt hair and hide armour, and his lip curled in contempt. Yorn was the quintessential Highlander, ignorant and uneducated – and yet somehow he had commanded more respect than Meredith himself. It made no sense. In fact, it bloody infuriated him.

'You're an absconder and a turncoat,' he said angrily. 'I despise you like I despise the rest of my countrymen. You are a *barbarian*.'

Yorn didn't react to the insult. 'I want to speak to Rayne,' he said again.

'Why?' Meredith spat. 'You think you can win his heart? With *what*, pray tell? Some appeal to brotherhood forged in whatever shithole spawned your ill-deserved reputation?'

'You ain't got a clue about Red Valley.'

Sir Meredith shrugged, causing his armour to clank. 'I should think it involves a war over empty land or ugly women. No doubt you triumphed over an opposing horde of feckless savages that could barely hold a sword between them. But they bellowed and waved their cocks like apes, oh yes, and consequently they were regarded as doughty warriors, and *you* were celebrated as if you'd stormed the walls of the Garden City itself. Pah!'

There was no anger in Yorn's voice, only an earnest curiosity that filled Sir Meredith with rage. 'Why're you so filled with poison, iron man? What happened to you?'

What happened to me? I believed in our legends, once. I believed in our people. But I learned that both are a lie.

'Defend yourself, savage,' he spat. 'Best me, and you shall be given leave to speak with Rayne. You have my word.'

'Your word?' Yorn repeated slowly.

'My word as a knight.'

Yorn studied him for a moment. Then he nodded and his face set in a grim mask. He raised his sword, and it glittered crimson in the light of the dying sun.

Sir Meredith smiled and lowered his visor.

Yllandris stumbled through the forest, her heart pounding so hard she thought it might burst. Stinging branches whipped her face, thick roots threatened to trip her and send her sprawling. She struggled to see through blurry eyes. Her face felt like it was on fire.

It hurts so much.

She looked around desperately, trying to count the children, but it was a difficult task. In the twilight gloom the Greenwild was an untamed, eldritch maze of immense trees that cast colossal shadows. 'Stay close to me,' she cried.

She led the children deeper into the great forest. Night stole the last of the light, and an owl hooted from somewhere high in the forest canopy above. The rustling of leaves and branches and the cries of nocturnal creatures awakening formed an eerie cacophony that helped disguise the patter of small feet stamping across the forest floor. Yllandris could hear whimpers of pain, and when she glanced back she saw the younger children being dragged along or carried by the older ones. Corinn gripped Milo with one arm and a snivelling girl with the other, pulling them behind her, her brow furrowed in concentration despite her obvious exhaustion.

Progress was agonizingly slow. Every so often they had to stop and help up an orphan whose small legs had simply given up. Each delay cost them time, but Yllandris refused to leave anyone behind. The sack over her shoulder felt as though it weighed more with every passing minute. She saw their faces in her mind's eye again.

Jinna. Roddy. Zak.

The small bones nestling inside that bag compelled her onward, forced her to endure despite the pain and the fever. She wouldn't abandon these children. She wouldn't fail them like she'd failed their friends.

'Are we there yet?' pleaded a small voice. It was Tiny Tom. His little chest was heaving with the strain of keeping up with the group.

'Almost,' she whispered. It was a hopeless lie. She had no idea where 'there' was. Perhaps they could find somewhere to hide and lose their pursuers; perhaps Yorn had somehow killed them all. She knew those were a child's hopes. But even a child's hopes were better than no hope at all.

All of a sudden the trees parted and a great clearing opened before them. Moonlight filtered down through the leaves above, casting a silver glow onto a large pool of water in the centre. A small stream fed the pool from the north side of the clearing, disappearing again to the south. Aside from the sound of trickling water and the happy noises the children made as they joined her in the clearing, it was perfectly silent. Tranquillity settled over them like a blanket, a dreamlike serenity that had no right to exist in this world of noise and suffering and senseless violence.

Yllandris stared around in wonder. Then she waved the children into the clearing. 'We will rest here a moment,' she called. 'Make sure you drink plenty. Corinn, would you help me refill our skins?'

The girl nodded. Yllandris placed the sack on the ground, and together the two women knelt down. The water in the pool was pure and unspoiled and tasted delicious. Yllandris splashed some onto her face, trying to soothe her burning wound. She caught sight of her reflection and recoiled in horror.

'It's not so bad,' Corinn said gently. She looked around, her eyes wide in wonder. 'I've heard stories about places like this in the Greenwild. They're called Nexus Glades. My mother told me about them.'

'Nexus Glades?'

'The spirits of the four elements are said to dwell here. Mother said the Pattern was weak in these places, whatever that means. Sometimes you can see the future in the water, or hear the ghosts of the dead in the rustle of the trees.'

Yllandris glanced down again but saw only her battered face staring back at her from the pool. 'I've seen enough of the dead already,' she said with a shiver. 'How did your mother come by such knowledge?'

Corinn shrugged and looked uncomfortable at the question, and Yllandris decided not to press the girl further. They sat in silence, watching the children taking refreshment at the edge of the pool. A few dipped tentative toes into the water. Tiny Tom reached in and cupped his hands, then glanced mischievously at Milo and flicked water at his friend's face. Milo shrieked in delight and splashed water back at him, and soon others were rushing to join the fun.

313

Yllandris met Corinn's eyes, and for the first time in many weeks something like a smile formed on her lips, though it made her face hurt even worse. She pointed at the sack resting on the ground. 'I would like to bury them here. It seems like the right spot. Do you think... could you...'

Corinn nodded. 'I'll help you,' she said.

'Thank you.'

Yllandris rose. She was bending over to retrieve the sack, preparing to move it somewhere away from the children's prying eyes and begin the unpleasant task of digging three small graves, when she spotted movement to the north. With mounting horror, she watched dark shadows melting out of the treeline. The children noticed the newcomers too, and ceased their play. Only one sound shattered the silence that followed.

Clank. Clank. Clank.

Something small and dark sailed across the clearing; it hit the ground with a thud just in front her. She looked down.

Yorn's bearded face stared up at her with dead eyes, his beard wet with blood.

'No,' she whispered. 'No...' Her legs began to shake. She wanted to run. They would kill her; the iron man would murder her like he murdered Yorn, cut off her head and—

'Daughter. Be strong.'

Her mother's voice seemed to float out of the very air, soothing her with those familiar words, words she had heard over and over again in her dreams.

'Be strong.'

'Take the children,' she whispered to Corinn. 'Follow the stream south. Don't stop for anything.'

Corinn hesitated, but a moment later, her voice shaking only a little, she ordered the foundlings to follow her. Tiny Tom and Milo loitered, gazing up at Yllandris with big eyes, but she shooed them away. She watched them depart the clearing and then, finally, she turned to face the approaching men.

'You're only delaying the inevitable.' Sir Meredith clanked forward and gestured at Yorn's severed head with the bloody edge of his sabre. 'He lasted longer than I anticipated, but in the end a true knight will always triumph over a barbarian. Your magic will not avail you now, girl.'

Yllandris saw that Red Rayne was with the iron man. He too wore a ring of demonsteel, the strange metal that made him immune to her magic. Her courage began to waver.

'Make me proud.'

Her mother's voice came to her again, chasing away her doubts, stilling the trembling that had threatened to overwhelm her. She evoked all her power and hurled it at the armed warriors, hoping beyond hope that it might work, that it would reduce them to ash—

Nothing. Her magic died as soon as it left her, absorbed by the absyssium around the fingers of the Kingsmen.

Sir Meredith glanced down at his gauntleted hand. 'Any warmer and that may have actually hurt. Impressive. Ryder will enjoy breaking your spirit, as befits his squalid nature.'

Yllandris stared down at her hands. Her magic had failed, as she knew it would. She remembered the massacre outside Heartstone, the awful fate of the sorceresses from the Black Reaching. *I'm going to die*, she thought dully.

But then the spirits stirred.

A gust of wind rustled her hair. The pool rippled slightly. The ground seemed to tremble beneath her. Like a geyser erupting from the earth, magic surged to fill her. Immense magic, greater than any she had ever known, more potent even than the binding spell the King's circle had worked on the Shaman. She wrestled with the sudden eruption of power, but it was uncontrollable, a raging torrent that threatened to tear her apart.

With a great scream, she let it burst free. It flowed from her, refusing to relent, a river gaining ever more momentum. A second passed and nothing happened. Another second passed, and a third, and then Sir Meredith shrieked. Rayne's scimitar clattered to the ground and he stared dumbly at his ruined hand, blood dripping from the stub where his ring finger had been a moment before.

An instant later her spell took effect. A raging column of fire exploded from her hands. The two Kingsmen were fast enough to dive out of the way, but the warriors behind them weren't so quick. The fire engulfed them and they died screaming.

Yllandris reached for more magic. It seemed as if the spirits would oblige, and she felt the power fill her once more – but just then there was a sharp pain in her side.

She looked down.

An arrow jutted from her waist. The twang of a bowstring sounded again, and this time something hit her in the throat. She reached up slowly to feel the wooden shaft lodged in her neck.

Time seemed to slow to a crawl. The world began to blur. The iron man stalked towards her, though she was on her knees now and couldn't see his face. It was too much of an effort to lift her head, so she focused on the dancing flames reflected on his breastplate. They reminded her of her parents' hearth, of the days long gone when she would sit beside the fire while they talked and dream of all the things she would do when she was a woman grown.

Her head felt so heavy. As it began to droop, her failing eyes settled on the sack on the ground in front of her. There'd been something she was going to do with that sack, she thought dully. She couldn't remember what it was now. Voices drifted to her, from somewhere far away...

'*I think she's ready.*'

'*It's okay, we're not angry. We forgive you.*'

'*You can come with us now. There's nothing to be afraid of. We're taking you to the better place.*'

Sir Meredith washed the blood from his sabre and stared down at his reflection in the water. He flinched at the face that gazed back at him. At the receding hairline and weak chin, at the ugly lines that marred his once handsome face. When had he aged so damned gracelessly?

He slammed his blade into its scabbard in cold fury, tore the damaged gauntlet from his hand and tossed it away. He examined his wounded hand by the orange glow of the fire spreading through the trees behind him. His finger was half-severed, white bone poking through where the demonsteel ring had shattered.

'Bitch,' he swore bitterly. 'Whore!' He knew he sounded like a barbarian, and his lack of erudition in the heat of his rage only made him angrier.

Rayne stumbled over, cradling his own wounded hand. 'The fire's spreading. If we don't move fast, we might not make it out. Shit, what the hell happened?'

Sir Meredith roared in frustration. He gave Yorn's head a vicious kick, sending it soaring into the pool with a splash. 'Where's that dog-faced bastard Ryder?' he bellowed.

'Here,' the tracker said, slinking out of the shadows. He flashed a yellow smile. 'Looks like I just saved your knightly arse. That sorceress would have turned you both to ash if I hadn't shot her.'

Sir Meredith stared at the smouldering remains of the three warriors they had brought with them from Heartstone. 'Our noble quest is a failure,' he said bitterly.

Ryder rolled his narrows shoulders and ran a callused thumb down his bowstring. 'You and Rayne head back to Heartstone. Get some healing. I'll finish the job.'

Meredith glanced at his mangled hand again and had to swallow a howl of anguish at the terrible sight. If he could find a sorceress in time, perhaps she could still save the finger. 'This forest will soon be a raging inferno,' he told Ryder. 'Your bravado will get you killed.'

The wiry tracker shrugged. 'I know the Greenwild better than anyone. Plus I got some friends nearby that might be willing to lend a hand. I might need to double back a-ways, but I'll catch 'em. Don't you worry, iron man.'

After a moment's thought Sir Meredith nodded. The loss of the handful of nameless warriors smouldering on the forest floor could be a written off as a small mishap, but if this mission ended up costing him his sword hand... why, *that* would be a bloody debacle.

Twenty-one Years Ago

'KING JAGAR IS waiting.'
The warrior's voice was muffled beneath the ceremonial helm covering his face. Brodar Kayne adjusted his cloak and tried not to let his nerves show as he followed the Kingsman, their footsteps echoing down the entrance hall. The floor was solid stone, the walls darkwood felled from the forests of the Black Reaching to the north. The Great Lodge was said to be the oldest building in town, built long before the coming of the Shaman to the High Fangs.

The weapons and shields of celebrated heroes and Wardens lined the walls, and Kayne allowed himself to wonder if his own blade might one day hang there in recognition of his service. Maybe that was why the King had summoned him to Heartstone: to congratulate him on ten years' service and honour him with a spot in this hall of heroes.

Then again, maybe his hopes were wide of the mark. He thought of his wife and son back at Eastmeet. Kayne had tried to reassure Mhaira that there was nothing to worry about. Her grey eyes seemed to suggest he was talking a heap of horseshit, and he couldn't rightly blame her for that.

He ought to be settling into his new life right about now. He didn't have the first clue about shepherding, barely knew one end of a sheep from the other, but Mhaira was looking forward to teaching him and just hearing the enthusiasm in her voice had been enough for him to go along with her plans. He reckoned he owed her that much, after all the years she'd waited for him, never knowing when or even if he might be coming home. Truth be told, though he sorely missed his brothers at the Keep, he was enjoying waking up each day beside her. And he relished spending time with Magnar. His son was growing up fast.

The Kingsman stopped before a pair of mighty oak doors. 'Go in,' he rumbled. Kayne took a deep breath and entered the throne room.

Jagar the Wise was sitting in his throne at the head of the long table that dominated the chamber. Kayne met the King's gaze and then almost faltered when he saw the other sets of eyes turning to stare at him. No fewer than seven chieftains of the High Fangs, a gathering of the most powerful men in the realm.

A few chieftains Kayne recognized from their visits to Watcher's Keep over the years. Mehmon of the North Reaching had been at the citadel the winter just gone. Galma Forkbeard was a frequent guest; the Lake Reaching and the East Reaching were neighbours, meaning Galma had a special interest in the fortunes of the Wardens. The chieftain of the East Reaching, Darnold Grint, had recently fallen ill and was not present at the table. Orgrim Foehammer had travelled to Eastmeet at his request. Rumour was that the High Commander was being groomed as Grint's replacement. Kayne wondered if he in turn was being lined up to replace Orgrim as High Commander. Was that what this summons was about?

He tried not to feel intimidated by the collective scrutiny as he marched down the side of the table and knelt before the King of the High Fangs.

'You may rise.'

The King looked much the same as the first time Kayne had laid eyes on him. Jagar's hair and beard had turned to grey, but his eyes were bright and he remained an impressively robust figure. 'I've heard many tales of your bravery, Warden,' the King said.

'Ex-Warden now,' Kayne replied diffidently. 'I served my time at the Keep. I'll always be grateful for the chance you gave me.'

Jagar nodded. 'I understand you killed Skarn and his gang. Alone, or so the stories go. They were torching a mead-maker's home when you fell upon them.'

Kayne remembered the burning house, the crumpled bodies on the floor. 'I did what needed to be done,' he said, trying not to let the guilt show on his face.

'The young man you pulled from the fire. Jerek, I believe. You are aware he volunteered for the Forsaken last autumn? Mehmon here took the boy's oath.'

'Aye?' Kayne replied, mildly surprised. The Forsaken was an elite group of hunters and rangers that kept the frontier of the North Reaching free of the strollers and ice ghouls that sometimes crossed from the frozen wasteland beyond. It was a dangerous and lonely path for any man to choose, let alone one so young.

Mehmon raised a thick hand. The chieftain of the North Reaching was said to be a formidable warrior, and it was an oft-repeated tale that he'd once killed a troll on the banks of the Blackwater – though others swore the 'troll' was actually a giant born with some kind of disease. Kayne had never met a troll in all his years in the Borderland. They were all but extinct now, though according to folklore they had been a common enough threat in the age before the fall of the gods.

The King nodded at Mehmon, granting him permission to speak. The big chieftain cleared his throat noisily. 'Jerek's patrol was ambushed by Blackwater pirates a few months back. The cowards attacked under the cover of darkness. The patrol was surrounded and outnumbered.'

Kayne's heart sank. 'Sorry to hear it. After what happened to him and his family I figure the boy deserved a better end than that.'

He didn't add that it was he who was responsible for leading Skarn's gang to Jerek's home. Somehow the passing trader who discovered the two of them lying on the road had got it into his head that the outlaws were burning the house down for their own amusement when Kayne showed up to stop them. By the time Kayne had recovered from his wounds well enough to correct him, the tale had spread through Watcher's Keep. He could've set them straight. He could've, but he hadn't.

Mehmon listened to Kayne's words with a puzzled expression. Then he grinned. 'Ah, but you never let me finish. The Blackwater turned crimson with the blood of pirate and patrolman alike. When it was over, one man walked away from the carnage. Just one man.'

'Jerek?'

'He struck me as an odd sort from the off. It weren't just the scars on his face, there was this queer look in his eye too. Anyways, he walks right back to Frosthold that same morning, painted head to toe in gore, looking more like a demon than a man. Hardly said a word about what happened, other than what I dug out of him. I sent another patrol to investigate, to see if his story held up. It did.'

Kayne listened in growing amazement. Jerek was only nineteen winters of age, hugely inexperienced when measured against the demanding standards the Forsaken required; the last man he might expect to survive that kind of tragedy.

King Jagar chuckled and the hall went silent. 'You and this Jerek have something in common, Brodar Kayne,' he said. 'You walk in the shadow of death, and yet somehow you always survive.'

Kayne winced at the King's words. He wasn't so sure he wanted to live in that particular shadow any more. He wanted to step into the light, now. Into Mhaira's light. Into Magnar's light.

The King clapped his hands together. 'On to business! It was not I that summoned you to this council.'

Kayne's brow furrowed in puzzlement. 'You didn't?'

'No. I did,' said a powerful voice Kayne had heard once before, many years ago.

The gathered chieftains lowered their heads as the Shaman emerged from the shadows at the far corner of the chamber.

The Magelord was just as Kayne remembered, a bronze-skinned, hulking slab of chiselled muscle wearing a pair of tattered brown trousers, wild hair falling around a blunt face. The glacial stare that fixed on him had seen countless kings come and go.

'The West Reaching has broken the Treaty,' the Shaman growled. 'Targus Bloodfist plans for war.' The Magelord moved to stand before Kayne, who, though he was half a head taller, felt small in the face of the immortal godkiller. As good as Kayne was with a sword, he knew the Shaman could break him in half if he chose. 'You kill without fear. Without mercy.'

'Ain't no use for either when it comes to fighting demons,' Kayne replied.

'Or men,' the Shaman replied. 'For years I have watched you. I was at your Initiation. I was there at your joining. I needed to be certain you were the one. That you were true.'

'I hope I am. True, that is,' Kayne stammered, caught off balance by the Shaman's revelations.

The Shaman crossed his mighty arms. 'I made a promise when I came to this land. A promise to keep its people safe. Safe but also strong, for life without struggle is death by inertia. Complacency breeds weakness – and weakness cannot be borne! Yet sometimes struggle must be averted for the greater good. I have been searching for a proxy.'

'A... a proxy?' Kayne didn't know what the hell a 'proxy' was, but it sounded like some kind of disease.

'A mortal to enact my will. A weapon to slay those that threaten the balance. You, Brodar Kayne, will be my *champion*.'

'Your champion?' Kayne echoed, dumbstruck. 'But... I got a family back at Eastmeet. I was gonna be a shepherd...'

The Shaman's piercing gaze seemed to see into the depths of his soul. 'A sword is not meant to steer sheep. A sword has but one purpose. To kill.'

'A home has been prepared for your family near Beregund,' King Jagar stated. 'You need never worry about providing for them again.'

Have I got a choice? Kayne wanted to ask – but he knew that he did not. And, if he was being honest, herding sheep wasn't the kind of future he'd dreamed about. No one remembered the names of shepherds. He thought again of the famous Highlanders and their arms hanging from the walls of the Great Lodge. Their legacies assured, destined to endure when all else had turned to dust and been forgotten.

Despite everything, he felt a flicker of excitement. 'I... I'm honoured. I'll do my best to serve.'

The King nodded and rose from his throne. 'I'll have a messenger dispatched to your wife.'

'A messenger?' Kayne repeated. Did that mean what he thought it meant? He suddenly felt an intense need to be with Mhaira and his son.

'Yes. It is important you begin preparations immediately. We march for the West Reaching without delay. Now, Galma has someone he would like you to meet.'

The chieftain of the Lake Reaching stroked his outlandish beard. 'One of my lieutenants. He's young and a bit rough around the edges, but fuck me if he isn't some kind of tactical genius all the same. His name's Krazka. We put our heads together and the Bloodfist won't know what hit him.'

'I'm all ears,' Kayne said dully. In truth he wasn't paying a great deal of attention to Galma Forkbeard. He was imagining the look on Mhaira's face when she received the message. Would she be excited for him? Proud? Or would she be disappointed? The one thing he'd sworn he would never do was disappoint her. Not after all she'd sacrificed for him.

As if he could read Kayne's thoughts, the Shaman growled

and fixed him with an expression that froze his blood. 'You answer only to me now, Brodar Kayne. You are my tool. My weapon. You are the *Sword of the North*.'

Mal-Torrad

'I THINK IT's healing.'

Jerek spat and slapped Brick's hand away. 'Ain't much left to heal after you butchered my leg. Should've just let the greenskin bite it off, likely would've made a cleaner job of it.'

Brick shrugged and turned away, and Kayne thought he saw the ghost of a smile on the boy's face. It was good to see the lad's spirits returning. He'd said little in the weeks that had passed since their 'escape' from the Bandit King's camp. With Grunt still sore over the loss of his mysterious egg and Jerek half-delirious from his leg wound, the three of them had made for grim company on the long ride north and west up through the Purple Hills.

'Reckon you can walk, Wolf?' Kayne asked. Jerek scowled down at his leg, which was wrapped in a thick padding. They'd removed the arrowhead and cauterized the wound and it looked like it was on the way to mending. The Wolf took a step and grimaced.

'Yeah.'

Kayne stared doubtfully at the rocky wilderness that rose slowly ahead of them. The naked hills were dark and jagged and entirely unwelcoming. The old trade route was just about visible despite centuries of neglect, cutting through the broken landscape to run the length of Mal-Torrad for a couple of hundred miles before the terrain rose even higher and the outskirts of the Greenwild appeared, marking the southern border of the vast country he called home. It was a hard and dangerous slog to get to that point.

'We could cobble together a litter, carry you some of the way. You know how dicey it gets further on.'

'You deaf as well as blind, Kayne? I said I can walk! Next thing I know you'll be hiding in the bushes waiting to wipe my arse for me.'

'Suit yourself, Wolf.'

They untied the packs from their mounts and then with heavy hearts they shooed the animals away, sending them galloping back south to the Purple Hills. It was a shame to part with the horses, but they would only slow them down once the going got tough and besides, there was little for the animals to graze on in the ruins.

Kayne's pack was filled to bursting with provisions; the Seer had provided them with food to last for weeks. Somehow she'd even arranged to have their weapons returned to them. The memory of the southern woman still made his skin crawl. He'd known some villains in his time, but the depth of Shara's evil had shocked him to the bone.

Slowly they made their way up the broken road. Every thousand yards or so it was punctuated by standing stones carved with runes in the language of the underfolk. The markers were signposts, detailing the hidden paths that ran beneath the hills and connected the ruins of the great underground cities far below the earth. Once upon a time Mal-Torrad had been the greatest kingdom in the north, but it was said to be home only to dark things now. The companions avoided the caves gaping in the hillside, steering well clear of the tunnels that led down to the ruins. As far as Kayne was concerned, whatever lurked among the bones of that shattered kingdom was best left undisturbed.

'You never told me what you and the Seer talked about back at the lake,' Brick said.

'You sure you want to know?' Kayne asked.

'Uh-huh.'

'A lot of stuff that ain't worth repeating. And some kind of prophecy about three kings.' He frowned, remembering the woman's words. The Bandit King was no mystery, and he reckoned he had a fair idea who the Butcher might be. He was damned sure he would never kneel before that piece of shit, not if his life depended on it.

Which left only the Broken King. The King he would send to his death. A shiver ran down his spine. It couldn't be him.

It couldn't be.

'You really think she could read the future?' Brick said, interrupting those dark thoughts.

Kayne glanced back at Jerek. The Wolf was limping heavily, sweat pouring from his bald brow despite the bitter chill in the air. 'I'm not sure anyone can say with certainty what the future holds. I figure if Shara had that kind of power she'd be ruling the world, not slumming it with an army of bandits.'

Brick bobbed his head in agreement. His red hair reached down to his shoulders now, and there was a hardness in his eyes that hadn't been there before. The boy was growing up fast. 'You don't mind that I'm travelling with you?' he asked cautiously. 'I've got nowhere else to go.'

Kayne gave the youngster a companionable pat on the shoulder. 'You're a free man, Brick. You can go where you please. I'm glad of the company.'

'Shit.' Behind them Jerek stumbled. Kayne was about to go and help his friend but Grunt got there before him, hauling the Wolf to his feet and putting a muscular green arm on his shoulder to steady him. The mute had kicked up a hell of a fuss when he'd found out he needed to leave his egg back at the camp, and for a moment Kayne had been worried the big green warrior would refuse to leave without it, placing them all in grave danger. Fortunately he'd calmed down eventually and fled along with the rest of them. He'd more or less returned to his old self since that morning, though he seemed a tad more glum these days.

'I thought Jerek and Grunt didn't get along,' Brick observed as they neared the next standing stone. This one had a circle carved below the harsh runes of the underfolk language. Though Kayne couldn't understand the words, he'd learned what the circle meant during his last trek through Mal-Torrad. The tunnel in the nearby hill led to some kind of auditorium – a vast open circle that must have served as a public meeting area.

'Takes the Wolf a while to warm to new faces,' Kayne answered. 'But when he decides you're all right, you're all right.'

'Does he have a wife? Any children?'

'Not as far as I can tell. He don't talk about himself much. Don't think he ever married. If he's got a son he don't mention him.'

'You don't talk about your son much, either.'

Kayne was silent a moment. 'Magnar and me, we had our differences. I thought... I thought he did something I couldn't forgive. But it turns out I might've been wrong.'

'About the thing he did? Or about forgiving him?'

'Both.'

Brick's green eyes were so earnest Kayne couldn't help but feel touched. 'He's your son. You should patch things up with him while you still can.'

Kayne rubbed at his bristled chin and stared into the distance. 'Aye, you're right. It's about time I— Hang on, who the hell's *that*?'

There was someone watching them from a ridge a little further ahead. Whoever it was, they were garbed head to toe in black and didn't look much like any bandit Kayne had ever seen. The mysterious figure's arm seemed to twitch, and then something skipped across the stone just in front of Kayne before coming to a halt near his boots. He reached down to pick it up. It was a dart, the point sharp enough to pierce steel.

'Get down!' he roared to the others, but his mysterious attacker had already disappeared over the ridge.

Brick had an arrow nocked and ready and was scanning the

hills around them. 'I think that was just a warning,' he said quietly. 'Whoever they are, they just mean to scare us.'

Jerek and Grunt joined them. The Wolf scowled at the dart and then spat in disgust. 'Coward's weapon, that. The tip's poisoned.'

Kayne placed the dart carefully back on the ground. 'Someone doesn't want us going any further. What d'you reckon, Wolf?'

'I reckon they can go fuck themselves,' Jerek growled.

'That's what I thought. We'd best stick close together. Brick, keep a lookout. If you spot movement, fire first and ask questions later.'

The youngster nodded and spat just like Jerek had. It seemed the boy was picking up some bad habits.

When they reached the next standing stone they stopped for a break. Despite a few obligatory grumbles Jerek immediately sat down and stretched out his leg while Kayne and Grunt examined the monument.

Kayne traced a finger down the seven-pointed star carved onto the rock. 'I wonder what happened to the underfolk?' he mused. 'Seems mighty odd for an entire people to just up and vanish.'

Grunt shook his head and ran a thick finger across his throat.

'They didn't vanish,' Brick translated as he checked the horizon again. 'They're all dead.'

'Aye, I figured that much. What made 'em all dead, is what I'm wondering.'

Grunt shrugged and then wandered off to take a piss. Kayne moved to inspect Jerek's wound, but behind him Brick suddenly hissed and he turned to see the black-garbed figure watching them from a rise less than thirty yards distant – well within bowshot range. Brick lined up his arrow, but with incredible agility the shadowy watcher turned and cartwheeled away to disappear behind a boulder, leaving them staring open-mouthed at thin air.

'Did... did you *see* that?' Brick asked in astonishment. 'Who is he?'

'I'm guessing we'll find out soon enough,' Kayne replied grimly.

*

As it turned out it was another hour before they encountered their stealthy observer again, and it didn't happen in the manner Kayne might've been expecting. The sounds of fighting reached Grunt's oversized ears and he brought a meaty fist down onto his palm to indicate trouble. Then he raised a finger to his lips and beckoned them to follow him. He clambered up a narrow path and led Kayne and Brick around an outcrop of jagged stone beyond which a fierce battle raged. Jerek limped along, unable to keep up.

The black-clad stranger who had been stalking them earlier was surrounded by a half-dozen men, bandits by the looks of it, bristling with swords and clubs and vicious daggers. The stranger at the centre of the melee appeared to be unarmed – but that didn't seem to hinder him, judging by the man already crumpled on the ground and another cradling a broken arm.

As the companions looked on, the stranger caught a sword thrust between his palms and wrenched the weapon away from his assailant, then punched out with an open palm, hitting him in the throat and dropping him in a heap. The stranger spun as another bandit stabbed, caught his wrist and used the man's own momentum to hurl him over his shoulder. One bandit managed to creep up behind and get in a good swing. His cudgel slammed into the side of his target, sending the mysterious black-clad figure staggering back. The stranger looked up then and noticed Kayne and the others, and though he wore a veil over much of his face Kayne could see that the person behind the veil was... unmistakably female.

'I could use a hand,' she called out in a voice that was strangely accented and slightly desperate.

Grunt growled softly and drew his swords. Brick looked at Kayne questioningly.

The old warrior sighed. This was none of their business: that was the truth of the matter. But he'd always had a weakness for women and children.

'I'm getting soft,' he muttered, giving Brick the nod and reaching up to draw his greatsword. The youngster's arrow took a bandit in the back as Grunt charged down the slope. Soon the mute's twin longswords were cutting down bandits from all angles, a display of swordsmanship Kayne would never have guessed the big greenskin capable of when first they'd met. The two remaining bandits quickly realized the tables had turned and made a break for it, fleeing for the hills before Kayne's creaking knees could carry him to the melee and leaving him looking like a bit of an idiot as his charge came to a staggering halt. He turned to the enigmatic woman in black.

'You hurt?' he asked evenly.

'Just some bruising,' she answered in her strange accent. Her dark eyes watched them warily. Though she relaxed her stance a little she still looked as if she could spring into action at a moment's notice. 'I must apologise for the incident with the dart. I thought you were with them. They were looking for someone.'

'Aye,' Kayne replied. 'Reckon I have a fair idea who.' He'd taken a good look at their faces during the fighting and thought he remembered one of the men from Fivebellies' gang. The Bandit King must have sent his cousin to search for them, just as Shara had warned.

A string of curses turned the air blue as Jerek limped down towards them, even more bad-tempered than usual at having missed the fighting. The Wolf didn't seem the least bit thrilled at encountering yet another wanderer on the road. 'Who are you?' he rasped. 'Show your face.'

'Very well.' The woman reached up with a gloved hand and removed her veil, revealing a pert nose and striking features that were very different from any other woman Kayne had ever met. 'I am Jana Shah Shan,' she said, pulling off her gloves and extending a bronze-skinned hand towards the Wolf in a gesture of greeting.

'Oh, for fuck's sake.'

Jana raised an eyebrow so thin it looked like it had been drawn in ink. 'Excuse me?'

Kayne cleared his throat noisily. 'Don't mind him. You don't look like you're from around these parts.'

'I hail from the Jade Isles.'

'You're far from home.'

'Further than you can imagine. I long to return to my betrothed, but I have a duty and I am sworn to see it done.'

'Duty, eh? I know or thing or two about that. Jana Shah Shan, you say? That's an odd name. No offence meant.'

'None taken. Shah is my father's clan name. Shan is my mother's. It is very important in my culture to know whence one came. Whence... Is that word correct? Do you understand me?'

Kayne's brow creased in confusion. 'Er... Aye, perfectly. What you doing in these parts, if you don't mind me asking?'

Jana's fist clenched in anger. 'I was sent by the Wizard-Emperor. An item of great value was stolen from the imperial treasury. A key capable of activating a terrible being imprisoned somewhere in these ruins.'

'Terrible being? You talking about some kind of demon?'

'Worse than that. A gholam.'

'A what?'

'It is a fell weapon of the gods,' Jana explained. 'Created during the Age of Strife by the Congregation to annihilate the armies of the Alliance. If the gholam were ever activated, there is no telling what devastation it might unleash.'

Grunt made a low moaning noise to get their attention. He turned to Brick and made a series of hand gestures.

'He knows this... gholam,' Brick translated. 'The gholam devastated the city of Azrath. Grunt barely escaped there with his life.'

'You must be mistaken,' Jana Shah Shan replied softly. 'The city-state of Azrath was destroyed six hundred years ago.'

'I think a wizard worked some kind of spell on him,' Kayne explained. 'I got a feeling he's older than he looks.'

Grunt nodded at that. He made another hand signal to Brick.

'The red wizard kidnapped him and put him to sleep for a long time. But he remembers the gholam. He still has nightmares about it.'

Kayne stared at the ruins and felt a shiver pass through him. He turned back to Jana. 'What makes you believe the gholam can be found here? Or this thief, for that matter?'

'The gholam was disabled and transported to Mal-Torrad for safekeeping after the Godswar,' Jana explained. 'The underfolk sealed it within a great prison in the deepest part of their kingdom. The key was kept in the imperial treasury, which was said to be unbreachable. Yet the thief managed to break in and steal the key. The thief has... peculiar appetites. It is not so hard to follow the trail of desiccated corpses they leave behind. Desiccated... is that a word?'

'Yeah. I think so.'

'The last corpse I found belonged to a bandit. I discovered it some distance to the south. The thief is heading north, towards the site where the gholam is buried.'

'Ain't no one guarding it now. The underfolk are long gone. They disappeared, just like the Yahan.' Kayne grimaced, remembering the lake of tar back at Asander's camp.

Jana shook her head. 'The fate of the underfolk is no mystery. The death of the gods broke the land and revealed vast treasures buried beneath Mal-Torrad. The seven great cities went to war over these riches. None survived. Now Mal-Torrad is a dead place – the endless halls haunted by the ghosts of the fallen.'

Brick was staring at Jana with a combination of curiosity and admiration. 'How did you learn to fight like that? I've never seen anyone take on a dozen men unarmed.'

Jana Shah Shan smiled, revealing a mouthful of white teeth. 'Not unarmed. I am a master of Unity, the sacred art taught to all the Emperor's agents. My body is a weapon, honed through years of practice and a deep understanding of the unseen energies which surround us all.'

'Would you show me?' Brick asked excitedly. He sounded like a boy once more, moved to childish enthusiasm at the discovery of another mystery to unravel. Kayne couldn't help but grin.

'Even the basics of Unity require many months of study. But if we are heading in the same direction, I could teach you a trick or two.'

'*And here it is*,' Jerek cut in, causing everyone to stare at him. 'Go on, Kayne,' he said bitterly. 'Just say it.'

'Say what?'

'Ask her to come with us.' The Wolf reached up and began tugging on his beard, his jaw tightening in anger. 'Thought we had a good thing going, just the four of us,' he said, nodding at Brick and Grunt. 'No one can say I raised a fuss about them coming along. Bit my tongue and got on with it.'

'Hang on, I remember you having a few choice words after—'

The Wolf was in no mood to listen. 'I can put up with a bandit's whelp what tried to murder us,' he ranted. 'Some big green bastard that might be a demon for all we know? Fuck it, he knows how to fight and he's all right as far as it goes, no skin off my nose if he tags along. But this—' He jerked a thumb at the attractive young woman staring at him in bewilderment. 'This is just taking the piss.'

Jerek spat and then limped away, bristling with righteous indignation. '*My body is a weapon*,' he said, voice thick with scorn. In a fit of anger, he turned and punched a nearby boulder. Even Grunt winced at the sound of Jerek's knuckles cracking. The Wolf just glared at them all, daring someone to say something as he tried to pretend he hadn't just busted a couple of fingers hitting a block of solid granite.

Kayne turned to Jana Shah Shan, who seemed perplexed by the whole spectacle. 'Don't take it personally,' he said gently. 'Jerek's always a bit on edge around strangers. You get used to it.'

Legacy of Gods

THE HOODED FIGURE sat in the shadowed corner of the tavern where the light from the globe above failed to penetrate and watched the men enter the common room. They'd been filing in for the best part of a bell now. Every miner who worked the Blight had been ordered to gather at the Black Lord's Re-Spite after the day's work was ended. The crowd's apprehension would soon turn to elation when the Mad Dogs delivered their news. Tomorrow they would all be sailing back to Thelassa – or at least that was what the miners would be told.

Davarus Cole knew better.

Another half-bell passed as he waited. The common room was heaving now, packed wall to wall with sweaty workers covered in filth. Cole received curious glances. A few men tried to speak with him or steal a look under his cowl. He drew back into the shadows and flashed his weapon at them and they quickly left him alone. He replayed Thanates' words in his head over and over again. He had only one chance to get this right.

Finally the door banged open and Corvac sauntered in. The blonde on his arm glared around the tavern with an air of hostility at odds with the tight, provocative clothing she wore. Cole flinched back at the sight of those two. A moment later he drew courage from the anger that flushed through him, remembering the things they had done to him that night outside this very tavern. He felt his anger turn to rage but quickly checked himself when he glanced at the glow-globe hanging from the ceiling.

Several of Corvac's lieutenants joined their leader as he made his way to the bar. All wore swords at their belts. That in itself was not unusual, but Cole knew the truth behind the enigmatic smiles on their faces, the eager glitter in their eyes.

He saw Smiler, and Floater, and Smokes, and others he knew well. Even were he to lower his hood they might not recognize him. He had emerged from Derkin's home a visibly different man after stealing Shank's soul. He was no longer the Ghost they remembered.

The Mad Dogs ordered a small area cleared around the bar and Corvac climbed onto a table to address the tavern. Goldie gazed at him adoringly, as if he were a king lording it over his subjects. Then she handed him a metal tray the bartender passed her, and Corvac drew his sword and clashed the two together, making a small racket. 'Silence!' he barked. 'I wish to speak.'

'Shut up!' Goldie screeched a second later, when the hubbub didn't immediately die down. That seemed to do the trick; the tavern quickly fell silent.

'I've got some good news for you, gentlemen,' Corvac said with an appalling smile. 'As you all know, the Mistress is nothing if not monogamous.'

'Monogamous?' someone shouted from the crowd, sounding amused. 'That's not what I heard! She was having it off with half those Sumnians!'

'Don't you mean magnanimous?' someone else yelled.

Corvac's face flushed red. 'That's what I said! Magnanimous! Clean your ears out, you sons of bitches!'

'He said *magnanimous*!' Goldie shrieked, spittle spraying from her mouth. One of the Mad Dog lieutenants leaned in to whisper urgently up to his captain. After a brief moment in which he visibly struggled with himself, Corvac managed to regain his composure.

'As I was saying... the Mistress is nothing if not *magnanimous*. Yesterday she sent word to the Trinity. I'm here to relay that message to you now. The White Lady has decided your work here is done. As from tomorrow, you are all free.'

'*Free?*' Smiler whispered, in the stunned silence that followed.

'That's what I said. Tomorrow you will all sail back to Thelassa and be granted a pardon from the White Lady. It's better than you lot deserve, but who am I to question the will of the Mistress?'

At Corvac's proclamation the tavern near exploded with cries of joy. Cole watched it all like a hawk, waiting for his moment to act. Everything was playing out exactly as Thanates had said it would.

Corvac gestured to the bar, where the serving wenches were busy filling tankards of ale. 'Since it's your last evening here, we've arranged a proper farewell for you. A reward for all your hard work, you might say. Free drinks for every man!'

'And free snatch for any man that wants it,' Goldie added with great sobriety. That brought even more cheers. Cole decided it was time. He took a deep breath, then rose and pushed his way through the crowd towards the table at the centre.

He spoke loudly and deliberately so that he could be heard above the din. 'I'm sorry, did you just say "reward"? I'd rather bugger a shambler than let my manhood anywhere near this shrew.'

The cheers evaporated almost instantly and the tavern fell silent again. Corvac's mouth dropped open. He looked dumbfounded that someone would dare insult him so brazenly. 'What did you just call my girl?' he whispered.

Cole gave a one-shouldered shrug. 'Nothing she didn't deserve. You're full of shit, Corvac. These men aren't being set free. You're planning to murder them all.'

Smiler flashed a grin that made no sense at all in the circumstances. 'Murder? What are you talking about?'

'The ale in those tankards over there is poisoned. Any man who swallows even a mouthful will quickly find his muscles seizing up. The Mad Dogs were planning to slit your throats while you're helpless.'

'Who are you?' Corvac screamed.

'The White Lady has decided that Newharvest is a failed experiment,' Cole continued, ignoring the question. 'After she learned the truth about the magic mined from the Blight she decided to close this place down. She's going to kill everyone. That includes you, Corvac, once your men have outlived their usefulness.'

There was a thud as Corvac leaped down off the table. The Mad Dog leader's face was twitching wildly now; he was near bursting with anger. 'Who the fuck *are* you?' he roared again.

Cole raised a gloved hand and pulled back his cowl. The man opposite him hesitated only a moment before realization dawned in his hate-filled eyes.

'Ghost,' Corvac whispered, his face filled with utter loathing. 'You son of a bitch.'

Cole's fingers tightened around Magebane's hilt. 'I know you sent Shank to kill me, Corvac. You're a coward. A coward and a bully.'

'I should have finished you myself,' Corvac spat. He sprang at Cole, who was expecting the move and dodged to the side, planting his boot firmly on the Mad Dog's arse and sending him sprawling face down on the floor of the tavern.

'You know something, Corvac?' Cole proclaimed. 'My friend Derkin said you were a decent man when you first arrived in Newharvest. A lot of you Mad Dogs were. But the Blight is poison to the soul. The Black Lord's taint doesn't just twist the land, it affects people too, makes them mean and crazy.'

'Why would the White Lady do this to us? I thought she was a just ruler.' The speaker was Floater, the big Thelassan who'd bought Cole drinks the night Corvac and his men had ambushed him.

Cole turned to the burly miner. 'You remember when you told me you felt more alive here than in Thelassa? The White Lady keeps everyone in the city drugged. Numbs your brains and suppresses thoughts she doesn't want you to have. The whole city is under her spell. She takes your unborn children, too. Performs experiments on them and erases your memories so that you can't remember any of it.'

Floater reached up to his head and pressed his fingers against his temples. 'Sometimes I have this dream. I dream I'm going to have another child, but my wife disappears right before she gives birth. When she comes back, there ain't a child in her belly no longer.'

Other Indebted were beginning to mutter darkly, staring at the floor with confused expressions or pursing their lips as if trying to think, to remember.

Suddenly, Goldie darted at Cole. Before he could react, she raked her nails down his cheek, leaving bloody scratches.

Rage flared inside Cole, a rage so intense he could barely stop himself from charging at the woman and cutting her to pieces. A memory stopped him. A memory of a kitchen knife plunging into Dull Ed again and again while Cole lay there helpless, the glow-globes above shining a sinister light in Shank's crazed eyes. He stared at the artificial light on the ceiling above.

It's the glow-globes, he reminded himself, forcing himself to be calm and remembering what Thanates hold told him. *They're created from magic mined from the Blight. They don't just radiate light. They intensify negative emotions.*

'Nice work, babe,' Corvac hissed. The Mad Dog leader had climbed back to his feet and was brandishing his sword at Cole, but before he could do anything more than squeal in surprise Floater grabbed him around the neck with a meaty fist.

'Does Ghost speak the truth?' Floater demanded. 'You planning to poison us? I'm supposed to go home next month. Home to my family.'

Corvac's answer was to twist around and plunge his sword into Floater's chest. The big miner gasped softly, and then bloody froth spilled down his chin and he collapsed to his knees.

That was the cue for all hell to break loose.

Cole scampered out of the way as Floater's friends charged at

Corvac. Though they were unarmed, thick muscles bulged beneath their dirty vests, and, as they stormed in, other miners began searching around for weapons. One man picked up a chair and broke it over the head of the Mad Dog opposite him.

Corvac's lieutenants responded by drawing their swords. Within seconds the tavern had become a seething cauldron of hatred, furious men bludgeoning, stabbing and choking each other to death while shouted obscenities and screams of visceral rage turned the air blue. The Condemned, Smokes, had lit a flame from somewhere and was now skulking around the edge of the melee, trying to set fire to the tavern.

Shit, Cole thought. This wasn't quite how he and Thanates had wanted things to play out, but it was done now. It was time for the next part of the plan. He made a break for the door and ducked outside. The evening chill caused his breath to mist as he hurried east across town. A few seconds later he ran smack into a patrol of Whitecloaks stumbling in the opposite direction, back towards the tavern.

Do they know about the Trinity's plans? Cole wondered.

Looking at Captain Priam's face, at his vacant stare, Cole doubted the man was even fully cognizant. He and the other guards could hardly stand, like Cole when he'd downed a dozen ales in the Gorgon back in his old drinking days.

'What's going on in there?' Priam slurred. The captain raised a shaking hand and pointed at the Re-Spite.

'The Mad Dogs are attacking the miners,' Cole replied uncertainly. He didn't want to believe Priam's men were in on the plot to murder the workers, but he couldn't be sure which way they would side.

Captain Priam hesitated for a moment. His eyes were glassy and there was something wet dribbling from his ear. 'Come on, men,' he said sluggishly. 'We need to keep the peace...' He staggered off towards the tavern, the rest of the Whitecloaks stumbling after him. Cole watched them go, wondering what the hell was wrong with them.

341

He continued east towards the outskirts of town where the huge metal silos that stored the magical ore loomed like silent sentinels in the night. Once he reached them, he hid behind their dark bulk and waited. He heard the flutter of wings a moment before he saw the tall figure emerge from the night.

Thanates adjusted his tattered black coat and nodded in greeting, then placed his hands on the silo nearest him. 'We don't have much time,' he said sharply. 'The Trinity will soon arrive. I must siphon as much as I can if I am to defeat them. The Unborn have fed well this night.'

'Fed?' Cole echoed, but Thanates ignored him and raised his cloth-bound face towards the night sky.

'Stand back,' the wizard ordered. His hands began to glow. Black fire pulsed down his arms, filling him with a baleful radiance. The silo began to shake.

Cole backed away and cast a glance back at town. Thick black smoke was beginning to rise from the Re-Spite. Miners and Mad Dogs alike were pouring out, both sides sporting bloody wounds, a few barely able to stand. Corvac was remonstrating with Priam and his Whitecloaks, clearly demanding they help subdue the miners. As Cole watched, more Mad Dogs arrived and began setting about the prisoners. Even more ominously, the fire devouring the tavern had begun to spread to the building next door.

Cole was about to turn to Thanates, to tell him he was going back to help the miners, when he noticed three white flickers racing across the Blight towards them. He felt a shiver of dread at the sight. 'The Trinity!' he said urgently. 'The Trinity are coming!'

Thanates turned just as the trio of handmaidens arrived. For a moment the Trinity faced the two men, as calm as a still lake, no sign of exertion visible on their porcelain faces. They hardly even seemed to breathe.

'You dare steal from the Mistress?' said one of the pale women tonelessly. There was something dark streaking her chin and flecking the top of her robes, as if she'd recently been feeding on something, or someone. 'This land and all the magic within are the property of the White Lady. The punishment for theft is death.'

Thanates' jaw clenched. 'I have cheated death for five hundred years. You won't stop me now, creature. Not when I am so close to discovering the truth.'

'The only truth you will discover is the cold certainty of the grave.'

Cole heard the wizard's heartbeat quicken, but from the three handmaidens he could hear nothing. Almost as if they were dead, like the shamblers back at the pit.

An idea occurred to him.

He stepped away from the cover of the silo and raised his arms in the air. 'I command you,' he intoned loudly, 'leave this place!' He waited expectantly as three pairs of colourless orbs turned from Thanates to regard him. Seconds passed and nothing happened. He began to feel a little foolish, so he decided to try again. 'I said turn back, dead things!'

The Trinity looked at each other. Cole frowned and slowly lowered his arms. This wasn't going according to plan. He was about to turn to Thanates and ask the wizard why his powers had stopped working when the nearest of the handmaidens suddenly leaped straight for him. Cole was fast but she was much faster, and as he fumbled with Magebane he knew he was a dead man.

But then there came a flash followed by the sickening stench of rotten meat burning, and the pale woman was on the ground, her perfect alabaster flesh blackened and charred. Despite her terrible wounds, somehow she climbed back to her feet in a strange, jerking motion. Thanates sent another blast of magical energy roaring towards her sisters, but they twirled out of the way with incredible agility and the bolt of energy dissipated harmlessly into the night.

'Go!' the wizard snarled at Cole. 'Help dispose of the Mad

Dogs. The Whitecloaks too, if you must – they are thralls to these creatures and death would be a release for them. If I do not return by morning, look for me at the Horn.' The air seemed to shimmer and there was the sound of something tearing, and then Thanates disappeared… only to reappear a hundred yards away. He disappeared and then reappeared again and again, blinking across the land as the Trinity began to give chase, until both hunters and hunted were swallowed by the Blight.

Cole stared down at his shaking hands. He might be god-touched, but without the wizard's intervention just then he would be dead. He couldn't allow himself to grow overconfident in his own abilities. He'd made that mistake before and it had always come back to bite him in the arse.

He hastened back to Newharvest. The miners and the Mad Dogs were involved in a pitched battle on the streets while around them the town burned. The prisoners were hurling debris at their attackers while Freefolk were running to and fro in the chaos, cowering in fear or trying in vain to put out the flames. Cole glimpsed Derkin and started towards him, but a Mad Dog suddenly leaped into Cole's path and took a swing at him with a bloody sword. Cole ducked under the blade and drove Magebane into the man's sternum. He *felt* the Mad Dog's life force sucked into the dagger as the man died, and a moment later a surge of energy flooded his own body. It was exhilarating. Exhilarating and terrifying and very wrong. He tugged Magebane free and let the corpse fall to the ground in disgust.

'Derkin!' he called. 'Derkin, I'm over here!' The corpse-carver looked up and Cole saw bright tears in his eyes.

'They stabbed my ma,' the little man said. 'The Mad Dogs came and she opened the door to them and they stabbed her.'

Cole felt a hollow sensation in his chest. Derkin didn't deserve this. He was perhaps the kindest and most selfless person Cole had ever met. It didn't matter that he was disfigured and cut up bodies for a living. Derkin was his *friend*.

'Is she still alive?' Cole asked desperately.

'She's hardly breathing. I don't… I don't know how to make the bleeding stop…'

'Come on,' Cole barked. He dashed off in the direction of Derkin's hut, dodging around groups of screaming men and piles of burning rubbish. He found his friend's mother lying in a pool of blood inside the kitchen. She smiled up at him through red teeth as he knelt down and examined the hole in her side. It was deep; the Mad Dog had stabbed her right through the liver.

'She's going to die,' Derkin sobbed.

Cole placed a hand over the wound and closed his eyes. He had no idea what he was doing, but he knew he had to try *something*. Thanates had told him that part of the Reaver's essence lived within him, that it fed on death. If he could take a person's lifeforce into his body then perhaps he might also be able to give it back. He concentrated, willing the vitality of the man he had just killed into the body of Derkin's mother. At first nothing happened and he was afraid he was going to end up looking foolish again, but then he gasped as he felt himself growing suddenly weaker. He glanced at his hands and watched the colour seep from his skin. He became frailer, his body sagging as his breathing became more laboured. It seemed that giving life was harder than taking it. He was feeling faint and close to collapsing when, behind him, Derkin placed a hand on his shoulder and gave it a squeeze. 'You did it,' he said, his voice a wet rasp. 'You saved her.'

'Babykins?' said Derkin's ma, her voice sounding much stronger. She stirred beneath Cole's hand and, as he finally opened his eyes, he saw that her wound had closed.

'Ma!' Derkin cried. He scrambled to her side and threw his arms around his mother, tears rolling down his cheeks.

Cole tried to rise, but almost toppled as the room swayed. 'I need some air,' he gasped. He stumbled out of the house and sank to his knees, listening to the sounds of screams echoing around him, feeling the heat washing off a nearby building wreathed in orange fire. He felt weak; so very weak.

Someone pulled him up, and then Derkin was hugging him tightly. 'You saved her,' he said again. 'I don't know what you did or who you really are, but thank you.'

'You're welcome,' Cole said. Though he felt a vague sense of embarrassment he returned the embrace, not least because he needed his friend's support to stop himself from keeling over.

A familiar voice shattered the moment. 'You two done hugging it out like a couple of bitches? You and me got some unfinished business, Ghost.'

Cole gently disentangled himself from Derkin and turned. Corvac was watching them from across the street, his eyes full of burning hatred. The Mad Dog leader whistled and three of his men abandoned the miner they were busy kicking to death to sidle over and join him. Goldie lurked just behind her man. 'Kill him!' she screeched. 'Kill that tiny dick!'

'It's not tiny!' Cole shouted back, though he immediately regretted wasting his breath as the Mad Dogs fanned out to surround them. Two made a move at the same time, one on either side. Despite his exhaustion, Cole pushed Derkin behind him and somehow managed to dodge a sword thrust. With his riposte he jammed Magebane into the stomach of his attacker – but the effort took most of his remaining strength and while he was recovering the other man's blade scored a nasty cut down his back, causing him to reel away.

'Got you!' the Mad Dog cried. 'Hey, boss, I got him—' His words were cut off in a gurgle as Magebane twisted through the air and found his throat, dropping him like a stone. Cole didn't have time to admire his throw. Corvac and the other Mad Dog were closing on him fast. He could feel the wetness already soaking his clothes from the wound he'd just taken, a deep one that would likely cause him to bleed out in minutes if he wasn't hacked down first.

'You call yourself Ghost?' Corvac sneered. 'Well, guess what. I ain't afraid of no ghost.'

'You tell him, baby! Slice him up good!' Goldie taunted. Cole stumbled back, almost fell. His dagger was a dozen feet away. He would never get to it in time.

Suddenly, Derkin cried out. With a mighty effort, the little man leaped at the Mad Dog to Cole's left and brought Bessie flashing down. It cleaved the man's skull apart in a splatter of brain and bone, cranial fluid spraying all over Goldie, whose taunts turned to shrieks.

Cole seized the moment. With every ounce of strength he had left, he dived towards the body of the last Mad Dog he'd killed and wrenched Magebane free of the man's throat. As his hands closed around the hilt, warmth seemed to envelop him and his vitality surged back. He felt a brief burning sensation in his back, and then somehow it no longer hurt.

Corvac reached him then. Cole blocked the Mad Dog leader's downward swing, and with a sudden surge of energy he pushed back, forcing himself to his feet. The two men moved at the same time, short sword and dagger coming together in a brief but deadly dance. They parted, and there was a moment of utter calm before Corvac stared down at the jewelled hilt quivering in his chest in disbelief. 'How?' he asked, his words bubbling from his mouth. 'I broke you... I made you my bitch...'

Cole shook his head. 'What you did to me doesn't make you strong, Corvac. It makes you the lowest of the low.'

'No one fucks Corvac!' the enraged little man gasped at him, blood dribbling down his narrow chin. 'No... one...'

He never had the chance to finish his sentence. All the anger that had been building up in Cole since that night outside the tavern suddenly burst out of him. He twisted a full circle, intending to roundhouse kick Magebane's hilt and drive it deep into Corvac's heart, but Goldie thrust herself in front of her man and caught the full force of Cole's boot right in the face. Broken teeth and red spittle exploded everywhere as Corvac and Goldie went down in a heap together.

Cole bent to retrieve Magebane, grimacing as the man's fading vitality flooded into him, an obscene sensation. Goldie was unconscious. Cole managed to resist the desire to thrust his dagger through her chest as well. It was more than a desire – it was a *hunger*. The realization scared him. That wasn't who he was. Was it the Blight filling him with such murderous urges, or something else? The divine essence sheltering within him?

Derkin was staring at the gore-streaked cleaver in his hands. 'What now?' he asked, still shocked at his own savagery of moments before.

Cole took a quick look around. The Whitecloaks had sided with the Mad Dogs and together they were getting the better of the miners, though Captain Priam's men moved sluggishly. Cole could see dark matter leaking from the ears of the soldiers, the tortured look in their eyes hinting at some horrible fate that wasn't yet fully explained.

That wasn't the only unpleasant revelation. Throughout the corpse-lined streets of Newharvest, another threat was becoming apparent. Blood-curdling moans joined the shouts of battle and the crackling of burning buildings: the dead were beginning to rise.

Cole turned to Derkin. 'Now we fight dirty.'

It was almost dawn when he finally made his way to the Horn, leaving the scorched town of Newharvest behind him. The survivors had gathered near the platform in the centre to await his return. They hadn't wanted to accompany him into the Blight. Cole glanced back at the army of corpses marching – or more accurately, shambling – silently behind him. All things considered, he couldn't really blame them.

To a man, the Mad Dogs and the Whitecloaks were all dead. The latter had hardly put up much of a fight at all. In fact, they seemed almost relieved when Cole's army of shamblers fell upon them. The expression on Captain Priam's face as he died suggested this was a moment he'd been waiting a lifetime for.

Cole had ordered the survivors to torch the bodies of the Whitecloaks. It didn't seem right, forcing them to serve him in death. He had a feeling there was a lot the wizard Thanates had yet to tell him about the soldiers, and besides, there were more than enough dead Mad Dogs to do his bidding. If the Trinity were still alive, they would need to fight their way through an army of the dead before they got to him. He hoped it was enough.

He paused as he came within sight of the Horn. The rising sun bathed the giant monument in an orange glow. Cole shielded his eyes and squinted, trying to work out why the tip of the Horn had somehow turned white while the rest of the giant landmark was as jet black as ever. As he got closer, though, he saw the truth of the matter.

The Trinity were impaled on the end of the Horn, their lifeless bodies stacked one on top of the other, pale robes falling uselessly around them.

Kneeling on the blasted earth before the Horn was Thanates. Cole thought he might be dead too – but with a great effort the wizard raised his head. 'It is done?' he asked hoarsely. 'Is the town secured?' The man's black coat was even more tattered and torn than before. He was covered in a dozen small wounds and looked utterly spent.

'Yes,' Cole replied. He stared at the dead handmaidens in wonder and then hurried over to the wizard. 'You're badly hurt.'

'Hurt? This is nothing. The White Lady had me lashed a hundred times before she hanged me from the walls of her city. After a few days had passed, once they thought me dead, the carrion birds and other predators began to feed on me. I claimed the soul of the crow that pecked out my eyes. This much I remember.'

Cole stared at Thanates in shock. 'The White Lady did that to you?'

'She did many things. The question is *why*.' The wizard sniffed the air. 'An army of the dead accompanies you. They will prove useful.'

'They will?'

Thanates clenched his jaw. With an iron display of willpower he climbed to his feet. 'A ship is due to arrive on the coast this morning. We will seize the vessel and use it to return to the City of Towers.'

'We're going to Thelassa?' Cole exclaimed. 'But what about the White Lady? If she finds out we're there in her city—'

'Oh, she will find out. I intend to make certain of it. But first there is something I must do.'

'What?'

Thanates pulled his tattered coat tightly about him and set off in the direction of Newharvest, walking with a pronounced limp. 'The White Lady is perhaps the most powerful wizard left in the north,' he called back without turning. 'I will require every scrap of magic ore left in Newharvest.'

The wizard's voice dropped to a deadly whisper then, and Cole had to hurry after him to catch his next words. 'I will have the truth. And then... I will have my vengeance.'

Revelations

'CREATOR'S COCK, IT'S the Halfmage! He'll have the answers we need.'

Eremul glanced at the small crowd that had gathered on the street corner and immediately regretted it. He should have put his head down and kept going, pretended he hadn't heard the desperate-looking fellow in the filthy rags that passed for clothes. The others with him were just as dishevelled. Mobs like these were growing increasingly common, and though the Halfmage wasn't in any particular fear for his safety, he was already running late.

'When are our loved ones coming home?' the man called out. 'It's been two months now! Please, you must know something about what's happening.'

Must I indeed? Who made me Halliax, Lord of Knowledge? Eremul didn't bother giving voice to his scorn. After all, Halliax had been a relatively obscure deity and these days few could name more than a handful of dead gods. Five centuries on from the Godswar and they were finally fading from memory.

Just like the city's jubilation at the death of the tyrant Salazar.

If Eremul had learned anything from years spent with his nose buried in books on history and philosophy, it was that contentment was the most transient emotion of all. The human spirit was not meant to float suspended in the calm waters of equanimity but rather to lurch wildly from one crisis to another.

'Please, Halfmage!'

The desperate plea tore him away from his ruminations. Eremul grimaced at the anguish in the man's voice. A father's pain, he guessed. Maybe a husband's. Both unfamiliar to him, but no less potent for that. More so, perhaps.

With a sigh, he slowed his chair and turned to face the mob. 'Look, you're asking the wrong person. I have no more insight into why the Pioneers have not returned than you.'

'You don't? But you're the Master of Magic. You can find out for us, can't you?'

The Halfmage tried not to wince at the earnest expression of hope on the man's face. He had preferred it when no one had expected anything from him except possibly a good laugh. 'I'm certain that if the Council had any news, I would be among the first to know,' he said. Actually, he would likely be the last to know if Timerus had his way. 'Perhaps ill weather delayed the return voyage. Perhaps the Celestial Isles are simply so rich with resources that it has taken longer than expected to catalogue everything.'

'You think so?'

'I'm no clairvoyant, but those strike me as the most logical explanations. Really, what's the worst that could have happened?' He didn't mention a couple of the more pessimistic theories that had occurred to him recently. He wanted to conclude his meeting at the old abandoned lighthouse before he spoke of his fears to Lorganna.

'I guess that makes sense. I'm just worried about my son. He means the world to me.'

'I can well understand,' Eremul lied, but it was the kind of lie that made his heart ache strangely. For some reason he thought of Monique, who was visiting him later at the depository for the very first time. He hoped Tyro hadn't made a mess.

'Do you have any children, Halfmage?' the fellow asked. It wasn't a question asked out of spite but rather honest curiosity, and Eremul forced himself to swallow the instinctive vitriol that welled up inside him.

'No,' he replied. And then for some reason, he added, 'Maybe I will one day.' *Creator's cock, what is happening to me?*

The man nodded and turned to the mob behind him. 'I think we've wasted enough of this hero's time,' he said happily. The small crowd began to disperse. Eremul noted with surprise that fresh hope had appeared on faces that moments ago were heavy with despair.

All because some crippled bastard they mistakenly believe to be a hero provided a few half-arsed words of comfort.

He actually found himself feeling sorry for them.

'Fare thee well, Halfmage,' said the leader of the mob, without a hint of irony. There had been a time when being told 'fare thee well' would have elicited a furious response from Eremul. Instead he smiled wryly and continued north towards Raven's Bluff.

As he made his way through harbourside alleys teeming with the poor and starving he wondered what had become of the two sisters he'd sent to Thelassa. They should have returned long before now. He'd not heard so much as a peep. It was just like the time he'd sent the small band to the Wailing Rift, he reflected. It was almost as if his quests weren't being treated with the gravitas they deserved. After all, in the bad works of fiction he kept hidden in the depository, if a stern-faced wizard arrived bearing tales of impending disaster, the chosen ones bloody well did what was asked of them. They didn't pocket the coin he had handed them and quietly bugger off Creator-knows-where like Sasha and her psychotic sister.

He ought to be annoyed but in truth he hardly cared. He had more important things on his mind, or at least so it seemed. He thought again of Monique. They'd met on three separate occasions since their 'date' – gods, he hated that word – at the Rose and Sceptre. He was starting believe she actually *liked* him. He just hoped she didn't run screaming if it ever reached the point where intimacy reared its ugly head.

'Spare a copper?' a hag squawked at him, too decrepit for any man to want to pay for a bite of her withered old cherry. Eremul patted down his robes but belatedly realized he'd forgotten his coin purse.

'I have no coppers to spare. But I can offer you my blessings.'

The old woman spat, revealing a gummy mouth sprouting crooked brown teeth. 'I can't eat blessings, can I? Thanks for nothing, cripple.'

Eremul merely shrugged and rode by. There was no point losing his temper. In a city where the half the population was struggling to eat and the other half was under constant threat of violence from Melissan's fanatics, insults were scarcely worth getting upset about.

As he left Whalebone Street and made his way up Raven's Walk, Eremul almost collided with a bunch of drunkards staggering from one of the cheap dives lining the bottom of the promenade. It was early to be drinking, but this was one of the poorest parts of the city and he couldn't blame the desperate for wanting to drown their sorrows.

A handful of glassy-eyed faces stared at him with varying degrees of despondency. One face looked vaguely familiar behind a wild growth of grey stubble, but just then another drunk barged into Eremul, almost knocking his chair over. The Halfmage had to throw his weight to the side to right the chair and avoid being dumped on his arse. 'Watch where you're going!' he hissed as drunken guffaws receded behind him.

A burly beggar covered head to toe in bandages and slumped against a wall stretched out a mangled hand to ask for coin, but Eremul rode right on by the fellow and whatever unfortunate incident had befallen him. There was only so much sympathy to go around.

His annoyance faded as he ascended the hill north of the harbour. He noted how much easier the journey was than the last time, his shoulders powering him up the rise with surprising ease. Before he knew it he had reached the top of Raven's Bluff.

The ruined lighthouse was exactly as he remembered: a

decrepit old tower overlooking the harbour, which few ever ventured near. Earlier in the year the White Lady had summoned him to this place for a clandestine meeting with her handmaidens. The Halfmage judged it the perfect spot to meet with Lorganna away from prying eyes.

The door was already a little ajar. He pushed it open and peered inside. A flickering torch illuminated the damp, circular chamber. Lorganna had her back to him, the woman's attention fixed on the fellow strapped to the chair in the centre of the room. The two guards Lorganna had evidently brought with her placed their hands on their weapons and scowled at him in that practised way of hired thugs the world over.

The Civic Relations Minister turned. 'Eremul,' she said. 'I thought you weren't going to show.'

'Never bet against a man with no legs.' Eremul wheeled himself over to the prisoner and raised an eyebrow in surprise. 'He's young. It would seem Melissan has started recruiting early.'

'Go outside and keep watch,' Lorganna ordered the two men. 'If you see anyone approach, raise the alarm.' The hired muscle exchanged a look and then left.

'Thank you for arranging this,' Eremul said. He'd never been comfortable expressing gratitude, but the woman had earned it. 'Doubtless your colleagues on the Council consider me crazy.'

Lorganna shrugged. She had discarded the long black robes of the city's magistrates for a plain brown tunic. She carried anonymity well, Eremul thought. There was nothing memorable about either her face or manner. 'If the Fade truly are returning to these shores, the Council will soon regret dismissing your concerns out of hand.'

Eremul reached forward and took hold of the leather strap gagging the prisoner. 'May I?'

Lorganna nodded. The Halfmage untied the strap and pulled it away from the fanatic's mouth. 'What's your name?' he asked.

The captive spat in his face.

Eremul wiped saliva from his chin and tried to control his

rising temper. It had been a while since anyone had dared spit on him and he'd forgotten quite how unpleasant it felt.

'They're all like this,' Lorganna said, shaking her head. 'The Grand Regent has authorized every kind of torture imaginable to force them to comply, but these fanatics won't give up a thing.'

'Their tongues might not talk, but it is not so easy to control one's thoughts.' The Halfmage placed a hand on the captive's head. Ignoring the fanatic's desperate thrashing, he summoned his magic. 'The last time I practised thought-mining was on our dearly departed Magelord. I doubt this young firebrand will prove any more obstinate.'

He probed, but try as he might he couldn't read anything except vague feelings of anger and, oddly, bewilderment. 'Where is the tattoo?' Eremul asked, sweat beading his brow.

'On his left arm, just below the shoulder.'

The door creaked open and one of Lorganna's hirelings poked his shaved head into the room. 'We caught some old drunk wandering around outside,' he said. 'Fellow's so pissed he almost fell off the edge of the cliff.'

'Give him a kick up the arse and send him on his way,' Eremul replied irritably. 'Or just toss him in the harbour.' Lorganna frowned at him. 'I'm jesting,' he half lied.

'See to it that he descends the hill safely,' Lorganna ordered. Her lackey bobbed his head and disappeared.

'Left arm, just below the shoulder,' Eremul murmured. He withdrew a knife from his robes and cut away the fanatic's sleeve. There it was – like a spider curled up tight beneath the skin. The Fade script.

'You plan to cut it out of him?' Lorganna asked, sounding apprehensive.

'Nothing so uncouth as that. I will tease it out using magic. In the event it somehow evades my grasp, be a dear and stamp on it. We must not let this one escape.'

The Halfmage took a deep breath and began channelling his

magic into the tattoo, muttering the words of a binding spell that would hold the thing in place as soon as it crawled free of its host's flesh. It was delicate work: an undertaking beyond the skill of many wizards. Though Eremul was always the weakest of mages when it came to raw power, he possessed a level of craft that had sometimes impressed even old Poskarus.

The 'script' began to writhe, just as it had on the corpse back at the morgue. Eremul held his breath and watched it like a hawk. As it crawled out of the prisoner's skin, the Halfmage triggered his spell.

'Got you,' he hissed triumphantly. He bent down to scoop up the bizarre object. It had a smooth metallic body with six serrated legs. Holding it up to his ear, he could hear a faint whirring noise coming from within. He realized then that this parasite wasn't a living thing – it was a construct, built by hands far more delicate than those of any human.

The prisoner jerked suddenly. 'Who are you?' he moaned. 'Where am I?' He tried to rise, then seemed to realize he was bound to his chair. 'What am I doing here?' he asked, his voice rising in panic.

Eremul and Lorganna exchanged looks. The Halfmage placed the tiny device carefully into one of his many pockets and stared down at the prisoner. The man's demeanour was entirely different now: nervous and afraid. 'That accent,' Eremul said. 'You're from Espanda?'

'Yes,' the boy replied fearfully. 'I was on my way to Tarbonne to celebrate the Rag King's coronation. Someone attacked me on the road. I remember a bag being pulled over my head. Then... nothing.'

'The Rag King was crowned over two years ago,' Eremul said slowly.

'Two years? That can't be possible... Wait. What year is this?

'The five hundred and first year of the Age of Ruin.'

The young Espandan paled. He looked like he was about to vomit.

'Tell me. Have you heard of Melissan? Do you recall *anything* of the last two years? Anything at all?'

'Nothing. Nothing except... nightmares. People burning. Voices whispering to me, making me do terrible things. What... what have I done?'

The Halfmage placed a hand inside his pocket, checking that the tiny device was still safely within. It felt strange. Alien. He turned to Lorganna, who was watching the captive with an intense expression. 'Call a council meeting,' he said triumphantly. 'I believe we have our proof.'

Knock. Knock.

He smoothed his robes one last time. This was it. There was no turning back now.

Eremul wheeled himself to the door, took a deep breath, pulled the latch, and yanked it open to reveal the slender, dark-haired figure of Monique. Her crooked grin and the smell of her perfume and the tight black dress she wore almost took his breath away.

'May I come in?' she asked in her lilting Tarbonnese accent. Eremul realized he'd been sitting there gawking at her.

Shit! I have the manners of an ape.

'Please do,' he said gallantly, backing his chair out of the way and accidentally running over a half-eaten bone Tyro had left on the floor. He swept an arm towards the interior of the depository. 'Welcome to my humble abode.'

He wheeled himself over to his desk and yanked open the bottom drawer. 'Carhein white,' he said triumphantly, pulling out the bottle within. The wine merchant at the Bazaar had charged a small fortune, but it was Monique's favourite and he wanted put his best foot forward, so to speak.

'Why are you smiling?' Monique asked curiously, and Eremul realized he was grinning at his own wit. Laughing at one's jokes was generally considered the mark of the insane or at least the insufferably smug. Whilst Eremul was reasonably certain he was guilty of at least one of the two, it couldn't hurt to keep Monique ignorant of his failings for a little while longer.

'How can I not smile when in the company of such radiance,' he declared, resisting the sudden urge to punch himself in the face. To his amazement, Monique's cheeks blushed red.

'You flatter me,' she said. 'I brought you these.' She held up a bunch of bright blue flowers, an exotic variety he had never seen before. 'They are found only in the northern mountains, where it is so cold nothing else may grow. They can survive for months without water before the flowers wither and die. Shall I place them here for you?' She walked across to his desk and set them down neatly.

'Er... thank you,' he said, silently cursing himself for not sprucing up the place a little more before their evening together. 'Would you join me for a drink?' He wheeled himself over to the desk and pulled out the spare chair Isaac had once kept in the back. Monique took the proffered seat and he poured them both a generous measure of wine.

'Where is your dog?' she asked, giving him a warm smile as she brought the glass up to her violet lips.

'Tyro? I locked him in the other room. He gets excitable around new faces.'

'Is it easy? Training a dog in your situation?'

'My situation?'

'I meant only... Oh, I am sorry. Please forgive me.' Monique blushed again and stared down into her wine.

'Nothing to forgive,' Eremul said magnanimously, fluttering his hands at her desperately. 'I was only teasing. Apparently it's common when a man... er... likes... a woman.'

Shit.

'So you like me?' Monique looked up from her glass and brushed a few strands of sleek black hair away from her face.

Now it was Eremul's turn to blush. He felt terribly out of his depth. 'I, ah... I value your friendship,' he finished lamely.

'Yes?' Monique raised a perfect eyebrow. Her dark eyes

danced with mischief. 'Friends are always good. But I had hoped that you might see me as more than just a friend. In what way do you like me?'

Eremul's heart began to hammer. He glanced around, searching for a distraction, hoping desperately that Tyro might somehow escape from the back room and start taking a piss on a few of the less valuable works of literature. Anything to get him out of this excruciating predicament. 'Er, well, that would depend on one's definition of "like". That, ah, that is to say—'

'Hush.' Monique placed a finger against his mouth. A moment later she leaned forward and her lips pressed against his. He felt her tongue probing and sat there in shock for a moment before he returned the kiss, tasting the faint hint of spice in her mouth. Though Monique's eyes were squeezed shut he had his wide open, and he felt strangely detached, as if he were a mere observer to the momentous event taking place. He watched her delicate fingers stroke his arm and then make their slow way down his robes; he felt himself respond in anticipation. He was simultaneously filled with dread and an undeniable, tingling excitement…

Shit, he thought. *Oh shit*.

There was a mighty crash from behind him and the wards that guarded the depository flared into life, triggering a series of pulses in his brain. He pulled away from Monique and turned, not needing the magical alarm to tell him there were intruders trying to enter the building. The door was hanging off its hinges; as he watched, stunned, a group of Watchmen burst in, the crossbows they held aiming straight at him. Monique gasped in terror, and it was her obvious distress that snapped Eremul of out his daze and filled him with a sudden rage.

'What the *fuck* are you doing?' he demanded of the soldiers in the red cloaks. 'Do you know who I am?'

'We know,' said the largest of the men. It was Bracka, the bushy-bearded Marshal of the Crimson Watch. His arm looked to be well mended now, judging by the crossbow he was pointing at Eremul's face, though he winced as he took a step into the room, his foot evidently still sore from kicking the door in. 'You make one false move and I'll have my men shoot you. Your woman too,' he added, as Eremul began to mutter the arcane words that would summon a protective shield around him. The spell died on his lips as the Marshal's threat registered.

'Why?' the Halfmage said in a strangled voice.

Bracka stepped aside and a ragged old fellow with a faceful of grey stubble pushed through the soldiers. It was the drunk who had jostled him on his way to the abandoned lighthouse. The Halfmage's eyes narrowed. He *knew* that face—

'Treason!' Spymaster Remy barked, pointing an accusing finger at him. The man's hand shook and he hiccupped as though he was still half-drunk, but there was an unmistakable glint of menace in his eyes. 'Your plot has been uncovered, traitor.'

'Plot? What are you talking about?'

'I followed you to Raven's Bluff. I know about your meeting with Lorganna.'

'What of it? The last time I checked I was still a free man. Half a man, perhaps, but free nonetheless.'

'You conspire to bring the city to ruin! Don't try to deny it. I've been spying on you for weeks, on the Grand Regent's orders. The evidence is quite overwhelming.'

Eremul stared at the soldiers and then at Monique. She looked as shocked as he was. 'I've been trying to uncover the nature of the threat posed by Melissan's rebels,' he said slowly and deliberately. 'Lorganna has been assisting me. I apologize if using magic in an interrogation offends your delicate sense of propriety, but it hardly qualifies me as a traitor bent on bringing the city to ruin.'

Remy sneered unpleasantly. 'You're a piece of work, Halfmage. A real piece of work.'

'That I'll grant you. It's your other claims I find so offensive.'

Dorminia's Master of Information took a step forward and leaned over; Eremul could smell the ale on his breath. 'She broke easily in the end, you know,' he growled.

'Who did?' Eremul snapped back, though he was beginning to feel a deep sense of dread.

'Lorganna. We arrested her before coming here. Oh, she did well to integrate herself into the Council, taking advantage of her position as Civic Relations Minister to help foment insurrection. Targeting her employees in the arson attacks was a fine piece of misdirection. But I've got a good nose for sniffing out a rat.'

It took a moment for Remy's words to sink in. 'Lorganna and Melissan are one and the same,' Eremul said numbly, realization hitting him like a hammer blow to the head.

How could he have been so stupid? It was the perfect ruse. And, like the witless cretin that he was, he had fallen for it.

'She's already confessed to everything. There's no point denying your guilt. You're coming with us.'

'What's going to happen?' Eremul asked. Monique met his eyes and the accusing look in her dark gaze made the situation immeasurably worse. *I'm innocent*, he wanted to tell her. But what was the point?

Remy hiccupped again and waved Bracka and his men forward. 'I think you already know the answer to that. It's the gallows for you, Halfmage.'

The Unborn

SASHA STARED OUT of the window, peering between the beads of rain that crawled down the glass. The autumn storm sent sheets of water pounding against the inn. She thought she'd heard shouts coming from the direction of the harbour, but the incessant roar of the downpour made it hard to be certain. Maybe it had just been the idle imaginings of her drug-starved brain; a sudden manifestation of the paranoia that stalked her, waiting for the slightest opportunity to create a thousand unnamed threats.

Sasha glared at the door and then turned back to the window and almost put her fist through the glass. The upper floor of the Siren was a good twenty feet above the street and there was nothing to grab hold of to break her fall, but after a week and a half locked in this room she was giving serious thought to just taking the plunge and hoping for the best.

She stared at her trembling palms. She needed a hit. She needed it *bad*. The Whitecloaks Ambryl had brought with her from the palace had turned the room upside down in their search and confiscated every last ounce of moon dust she'd been able to hide away. She'd screamed and scratched at them, but the guards had only continued to restrain her while her sister had calmly stated that either she accepted a fortnight of isolation in the inn or she would be taken to a cell with nothing but a dirty bedroll and shit-stained bucket by way of comforts.

She grabbed a pillow and was about to hurl it across the room when she glimpsed movement on the white marble streets below. A Whitecloak patrol was hurrying west towards the docks, their booted feet sending up great splashes of water. Without warning the sky suddenly lit up, heavy black clouds rendered an eerie blue for the blink of an eye. She thought it might have been lightning, but the tremors that shook the inn a moment later put paid to that notion. The vase she had purchased at the market to replace the one Ambryl broke toppled over, rolled a few times on the table, and then tumbled off to shatter on the floor.

Sasha felt the room spin as panic gripped her. *Alchemy*, she thought in terror. Memories of the Wailing Rift and the night Dorminia burned flooded back. Her breath quickened; her trembling palms began to perspire. She thought she'd resigned herself to another few days between the deathly dull confines of these four walls, but the sudden anxiety that overwhelmed her made a mockery of that resolution. Not even the threat of her sister's wrath was enough to quell the frantic impulse to flee, to escape this building by any means necessary.

She called for Willard, but received no response. The inn shook again. She rushed across to the door and pulled desperately on the handle. The door was locked tight, as she knew it would be.

'Someone let me out!' she cried, rattling the handle desperately, giving the door a hard kick for good measure. In Dorminia one of the other guests would surely have answered her cries, if only to tell her to shut her whore mouth or something similarly charming. Not so in Thelassa. If the inn had other guests, they were content to mind their own business.

There was another flash of light from somewhere off in the city. She was certain she could hear distant screams, now. She picked up the small round table the vase had been resting on, thinking to ram it through the window and follow up on her earlier plan, wondering if she might force the straw mattress or at least a pillow through the opening to break her fall. Then she spotted one of Ambryl's hairpins on the floor near the bed.

She put the table back down, hurried over to the bed and scrabbled around until her fingers closed around the thin piece of metal. She pulled away the few strands of red-blonde hair caught in the pin and tried to recall the lecture Cole had given her on how to pick a lock. As always it had been more an excuse for him to boast about the new skill he'd learned than any real desire to impart his newfound knowledge, but Sasha had been blessed with a keen mind for details. She'd been blessed with a keen mind for many things, when it wasn't half-baked from narcotics.

She bent the end of the hairpin a little so that it stuck out at an angle, and then she carefully inserted the makeshift lockpick into the door's keyhole and wiggled it around until she felt the locking mechanism catch. Despite her nerves, she managed to keep her hand steady long enough to gently ease it apart until finally it clicked. With a shuddering sigh of relief, Sasha thrust open the door and raced down the stairs into the common room.

It was empty save for Willard. The manager of the Lonely Siren had his back to her and was standing in the open doorway, staring out into the pouring rain. Sasha was about to ask him what the hell was going on when Lyressa emerged from the kitchen.

'No need to be alarmed, dear,' the innkeeper said brightly. 'Probably just some troublemakers that have had too much to drink. The handmaidens will deal with them.'

Sasha stared, open-mouthed. She hadn't laid eyes on Lyressa since the Seeding Festival over a month past, when the White Lady's handmaidens had come for the woman in the middle of the night and taken her away. Yet here she was, back in the Siren as if nothing had happened, a kindly smile on her face and everything about her exactly as Sasha remembered it. Everything except one important detail.

'You...' she began in astonishment, hardly believing what she was seeing. 'You were heavy with child...'

Lyressa rested a hand on her stomach. Where before it had been visibly swollen in late pregnancy, now it was almost flat.

'Heavy with child?' the innkeeper laughed. 'I know I haven't got the body I did ten years ago, but you wait till you get to my age, missy! Willard doesn't seem to mind that I've put on a few extra pounds.'

At his wife's mention of his name, Willard turned from the doorway. There was something strange about his face, Sasha thought. His eyes seemed... glassy. As did Lyressa's, now that she examined the woman more closely. A shiver ran down her spine. Something was very wrong here.

'You were at least six months pregnant,' she said, trying to remain calm. 'You went missing the night of the festival. I was upstairs when they came and took you away. I found Willard on the floor. He was in tears.'

As Sasha spoke, a strange thing happened. Lyressa began to blink. Slowly at first, but then more rapidly. Willard, too, was in the midst of some kind of internal turmoil, his eyelids flickering dementedly, his face shuddering as if there was something beneath his skin trying to break free. Sasha's sense of unease deepened to a rising dread.

'You're mistaken,' Willard snapped. 'Your sister said you had to be kept locked up in your room. It's the drugs, isn't it? You're a *hashka* junkie. Your mind's playing tricks on you. I'm not judging you; we all have our problems. But you can't come down here saying crazy things. You understand me? You can't come down here saying crazy things!' There was something frantic in the man's tone, a rising mania like a kettle of water about to boil over.

Sasha reached up to her face and massaged her throbbing skull. Was Willard right? Could years of abusing every substance she could get her hands on finally have turned her crazy? She'd suffered hallucinations before, during her worst excesses. But they'd always passed quickly, leaving her in no doubt as to their source. She spotted the chair with the broken leg, the one that had been damaged the night Lyressa had been abducted, and she knew with utter certainty that she hadn't imagined it.

'I... apologize,' she said slowly and deliberately. 'You're right; I'm talking nonsense. Excuse me. I need to go outside and get some air.'

Like the sun suddenly emerging from behind a thunderhead, Willard's tortured expression relaxed into one of utter serenity. The abrupt change in his mood was every bit as unnerving as his crazed behaviour a moment before. 'Go outside? Why, it's storming something fierce! You'll be soaked to the bone.'

'Listen to Willard, dear,' Lyressa added. Dark blood had begun leaking from her nose, but she appeared not to have noticed. 'There's trouble out on the streets. Why don't you sit here a while? I'll brew you a mug of hot tea.'

'No, honestly, I enjoy the rain,' Sasha said hurriedly, watching the blood dribble down Lyressa's chin and patter to the floor and trying not to shudder. 'I just need to clear my head. I won't go far, I promise.'

That was a lie. As it happened, she did plan to go far – about the width of Deadman's Channel away in fact. The *hashka* she had somehow possessed the foresight to hide in a nearby alley ought to fetch her enough coin to pay for passage back to Dorminia, if she could find a buyer. She wanted out of this city as soon as possible, with or without Ambryl.

Willard made no effort to block her path as she hurried past him and out into the late-afternoon storm. Her dark hair almost instantly became a sopping mess in the hammering downpour, and she squeezed her chin into her chest and tried to ignore the water soaking her boots as she splashed her way up the street. Another flash lit up the sky and she glanced back to see yet more Whitecloaks emerge from a side road and turn west towards the harbour, though she could make out nothing of the docks through the endless veil of rain.

As Sasha closed on the alley where her stash was hidden she drew level with one of the soaring spires for which Thelassa was renowned. This particular tower was small in comparison with those nearer the centre – not even half the height of the Obelisk back in Dorminia. She paused a moment to gaze up at the rain-shrouded pinnacle. Suddenly the entrance door creaked open and one of the White Lady's handmaidens glided down the short row of steps leading up to the tower. The rain seemed to fall *around* the pale woman, leaving her white robes untouched.

The handmaiden stopped just in front of Sasha. 'Return to your home,' she said coldly.

'What's happening?' Sasha asked, partly to buy herself some time to think in the event of any awkward questions.

'There is a disturbance at the docks. A hostile wizard has arrived in the city. He will be neutralized shortly. Until then these streets are not safe.'

'My house is just up ahead,' Sasha lied. 'I'll return there now.'

The handmaiden stared at her for a moment with those colourless eyes. Then she drifted past Sasha, gliding west towards the harbour, eventually disappearing behind the grey curtain of rain.

Sasha heaved a sigh of relief and shook her head, sending droplets of water flying everywhere. The alley beckoned close by. She was about to hurry down it when she noticed the tower's door was slightly ajar. The handmaiden had neglected to close it behind her.

'*Don't be a fool*,' she whispered to herself. No one knew what lay within those soaring spires. Or if they did, none ever spoke of it. The White Lady's handmaidens were an enigma, but they were far from the only secret this city kept hidden behind its bright exterior.

She hesitated and looked around again. The streets were empty. She asked herself what Cole would have done in this situation, knowing the wisest course of action would obviously be to do the exact opposite. But the tower seemed to beckon to her. With a final check to be sure no one was watching, she dashed up the stairs and darted inside.

Her eyes took a moment to adjust to the gloom. Outside, the roar of the rain continued unabated. Inside it was silent, and all but bare of decoration. Only a single torch on the opposite side of the circular chamber provided any illumination. It revealed a stairwell in the centre, with several doors positioned at equal distances around the circumference of the floor. After a moment's hesitation, Sasha tried one of the doors and found it locked. Further inspection revealed a wooden panel positioned at head height. Sasha fiddled with it and discovered that it slid open to reveal clear glass, affording a perfect view of the room beyond. The room was well adorned with a bed and a sofa and small bookshelf in the corner, though it was currently unoccupied.

Sasha selected another door at random and slid back the panel to stare through the glass. This room was identical to the last – but this time there was a heavily pregnant woman lying on the bed. She appeared to be crying, though no sound penetrated beyond the room. Sasha banged on the glass, trying to get the woman's attention, but it seemed that the door cancelled noise from both sides. The woman couldn't hear her.

Wary of lingering too long in one place, Sasha abandoned the room and its occupant and climbed the stairs to the next floor, which was somewhat more brightly lit than the ground floor. Life-sized statues of the White Lady stared down from alcoves cut into the walls, capturing the likeness of the Magelord in a variety of poses from the serene to the vengeful. None truly did justice to the immortal ruler of Thelassa, though with all she had witnessed in the last few weeks Sasha was convinced that beneath the White Lady's outward perfection lurked something warped and unspeakably ugly.

There were only two doors on this floor. Both were plain and featureless with no panels to slide back and see inside. Sasha found them both locked when she tried their handles. She thought she could hear whimpering from behind the door to the left, as well as a strange metallic snipping sound, but the last thing she wanted was to draw attention to herself by knocking on the door so she quickly moved away.

She was climbing the stairs to the third floor when she became aware of a foul odour in the air. It reminded her of the terrible smell that had infiltrated Dorminia in the days following the liberation of the city: the carnal stench of old blood going bad and corpses rotting on the streets.

Despite the warning her nose afforded her, Sasha was nonetheless unprepared for the horror that greeted her when she emerged from the stairwell.

With the exception of the stairwell and a narrow walkway adjacent to it, the top half of the tower was surrounded by thick glass. It formed a giant tank that rose to the apex of the building. Behind the glass, a thick and evil-smelling liquid oozed from somewhere far below, filling the tank to the top. As Sasha brought a hand to her nose to shield it from the stench, she realized with sickening certainty that the fluid was blood. A vast quantity of the stuff, enough to fill the rooms of Garrett's estate with plenty to spare.

Something bumped up against the side of the tank. With rising horror, Sasha saw a tiny, vaguely humanoid shape scrape along the side of the glass, its misshapen limbs wrapped around a foetal body as it spun slowly in the sluggish current.

'What the *fuck*?' she whispered, and then she jumped as something struck the glass right in front of her. She stood paralysed in terror and stared into the face of an adult woman, naked and covered in blood except for the eyes, which were shockingly white and very dead, right up until the moment they swivelled slightly to regard her with an expression that almost stripped away her sanity right there and then. The woman's mouth suddenly burst open; her lips formed a silent scream.

Sasha turned and ran. She took the stairs two at a time, desperate to get away from this tower of horrors. Such was her single-minded determination that she almost didn't see the man preparing to climb *up* the stairwell. She smacked into him and almost knocked him down in her mad haste to escape the nightmare she'd just witnessed.

'Who in the blazes are *you*?' he demanded in a surprisingly distinguished voice. He was tall and sharp-featured, with a high widow's peak. The white apron he wore was spotted in blood – as were the sharp metal scissors he carried in his slender fingers.

She stared at him for a moment, her mouth working soundlessly. 'I...' she trailed off, overcome with revulsion.

'State your name!' he demanded again. 'If I have to call for the guards, why, you can consider yourself fortunate if you're still able to feed yourself come the morrow. No memory suppressants for you, I'm afraid. No, I'll go straight in through the skull.' He gave the scissors a snip.

'Cyreena,' Sasha blurted out. She wasn't sure why. The lie was on her lips before her brain had even caught up with what was happening.

'Ah-ha. So you're the Mistress's new favourite. I wasn't expecting you for a few more weeks yet. The clandestine work we do does not agree with everyone's palate, at least at first. In my experience acceptance, even enthusiasm are only a matter of time. My name is Fergus. You might consider me a pioneer of sorts. A man of science. My work enables Thelassa to safeguard its autonomy in this cold and merciless world.'

'Your work?'

'The Unlife Chamber is quite something, is it not? Who would have imagined the blood of a dead god could have so many *uses*. At our current production rates the Mistress should possess in excess of one hundred Unborn before the year is out.'

'The Unlife Chamber... That... that tank? You're creating more of the White— the Mistress's handmaidens?' The realization of what was happening in this tower appalled her. How many other places like this were there? What kind of monster was the Magelord of Thelassa?

'Naturally our output is restricted by population considerations. The Seeding is an effective means of maintaining a sustainable level of female candidates for the change. Ply a man or a woman with the correct substances, provide them with an excuse to discard the social constructs that moderate our impulses and separate humans from the lesser beasts – why, the results are remarkably easy to predict. It is simply a case of stimulating the brain to achieve the desired outcome. Thelassa is more efficient than any city its size in the entire course of human history. The Mistress could never abide the ugly dictatorship practised by the Tyrant of Dorminia and his ilk. Her methods are so much *cleaner*.'

'I should go,' Sasha said. She forced herself to keep her tone neutral, though a part of her wanted to bend over and vomit. Another part wanted to throttle this Fergus with her bare hands.

'As I said, it does get easier. The next time you are here I will demonstrate the procedure for removing a babe from the womb and preparing it for submersion in the blood of the Reaver. Some wastage is inevitable, but I'm happy to say the ratio of successful Unborn to Abandoned is ever improving.'

'I'm pleased to hear it,' Sasha said numbly. As she walked past Fergus she caught a glimpse of a woman tied to a table through the door he must have just come through. There was a pool of blood forming between her open legs. Sasha looked away, somehow resisting the urge to snatch Fergus's scissors from his hands and drive the sharp end straight through his windpipe.

'Remember,' he called after her. 'Drink only the water provided by the Consult. While the drugs we pump into the city cisterns are not dangerous, it is better for members of the Consult to serve the Mistress with a clear head.'

As Sasha exited the tower and let the rain wash away the tears that now rolled freely down her cheeks, a clear head was the very last thing on her mind.

Fourteen Years Ago

'PA, WHAT'S THE matter? Pa!'

He heard Magnar's voice, but what he saw were the faces. So many faces, some of them not much older than the one staring back at him just then.

He'd given the order. There hadn't been any choice in the matter, not when it came right down to it. Once a man gave his word, he stuck to it or it wasn't his word any longer. The Shaman's instructions had been clear. Seven years of blood needed answering with blood.

And so he'd given the order, and men hardly older than his son had died beneath the eager swords of Krazka and his men. The nightmares kept him awake at night, and now they were following him into his waking hours. He ran a rough hand down his face. It came away slick with sweat. 'We're done for the morning,' Kayne rasped. 'Go help your mother.'

'You promised to teach me!' Magnar pouted. He was barely ten winters of age and already he was tall enough for his head to reach his father's chest.

'I said we're done for the morning.'

Magnar threw his wooden sword to the grass and turned his back on his father.

'Pick that up.'

'Why? You were never around! Now you're back and you don't even care. All you and Ma ever do is argue.'

'I told you to pick it up,' Kayne said, his voice dangerously soft.

'I heard Mother say you're not the same since the war,' Magnar hissed. It was a boy's instinct, that ability to hurt a parent precisely where they were most vulnerable.

Kayne wrestled with the sudden rage that swelled within him. Ever since Red Valley it had lurked there, waiting for any excuse to burst free. Watching countless friends die and ordering five thousand put to the sword had broken the ice that slaked his fire. These days he found himself getting incensed at the smallest things.

He took deep, measured breaths and tried to compose himself. The spring sun was pleasantly warm after the hard winter, and the gentle birdsong helped soothe his fury. 'When did she say that?' he asked, as calmly as he could manage.

'She was speaking to Aunt Natalya. Aunt Natalya said some bad things about you and Mother was crying.' Magnar's anger faded, forgotten as quickly as it had come. 'Sometimes I don't like Aunt Natalya.'

Kayne's eyes narrowed. His fingers tightened around the hilt of the practice weapon he clutched until he felt the wood crack. 'You and me both, son.'

Mhaira's cousin Natalya and her husband had built their house nearby, on the land granted Kayne by the King. Keeping his wife's family close had seemed like a good idea at the time, a way of making sure she wasn't lonely while he was away in the West Reaching, especially after her sister Lellana had died so unexpectedly. He knew that Natalya bore him a grudge and he couldn't rightly blame her for that. But poisoning his own wife against him: that was low.

'I'm going inside,' he said abruptly. 'Put your sword back with the others. You can throw this one away. It ain't no good now.' He approached Magnar and handed him the split hilt of the practice weapon. Then he hesitated for a second before placing a weathered hand on his son's head. 'I'm sorry I wasn't around more,' he said. 'I love you and your ma more than anything. There wasn't a day that passed when I didn't think of you. You know that, aye?'

Magnar nodded. 'I know, Pa.'

Kayne smiled and patted Magnar on the shoulder. 'We'll practise again tomorrow.'

He crossed the field to the house, pausing a moment to inspect the wreath hanging on the door. He recalled their joining: Borun walking Mhaira down the aisle and her beauty near taking his breath away.

Kayne pushed open the door and padded silently inside, thinking to surprise Mhaira, to sneak up and throw his arms around her like he had when they were younger. He spotted the hole he'd punched in the wall and winced. He'd seen and done some terrible things in the war, but that was no excuse. He needed to master his temper. Before he did something that couldn't be fixed with a hammer.

There was no one inside the house, so he continued on through the hall and out to the garden at the rear. The flowers were in full bloom this time of year, expertly tended by Mhaira's loving hands. He wished he had half her skill at running a household or growing a garden or even raising their son.

He slowed when he saw Natalya and her husband Gared. Kayne had never much liked Gared. The man had wedded Mhaira's cousin just as soon as he learned she was coming into some land, or so it had seemed to him. Now he was nodding along while his wife spoke, the two with their backs to Kayne. Mhaira was opposite them, sitting on the bench under the old apple tree in the corner of the garden.

'Hope I ain't interrupting anything,' Kayne said politely. Gared jumped and Natalya whirled around, a guilty look on her face.

'Brodar,' Gared stammered. 'Well met! We thought you were out practising with young Magnar. Teaching him to be a famed warrior like his father, eh?'

Kayne stared at Mhaira. She looked like she might've been crying again.

'We were just leaving,' Natalya said curtly. She gave Mhaira a long, meaningful look that for some reason filled Kayne with dread. 'I'll speak to you soon, cousin.'

'Good to see you,' Gared babbled. 'We should catch up some time.'

Kayne watched them go and turned to his wife. 'What was that about?'

Mhaira rose slowly. 'I need to prepare dinner.'

'Mhaira… I ain't a stranger. I'm still the man you married.'

She stared at his face, as if searching for something. 'Natalya brought Gared to speak with me.'

Kayne froze. 'What about?'

The sorrow in Mhaira's eyes might have broken his heart if her next words hadn't filled it with rage. 'You've changed. You… you *scare* me. Some of the things Gared told me, about Red Valley—'

'What a-fucking-bout it?' Kayne roared, all the pent-up anger pouring out of him like a river bursting through a shattered dam. 'It was a war! The Bloodfist and his army weren't for giving an inch! Men like that, you need to send them a message.' He realized he was shouting and lowered his voice. 'There were thirty of us, Mhaira. Thirty. All that was left of the army that marched on Reaver's Gate. A couple minutes more and I wouldn't be standing here at all. If Mehmon's reinforcements hadn't arrived…'

'You ordered all those men killed,' Mhaira said accusingly. 'Even those that surrendered.'

'If I hadn't, the war might've dragged on another seven years.' He spoke quietly, not wanting to hear the words even as he uttered them. They might be true, but that didn't matter. Not now. 'They were my orders. The Shaman's orders. I'm the Sword of the North now, Mhaira. I ain't a Warden no more.'

'Natalya and Gared asked if Magnar could move in with them,' Mhaira whispered. 'They don't think it's safe for him to be around you.'

'They… they *what*?' Kayne struggled to speak. He was

shaking with fury now, like a great volcano about to explode. 'After all I've done for them. For *you*.'

'You left me here alone,' she said.

He raised a hand, and before he knew it, before he could stop himself, he slapped her.

An instant later he knew he'd made a terrible mistake. Mhaira didn't move, didn't react at all. She only stared at him uncomprehending. And that was about the most heartbreaking reaction he could imagine.

'Mhaira,' he said, distraught, overwhelmed with disgust for himself. 'I'm sorry. Please. I'm sorry.'

She walked slowly past him. Crossed the garden and didn't look back, not until she was standing right beside the door leading back into the house. Then she turned to him, and her face as white as a ghost. 'I told them no,' she said quietly.

Kayne stared at his stinging palm in horror. There was a rustle of movement, and he looked up.

To see Magnar watching him from the wall near the door. His son's grey eyes were filled with something that made the Sword of the North, the most feared warrior in the High Fangs, want to scream in anguish.

It was hatred.

Friends Old and New

'ALL RIGHT, LAD?'
Brick glanced up and nodded. The boy was restringing his bow by the light of the campfire, his tongue poking out in concentration. Kayne considered clapping him on the shoulder, then thought better of it and wandered over to sit by Jerek. His knees creaked as he lowered himself to the hard, stony ground. The Wolf gave him a nod and shot a dark glare at the lone female face beside the fire.

Jana Shah Shan had been travelling alongside them for days now. In all that time, Kayne couldn't recall Jerek uttering a single word to her. Even Grunt had made more of an effort to communicate, a sorry state of affairs considering he didn't even have a tongue.

Jana didn't seem to be enjoying the biting cold that had descended on them as they travelled north through the ruins. The Jade Islander wore a stoic expression, pretending to be unperturbed by the sudden drop in temperature – but the way she kept inching nearer the fire, rubbing her hands together when she thought no one was watching, told a different story.

'Want to borrow my cloak?' Kayne asked. 'It's a bit dirty but it'll keep you warm.'

Jana stuck out her chin. 'With my training I need no protection from the elements. Discomfort is but a state of mind.'

Jerek muttered something under his breath. 'I'm going for a piss,' he announced, climbing to his feet. At least his wounded leg was looking a good deal better now. If there'd ever been a harder man in the High Fangs, Brodar Kayne had yet to meet him.

Jana crossed her arms and watched the Wolf's departure with a frown. 'Your friend doesn't seem to like me,' she observed.

'He don't like many folk.'

'Is it because I am a woman? Or because I am from the east?'

Kayne shrugged. 'If I had to guess, probably both.'

'You seem like a man of principle. I'm curious why you would keep the company of such a close-minded sort.'

'Jerek hates everyone,' Brick piped up unexpectedly. He examined his bow and nodded in satisfaction. 'He's an angry bastard. But he's all right when you get to know him.'

Grunt murmured in agreement. Jana seemed to be expecting one of them to add something more. When they didn't, she shook her head in exasperation. 'The men from this part of the world are most peculiar. I'll be glad to return to my betrothed once my mission is complete.'

'What's he like, this young man?'

Jana rested her chin on her palm and stared into the fire. 'He's not so young. But he's a good man, and honest.'

'Ain't too many of them around nowadays. Not in this part of the world and I'm guessing not in the Confederation, neither.'

'We live in difficult times, it is true. My betrothed… taught me a great deal about myself, and many other things besides. Our relationship is not without its complications.'

Kayne grinned. 'Just till you're married.'

Jana's eyes narrowed slightly, but a moment later she seemed to catch the joke and smiled sheepishly. 'I would ask you a question. Please be honest with me.'

'I'm all ears.'

'The Imperial Academy requires that every student learn the language that you westerners call "Common". Do I speak it well? At least well enough to make myself understood?'

Jana must have mistaken the confusion on Kayne's face for

379

something else, as she reddened and appeared slightly ashamed. 'I rarely had the opportunity to practise your language before I departed the Isles. I apologize if I sound foolish.'

'No, no, that's not it at all,' Kayne said, waving his hands in embarrassment. 'To tell the truth, I ain't that familiar with the nations beyond the Unclaimed Lands. Never occurred to me that your people might not speak the same language as us. You say you speak two languages?'

'All who graduate from the Academy must be fluent in at least three languages. I speak six. Though as you've heard, my Common is a little rusty.'

'It sounds damn near perfect to my old ears. What d'they teach you at the Academy, other than languages?'

'Everything a man or woman needs in order to serve their emperor. Only the brightest and most talented are accepted. It is a great honour for one's family.'

'This Unity you spoke of. They teach that at the Academy, too?'

'Yes. It is a tradition dating back to before the Cataclysm, when the iron mages of Gharzia turned our own weapons against us.'

'The Cataclysm? I'm guessing you mean the Godswar.'

Jana nodded. 'The Cataclysm shattered the two great empires of the east. Gharzia and the Jade Isles are at peace now, but Gharzia still has its iron mages and a wise ruler knows that friends can quickly become enemies.'

A shadow fell across them as Jerek returned. The Wolf hunkered down and then poked at the fire with a stick, checking the bubbling pot hanging above it. 'Stew's almost ready,' he grunted. He rummaged around in his backpack and withdrew a loaf of rock-hard bread. From across the fire, Jana groaned.

'This is the seventh night in a row that we're eating warm stew with a heel of bread. Don't you ever tire of such food?'

'I like stew with a heel of bread!' Brick said reproachfully.

Jana reached into her own backpack and pulled out what appeared to be a fruit. It was yellow and covered in black bruises and, if Kayne were to be honest, brought to mind a certain unflattering part of the male body. 'This is the *nana* fruit. It grows on trees in the islands south of my homeland. Even after it is picked, the fruit remains fresh for months within the skin.'

Kayne stared at it doubtfully. In his view, eating anything that yellow probably couldn't be good for a man's stomach.

'I wonder if my angry friend would care to try?' Jana said, tossing the strange fruit across the fire to Jerek, who stared at it as he might a venomous snake that had just dropped into his lap. 'You remove the skin and eat the fleshy part.'

'I ain't eating this shit,' the Wolf rasped. 'Probably some kind of poison.'

'I assure you that the *nana* fruit is perfectly good for you. It is highly nutritious and even helps the body to cleanse itself.'

'Cleanse itself?' the Wolf grunted.

'I think she means take a shit,' Brick explained.

'Fuck it then.' Jerek ripped the skin off and took an experimental bite. 'Ain't bad,' he said grudgingly, swallowing it down. 'Tastes sweet.'

Jana smiled. 'You swallow too fast,' she said. 'You need to masticate it first.'

Jerek instantly froze, the *nana* halfway to his mouth. He stared at the fruit in horror. 'The fuck did you just say?' he whispered savagely.

'You need to masticate it first.'

'I don't think she means what you think she means,' Brick cut in desperately, but the Wolf was already on his feet, the half-eaten *nana* fruit raised like a weapon.

'I'll shove this up your arse!' he bellowed. Jana Shah Shan leaped to her feet and took up a fighting stance, arms outstretched and legs tensed to spring into motion at any moment. Things were about to turn ugly.

Kayne tried to scramble up, thinking to put himself between them and calm things down, but a sudden sharp pain in his chest stole the breath from his lungs and he almost pitched into the spitting campfire.

'Kayne?' Jerek rasped, his rage immediately forgotten. The Wolf was across to him in an instant, taking his weight effortlessly, his bald brow furrowed in concern.

'I'm all right,' the old barbarian said, though his legs felt like water. He sat back down, breathing hard.

Jana Shah Shan hurried around the fire and crouched over him, then began to massage his chest and arms, her deft hands rubbing life into his tingling limbs. 'Your body needs rest,' Jana said. 'You push yourself too hard for a man of your years.'

'I ain't that old,' Kayne complained, but the truth was he felt ancient. Once Jana had finished checking him over, he lay down on his back and stared up at the bright stars in the night sky overhead. A long silence followed, everyone shocked by what had just happened.

Eventually Brick broke the silence. 'What's your home like?' he asked. 'Your house, I mean. Up in the mountains. You have houses, don't you? My uncle said the Highland people are savages who dwell in caves.'

Kayne chuckled, though it hurt to laugh. 'Aye, we got houses. It's not so different up in the mountains than down in the Lowlands. I had a house, a decent-sized one with a garden and fields and all. Got a lot of memories of that place, not all of 'em pleasant.'

'I wish I had a home,' Brick said glumly.

'Home's wherever your heart says it is,' Kayne replied. 'Find someone that makes you feel like you belong and you'll never want for a place to call home again.' He turned to Grunt. 'Where's home for you, friend?'

The big green mute pointed a thick finger towards the north. He made a series of movements with his other hand, his yellow eyes filled with sadness.

'He says his people lived a nomadic life on the southern steppes before the coming of the Yahan,' Brick translated. 'But eventually the humans grew too many and his people had to flee their homeland. They went north, beyond the frozen sea. Those that remained behind scattered and slowly died out. Grunt's ancestors were among them. He thinks he might be the last of his kind, at least this side of the Frozen Sea.'

'Ain't nothing beyond the Frozen Sea,' Kayne said doubtfully. 'Just ice. The world ends at the High Fangs.'

Grunt gestured again and made a flapping motion with his oversized hands. 'He says the distance is vast and impossible to cross by ship. But there is another land far beyond the ocean of ice. He thought he could fly there on the back of a giant... lizard. Is that right? Lizard? I don't how to translate that.'

Jana Shah Shan raised her head from where she lay perilously close to the fire. 'My people have a similar legend,' she said quietly. 'A legend of great flying reptiles whose kind ruled the world before the Ancients and their machines. They were called dragons.'

They rested the next day and the morning after that. The temperature continued to drop, the chill claws of autumn gripping the land and bringing with it an icy wind that blew down from the mountains. Kayne was feeling a good deal better by then, and so they finally broke camp and resumed their journey deeper into the ruins. The hills grew steeper and more treacherous as they progressed north, passing more of the standing stones along the way. Now and then Jana would translate the underfolk script, which as it turned out was one of the six languages she had learned back at the Academy.

'This tunnel once led to the residences of the nobles,' she was saying now. 'The underfolk had a strict caste system. The only way to advance in their society was through the relentless accumulation of gold.'

'Swap gold for blood and I reckon the same applies to the High Fangs,' Kayne muttered. Most of the chieftains he'd known over the years had achieved their positions largely through prowess in battle. The problem with that approach was that once a man became good at killing, it was hard for him to stop. The likes of Targus Bloodfist and Krazka One-Eye weren't ever satisfied. Even the Shaman's will hadn't always been enough to thwart their ambitions. He thought of Red Valley and flinched.

An hour later they reached the next standing stone. Jana checked the runes carved on the stone and announced that it marked the site of a major crossroads of some kind. They were about to move on when suddenly Grunt let out a low growl and his amber eyes narrowed. He cocked an oversized ear and appeared to be listening for something. Then he pointed to the tunnel entrance cut into the hill far below them and gestured frantically to Brick.

'There are men coming down that tunnel,' the youngster translated. 'A lot of men. We should hide.'

They sought cover behind the standing stone and waited. Sure enough, a minute later a stream of bandits began to pour from the cave mouth. Kayne's failing eyes couldn't make out their faces, but he counted at least fifty. One of the men was unmistakable, as wide as any two of his fellows put together. 'Fivebellies,' he muttered.

'Thought they let us go,' Jerek growled. 'Looks like those pricks followed us here.'

'The Seer arranged our escape,' Kayne explained. 'That don't mean Asander was in on the plan. I reckon the bandits that attacked Jana were part of this group.'

As they watched the men swarm from the tunnel, it quickly became clear that something was wrong. The bandits were breaking in all directions, their faces pale with terror. A few began to climb the hill just below, scrabbling desperately to get away from whatever was down in the tunnel with them. Fivebellies himself was in the lead, setting the pace despite his great bulk.

Just then the ground trembled, and the source of the bandits' hysteria emerged into the afternoon light like a nightmare of fire and shadow stepping into the waking world.

'Shit,' Kayne whispered, horrified. The *thing* that came out of the tunnel was humanoid in shape and not much bigger than a man – a good deal smaller than some of the abominations and giants he'd fought over the years. But looking at it, staring beyond the flames that wreathed its shadowy form, he felt as though he was gazing into the abyss. It wasn't what he saw that made his heart hurt and set his teeth on edge; it was what he didn't see. The complete absence of light and warmth, as if he were staring into an empty void.

The horror seemed to flow across the ground, leaving a trail of scorched stone in its wake. It reached out a nebulous arm and wrapped it around an unfortunate bandit who hadn't fled quickly enough. The man screamed, a long-drawn-out sound that rose to an inhuman screech. Seconds later his skin began to smoke and then he began to glow as fire consumed him from within. The bandit grew brighter and brighter, until a thousand tiny cracks ruptured his flesh. Then he simply collapsed inward, leaving nothing but a drifting cloud of ash.

'The gholam,' Jana said, her voice thick with dread. 'Someone activated it.'

'Can you stop it?' Kayne said urgently.

Jana shook her head helplessly. 'Only the key that was stolen can deactivate the gholam.'

'Then let's get the hell out of here.' The companions turned and fled, half running, half climbing the jagged terrain that rose ahead of them. As the minutes stretched on and they ran, Kayne found himself falling further and further behind. Jana was a speck far in the distance, Grunt a green blur just behind her. Jerek and Brick were behind them but still a hundred yards ahead of Kayne. The red-haired youngster glanced back, and a moment later he slowed right down.

He's waiting for me, Kayne thought in horror. He waved a furious hand at the boy. 'Go,' he shouted. 'Don't worry about me.' But if Brick had heard him, he didn't move. 'Go!' Kayne roared again. This time Brick hesitated, and then he turned and sped off after the others.

Kayne tried to keep up but his legs didn't want to obey him. Every step he took felt as though he were wading through the tar lake back at the bandit encampment. He reached the next standing stone and had to stop to catch his breath. He leaned on the marker, sucking air into his lungs.

He took a quick look around. The others had disappeared. 'Sod it,' he gasped, lowering himself against the monument and letting it take his weight.

He wondered if the gholam was still out there somewhere. Chances were he wasn't doing himself any favours by sitting there on his arse waiting to find out. He placed his palms on the stone and tried to push himself up.

'Urgh,' he said, and he collapsed back down.

He just needed to rest for a minute, that was all. Just a minute to let his thumping heart calm a little, and then he would get right back up and be on his way.

Something cold pressed against his neck. He jerked awake, accidentally banged his head on the solid block of granite behind him. For a second he was disoriented. Then his eyes focused on the multiple chins wobbling just beyond the length of steel shoved against his throat and a face bled into view.

'Where are the rest of you?' Fivebellies demanded. He had a haunted look in his piggish eyes.

Kayne held his breath. One false move and the bandit would open his neck like a hog during Beregund's Midwinter Festival from years gone by. 'Beats me,' he croaked.

Fivebellies glanced around nervously. He wouldn't stop fidgeting, Kayne noticed. It was hard not to notice a quivering razor-sharp edge an inch from your throat. 'Slowing them down, were you, greybeard? I don't know how you escaped back at camp, but you aren't getting away again. I need you as bait.'

'Bait?' Kayne echoed. That didn't sound promising.

Fivebellies nodded and a muscle beneath his left eye twitched. 'Something came for us,' he said brokenly. 'While we was planning to ambush you.' The bandit's voice dropped to a terrified whisper. 'I'm the last one. The rest are... they're dead. Gone.'

Kayne swallowed carefully. 'You reckon it's still after you?'

Fivebellies shook his head in despair. 'We split up and we laid traps for it and we still couldn't lose the fucker. It can't be hurt. It can't be stopped.'

Such was the horror on the man's face that Kayne almost pitied him, right up until his very next words.

'You're going to lead it away from me.'

'I ain't in much of a condition to lead anyone a chase.'

'Shut up!' Fivebellies screamed, his meaty jowls quivering. It dawned on Kayne then that Fivebellies had been pushed beyond breaking point; the bandit's mind had been cracked by whatever he'd witnessed down in those tunnels.

Fivebellies nodded at Kayne's left hand. 'Hold it up,' he said. 'Place it against the stone.' His manic eyes not leaving Kayne, Fivebellies reached down to his belt with his free hand and drew an evil-looking machete.

Kayne's heart sank. 'Not bloody likely.'

Fivebellies pressed the scimitar close against his flesh and Kayne felt a warm trickle of blood run down his neck.

'Your hand or your head, greybeard.'

Very slowly, Kayne raised his left hand and placed it palm up against the monument. 'You don't have to do this.'

'I'm not stupid! First chance you get, you'll draw that greatsword of yours. You know what? I think I'd prefer you with no hands.'

'No hands?' Kayne repeated, horrified. 'You want to chop 'em both off?'

'I'm not for taking any chances.'

Kayne's mind whirred, searching for a way out of this predicament. For the first time since the day of the Shaman's pyre, he felt truly powerless. He thought of Mhaira and his eyes blurred with tears. He was so close to the High Fangs, now. He didn't fear death, hadn't feared it for many a year, but he didn't want to die without seeing Mhaira's face one last time.

Without telling his son he was sorry.

Fivebellies rested the serrated edge of the machete against Kayne's wrist. 'This will hurt, but I'll warn you now: you make a fuss, and I'll do to you what I did to that dandy Glaston—'

Fivebellies gasped and something splashed into Kayne's eyes. It was warm and wet, and it took all his willpower not to move his free hand to wipe it away. Instead he blinked wildly. When his vision cleared, he saw something sticking out of the bandit's monstrous gut. It was an arrowhead, glistening with blood. It had struck him from behind and gone near straight through his body.

A second later Fivebellies toppled backwards and began to scream. Maybe it was Kayne's imagination, but he fancied the earth shook a little as the man's prodigious bulk struck the ground.

A pair of familiar faces appeared over the hill, one bald and fire-scarred and looking decidedly pissed off, the other young and freckled.

'You came back,' Kayne gasped.

Jerek scowled and scratched his short beard. 'Brick said you was struggling. I've spent two years saving your sorry old arse. I figured what's one more time.'

'I told him to run,' Kayne said, nodding at Brick. The boy was staring at Fivebellies, a strange expression on his face.

'Kid was determined to help. Reckon he's just about as stubborn as you.' Jerek's eyes narrowed on Fivebellies. 'The *fuck*, Kayne? You got blindsided by this bag of shit?' The Wolf gave the stricken bandit a quick boot in the ribs. Fivebellies twitched and let out a groan. 'Arse the size of his, even your useless old eyes ought to be able to spot him a mile away.'

'I got careless,' Kayne replied. He'd got old and weak: that was the truth. With a tremendous effort he pushed himself to his feet. 'Where're the others?'

'Waiting up ahead,' Brick said distractedly. 'Shall I finish him?' The boy reached for his quiver.

There was something in Brick's voice that Kayne hadn't heard before and didn't much like. There was killing and then there was killing, and while Kayne could understand the boy's hunger for revenge, it was a line that once crossed changed a man forever. 'I'll do it,' he said wearily. He was reaching over his shoulder to draw his greatsword when Jerek placed a hand on his arm, stopping him short.

'You two go on,' the Wolf snarled, clutching his axes and fixing Fivebellies with a look that chilled the blood. 'I'll catch up. Me and this prick got some debts need repaying.'

The sky was darkening by the time they found Grunt and Jana Shah Shan close to a stone marker that had somehow toppled over. It was on the verge of a steep rise that quickly fell away just beyond. Jana balanced dangerously on the edge of the upturned monument, standing on the tip of one foot with her arms spread wide and her head turned towards the moon.

'Slowly,' she said calmly, without moving an inch. 'You don't want to startle them.'

'Startle who?' Kayne asked. He met Grunt's amber gaze. The big mute was sitting on the fallen stone, his elbows resting on his knees and a glum expression on his blunt face. He gave an apologetic shrug and tossed a pebble at a rock twenty feet distant. If the collection of stones scattered around his target was any kind of measure, he'd been at the game a fair while.

'Startle who?' Kayne repeated as he reached the marker – but as the depression beyond the rise came into view, he saw exactly what Jana referred to.

A large group of children sat huddled together on the stony ground. He counted two score, at least – all thin to the point of starving and coated in layers of grime. The poor things looked more exhausted than he was. The faces of some of the children held a haunted quality that reminded him of Fivebellies, and many drew back in fear as he crested the rise.

'Don't be afraid, young ones,' called Jana, as Jerek and Brick joined Kayne on the rise. 'These men are friends.'

Dozens of eyes stared at the three of them. Jana somersaulted from the monument, landing on her feet with the grace of a cat. A few children clapped. Most continued to watch the newcomers nervously.

'You look familiar,' one of the children said hesitantly. She was more a woman than a girl, in truth: blue-eyed and blonde-haired, likely the eldest. 'You remind me of the old King.'

Kayne's eyes narrowed. 'Old King? My name's Brodar Kayne. My son Magnar rules the High Fangs.'

The girl shook her head. 'Krazka's king now. We fled town to get away, but Krazka sent his Kingsmen after us.'

A sudden pressure weighed in Kayne's chest, and his next words emerged as a croak. 'What happened to Magnar?'

'Krazka hurt him. Cut him bad.'

Kayne reeled as if he'd been punched. 'How badly? What the fuck did that bastard do to my boy?'

The girl flinched back, suddenly afraid. 'Krazka kept him in a wicker cage. Yllandris said he took some of his fingers, and did some worse things, but she never said what. I'm sorry, I don't know.'

Kayne became aware of his own breath rasping inside his chest. Memories of the wicker cage flooded back to him – an endless nightmare of pain and terror that had threatened to drive him mad. Most men broke after a week inside that terrible device. Kayne had somehow survived a year. He remembered the Shaman's words outside Dorminia.

I must return to the High Fangs. Heartstone is in grave peril.

Was that the moment Krazka had seized the capital? Seized

the capital and placed his son inside a wicker cage? He felt himself shaking, and realized that his fists were bunched together.

A rough hand squeezed his shoulder and then Jerek was right there beside him, his voice softer than Kayne had ever heard it. 'We ain't far from the Fangs now. We'll get him out of there, Kayne. You can count on it.'

Kayne took a deep breath. Somehow he relaxed his fists and let go of the terrible rage. 'I'm sorry, lass,' he said. 'I shouldn't have snapped at you like that. Why hasn't the Shaman taken Heartstone back? I saw him return north. Him and the Brethren. There's not a man that could keep them out.'

'Krazka has demons with him. He made some kind of pact with one, the Herald. It fought the Shaman and chased him away. I think the Shaman's with Carn Bloodfist's army now, in the West Reaching, but... they say he's dying.'

Kayne took another deep breath. Highlanders siding with demons. The world had changed beyond all recognition. 'What's your name?' he asked.

'Corinn,' she replied timidly.

'Well now, Corinn. Why's Krazka sending his Kingsmen after you and the rest of these children?'

Despite her own trepidation, the girl approached Kayne and lowered her voice so that the younger children couldn't hear her next words. 'They want to sacrifice us to the Herald. Yllandris led us away from town. The iron man caught up with her in the Greenwild and set fire to the forest. We only just made it out.'

As Corinn came nearer, Kayne saw the bright tears in her eyes. 'I think Yllandris is dead,' she continued. 'We've been fleeing south but our food has run out. Tiny Tom and some of the others, I think they're starving.' Her voice cracked as the brave mask she was wearing finally began to slip, and Kayne was overcome with sympathy. This Corinn had barely seen thirteen winters, yet if her story were true she'd guided them through a hundred miles of the roughest terrain imaginable, all the while being pursued by the most formidable warriors in the King's Reaching.

Kayne swallowed his own anguish then, forcing it deep inside him. These children were counting on him now. 'You're gutsy to have come this far,' he said gently. 'But there's nothing south of here for near a thousand miles.' He didn't mention the gholam. Nothing good would come of that. 'Me and my friend Jerek are heading north, back to the mountains. I reckon you'll be safe enough in the West Reaching if we can circle around. Carn Bloodfist ain't ever been a friend of mine, but he's fair enough with those he's got no quarrel with.'

'What about the iron man? And the other Kingsmen? I think they killed Yorn, too.'

Yorn. That name brought back memories. Holding the valley against overwhelming odds. Red Rayne to his left, Taran behind him and Yorn to his right. Yorn had joined the town guard after the war. He'd been a solid sort. It was funny how the solid sorts were always the ones that died youngest.

Kayne cleared his throat. 'Anyone wants to harm you, they'll have to go through me and Jerek first.'

There was a growl and then Grunt joined them on the verge. 'Him too,' Kayne added.

'Don't forget about me,' Brick piped up, trying his best to sound tough. He nodded gravely at the three men towering above him and puffed out his small chest. Then he caught Corinn staring at him and his ruddy cheeks turned a bright red.

Kayne turned. 'Jana, you in?'

The Jade Islander looked guilty. 'I must bring word to the Emperor of what has happened. A larger party will need to be sent. The thief must be found and the key recovered or there is no telling what the gholam may do.'

'Women,' Jerek rasped in disgust. 'This is why you don't bring 'em along. Only one thing you can count on a woman for and that's let you down when you need 'em most.'

Jana went stiff. 'You didn't let me finish,' she said coolly. 'I'll help you deliver these children to safety before I return east. Perhaps the thief is yet ahead of us.'

Kayne looked from Jana to Jerek. It might've been his imagination, but he thought he saw the ghost of a smile on the Wolf's face.

What Lies Beneath

DAVARUS COLE STAGGERED from the impact of the blast but somehow managed to keep his feet on the slippery marble. On the street just ahead, the remains of the Whitecloak patrol that had been standing there a moment ago oozed over the wet flagstones. Blood and viscera bubbled gently, pooling around torn fragments of cloak and lumps of twisted metal and chunks of blackened bone.

Cole stared at Thanates, horrified. The wizard crackled with energy, filled to bursting by the prodigious quantity of magical ore he had siphoned from the silos back at the Blight. A baleful radiance shone through the scarlet rag that covered his eyes. Tiny arcs of black fire danced up and down his tattered overcoat.

'Did you need to do that?' Cole remonstrated as forcefully as he dared. 'Those men probably had families.'

You set the shamblers on the Whitecloaks back in Newharvest, a treacherous voice in his skull reminded him. That had been different though. Priam's men had been going to kill him.

He frowned down at the steaming remains, swallowing the nausea that rose within him. In all likelihood, those men had been about to kill him too. Scarcely a year ago the world had seemed so black and white. Now every choice he made seemed to be the wrong one.

The wizard's voice was as hard as iron. 'It is the lesser evil. Whitecloaks are not permitted families. They are thralls, cursed to wither away their brief lives in dire servitude, their blood and seed and eventually their very essences fed upon by the White Lady's handmaidens in order to preserve their unnatural existence. Those men are better off dead.'

Cole remembered the strange fluid leaking out of the ears of Priam and his men back at Newharvest. He remembered Thanates' words.

The Unborn have fed well this night.

It took all his self-control to stop himself emptying his stomach on the streets then.

Thanates turned to the large crowd gathered on the edge of the docks. Behind the crowd the ship they'd commandeered near Newharvest lurched crazily in the harbour, battered by the endless gusts of wind and the torrential rain.

'You are Freefolk now,' the wizard boomed. Somehow his voice carried above the storm. 'Those of you who wish to flee are advised to seek shelter from what is to come. Those with homes may return to them.' Thanates raised a hand and curled it slowly into a fist. When he continued, his voice had grown even louder. It seemed to thunder from him, the black fire that wreathed his body flaring angrily with every word. 'Those of you who lost loved ones in the Blight, those of who you feel an absence in your heart you cannot explain – remember what I told you. Remember what the woman who rules this city has done. Soon your stolen memories will return. I cannot promise that you will not feel grief. I cannot guarantee that the rage you will feel will not consume you. But I offer you this: join me as I seek answers, and I promise to make the White Lady pay for each and every wrong she has done you!'

As the wizard finished speaking the crowd erupted into cheers. Cole saw determination in the eyes of many. An Indebted whose name he didn't know took a step forward. It was one of Floater's friends, he realized. 'I lost a good friend back there. I haven't got a family of my own, but Floater did. I owe it to him to get revenge on that bitch.'

That won a fresh round of cheers. Another Thelassan stepped forward. 'Floater was my friend too. The White Lady's got to pay for what she's done. She's got to pay!'

More cheers roared across the dock. A consensus was beginning to form, the anger of the crowd turning it towards a singular purpose, a singular path of action.

Suddenly, Smokes stepped forward. 'I'll burn this fucking city to the ground!' he snarled. 'And every man, woman and child in it!'

The sound of someone clearing their throat was the only noise to break the silence that followed. 'For what she done!' Smokes added belatedly. He looked around, desperate for someone to back him up.

'That seems a little... extreme,' Cole said slowly. 'Besides, the city is constructed from marble. It'll never catch fire. Especially not in this weather.'

Smokes sagged and a moment later shuffled shamefacedly back into the crowd, which now looked rather deflated.

Cole took a deep breath. It was up to him to salvage things. 'I know all too well the depths of the White Lady's evil,' he began hesitantly. 'I served her faithfully. But after she was done with me, she tried to have me murdered. She almost succeeded. Almost, but not quite. I survived. Thanks to this man, I survived.' Cole gestured at Thanates. 'I owe it to him to stand with him now. As do you! Months ago the people of the Trine toppled one tyrant. Today we can topple another.'

Much to his surprise the crowd reacted to his words with fresh cheers. He'd half expected peals of laughter. He couldn't imagine why any man would pay attention to him, a common bastard. Perhaps they were simply intimidated by his mastery of the dead. There was a time when being feared would have gratified his ego, but of late he had come to realize that anyone who inspired loyalty through terror was probably not a very good person.

Smiler melted out of the crowd and approached him. 'You're a hero, Ghost.'

Cole shook his head. 'I'm no hero. I just do the best I can with what I have.'

'You've certainly changed your tune. You were the cock of the walk that night at the tavern.'

'I was a fool,' Cole said sombrely.

Smiler jerked a thumb behind him towards the harbour. 'I wish you luck in any case. I'm sailing back to the Grey City once this weather lets up. My cousin Moryk's there somewhere, I know he is.'

Cole nodded. 'You've been a good friend to me. What does your cousin do?'

Smiler gave a gap-toothed grin. 'Moryk? You might say he's a miner, too, of sorts. He'll force himself through any hole.'

Something about that sounded odd to Cole's ears, but he let it pass. 'Well, I hope you find him. Look out for Sasha while you're in Dorminia. She has long brown hair and eyes a man could lose himself in. If you see her, tell her... tell her I'm coming home as soon as I can.'

'It'll be my pleasure,' Smiler replied. Cole exchanged a companionable nod with the fellow. Despite all that had happened, it was reassuring to know there were still decent men like Smiler around. He reminded Cole of his erstwhile henchman Three-Finger, before the cruel truth of the world had broken his spirit.

The survivors of Newharvest said their farewells. Those who lacked the stomach for a fight sloped off into the rain while those who remained looked expectantly to Thanates. The wizard nodded at Cole and then pointed to the ship. 'It is time. Call your minions from the hold.'

Cole shifted uneasily. 'I don't want any innocents to get hurt.'

Thanates clenched his fists angrily and dark fire danced around his knuckles. 'It is vital that we as create as much chaos as possible on the streets! I need the Whitecloaks and the Unborn drawn away from the palace. But first you will take me to the Hall of Annals. I understand it lies somewhere in the ruins of Sanctuary.'

'I don't know the way.'

The sinister glow that shone through Thanates' rag flared dangerously. 'You told me you were familiar with those ruins,' he hissed. Despite the fact he had Magebane tucked safely at his belt, Cole couldn't help but shrink back in the face of the wizard's ire.

'The pale women escorted me there! They used some kind of device to conceal the path from me. All I remember are shadows and mist, and children crying.'

'I can show you,' piped up a small voice.

Cole and Thanates turned. Gazing up at them with his watery eyes was Derkin. 'Ma and I spent years living in the ruins,' he added. 'I'll guide you there.'

The western section of the ruins of Sanctuary was much the same as the other parts Cole remembered. Ancient walls constructed of sandstone and other weak materials had begun to collapse long ago, resulting in leaning buildings that were supported only by the weight of their neighbours. Rubble and rotting timber covered the abandoned streets. The storm had penetrated even here; water rained down from hundreds of feet above, percolating through cracks in the artificial foundations that separated the City of Towers from the corpse of the dead city beneath. There was little in the way of natural light, but the torch Derkin carried provided sufficient illumination for the three of them to navigate the ruins. Derkin's ma waited back at the docks, still too weak from her recent brush with death to risk venturing down into the undercity.

'The White Lady was once the high priestess of the Mother,' Thanates said as they made their way deeper into the skeleton of the holy city. 'Politically and magically she was perhaps the most significant figure of our time. That much I learned from my research in Dorminia.'

For a second Cole thought he glimpsed something moving just beyond the edges of the light. He stared at the darkness but saw nothing. He decided it was probably just his imagination.

'There's something I've been wondering about,' he said. 'Does the White Lady have a name? She can't have always been the White Lady. She must have had a real name at one time.'

Thanates shook his head. 'If she did no one remembers it, least of all me. Until recently I could not even recall my own.'

Cole's eyebrows rose in surprise. 'You couldn't remember your own name?'

'For close to five hundred years I lived as a crow, my consciousness lost in the mind of my familiar. I came to the Grey City searching for clues as to my true identity.'

'What did you discover?'

'My real name, among other things. With the help of another I began to piece together my fractured mind. My memories are still incomplete. I trust I will find the answers I seek in the Hall of Annals.'

'The person that helped you rediscover yourself. What was his name?'

'Isaac.'

Cole stopped dead. 'I knew an Isaac!' he exclaimed. 'He was about my age, maybe a little older. He was...' Cole paused. He couldn't remember what Isaac had looked like. All he recalled was a face of devastating blandness. Absolutely nothing about the Halfmage's manservant had stuck in his mind, other than the fact he had seemed intent on ingratiating himself with the old barbarian Kayne and the rest of the group of rebels. 'I don't remember,' he admitted, feeling stupid.

Thanates cocked his head in that peculiar manner of his. 'You cannot describe his appearance either? Strange. This Isaac was an enigma. In return for his help he had me perform various favours that made little sense at the time. I now believe he was planning something. Preparing a strategy. He was brilliant, a man of endless talents.'

'I thought he was an ass,' Cole mumbled. Something occurred to him then. 'Why did you save me? When you found me dying, I mean.'

'I believed I could use you.'

'Use me?' Cole said warily. He had an unpleasant feeling he knew where this was heading.

'You killed Salazar. You toppled a Magelord. As such, you are a beacon of hope that I will light when the time is right. And you have strange powers of your own. You are a potent tool, child.'

'I'm not a tool!' Cole snapped back. 'And I'm not a child. I'm sick of people trying to control me. Trying to use me. It's almost got me killed on countless occasions. I just want to be left alone.'

There was a hint of amusement in the wizard's voice. 'For a boy who wants to be left alone you have an uncanny knack of finding yourself at the heart of events.'

'Not any more. After this is over, I'm settling for the quiet life.'

'You carry a god's essence within you, Davarus Cole. The quiet life is no longer yours to choose.'

An uncomfortable silence followed. Cole looked down at his hands. They were beginning to lose their colour again, the vitality he had stolen from Corvac fading away. What was it Thanates had said to him?

Death itself resides in you. Feed it and you will grow stronger. Resist... and it will feed on you.

He shook his head angrily. He was determined not to feed *anything*. He would refuse to become a killer like the Reaver's essence seemed to want him to be. He hadn't asked for this.

Suddenly, Derkin gasped and raised his torch as high as his stunted arms would allow him. 'The Abandoned are coming,' he whispered.

Cole glimpsed dark shapes at the edges of the torchlight. He concentrated and thought he could hear heartbeats. Dozens of them, faint and highly irregular. 'The Abandoned?' he whispered.

'They rarely venture into this part of the ruins,' Derkin explained. 'Something must have drawn them here.'

Cole placed a hand on Magebane's jewelled hilt. 'Are they dangerous?'

'They feed on waste from the city above and normally avoid people. But they can be dangerous if they haven't fed in a while.'

The misshapen figures inched nearer, drawn to the three intruders like moths to a flame, though they seemed reluctant to step inside the circle of light. Cole became aware of a faint rasping sound, like a dying man gasping for breath. A tense moment passed. Then the first of the Abandoned stepped into view.

Cole recoiled in horror. The *thing* that emerged from the shadows was the size of a large child. It was entirely naked, its pale flesh so thin that it was nearly translucent, revealing the dark shape of vital organs beneath. Oversized eyes the colour of soured milk stared from a face the features of which were poorly defined, as if the creature were somehow incomplete. Every breath seemed a tortured rattle in its underdeveloped lungs.

The Abandoned raised a hand, its webbed fingers reaching towards Cole, who drew Magebane and held it protectively before him. 'Back!' he shouted. 'I don't want to hurt you.' Surprisingly, he found that he meant it. Something about this apparition brought to mind a lost child. A twisted mockery of a child, but a child nonetheless.

The horror inched closer. It opened its mouth, a simple hole in its face that contained no teeth, only a tongue that flopped out, drooling thick white mucus. In a broken voice it rasped a single word.

'FaaAAAther...?'

A moment later there was a blinding flash. Cole reeled away, clutching his face. When his vision cleared, he turned back to see the creature smouldering on the ground, one smoking arm extended in the act of reaching for Cole before it died. The rest of the Abandoned were nowhere to be seen.

'They've fled,' Thanates said. 'At least for the moment. I fear not these wretches, but I can ill afford to expend my magic chasing them off.'

Cole was still staring at the corpse. Something was troubling him 'Did... did that thing call me *father*?'

The wizard shrugged. 'There are many mysteries in this city yet to be solved. Perhaps the godly essence you carry within you is in some way related to these creatures.'

Cole couldn't help but sigh at that. 'Great,' he muttered.

'Don't let it concern you now. We must hurry to the Hall of Annals.'

'It's just ahead,' Derkin said. He hesitated a moment. 'The Hall is forbidden. The White Lady's handmaidens hunt down anyone that dares go near it. A whole community of us disappeared three years ago after someone trespassed there.'

'Then my instincts prove sound,' Thanates replied grimly. 'If there still exists a place where the truth of what happened to Sanctuary all those centuries ago might be found, it is the Hall of Annals. The White Lady wanted to erase history... and yet I suspect she could not bring herself to destroy everything. A tiny part of her clings to the memory of that which she once cherished. In this she is not unlike other women.'

'How do you know that?' Cole asked.

When Thanates eventually answered, Cole thought he heard something like uncertainty in the wizard's voice. 'The White Lady and I once were lovers. This I remember.'

The shelves stretched out as far as he could see, disappearing into the darkness at the far reaches of the cavernous chamber. Cole stared at the towering bookcases in wonder as Thanates led him and Derkin deeper into the Hall of Annals. They had found the great doors unlocked, but the thick carpet of dust coating the floor suggested no one had seen the inside of the great domed building for many years. In contrast to the rest of the crumbling ruins, the Hall of Annals was in a near perfect state of repair.

'A holding spell,' Thanates announced, sniffing the dry air. 'The walls of this place are kept in perpetual stasis by the White Lady's magic. They will not falter until she does.'

402

'Stasis?' Cole repeated. 'Salazar had something he called a Stasiseum in the Obelisk. There was a giant egg suspended over a fire frozen in time. And a big green savage imprisoned behind glass. He was unmoving, like a statue. But he looked real enough.'

'I dare say he *was* real,' Thanates replied. 'I wonder what became of this creature. Orcs once ruled the north. I had believed them long extinct.'

'Orcs? I thought they lived in the frozen sea beyond the High Fangs. They're a kind of whale. I read about them in a book once.'

The way the wizard's jaw clenched angrily made him shrink back slightly. 'You are confusing two different words,' Thanates growled. 'Don't test my patience.'

Cole stared down at the floor glumly. Then he remembered Corvac had made similar mistakes and a shiver passed through him.

Surely it's just a coincidence, he thought. I got confused, that's all.

They continued down the long aisles between shelves. Glow-globes in the gently arched ceiling high above provided a soft light. At first Cole had been afraid they were the same as the glow-globes in Newharvest, produced from the tainted magic of the Blight. Thanates had stated that was not the case and the globes had in fact been created centuries ago, much to Cole's relief. The blind mage hardly needed further provocation to stir the flames of his hatred. It was visible with every flicker of black fire across his body, every crunch of his teeth grinding together. He was a man skirting the edge of a precipice, liable to lose himself to sudden and terrible rage at any moment.

Cole slowed his pace to walk alongside Derkin, who was struggling to keep up. 'This place is huge,' Cole observed. 'I thought there were a lot of books in the Obelisk's library, but there must be ten times as many here. A hundred maybe.'

'It is the largest known collection of books in the world,' said Thanates. 'Even the imperial library of the Wizard-Emperor cannot compare. According to Isaac, the dwarves of Mal-Torrad once had a collection to rival it – but it went up in flames during their civil war. Isaac's knowledge of history was astoundingly complete, in stark contrast to your ignorance.'

Cole frowned and kicked up a cloud of dust. Gods, he hated that bastard Isaac. Derkin began to cough and he immediately regretted his act of petulance. He leaned over and slapped his friend on the back as Derkin choked on the dust he'd just thrown up. 'Sorry,' he said meekly once the little man had recovered.

'It's fine,' Derkin replied, blinking his mismatched eyes. 'I got used to it when I lived down in the undercity.'

Thanates stopped suddenly, and Cole had to grab hold of Derkin to stop his friend blundering into the back of the wizard. 'Here. *This* is what I am searching for.'

The row of books beside them looked much the same as any other. 'How can you be certain?' Cole dared ask.

'Watch.' Thanates reached towards the shelf before him. Silver sparks immediately crackled into life around his gloved hand and he flinched away, smoke steaming from his scorched fingers. 'The White Lady warded these tomes for a reason. I could dispel her magic and remove the wards, but it is hardly necessary. Not when I have you.'

'Me?' Cole replied uncertainly.

'Unsheathe your dagger. Place the point against the bookshelf.'

Cole did as he was asked, bringing Magebane hesitantly forward until the tip was almost touching the spot where Thanates had activated the ward. At any moment Cole expected silver sparks to burst into life and fling back him backwards. Instead, all that happened was that the hilt in his palm grew warmer as Magebane absorbed the magic. Just as it had the night he'd assassinated Salazar.

'As I said,' Thanates remarked 'a powerful tool.' It wasn't clear if the wizard was talking about Magebane or Cole. 'That should suffice. Now put that weapon away. If it should happen to touch my flesh while you are holding it, the consequences would be disastrous.'

Cole sheathed his dagger and moved out of the way. Thanates ran his hands along the spines of the ancient tomes for a moment and then pulled out a large green volume. 'This one,' he said. 'What does it say?'

Cole peered at the spine. '*The Dalashran*.'

'Open it.'

Cole suppressed a sigh and thumbed the book open at random. 'It's a history of some place called Dalashra,' he said. 'It doesn't look very interesting. Wait, what's this? There are some illustrations.'

'What do they depict?'

'Men. Kings seated upon their thrones.' Cole squinted. 'This... this one looks like you. He's younger and well, he doesn't look blind, but... Yes. It *is* you.'

Thanates nodded and turned to Derkin. 'Can you read?'

'Yes,' Derkin said proudly. 'My ma taught me how. We only ever owned three books but I read them cover to cover more times than I can count.'

'I want you both to pull out every book on this shelf. Find anything that relates to Dalashra or the White Lady's personal life. Anything that documents events in and around Thelassa in the time leading up to the Godswar. I want to know who I was. I want to know why she did this to me. Why she stole my memories and extinguished all hope from the world.'

'There are a lot of books here,' Cole said doubtfully.

'Then you had best get a move on,' the wizard replied.

Angels and Demons

SHE SQUINTED THROUGH the rain and the tears that blurred her vision. The palace was just ahead.

Screams and shouts tore through the city as she walked unsteadily down the broad avenue in which the Seeding Festival had taken place months earlier. Soldiers streamed past, the cloaks they wore as white as the wet powder smeared over her nose. No one made to stop her. If they tried, she would kill them. She had killed before, on the battlefield outside Dorminia's gates. Put a sword right through a man's face. The image had kept her awake sometimes. It wouldn't any longer. There were worse fates than an honest death to cause her sleepless nights now.

In her mind she saw the nightmarish visage of the woman in the tank, her mouth yawning open, tortured scream swallowed up by the putrid blood surrounding her body. She saw again the tiny body of an unborn child scraping against the glass. She wondered if the woman tied to the chair in Fergus's laboratory might have been its mother.

Sasha thought she heard the cruel *snip* of scissors then and looked around wildly – but no, it was just the clank of a Whitecloak's sword as he hurried by.

One face above all was fixed in her mind. It was achingly beautiful, with bewitching violet eyes and perfect skin, and she wanted to smash it apart, shatter the lie it told, tear away that outrageous façade of benevolence and expose the ugly truth for the world to see.

The White Lady's servants would stop her before she reached the Magelord, she knew. Maybe her own sister would be the one to do it.

Sasha didn't care. Ambryl was a monster too. There was no point lying to herself any more. There'd been enough lies. This entire city was built on lies.

Somehow she reached the stairs leading up to the palace gates. There were no guards on duty; whatever chaos was unfolding elsewhere in the city had drawn them away. She pushed open the gates and strode through the entrance hallway, ignoring the rainwater that dripped from her soaked clothes, the muddy footprints her boots left on the lustrous marble floor. She wanted to smear the whole palace in filth. Everything was so damned clean in Thelassa, so pristine. It sickened her. She had never imagined she would miss Dorminia, but at least there was no pretence in the city of her home. No demons wearing the faces of angels.

Her nose burned. She wiped it with the back of her hand, glanced at it and saw that it was smeared with blood. She'd snorted the entire bag of *hashka* back in the alley. Inhaled it right there in the rain, desperate to take the edge off the horror. The silver powder had chased her terror away... but now that the fear was gone, only anger remained.

She approached the pair of gilded doors that she knew must lead to the throne room. There was a guard standing before them, one of the White Lady's handmaidens.

One of the Unborn.

The pale woman moved to intercept her, but Sasha didn't slow. She wasn't afraid of these creatures any more.

'You are not permitted to be here,' the Unborn stated in her emotionless voice. The woman's colourless gaze met her own. That gaze that had once filled her with dread now brought only pity.

Sasha didn't hesitate. She stepped forward and embraced the White Lady's handmaiden. 'I'm sorry,' she whispered. 'I'm so sorry for what they did to you.'

The Unborn seemed to flinch. It could have flung her away as if she were a leaf blown in by the wind. Could have broken her in half like a stray twig. But it merely stood there unmoving as Sasha pulled the gleaming dagger she'd stolen off Ambryl from her belt and drove it through the back of its skull. She gave the hilt a twist, heard bone crack. Black blood ran over her hands. The sudden stench of rot and decay and death filled her burned nostrils, but she ignored it, resisting the urge to drop the body and reel away gagging. Instead she lowered the shuddering creature to the floor as if it were a child.

'I'm sorry,' she said again. There was something in the hand-maiden's expression that brought tears to her eyes, something very much like gratitude.

Sasha's anger returned, fiercer than before. The dagger she clutched still dripping with black blood, Sasha kicked open the doors to the throne room and stormed through to confront the Magelord of Thelassa.

The object of her fury was sitting on a delicate throne carved of ivory on a dais overlooking the chamber. Overhead, a mosaic of heavenly figures stared down majestically from the vaulted ceiling. Directly above the throne itself, a large circular window set into the ceiling revealed a violent blue-grey sky beyond. Streaks of rain crawled down the glass as the tempest continued unabated above the city. As Sasha marched towards the Magelord, a flash of lightning lit the chamber and the White Lady's head shot up. She fixed her with those violet eyes. Despite the numbing effect of the *hashka* and the cold, hard anger knotting her stomach, the weight of that immortal gaze stopped Sasha in her tracks.

'Sister?'

She was only distantly aware of Ambryl's astonished voice amongst the crowd of attendants seated on the benches arranged before the raised throne. A devastating tide of hopelessness swept over her. The utter contempt on the Magelord's face dug up old memories; painful memories she'd sought to bury with moon dust and devil's breath and anything else she could get her hands on. Always the memories returned, fiercer than before, seeking to drag her down to a place where she was worthless, barely human. Hardly a person at all.

The White Lady rose from her throne with consummate grace. She raised a flawless hand to halt the pair of Unborn that had melted from the statues beside the dais. The Magelord's voice was curious. 'It is forbidden to bring naked steel into my presence, child. You test the limits of my forbearance. Explain yourself.'

Sasha opened her mouth, but despite the anger that had driven her this far, no sound emerged. She was once again helpless before the ruinous sight of the ruler of Thelassa. A girl once more, knowing she was too weak to fight back. Too weak to do anything except squeeze her eyes shut and hope it would soon be over.

'Mistress.' Ambryl hurried over to her sister. 'Please, forgive my foolish sister. She has lapsed again. Allow me to escort her away from here and I promise to fix her.'

Fix me? You can't fix me. I'm broken. The dagger quivered in Sasha's hand.

With supreme elegance, the White Lady descended the handful of stairs leading from the dais and approached the two sisters. Her purple eyes lingered for a second on the bloody blade Sasha carried. 'You claim your sister is weak, and yet somehow she slew one of my Unborn.'

The White Lady gestured and the dagger was torn from Sasha's grasp. It floated slowly towards the Magelord, murky droplets of putrefying blood rolling off the steel blade to hang suspended in the air. 'The punishment for destroying my property is death,' she finished calmly.

'*Your property?*' Sasha managed to whisper, aghast. 'That was a person once. A... a baby.'

'Mistress,' said Ambryl. 'I beg you. Don't hurt her.'

Sasha stared at her sister. For the first time since they'd been reunited, she had heard a glimmer of the old Ambryl. The Ambryl who would fix her hair and joke with her about boys and comfort her during a thunderstorm.

The White Lady tapped the dagger against her perfect fingernails and frowned down at Sasha. 'You know too much. I could have you taken for correction. Some, such as Cyreena here, see the light with their eyes wide open. Others require... encouragement.'

'No,' Ambryl gasped, white-faced. 'Please. Not that.'

The Magelord reached out a hand and laid it upon Sasha's brow. 'Bow before me, child,' the White Lady said serenely. 'Swear to serve me and you shall arise as one of the Consult, your indiscretions forgotten.'

Sasha looked up at the ceiling, at the assorted gods depicted there – deities murdered by the wizard whose hand was upon her head. She thought of the poor and starving on the streets of Dorminia, of the families torn apart as husbands and wives were forced to board ships to the Celestial Isles because of a crisis the White Lady herself had engineered. She thought of mothers and fathers so heavily drugged they couldn't recall the horrors that had been visited upon them. Couldn't even remember what it was they'd lost.

'No,' she said.

'No?' The White Lady withdrew her hand. A terrible anger flared in her purple eyes. 'I saved the world from the depredations of the gods. I overthrew the tyrant that ruled your city. I am the light that keeps the darkness at bay! And yet you, you worthless little junkie, you stand before me and refuse my patronage?'

'Yes.'

'*Why?*' The Magelord's voice was a deadly whisper.

'Because...' Sasha met the White Lady's gaze and her courage deserted her. She looked away.

Looked away to see the two Unborn by the throne. Remembered the tiny body in the tank and the woman tied to the chair, blood pooling around her ankles.

'Because you're an evil cunt,' she snarled. Her hand shot up and caught the immortal wizard a stinging slap across the face, the sound reverberating through the chamber like the dying breath of a god.

A moment of utter silence followed. Then shocked gasps erupted from the Consult, a few of them fainting on the spot. Very slowly the White Lady raised a disbelieving hand towards the ugly red mark on her cheek.

Sasha's head was yanked painfully back. 'You fool!' Ambryl screamed at her, dragging her by her hair. 'You've ruined everything!'

Sasha tried to twist around, but suddenly the White Lady loomed before her and all the *hashka* in the world wouldn't have lent her courage in the face of the Magelord's fury. She closed her eyes, praying for a quick end.

The world seemed to explode.

Ten Years Ago

THE FIRST THING he noticed were the overgrown fields. If it hadn't been for his boots, the grass might've tickled his ankles as he dismounted his old mare and stretched the stiffness out of his legs. The ride back from the Blue Reaching had taxed him more than he cared to admit. He was getting old, an unpleasant realization that was driven home as he unpacked the knife he'd fashioned for Magnar and saw his reflection in the cold steel. There was a good deal more grey in his hair than when he'd departed with a heavy heart for the Sky Reaching six months past.

He tethered his horse to a post and walked somewhat stiffly to the front door of the house. Truth be told, the Shaman's summons hadn't been entirely unexpected. The border dispute between the neighbouring Blue and Sky Reachings had been threatening to erupt for years now. Even so his heart had sunk when the transcended eagle had landed, a sealed note signed with Jagar's increasingly erratic handwriting tied around its leg.

He didn't want this any more. Not the travel. Not the endless bickering about boundary lines or fishing rights or a hundred other finer points of the Treaty. Not the knowledge that another family would be mourning the loss of a husband and father when diplomacy failed, as it always did. Torm had been a decent sort, a chieftain who had genuinely cared for his people. But he had proved too stubborn, and now, like Targus Bloodfist, his life had come to an abrupt end on the inexorable edge of the Sword of the North.

He recalled Torm's last staggering steps. The way the chieftain's hands tried desperately to cover the gaping wound in his throat while his guards died noisily nearby. The awe on the faces of Hrothgar's men as Kayne had left the tent, fresh blood painting his new armour, the wyvernscale the Shaman had gifted him. He hadn't wanted their admiration. He didn't want the songs the bards had composed about him, songs they'd decided he might want to hear as he turned his back on them and mounted his horse and tried to shut out the horror of what he'd just done.

He just wanted to be left alone.

Kayne walked straight through the hall and out into the garden at the rear, expecting to find Mhaira there. He stopped in astonishment when he saw the garden. His wife's pride and joy was in just as bad a state as the fields to the front of the house. The grass was long and wild, and the flowers Mhaira tended so keenly were dying from lack of water. Even the apple tree near the bench was overgrown. It looked as if no one had touched the garden for weeks.

Brow creasing in confusion, Kayne went inside – and almost walked straight into Magnar.

'Son!' he exclaimed happily. He moved to embrace his boy, but when Magnar made no move to return the gesture he turned it into an awkward pat on the shoulder instead. 'Spirits above and below, lad, you've grown.'

Magnar's grey eyes were almost on a level with his own now. His son still possessed a boy's frame, but he was beginning to fill out.

'Pa. You're back.' Magnar's voice was deeper than he remembered, and it sounded uncertain. Kayne reckoned he knew why.

'Happy naming day, son,' he said lamely. 'I'm sorry I couldn't be here. I rode as hard as I could. The King wanted me to bring him a report and, well... you ain't interested in that, I'm guessing. I made you this. Braxus himself forged the blade.' Kayne held the knife out. Magnar looked at it but didn't move.

'I never forgot,' Kayne said pleadingly. 'You know I wouldn't forget. I'd have given anything to be here. Here, take it. It's yours.'

'I don't want the stupid knife,' Magnar blurted out. His grey eyes were clouded with anger. 'Keep it. You might need it to kill someone.'

Kayne blinked in shock. 'I said I'm sorry, son. I ain't claiming to be the greatest father in the world, but I did what I could.'

'You weren't here! You're never here. My tutor told me they're singing songs about you now. The others look at me like I'm lucky to have the Sword of the North as a father. I'd rather it was anyone *but* you.'

Kayne found himself shaking. He and Magnar had argued before, but never in a fashion this ugly. He thrust the knife back in his belt. 'It's on account of your old man you got one of the best tutors in Beregund. You might want to remember that.'

'How can I forget? Everyone always says how great you are, but you never cared about being a father. You never cared about my mother. You're not around for her.'

Kayne felt his fists clenching at his sides. 'Well, ain't that some gods-damned gratitude. You got no idea about the sacrifices I make to keep the Shaman happy. You think it was my own choice to travel all the way to the Blue Reaching just to cut a good man's throat, you ungrateful little shit?'

Magnar flinched, but then a moment later his anger seemed to return twofold. 'You're good at cutting men's throats. It's about all you can do. Are you going to hit me like you hit her?'

Kayne staggered as if he'd been punched. 'What did you say?' he rasped. 'What did you fucking say?' He realized he had his hands on Magnar's shoulders, saw the sudden fear in his son's eyes. The fear of a boy faced by the fury of the most feared killer in the High Fangs. The realization hit him like a hammer. 'I'd never strike you,' he said, almost choking in shame. 'You know that. What happened that afternoon, I wasn't myself. I promise you I'll never do anything like that again. You and your ma are everything to me. Where... where is she?'

'Sleeping,' Magnar said. His voice seemed to crack a little. 'Pa...'

Kayne paused with his hand on the door of the room he and Mhaira shared. 'Aye, son?

'She's sick. Ma's really sick.'

He froze. The world seemed to rock around him. 'Sick?' he repeated, dumbstruck.

'When I returned from Beregund a few months ago, she wasn't herself. She kept coughing. She tried to hide it, but I saw blood. I think... I think she might not make it, Pa.' His voice became a sob.

Brodar Kayne closed his eyes, feeling as though a pit were opening beneath him and he were seconds from oblivion. It took all the courage he had to push the door open, to walk slowly over to the bed. In the dim light he could make out a shape beneath the thick furs. Too many furs for the height of summer.

'May?' he whispered. There was no response. Mhaira didn't seem to be moving. He couldn't hear her breathing. Sudden, animal terror filled him.

'May?' he whispered again, voice breaking. He was shaking, the pressure building in his head until he thought it might burst. He reached towards her with a trembling hand. He couldn't remember when he'd last told her he loved her. What if she'd heard them arguing and it had proven too much for her, what if—

'Brodar...?'

Mhaira's voice was a faint whisper. She shifted slightly, and then opened her eyes to stare up at him. Not with anger or bitterness or accusation. Only honest, heartbreaking love. 'You're back,' she said. Her face was thin, much too thin. She was shockingly frail.

But despite everything she smiled up at him, a heartfelt expression of such happiness that all he could do was fall to his knees and gather her gently in his arms, tears streaming down his cheeks, his body racked by silent sobs.

He didn't move from her side for two weeks. Not until the worst had eventually passed, and she was strong enough to rise from the bed.

Sundered

'MILO, LEAVE HIS ears alone!'

The little orphan grinned at Corinn and finally let go of Grunt's big flapping ear. On the big mute's opposite shoulder, Tiny Tom was babbling excitedly to his new best friend about everything under the stars. Every so often Grunt would nod or stifle a sigh or just cast a despairing look around. In truth, he had volunteered to carry the smallest of the orphans upon his broad shoulders and Kayne reckoned he was secretly enjoying being the centre of attention.

He caught Brick glancing at Corinn while she scolded Milo. The flame-haired archer and the blue-eyed girl kept looking at each other when they thought the other wasn't watching. Kayne smiled mischievously and leaned in close to Brick. 'Pretty lass, that one,' he whispered. 'Reckon she's about your age.'

The youngster feigned a look of surprised disinterest. 'Is she? I can't say I'd noticed.'

'She likes you.'

Brick's face began to flush crimson. 'She doesn't! Besides, she's a Highland girl. I thought they were all crazy.'

'That ain't just Highland women, lad, that's women in general. But take it from someone who knows – I've been married to a Highland lass for over twenty years and there ain't a day gone by I regret it. You'd do well to find a wife like Corinn there.'

'A *wife*?' Brick said, aghast. 'I don't want to get married!' He slowed his pace, falling back to walk alongside Jerek.

'Nice to see you two getting along,' Kayne muttered. Behind the three of them, the band of orphans clambered over the broken ground in a snaking line, Jana Shah Shan bringing up the rear. Their progress was torturously slow. The fact they were turning back the way they had come hadn't gone down well with some, even though Corinn had tried to explain that they were being taken to a safe place. A few had cried or thrown tantrums until Jana went into her packs and handed them her remaining *nana* fruits, which quieted them for a time.

The stars in the night sky shone like diamonds overhead as they inched towards the Greenwild in the distance. It was a dark blur on the horizon now, growing larger with each passing hour. They saw more standing stones on the way, though Jana no longer took the time to translate the runes carved onto them. All her efforts were focused on ensuring the children made it across the dangerous terrain safely.

Appalling visions of Magnar trapped in a wicker cage occupied Kayne's thoughts constantly. He felt his muscles tighten and forced them to relax. Whatever hurt that bastard Krazka had done to him Kayne would return tenfold. He'd made a promise to Mhaira once: a promise he would keep or die trying.

'Ain't long now. We're almost to the Greenwild.'

Jerek was right beside him, keeping pace with Kayne as the old warrior trudged on lost in his thoughts. The Wolf gave him a small nod. He'd never say it outright but Kayne knew that Jerek was concerned for him. The grim Highlander never showed any sign of weakness, would rather walk across hot coals than admit to feeling sympathy. But the Wolf knew all about promises. His word was his bond, and depending on where a man stood it could be either a death sentence or the greatest gift. He might be the angriest, surliest son of a bitch Kayne had ever known, a fearless warrior seemingly without peer, but Jerek was also the truest friend anyone could wish for. When it came right down to it, that was how you judged a person: not through their words but through their deeds.

Kayne cleared his throat as they walked together. 'I've been meaning to thank you. I couldn't have made it this far without you.'

Jerek merely grunted, his eyes betraying nothing.

'When everyone else abandoned me, you stayed true. I don't know what it cost you to free me from the Shaman's cage and drag me away from the Fangs. I don't know what you had to leave behind when we fled south. But words can't express how grateful I am.'

Jerek glanced at him then. 'Shit, Kayne,' he grumbled, 'I said you was turning into a right old pussy.' He hesitated for a moment – and then, much to Kayne's shock, the Wolf reached across and gave him a companionable pat on the shoulder. 'I made you a promise on account of what you did for me,' Jerek said quietly. 'Besides, friends watch out for one another, aye?'

'Aye,' Kayne said. And then the two men said nothing, walking side by side in that easy silence of brothers-in-arms who have been through hell together.

Milo's small voice reached them from somewhere up ahead, interrupting the peaceful calm. 'Who are those men?'

Kayne saw Grunt's head turn to stare off into the night. Then the big mute stopped dead in his tracks and gave a growl of warning.

Kayne squinted as he drew alongside Grunt. Shadowy figures were descending the hill ahead of them. Heart heavy with foreboding, the old warrior unsheathed his greatsword. Behind him, Jana Shah Shan called the orphans to an abrupt halt.

'Who's there?' Kayne shouted at the advancing figures. 'Best state your intentions, before I make up my own mind and act accordingly.'

The silence that followed was broken by a sharp, barking laugh that sounded more animal than man. 'Red Rayne ain't gonna believe this,' said a voice that poked at old memories.

'Red Rayne? What d'you know about him? Who the hell are you?'

The nearest of the approaching figures slunk into view just as the silver plate of the moon emerged from a passing cloud and bathed him in a hoary glow.

He was rake lean and leathery skinned, as old as Kayne himself. Sharp yellow teeth flashed a smile in a face that seemed distantly familiar. 'They call me Ryder. You and me go back a-ways. Remember Skarn?'

'Skarn?' Kayne repeated, his throat suddenly raw. 'Aye, I remember him. Broke his skull with my bare hands. You threaten a man's family, you can't be surprised at the things he'll do to make certain you never get the chance to carry out those threats.'

'I told him. After you fled to that house, the one we set fire to, I told Skarn to smash the door down and stick a blade in you. You know what Skarn was like though. Never one to pass up the chance to wreak a little havoc. It was his undoing in the end. You cut off my bloody ear, remember that?'

'I thought you were dead.'

'Dead? Ha! I was the one that got away. Though I won't lie, my head hurt like a bitch for months. I fled south, all the way to the Greenwild. Spent years there, living among the Wildfolk till I judged it safe to poke my head back out. Fortunately the new King is happy to let old grievances lie. Except where your boy's concerned. He's taking his sweet time getting his payback on that one.' Ryder laughed again, a high-pitched bark that set Kayne's teeth on edge.

'Who are these others with you? More of the imposters Krazka calls Kingsmen?' Kayne could feel his old anger starting to build, the terrible rage threatening to return. He'd managed to keep it under control for many a year, ever since that terrible day he'd returned from the Sky Reaching. The day that had changed him forever.

'Naw. These are friends from the Greenwild. They attack outsiders on sight, but they remembered me. The sorceress that helped those foundlings escape burned down their homes and now they want blood, don't you, lads?'

Right on cue, the Wildmen approached. They were naked beneath their thick fur coats, wooden cudgels and simple hand axes clutched tight between hairy knuckles. They reminded Kayne a little of the hill-men from the Badlands, though they weren't as broad.

'I dreamed of the day I'd run into you again. Skarn called you angel eyes. Let's see if they look so pretty when they're full of arrows.'

Kayne saw Ryder draw his arm back, heard the twang of a bow a split second later. He was already diving to the right when he felt the arrow whistle by his cheek, missing by a matter of inches. 'You always go high with the first shot,' he growled, rolling to his feet. Ryder cursed and fell back behind the Wildmen, who rushed Kayne like a pack of feral dogs.

He cut down one, turned and caught the cudgel of another with the cross-guard on his greatsword. Someone stood on his shoulder and then Jana Shah Shan somehow sailed over his head, spinning in mid-air to kick his assailant in the face so hard Kayne heard the man's jaw break. Jana landed and caught the axe of another attacker between her palms. She jerked the weapon away from the Wildman, chopped down with both hands right on his neck, dropping him like a stone.

Ryder was backtracking whilst attempting to nock another arrow, a feat that would have been mightily impressive any other time. Kayne didn't pause to admire the man's skill. He charged right at him, desperate to reach the archer before he could release his arrow. He got there just in time and the outlaw-turned-Kingsman turned to flee, a smidgen too slow. Kayne's greatsword would have cleaved him in half, but at that exact moment another Wildman leaped out and disrupted his attack. Instead of taking off Ryder's head like he intended, Kayne caught the man's remaining ear with his sword. The mass of skin and gristle sailed away as Ryder twisted free, newly earless and none too pleased by the fact, judging by his howl of outrage as he fled.

This newest Wildman was more skilled than his fellows. He

and Kayne exchanged a few blows, the old Highlander taking the measure of his opponent before eventually picking him off, driving the steel blade through his sternum with a vicious popping sound.

Kayne dislodged his greatsword from the Wildman's body and took stock of the situation. He wondered if he might catch up with Ryder before the bastard escaped, but it didn't seem likely – he'd only been fighting a few minutes but already his breathing was laboured and he doubted he would be able to sprint more than a hundred yards before he was knackered.

'Well, that was easy,' Jana Shah Shan proclaimed, dusting her hands together. No fewer than four Wildmen lay unmoving at her feet. Kayne's eyes scanned his friends, making sure everyone was unhurt.

When his gaze settled on Jerek, however, his blood went cold.

The Wolf was staring at him with an odd expression. It was part grief and part utter fury. For a moment Kayne was confused, but then he remembered his exchange with Ryder and a terrible understanding dawned.

'You told me it was my family they were looking to kill,' Jerek whispered, his voice hollow, matter-of-fact, as though he were pointing out some trifling detail. 'You told me you happened across them just as they was burning down the house.'

'Jerek,' Kayne began, searching for the words. But there weren't any words. Ryder had said all that needed to be said. The lie he'd allowed to fester for years, for decades, had been exposed, and every inch of its ugliness was revealed in the agonized expression on Jerek's face.

'You let me think you got involved to try and save them,' the Wolf grated. He took a step towards Kayne, coal-black eyes never leaving his face. 'Twenty-five years you let me believe a lie. Twenty-five fucking years.'

'Listen, it weren't like that. I fled there seeking shelter. I didn't know they would set fire to the building. And I came back for you. I came back for you and your family—'

'Fuck you,' Jerek snarled. There was a pain in his voice Kayne had never heard before, a pain he had never imagined the grim warrior was capable of. 'I risked my life for you countless times. I thought I owed you a debt. Turns out you treated me like a cunt. Fuck you.'

'Jerek—'

The Wolf was on him in a flash. Steel axes slashed down with terrifying speed, a flurry of devastating blows that would have ended a lesser warrior in seconds.

Brodar Kayne blocked them all, first one axe and then the other, edge scraping against edge and forming a screaming song of steel. For a moment their weapons locked together. With a roar, Kayne pushed back and the two men came apart.

'I thought we was friends,' Jerek rasped, his voice raw with grief. 'I thought we was brothers. You played me for a fool, Kayne. One of us ain't leaving here alive.'

'Stop it! Don't fight!' Brick yelled at them. Children were crying now. Kayne caught a glimpse of Grunt's amber eyes, wide in confusion. Jana's face was pale with shock. The Wolf's gaze held only burning fury, a promise of death Kayne had seen countless times before. But he was the Sword of the North, and death was as familiar to him as an old blanket.

Jerek came at him again, a whirlwind of cutting, biting axes, countless blows raining from every angle, bone-jarring strength behind every blow. Kayne's hands began to hurt from the impact of blocking the relentless assault, his eyes blurring from the effort of trying to follow the attacks. He saw an opportunity for a counter, a riposte that had defeated countless men in the past, and in desperation he seized the moment, waited for the Wolf's error to leave him vulnerable and deliver that deadly blow.

Somehow Jerek anticipated his counter, turning it aside before it landed. They came together in an embrace, the Wolf's breath warm on his face, too close for either man to bring his weapons to bear. 'You got my family killed,' Jerek rasped, his eyes seeming to bore into his skull. 'My parents. My sister.'

'I'm sorry, Wolf,' Kayne gasped, sucking in air. 'I can't tell you how sorry I am.'

'Shove it up your arse, Kayne.'

He felt Jerek's muscular arms close tight around him. A moment later he was lifted bodily off the ground and flung away. He hit the earth hard, somehow managed to turn the impact into a roll and came back to his feet just as Jerek charged. He saw the glint in the Wolf's eyes and knew exactly what he intended. It was a combination that had slain countless men over the years, a brilliant chain of attacks, near impossible to parry unless you knew exactly how it went.

Overhand slash with the right, swing in low from the left, pivot and then back to the right for the reverse stroke...

He parried the third and final attack, lashed out with the pommel of his greatsword and smashed it right into Jerek's face. That should have ended the fight right there and then. The Wolf's nose broke with the impact, blood spraying out to splatter all over his chin – but the relentless warrior might as well have been hit in the face by a stray leaf for all that it fazed him. Even as his nose shattered Jerek kicked out, catching Kayne hard in the stomach and sending him staggering away.

'Stop it!' Brick screamed again, his voice cracking.

Just then there was another scream. It came from somewhere off in the night, and it sounded like Ryder.

A malevolent glow appeared on the other side of the hill, moving inexorably towards them. Kayne and Jerek tore their attention away from each other and turned to watch the approaching menace. It flowed around the hill and finally came into view. Intense flames danced around an endless void shaped like a man – a god-forged weapon of infernal wrath with but a solitary purpose, to eliminate life from the world, body and soul, leaving nothing but dust and memories.

The gholam had come for them. And Milo and Tiny Tom were directly in its path.

Kayne screamed for the boys to run, but they were transfixed by the horror bearing down on them and didn't seem to hear him.

There was a green blur and Grunt suddenly barrelled towards the youngsters, thrusting them out of the way just as the gholam surged forward. Grunt placed his body in front of the children and the gholam engulfed the big mute, who fought with all his prodigious strength but couldn't disentangle himself from that ruinous grasp. Soon he began to smoke, his green skin turning a darker shade of olive as he was incinerated from within. He opened his mouth and let out a heart-rending cry, a sound that no man or beast should ever make. Kayne caught a final glimpse of those brilliant amber eyes staring out from his blunt and honest face. And then Grunt began to crack, and the sight was so awful he had to look away.

Moments later the gholam let the ash that had been Grunt fall from its hands and turned towards Brick. Corinn and the rest of the foundlings huddled behind him, frozen with terror. Jana Shah Shan was on her knees, hands covering her face, her earlier bravado a distant memory. She knew better than anyone what the gholam was capable of. She knew it was over.

Kayne lifted his greatsword for what he knew would be the final time and prepared to charge the gods-forged killer. Maybe he could buy the others a little more time. Just a little more.

'Kayne,' rasped Jerek's voice. The old warrior turned to stare back at his friend.

The Wolf was watching him, blood pouring from his nose, his bald head bathed in the orange glow of the gholam's fire. There was a strange look in his eyes: an odd acceptance, as if he had come to some decision. He raised an axe and gestured at the tunnel nearby. 'When I move, round up everyone and get the fuck away from here. I'll keep it busy as long as I can.'

'Jerek—'

'I don't want to hear it. I ain't doing this for you. If I ever see you again I'll kill you. That's a promise. Now fucking move.'

Without another word the Wolf turned and stalked towards

the horror that had levelled entire armies. At first it ignored him as it closed on Brick and the foundlings. The youngsters were frozen in place, paralysed by terror. But Jerek raised an axe, took aim, and sent the weapon whirling end over end. It disappeared into the void that was the gholam's body and the nightmarish being stopped dead – and then very slowly turned to face this new annoyance.

Time seemed to stand still. Kayne met Jerek's gaze one final time, and what he saw there made him want to weep for his friend. There no anger in the Wolf's eyes now. Only a deep sadness that something he had once cherished had been broken, never again to be made whole. A brotherhood sundered.

What followed would etch itself in Kayne's memory for the rest of his life. Jerek stood before the gholam, alone and defiant, a fire seeming to burn in his own dark eyes as he turned his unflinching gaze back onto this fell creation of the gods. The deadliest weapon of destruction the world had ever known.

'Come on, you motherfucker,' the Wolf snarled. 'Let's see what you got.'

The gholam began to flow towards Jerek, covering the rocky ground with terrifying speed, leaving the stone scorched and blackened in its passing. The Wolf's jaw set in utter determination and then he turned and sped off, sprinting towards the tunnel. He reached it twenty yards ahead of his hunter. Stepped into a personal hell at the end of which waited only his death. And he didn't hesitate even for a moment.

The gholam followed him into that dark maw and once again the night was still and silent, as if the madness of recent events belonged to a nightmare that was thankfully over. But the pile of ash that had once been Grunt and the petrified faces of the children opposite Kayne revealed that lie for what it was.

He spurred himself into action, raced over to the foundlings and yelled at them to get moving. Brick recovered the quickest and immediately set about rousing the others. Jana Shah Shan climbed unsteadily to her feet, her body still trembling. To her credit she quickly mastered herself and within moments she was herding the orphans northwards. Kayne brought up the rear, his greatsword clutched tightly in his sweating palms in case the gholam returned, though he knew it would do him no good. He was exhausted, the various blows he had suffered in his fight with Jerek causing his body to ache fiercely as he ran. Yet it was as nothing compared to the agony in his heart at seeing two friends lost, their lives sacrificed because of him.

'I'm sorry,' he whispered.

The Returned

THE STORM WAS still raging above the streets of Thelassa when Cole finally emerged from the ruins of Sanctuary, Derkin stumbling breathlessly behind him. Thanates' anger had been terrible to behold. For a moment Cole had been convinced the wizard was going to take out his fury on them. Instead he'd twisted away and began laying waste to the Hall of Annals. The great library was well on the way to becoming a red-hot inferno when Cole and Derkin had finally fled.

Thanates had come to that place seeking truth. In the end, the truth had pushed him over the edge.

The streets were cloaked in rain as the two friends exited the abandoned building. The cellar below connected to Sanctuary, one of several such access points across the city. The torrential downpour battered them as they walked, washing away the grime of the ruins. Above the howl of the wind and rumbling thunder, screams could be heard. The fighting had spread beyond the harbour. Cole ducked down behind a wall as a group of Whitecloaks came marching down the avenue that led to the palace. The army of the dead he'd unleashed were still occupying the city's defenders, just as Thanates had demanded. Across Thelassa, the freed miners were running rampant. The thought of the Condemned wreaking havoc in this peaceful city made Cole deeply uneasy. He remembered the blonde-haired noblewoman back in Dorminia whom he had rescued from a Sumnian looter. Technically the southern mercenary and Cole had been on the same side, but sides had become meaningless when confronted with the brutal truth that an innocent woman was about to get her brains scrambled by a chair leg just because she served the wrong man.

It is the lesser evil, Thanates had said. It seemed to Cole there was no 'lesser' evil – just evil. He was tired of people trying to justify their dark deeds to him.

There was a flutter of wings overhead and Cole glanced up to see the black shape of a crow winging its way towards the palace.

'Thanates,' he muttered.

'He's going to confront the Mistress,' Derkin said. 'To seek his revenge.'

'Revenge,' Cole echoed. The word tasted sour in his mouth.

'I'm heading back to the harbour. I need to check my ma is okay. We're going to cross the channel and try our luck in Dorminia.'

'I'm going with you.'

Derkin looked at him in surprise. 'But this is your chance. Your opportunity to get back at the White Lady for what she did to you.'

Cole stared at his palms. He thought of Thanates and the woman he had once loved and the tragedy of what had befallen them. 'I'm tired of violence, Derkin. There are more important things than pursuing a grudge. Sasha's waiting for me.'

Derkin grinned at him. 'Come on then,' he said, his big eyes bright with enthusiasm. 'Let's get you home.'

Together they set off west towards the docks. They'd only gone a short distance when they ran into an unexpected face. Sitting on the soaking wet ground cradling the body of a cat was a huge bear of a man, his sobs audible even above the sounds of the storm. The animal he held in his arms was blackened and charred, as if it had been caught in a fire.

'Ed?' Cole said incredulously.

The big simpleton turned to stare at him. 'Ghost!' he squealed.

Cole could see the thick bandages covering his chest, splotches of pink bright against the sodden dressing.

'You should be resting back on the ship. You almost *died*, Ed.'

Dull Ed shrugged his massive shoulders and wiped at the snot hanging from his nose with the back of one hand. 'I heard people yelling. I thought someone might need help.'

'What are you doing with that thing? It's dead.'

'Smokes did it!' Ed rumbled, his voice angry. 'I found him hurting the kittens and I chased him off... but mummy cat was already dead. He burned her.'

'Where are the kittens?'

'I hid them somewhere safe. Somewhere dry and warm.' Ed's expression became one of childish hope. He held out the remains of the cat. 'You can bring her back, can't you? Make her move like you did the dead people.'

'It doesn't work like that, Ed. I can command the shamblers from the Blight, but I can't raise dead bodies. And I can't return anything to life.'

'Oh.' So crestfallen was Ed's face that Cole couldn't help but feel guilty. Before he could do or say anything to cheer the big man up, a flash of silver fire lit the skyline near the palace and the city streets suddenly trembled.

'That wasn't thunder,' Derkin said slowly.

'Ed, we need to go,' Cole said hurriedly. 'The city isn't safe. Put that thing— er, mummy cat down. You can't help her now.'

'What about the kittens?' Ed asked.

Cole sighed and blinked rain out of his eyes. 'You said they're somewhere warm and safe. Kittens hate the rain and they're scared of loud noises. They'll be happier inside until this storm stops. We can come back for them later.'

Ed's heavy brow creased. 'You promise?'

'I promise.'

Dull Ed placed the dead cat carefully down on the ground and stood up. Another flash of silver lit the sky, and this time it was met with an answering burst of black fire. Cole glanced in

430

the direction of the palace and swallowed nervously. 'Time to go,' he said.

Sasha opened her eyes. Somehow she was still alive. She was on the floor, Ambryl groaning beside her. Screams floated above the roaring in her ears. She blinked twice and saw that she was surrounded by rubble. Thick dust still sprinkled down from the damaged ceiling above. The southern wall of the throne room had been reduced to a smoking ruin; the golden doors were a mangled heap nearby, bent almost beyond recognition.

Standing in the blasted remnants of the doorway was a man. A tall, severe-looking man wearing a tattered black coat and a red cloth around his face. Black fire danced across his body and Sasha knew straight away that he was a wizard. A wizard, or some kind of demon stepped right out of hell.

'Beloved,' he boomed, giving voice to a fury that made her earlier anger seem like a child's tantrum. 'I have returned for you.'

Sasha scrabbled to her feet, cutting her palms on the broken glass strewn across the floor. The great window above the dais had shattered and rain streamed through the opening to fall around the target of the wizard's wrath.

The White Lady seemed unharmed by the magical assault that had just levelled half the chamber. Even so, her voice was thick with disbelief. 'Thanates,' she whispered. 'You were dead.'

'Dead?' The newcomer laughed bitterly, a sound uncannily like that of a crow's croaking cry. 'A wizard of Dalashra cannot be so easily killed – and I was a king among wizards. You underestimated me, Alassa.'

'How do you remember my name? I took it from you! I erased our names from the world! Stripped them from the memory of every living thing!'

'Yes,' the wizard agreed. 'And that spell near broke your mind as it did my own. But you left the truth in the Hall of Annals. You wanted it preserved somewhere, a reminder of the love we once shared.'

'Lies!' the White Lady shrieked. 'You lie! I've never loved any man!'

'You loved me enough to carry my child!' Thanates roared in answer. He managed to compose himself, and when he continued a deep melancholy filled his voice. 'We could have averted war between the Congregation and the Alliance. We could have stopped the tragedy that followed. But you tore Sanctuary apart in your fury, slew every priest and priestess within its walls. And when I attempted to restrain you, you turned on me.'

A long moment of silence met his words. 'The Mother betrayed me,' the White Lady said eventually, her voice heavy with unexpected grief. 'I was her mortal representative, yet she rewarded my devotion by taking the one thing I could never accept. As I watched her die, I asked why. Why of all women she would take *my* baby in childbirth? Do you know what her answer was? "The Pattern wills what the Pattern wills." But we broke the Pattern, and therein we revealed the truth of her lie.'

'Foolish woman!' Thanates spat back. 'The Alliance broke the Pattern to reach the heavens and in doing so you brought upon us all this Age of Ruin!' The wizard took a step forward and the black fire wreathing his coat flared again. 'For what you did to me – for the fate to which you have doomed this world – I will have my revenge.'

The White Lady's perfect features twisted into an ugly sneer. She gestured and the Unborn gathered around the dais suddenly surged towards the wizard. He raised a hand as they converged on him. Black fire burst from his fingertips and somehow, despite his apparent blindness, his aim proved unerring.

Where the black fire touched the pale women they ceased to exist. Body parts disintegrated. Entire torsos suddenly disappeared, causing newly detached limbs to wheel wildly away in explosions of pale white flesh and dark, rotten innards.

The last of the Unborn was almost within touching distance of Thanates when her head simply vanished. Her flailing body sprayed black blood all over the marble floor before collapsing.

The smell of the grave filled the air and even with her *hashka*-ruined nose Sasha couldn't stop herself gagging from the overpowering stench. Over by the benches the Consult were doing the same.

Thanates, however, was indifferent to the sickening odour. The wizard raised his arms and seemed to brace himself. 'I have waited five hundred years for this moment,' he growled. 'I shall not be denied now.' He screamed a word, and hurled a raging torrent of black fire towards the White Lady.

An answering stream of silver fire shot out to intercept it. For a few tense seconds the two opposing beams roared into each other, monumental manifestations of magical force struggling for supremacy. Then the silver fire began to inch forward, eating up the black fire, gaining momentum. Thanates' face dripped with sweat, while in contrast the White Lady appeared unflustered. 'I remember now why I had you tortured,' she said coolly, having recovered her earlier poise. 'Your arrogance grew insufferable. If you understood what it meant to storm the heavens and succeed, you would never have presumed you could defeat me. Not if you had siphoned all the raw magic in the Trine.'

As if freed from invisible shackles the silver fire surged forward and struck the wizard, hurling him back through the gap vacated by the shattered doors. He disappeared from sight, his final cry of outrage echoing through the chamber.

The White Lady lowered her arms and the silver stream vanished. Her eyes flicked to Sasha, who recoiled in fear – but it seemed Thelassa's ruler still had other matters to demand her attention. Her lips forming a grim line, the Magelord stepped down from the dais and exited the chamber.

As soon as their mistress had left, the Consult began peeking out from behind the benches where they'd been hiding. Chaos broke loose as men and women fled the throne room.

'Follow me,' said a familiar voice behind her. Sasha turned to find Ambryl staring at her, her expression unreadable. Without another word her sister sped off towards a door at the rear of the chamber. Sasha followed, stepping around chunks of rubble and over the severed limbs of the Unborn. She skirted the dais, which was wet and slippery from the rainwater pouring in from above.

Ambryl led her through a maze of winding, narrow corridors that seemed to connect to every room in the palace. Other members of the Consult raced to and fro, a few giving Sasha dark looks as they passed by. 'Where are we going?' she asked once they finally emerged into the biting rain somewhere west of the palace.

'To the docks,' Ambryl replied acidly. 'I can only hope we find a captain foolish enough to cross the channel in this storm.' Despite her obvious fury her sister's words came as a welcome relief to Sasha.

'Thank you. We'll be much happier back in Dorminia, you'll see.'

'*We?* I'm going nowhere.'

Sasha blinked rain from her eyes and stared at Ambryl in shock. 'You're not?'

'No. After today, you are on your own.'

'But you're my sister. We stick together no matter what. That's what you said.'

Ambryl's mouth twisted. 'I have no sister. You are a selfish, impulsive fool. A junkie and a harlot, beyond help or good reason. I will see you safely away from here, for the memory of our parents if nothing else. After that, we're done.'

'Ambryl—'

'Shut up. You've been nothing but a disappointment to me. I should have turned the other cheek back in Dorminia. I should have let the rapist have you.'

Sasha's mouth gaped open. She felt like she'd been punched in the gut. Of all the things her sister could have said to wound her, that – *that* was the most devastating. Tears filled her eyes, but her sister merely turned away. Turned her back on her and set off again without a backward glance.

They hurried through the streets, neither saying a word as

they passed men, women and children scattering in all directions. Every so often an explosion would rock the city and bright lights would flash somewhere to the east, an ominous warning that hinted the battling wizards were not yet done with each other.

As on the night Salazar had died, looters had taken to the streets. Sasha witnessed doors being kicked in and homes robbed. One man was trying to set fire to a house with little obvious success. She thought she saw an exceptionally dishevelled figure crouching down and gnawing on a body, but that might have just been a trick of the *hashka* clouding her brain.

They were hurrying down a side street when she slipped and fell. She reached down and probed her ankle, felt the swelling and knew immediately that it was fractured. She tried to rise, but even with the deadening effects of the moon dust the pain when she attempted to put her weight on the ankle was intense. 'It hurts,' she gasped at her sister. Ambryl was frowning down at her, as if she were a wounded animal that it might be kinder simply to put out of its misery.

'I should leave you here,' her sister said quietly. 'The Mistress will not forget what you did. If I am found to have helped you, everything I have dreamed of will be in ruins.'

Sasha looked up at Ambryl. 'Go then!' she said angrily. 'Leave me. I'm sorry I couldn't be who you wanted me to be. I should have died that night. The truth... the truth is I'm broken.'

Ambryl's eyes narrowed. She reached down, grabbed Sasha by her hair and pulled her roughly up despite her protests. 'Don't you ever say that,' she spat. 'You say that again and I'll kill you. Now put your arm around my shoulders and don't let go.'

Sasha did as her sister ordered and together the two of them continued west towards the harbour, moving as best they could with Sasha's injury. They hadn't gone far when a blinding flash lit up the streets and a howl of rage tore through the air. Sasha looked up and her breath caught in her throat. She felt Ambryl's fingernails dig into her arm as she too saw what was happening above them. The sisters stumbled to a halt and stared at the devastating contest playing out in the skies above Thelassa.

The White Lady and Thanates were circling each other hundreds of feet above the city. As Sasha watched, dumbstruck, the Magelord of Thelassa hurled a javelin of silver fire at her former lover. Thanates dodged to avoid it and the deadly projectile soared away into sky. Undaunted, the wizard tilted his head back and twin jets of fire exploded from his hands, propelling him up into the black clouds above. He disappeared from sight. The world seemed to hold its breath in anticipation.

Thanates reappeared directly above the White Lady, plummeting straight down. He collided with the Magelord and wrapped his arms around her body and the two of them dropped from the sky like stones, locked in a deathly embrace. Down and down they fell, twisting and turning, until eventually they vanished behind one of the great marble spires.

'Is it over?' Sasha whispered. 'Is she dead?' *Please be dead*, she prayed silently. *Please be dead*.

She received her answer moments later. Like a vengeful angel, the silvery figure of the White Lady rose up to float beside the tower. She was clutching something in her hand, something red. 'You should never have come here,' she thundered, her voice carrying like a hurricane. 'This place will be your tomb.' The White Lady released whatever it was she was holding and it floated slowly down through the wind and the rain. It was a cloth, Sasha saw. The red cloth Thanates wore around his eyes.

The Magelord raised her arms and began to chant arcane words, working a mighty spell. There was a tremendous crack and then, to Sasha's horror, the great spire beside the floating Magelord suddenly rose into the sky. A thousand tons of marble, torn from the ground in an absurd display of power. Rubble rained down as a fresh wave of screams erupted on the streets.

When the tower was half a mile above the city the White Lady moved her hands in a circular motion. Three hundred feet of stone turned slowly in a colossal arc so that the pinnacle pointed down at the ground. The Magelord aimed it like a spear: a spear capable of slaughtering an army.

Don't do it, Sasha thought, appalled. *You can't. You'll devastate the entire city.*

It seemed the Magelord of Thelassa was beyond caring. With a scream like the death wail of a banshee the White Lady hurled the tower from the sky. For a split second a shadow seemed to swallow the earth, as if the moon itself were falling.

The noise when the great spire collided with the city below was like a hundred firebombs exploding all at once. The street lurched, sending Sasha crashing into the side of a building. Out of sheer instinct she tried to steady herself with her injured foot, screaming in pain as her ankle buckled. The wreckage of the pulverized tower rained down from above, stones striking her and dust filling her nose and mouth until she was choking on it. She heard something huge crash into the house behind her. There was a pregnant pause – and then a terrible creaking sound as the top half of the building began to sag.

Sasha could only watch transfixed as it toppled forward, a wagon-sized chunk of marble embedded in the roof. She was directly in its path. Her brain screamed at her to move out of the way but her body refused to act and she knew then that she was going to die, alone in a foreign city with no friends or family except a sister who surely hated her. She'd ruined things for Ambryl. Just as she'd ruined things for everyone who'd ever been close to her. She closed her eyes and waited for the end, the end she deserved.

It never came. Suddenly Ambryl was there, shoving her aside and covering her younger sister with her own body. Sasha caught a glimpse of her sister's face an instant before the house crashed down. Ambryl's expression was perfectly calm and there was a strange look in her eyes, as if this was a moment she had been waiting a lifetime for. The years of bitterness and hard living and dark deeds melted away, and in that instant she was the old Ambryl again, the young woman who would do whatever it took to keep her little sister safe.

'Ambryl!' Sasha screamed as the avalanche of stone and timber and the giant section of the shattered tower fell onto her sister. Ambryl's body shielded Sasha from the bulk of the collapsing house as Sasha tried to roll away, innumerable bits of rubble striking her painfully, leaving her bloody and bruised but somehow still alive. She rose shakily from the ground, heedless of the hundred agonies threatening to tear her apart. Where Ambryl had been standing there was now only a vast pile of debris.

Fresh agony exploded in Sasha's ankle as she stumbled to the wreckage but she ignored it; she went to her knees and began to claw away the rubble with her bare hands. Tears streamed down her face as she called her sister's name again and again. This time there was no one to rebuke her. No sound at all except the patter of the rain and, a minute or two later, an ominous groan from somewhere far below the city.

There was a commotion at the end of the street and a crowd suddenly appeared, fleeing towards the harbour. One man glanced at her as he ran by. 'The city's collapsing,' he shouted. 'Get out of here while you can.'

Sasha paid him no mind. She continued to dig, tearing her nails and bloodying her hands, lost in grief. She knew it was hopeless. No one could survive being buried alive beneath all that stone.

With a despairing sob she crumpled against the fallen building, rolling onto her back and letting the rain wash over her face. The city groaned again and this time she felt the earth tremble. More people raced down the street. She briefly considered joining them but knew she wouldn't be able to make it twenty yards without help. If she was going to die it might as well be here, beside her sister.

Another man ran past her, a straggler wearing a hood over his face. He glanced briefly in her direction and kept going for a few seconds. She couldn't explain it but as she stared dully at the man Sasha felt a flicker of familiarity, as if she ought to know him.

It appeared the hooded figure was having similar thoughts. He did a double take before turning and starting back over to her.

'Don't worry about me,' she said hoarsely. 'Save yourself.'

The hooded man's voice was thick with disbelief. 'Sasha?'

How does he know my name? There was something familiar about that voice. The figure reached up and thrust back his hood.

'C... Cole?' For a moment she was too shocked to say anything more. Then it all came pouring out in a mad rush. 'I thought you were gone,' she said, her voice cracking. 'I looked everywhere for you. I didn't know if you were dead or maybe if you'd abandoned me. I'm sorry I treated you badly. I'm a fuck-up, I know that. Please don't—'

'Hush. I would never abandon you. Why would you even think that? I ran into a little trouble but I'm here now.' Cole came closer and inspected her injuries and the concern in his grey eyes almost made her cry again. 'You're badly hurt.'

'My ankle's broken.'

Cole inspected the injury and winced. 'How did that happen? Never mind, I'll get you out of here.' He turned and called to an odd pair waiting a little further up the street and together they ambled over. One was clearly a hunchback, with an oversized brow and big, watery eyes. The other—

'Ed,' Cole said patiently. 'Why'd you take your top off?'

The big fellow Cole referred to as Ed stared down at his badly scarred body. He looked as though someone had recently tried to carve him up with a knife. 'I wanted to show your girlfriend my scars,' he rumbled.

Cole gave Sasha an embarrassed look. 'I never said that. That you're my girlfriend I mean. Damn it, Ed, just help her up! Derkin, you lead the way. You know these streets better than me.'

Sasha gasped softly as Ed lifted her from the rubble with a combination of fearsome strength and surprising gentleness.

Her body hurt all over but seeing Cole's face again soothed her pain and for the first time in months she felt safe, despite the fact the city was collapsing and an angry Magelord was still circling the skies above.

'You're pretty,' Ed rumbled. He sounded like a child. Sasha looked up at his simple face and forced herself to smile.

'Thank you,' she said. She glanced at Cole. There was something different about him. 'Are these men your new henchmen?' she asked, remembering Three-Finger and suppressing a shudder.

'Henchmen?' Cole looked puzzled. 'No. These are my friends.'

Sasha stared at Cole again. He had changed; she saw that now. The way he carried himself, the way he spoke... he was less certain. Less sure of himself. 'What happened to you?' she said quietly.

Cole hesitated and then shook his head. 'There's no time to explain. We need to get to the harbour before this place falls apart.'

They joined the mass of people stampeding through the streets towards the docks. Sasha looked back one final time at the collapsed house, at her sister's tomb. Cole must have noticed the tears in her eyes. 'What's wrong?' he asked. 'Why are you crying?'

'Someone dear to me is buried underneath that rubble. She... she sacrificed herself to save my life.'

Cole slowed and looked as if he were about to turn around. 'We can go back if you want. Maybe she survived. Maybe we can dig her out—'

'No. Please, Cole. It's over. She's gone.'

Cole's mouth opened and he looked like he might argue, but a moment later he bit his lip and nodded. The old Cole would never have shown such restraint and she wondered again at the change in his personality. Then her thoughts returned to her sister.

'*Goodbye, Ambryl,*' she whispered, blinking back tears. To

her surprise Ed squeezed her tighter as he carried her in his arms, a gesture meant to comfort.

They hurried on, saying little as the rain continued to pour down and those fleeing the city converged on the harbour. It was heaving with people when they finally arrived, soaking wet and short of breath, especially poor Derkin. An elderly woman waved at him and he broke away from the group to join her, protesting animatedly as she smothered him in hugs and kisses.

Despite the stormy conditions, several ships were already full as city folk sought the sanctuary of the open sea. Those already on the ships stared back at the crowded docks with sympathetic faces. No one wanted to be on solid land in the event the city's foundations gave out.

Sasha gazed out across the churning green water as Ed carried her across the soaking wooden boards that formed the docks. The endless sheets of rain made it hard to be certain, but as her eyes scanned the ships floating in the harbour she thought she could make out large shapes approaching through the grey haze of mist beyond.

The captain of one of the smaller vessels leaned over the rail and waved at the crowd waiting on the docks. 'No need to panic,' he called out. 'More ships are returning to harbour. At least three. Hang on, make that four. Wait... what in the hells?'

Uproar broke out on those ships whose passengers were close enough to get a good look at the approaching fleet. Seconds later screams rolled across the wharf, a tide of panic rising like flood-water as the crowd finally saw what it was that approached.

'Let's get closer for a better look,' Cole suggested, and he and Ed pushed their way through the crowd. Sasha clung tightly to the big simpleton, and as he barged his way to the edge of the docks she looked up to see a large crow soaring overhead, its wings badly damaged and its dark feathers singed as if it had been caught in a fire.

Sasha's attention snapped back to the harbour as she heard Cole's horrified gasp. A moment later her own breath caught in

441

her throat. All around them people were shouting. No small number were retching, sickened by what they saw drifting towards them.

The ghost fleet was empty of both crew and passengers, or at least of those still among the living. All the ships contained were heads. Hundreds of heads piled high in grisly pyramids, their worm-eaten eyes staring out unseeing above sallow cheeks turning green with rot.

Yet more ships came into view, all of them carrying the same ghastly cargo. The dead must have numbered in the thousands, men and women who only a few months ago had set sail from Dorminia dreaming of untold riches or just a warm meal to fill their family's bellies.

'The Pioneers,' Sasha said numbly, almost choking on bile. The ships sent to the Celestial Isles had returned.

The Better Man

Sir MEREDITH FLEXED his hand as he approached the hill, marvelling at how strong it felt. Shranree had done an admirable job of healing the terrible injury he had brought back from the Greenwild. The sorceress had teased the bone back together with fingers as supple as her tongue and sealed the wound with a brief unveiling of magic that had eased the pain. Now, a scant few weeks after the tragedy, he was restored to his glorious best.

The guards at the west gate huddled miserably against the wall, trying to escape the biting wind that brought with it endless flurries of snow. Sir Meredith sneered at them behind his helm, wondering at the lack of mental alacrity that would compel a man to such menial duty. He hoped these two performed their roles with greater enthusiasm than the previous guards. He noticed their bodies in the corpse pit as he passed it. The thick snow hid their wounds, and he considered that something of a shame. He rather enjoyed admiring his handiwork.

Red Rayne caught up with him as he was halfway up the hill. A glance at the wretch's face confirmed that he was high on *jhaeld* again. Sir Meredith shook his head in disgust and ignored Rayne's muttered greeting. Attending the King in such a state bespoke a man of abhorrent character. Admittedly, neither of them was supposed to be present at Krazka's side this day. But a knight's devotion never wavered, which was exactly why Sir Meredith's armour had already been polished and donned when

Krazka's unexpected summons arrived. Rayne on the other hand looked as though he had just crawled out of a brothel, which in all probability he had. Sir Meredith consoled himself with the knowledge that Shranree's ministrations had been less successful when it had come to the fireplant-addicted degenerate; Rayne would never hold a sword in his right hand again.

When the two men reached the top of the hill, they found Krazka staring out across the snow-blanketed fields of the King's Reaching. Bagha and the pasty-fleshed Northman, Wulgreth, were guarding him. Orgrim Foehammer stood nearby, concern plastered over his face.

Shranree was also present. Sir Meredith amused himself wondering if the sorceress still walked with a slight limp after the night they'd spent together. Her appetites were surprising indeed, but then a knight understood how to treat a lady. Knew how to unlock all the hidden passions his artless countrymen couldn't even begin to comprehend.

Disappointingly, Shranree didn't seem pleased to see him. Her eyes met his, and he thought he glimpsed worry there before they flicked away.

Krazka finally turned, the white cloak he wore dancing wildly in the strong wind. The King held a strange device in his hand. It looked like a brass tube, tapering somewhat along its length. There was a thick layer of glass at the wide end. The King must have noticed Sir Meredith's puzzled expression, for he tapped the strange gadget and smiled a humourless smile.

'You ain't never seen my looking tube before, sir knight? Here.' Krazka tossed the device at Sir Meredith, who after a heart-stopping moment in which he almost fumbled the tube to the snow managed to catch it in his gauntlets.

He stared at it for a moment, examining the bronze casing. Then he raised his visor and brought the tube up to his face. He squinted through the glass but saw only a blur. 'It's broken.'

'The other end,' Krazka said patiently. Bagha grinned at his error, a blatant expression of ridicule that had Sir Meredith itching to knock the brute's oversized teeth out of his mouth. He turned the device around and brought the narrow end up to his eye.

The world seemed to grow fivefold. The row of pines on the hill over the river loomed large enough for him to make out individual trees. He turned slowly, staring out over Heartstone in wonder. Even at this distance, he could make out the faces of the townsfolk. It was as if someone had granted him the vision of a hawk. He scanned the buildings until he found the Great Lodge, then directed his gaze to the pinnacle. He spotted what he was looking for on the roof. A wicker cage housed a naked and filthy prisoner. Sir Meredith could make out the lacerations on the young man's body, the fresh shit that had been smeared into his wounds.

'This has to be some kind of magic,' Sir Meredith exclaimed, lowering the looking tube and turning it over in his hands. Bagha guffawed at that, and the knight's good humour drained away like piss down a latrine. 'Mock me again and I swear to you, brute, I shall break this over your ugly head!' he roared.

The King's lone eye narrowed on him. 'That's one of a kind. You damage it and I won't be happy, sir knight. Wulgreth found it in the same place he found this.' Krazka reached down to his belt and patted the handle of the long-barrelled projectile weapon with which he'd put a hole in the Shaman. The strange artefact still made Sir Meredith nervous. It struck him as perverse that such devastating power could be housed in so small a form.

'To answer your question,' Wulgreth said softly, 'it is not magic. The hidden grotto I discovered while lost in the North Reaching contained all manner of strange objects. Long before men walked these mountains, another race dwelled here. In that cave were paintings of a forgotten people. They were tall and white-skinned, with eyes like obsidian. And they built weapons that could humble the gods.'

Sir Meredith listened with gritted teeth, hating Wulgreth and the foul perversions he knew sickened the man's mind. The bastard struck him as too smart by half and there was something about his eyes, always bloodshot and *hungry*, that bothered the knight, that offended his honour.

'There's something I want you to see,' Krazka grated. He gestured at the looking tube. 'Twist the end. It changes the distance. Set it as far as it'll go and take a gander due south.'

Sir Meredith did as the King commanded. Shranree looked uneasy, which was a strange sight indeed in a woman who had proven so hard to shock in the bedroom. He rotated the end of the tube until it clicked and would go no further, and then he peered through it. This time he couldn't suppress a gasp. He could see for miles, the excellent vantage the hill provided offering him a breathtaking view of the King's Reaching.

There was something odd about the horizon. A dark cloud of grey was visible beyond the white sheets of snow, and it took him a moment to realize that it was smoke. Too much smoke to come from any single village. No, it had to be the work of a great many men. An army, less than a day's march away.

He heard a clicking noise on the hill behind him. He lowered the looking tube and turned – only to stare down the barrel of the King's deadly weapon.

Krazka's disfigured face twisted into a scowl. 'Some stupid fucker decided to go and murder a bunch of Greenmen and their wives and children. You might not have heard but they call me the Butcher of Beregund down there. I weren't a popular man as it was. Turns out even I'm less popular since half my Kingsmen went on a murdering spree.'

'The Green Reaching has responded by revoking its neutrality,' Wulgreth said in his smooth voice. 'It has declared for the Shaman.'

Sir Meredith swallowed hard in the silence that followed. Could it be that he'd miscalculated? The Greenmen were supposed to come crawling back to Krazka, begging for his mercy after they'd been brought to heel. The stratagem had always worked for the Rag King back in the old days.

The King pointed his weapon at Red Rayne, the other man to have accompanied Sir Meredith on their ill-fated quest and returned to tell the tale. That dog-faced bastard Ryder had apparently not made it out of the Greenwild.

'I thought about sending your heads to Southaven as a peace offering,' the King mused. 'But I reckon we're beyond salvaging the situation. Their army's already camped out in my own Reaching, ready to attack as soon as they've marshalled their forces. I got that cocksucker Carn Bloodfist to the west, Mace to the north, and now Brandwyn the Younger to the south. All I need is the Shaman miraculously recovering and the Sword of the North showing his face and this little clusterfuck will be complete. Lucky for us the Herald's on its way back soon. We just need to hold out for a while longer.'

Sir Meredith breathed a small sigh of relief, thinking the conversation was returning to calmer waters. His respite proved short-lived as Krazka swung the weapon back towards him.

'I want to know which of you is responsible for ignoring my orders. I can tolerate murderers and sadists and even a shit-for-brains like Bagha here. But if there's one thing I ain't gonna stand for, it's an independent thinker. You never get anything done with men like that at your back. We all know Ryder weren't no leader. It was one of you two that fucked up.'

Red Rayne pointed a trembling finger at Sir Meredith, the mangled digit next to the ruin of his ring finger. It wasn't clear if he was shaking from fear or the *jhaeld* in his system. 'It was his idea. The iron man. He said they was your orders.'

Krazka shifted the barrel back towards Sir Meredith. 'That right, sir knight?'

Sir Meredith's heart was racing now. Sweat beaded his brow; he could feel it soaking his under-tunic beneath his mail. He couldn't take his eyes off the lethal weapon pointed at his face. 'He's lying,' he replied, though he heard a slight tremor in his voice and inwardly cursed. He was a *knight*. He wouldn't show weakness in the face of this savage!

'I implored that witless cur to focus on the quest in hand!' Meredith snapped, recovering himself somewhat. 'The fireplant resin coursing through his feeble brain turned him into a rabid dog. He raped and murdered his way through so many poor families that Ryder and I lost count. The delay his reprehensible actions cost us allowed the foundlings to escape to the Greenwild.'

'You weasel-tongued bastard!' Rayne roared. His hands shot to the scimitars at his sides a moment before he realized he could no longer use his right hand, his stronger hand. 'That's bullshit and you know it!'

Sir Meredith reached for his own sabre then. 'I will not be called a liar by a reprobate such as you!' he barked. He knew Rayne didn't stand a chance, not with his mutilated hand. The man's days as a worthwhile member of the Six were past, if indeed they had ever been present. 'Let a contest of steel reveal the truth of your deception!'

The King shook his head. 'There'll be no duelling. That'd hardly be fair on old ninefingers there. No, we're gonna take a vote. Like civilized men.'

'A vote?' Meredith said uncomfortably.

Krazka raised an eyebrow. 'You know, it don't hurt to address your king with a bit of respect. Seeing as I pay you handsomely and all.'

'You pay me what I deserve,' Sir Meredith replied, the words tumbling out of him before he'd given them proper consideration. He stared at the weapon the King carried and swallowed hard.

The King's eye flashed in anger, but he smiled and turned to Bagha. 'What d'you reckon, bearface? Who's to blame for bringing the goat-fuckers to my doorstep?'

Bagha scratched his head. 'Huh. I think the iron's man guilty.'

What you think is worth less than a goat's shit, Sir Meredith wanted to bark, but he managed to keep the words inside this time.

The King leered at Sir Meredith, who was suddenly reminded

of dark nights long ago. His knightly courage began to waver as the memories flooded back. 'No,' he whispered. '*No*.'

'What's that? You say something?' The King shook the barrel at him, and the sudden movement made Sir Meredith jump.

I'm a knight, he thought desperately. *Knights fear no one.*

'Wulgreth,' the King said abruptly. 'What's your opinion?'

Sir Meredith could see that the Northman knew the truth. He could read it in his bloodshot eyes and the smirk on his face. But when Wulgreth answered it wasn't the response the knight had been dreading. 'I believe Red Rayne is guilty, my king.'

Krazka nodded. 'That's one vote each. What about you, Foehammer?'

Orgrim Foehammer shook his head. The former chieftain of the East Reaching looked like a broken man. As if everything he had ever believed in had unravelled right before his eyes. 'I don't care.'

'Now, don't be a spoilsport. You get a vote here the same as everyone else.'

The big Easterman crossed his meaty arms and spat. 'I got no say in any of this. I shouldn't be here. I should be back at Eastmeet, back with my people. Fighting to keep the Fangs safe. Fighting to turn back the demons you permitted to invade our land.'

'Don't make this all about you, Foehammer. I got more than one bullet for this weapon, if you catch my drift. Give me a name.'

Orgrim's shoulders sagged. 'Him,' he whispered, nodding at Sir Meredith.

'Shranree?' the King asked.

The sorceress cleared her throat. 'My king, Red Rayne is clearly unbalanced. His fireplant addiction makes him a liability and his loss of fighting skill means he is no longer fit to guard you. Sir Meredith is without question the better man.'

'Bullshit!' Rayne roared again. His face had turned as red as his epithet, the *jhaeld* in his blood pushing him to the brink of a berserker rage.

Krazka's eye narrowed and he stared off into the blizzard as if deep in thought. 'That's two votes each. Looks like I get to cast the deciding vote.' There was a terrible pause before the King's weapon swung back to Sir Meredith. 'Think that metal armour will protect you, sir knight?'

Meredith felt a warm trickle beneath his cuisses and he realized he had pissed himself. He squeezed his eyes shut, waited for the end.

The blast sent him crashing to the ground in an armoured heap. He lay flattened for a moment, his ears ringing from the thunderous noise, too shocked to move. Then he rolled over and groaned. He reached out to push himself up and felt something soft and spongy beneath his gauntlets. He opened his eyes.

The grey, snaking mess of Rayne's brains were splattered all over the snow. The man's body was crumpled nearby, dark matter hanging out of the shattered remnants of his skull. There was blood everywhere.

A shadow loomed over him. It was Krazka, the barrel of the terrible weapon he clutched smoking gently in his hand. 'You may be the better man,' he drawled, 'but if you ever pull a stunt like that again, it'll be your corpse lying headless on the snow. We understand each other, sir knight?'

'Yes,' Sir Meredith managed.

'Yes what?'

'Yes... *my king.*'

He drove his sword home again and again. Krazka's face filled his world as he thrust, gasping with effort, sweat pouring down his face. 'Die,' he rasped. 'Die, you bloody savage.'

The King tried to scream but no sound emerged. Sir Meredith smiled and thrust harder, revelling in his mastery, relishing the restoration of the natural order of things. He was a knight. Knights did not cower before barbarians.

He felt a sudden sting on his face. He snapped out of his reverie to see Shranree's nails clawing at his cheeks, her body writing beneath him. His hands were wrapped around her throat, choking her as agreed, but he'd got carried away in his fantasy and now she was turning red, no longer able to breathe. He relaxed his grip and turned away from the woman, rolling onto his back to stare up at the wooden ceiling while she coughed and spluttered on the bed beside him.

'You almost strangled me,' she gasped, rubbing at her neck. 'A few seconds more and the King would be searching for another Kingsman. You are a good fuck, but you are not worth dying for.'

As if to reinforce the threat in her words, Shranree's hand glowed briefly. A moment later the red marks around her neck faded. Sir Meredith stared at his rapidly wilting manhood and wanted to scream. How many more times was he going to be emasculated this day?

As his desire slipped away, Meredith was glad for the robe Shranree pulled on to cover her fleshy figure. He barely found her attractive at the best of times, and in truth was still confused as to why he had agreed to meet with her at all. After his humiliation earlier that day company had been the last thing on his mind. He ought to be preparing himself for the war to come, not lying here ploughing this shapeless sack of flesh.

Shranree's heavy cheeks were still flushed from the ferocity of their lovemaking. He flinched as she placed a hand on his forearm. 'The King was not jesting earlier,' she said quietly. 'If you go against his will again, he will kill you.'

Sir Meredith felt his teeth grinding together. 'The King is insane,' he replied bitterly. 'A madman. In Carhein the city's physicians would lock him in an asylum and throw away the key.'

'At first I too believed him mad. I have since learned the opposite is in fact true. Most see the world through a prism constructed of a hundred thousand lies, but Krazka sees only reality. Great men must embrace reality in order to shape it to their will.'

Sir Meredith frowned. 'And what is reality, woman?'

'We live in a godless world. A dying world. When hope fades, it is better to submit to the darkness than to resist. The King knows what he wants and he lets nothing dissuade him from it.'

'What do *you* want?' Meredith asked. The woman was beginning to irritate him. She sounded like one of the Nameless cultists back in Grantz, with all her talk of submitting to the darkness. He was a knight. *He* would forever walk in the light.

'Power,' she said simply. 'When the Lowlands eventually fall, I will claim a dominion of my own down south.' She briefly rose from the bed and her robes fell away to reveal her soft curves beneath. 'I should like a consort to rule beside me,' she said, reaching towards his flaccid member. 'Perhaps we could claim one of the Shattered Realms. Maybe even Tarbonne. Would you like that, lover?'

The thought of his beloved Tarbonne befouled by an army of his countrymen and a horde of demons filled Sir Meredith with horror. It was too precious a jewel to be desecrated by fiends and barbarians.

He had made a mistake in coming back, he saw that now. This was no land for a knight.

Shranree's round face creased in confusion as he batted away her hand. 'What are you doing?' she asked, as he bent down and retrieved his sword belt from the floor.

'I'm done here,' he said crisply. He *was* done, in more ways than one. He began to gather up the pieces of his armour.

'You can't just walk out,' Shranree hissed. Her voice had turned ugly. 'Who do you think you are?'

'I, milady, am a *knight*,' he snapped.

Shranree rolled off the bed. Her feet struck the floor with a hefty thump, and she leaned down to gather her discarded robes. 'A knight,' she said, her voice thick with scorn. 'Why, you didn't look like a knight earlier. I saw you piss your pants.'

Sir Meredith stiffened. 'Watch your whore tongue,' he rasped, his hands twitching.

Shranree finished gathering up her robes. As she straightened, something seemed to occur to her. Without turning, she said, 'I always wondered why your mother gave you a girl's name. Now I know.'

Shranree was still snorting with amusement when Sir Meredith's sabre burst through her back.

The snow had stopped falling at last. The night was still and silent, the town buried beneath a blanket of white. Sentries were posted on the walls, their torches casting long shadows over Heartstone, but their attention was directed towards the north and the south and the west, where the armies of three hostile Reachings were encamped.

It was to the east where Sir Meredith's eyes were fixed. The burden he dragged behind him left a deep furrow in the snow. '*Why did I come back?*' he muttered feverishly to himself, over and over again, sweat rolling down his brow and dripping from his chin. If only that bitch hadn't opened her fat mouth.

'Insolent whore!' he swore, instantly clamping a hand over his face, afraid that someone might hear him. He took a deep breath and tried to focus. He needed to get the body out of Heartstone and dispose of it before anyone discovered Shranree was missing.

He slowed as he neared the east gate. The guards on duty recognized him and threw hurried salutes, no doubt keenly aware of the fate that had befallen their counterparts on the west gate. They stared at the sack Sir Meredith hauled with curious expressions.

'What ya doing?' one dared asked, his rustic manner of speech making Sir Meredith shudder.

'The King's business,' Sir Meredith shot back. 'Get that bloody gate open – and learn some eloquence, damn you!'

The guards hurried to obey. One of them kept glancing at the sack, a deep frown on his bearded face. The knight memorized the man's features, thinking that he might need to make him vanish if the opportunity presented itself.

'Need some 'elp?' asked the first guard as Sir Meredith hauled his burden through the gates. The dropped 'h' was simply too egregious after everything else that had transpired that day. Meredith spun and backhanded the guard across the face with his iron gauntlets, cracking his jaw and knocking out several teeth.

'When a knight gives you an order, you obey it,' he said furiously.

He dragged Shranree's corpse away from the gate and down the road a short distance, and then descended the shallow embankment south of the road. There was a small stream just ahead. It wasn't ideal, but it should serve to hide the evidence. In his mind's eye he saw Rayne's brains seeping out of his skull, and he shuddered.

He reached the stream and let the sack go slack. He rubbed his aching back, cursing the day he had decided to lower his standards for such a woman. For a moment he had the uneasy thought that perhaps he was going native. Would he soon be trading wine for mead and stumbling home excited by the prospect of a toothless mouth gumming his manhood? The image filled him with revulsion.

Yet another reason to leave this accursed land as soon as possible.

He grabbed hold of the sack and was preparing to drag it into the water when he noticed the stream was frozen solid. He stared at it in disbelief. How could he have been so stupid?

'Shit,' he said. This had gone well beyond a debacle. Now it was a damned *calamity*.

He was searching desperately for another spot to dump the corpse when he noticed someone approaching from the road. He drew his sabre, knowing that if he was discovered and word got back to the King, his life would be forfeit.

It was that bastard Wulgreth. The Northman was dressed for travel, a thick cloak thrown over his hide armour and a satchel slung over his shoulder. And yet he wasn't carrying his spear, or indeed a weapon of any description. Sir Meredith was both surprised and elated. He would make quick work of this fool.

For some reason, however, Wulgreth seemed amused. 'Iron man. I thought as much.'

Sir Meredith looked around to be sure no one was with Wulgreth. 'Did the guards raise the alarm?' he demanded.

'They never saw me leave.'

Meredith's eyes narrowed. 'You are a fool to travel unarmed.'

'Weapons come in many forms.' Wulgreth's eyes settled on the sack. Even in the darkness, they seemed to have a reddish tint. 'You murdered his favourite sorceress. The blood is still fresh.'

'She impugned my honour. That may mean little to you – but to a knight it is not something that can be borne. She left me little choice but to kill her. As do you.'

'Do not threaten me, iron man.'

'A barbarian threatens. A knight *asserts*.' Sir Meredith stormed forward, preparing to drive his sabre through this arrogant Northman's pale flesh.

Wulgreth uttered a single word that made no sense. Suddenly the hilt of Sir Meredith's sabre glowed red hot and he dropped the weapon, yelping in pain. The Northman's eyes were a brighter red now, like two hot coals sparking to life.

'You... You're a wizard?' Meredith asked hoarsely.

'Of a kind.'

'Why are you here?'

Wulgreth reached up to his neck and fondled the key that was hanging on a thin chain there. 'My work in this part of the world is finished. The gholam is free and the markers are in place. I was preparing to follow the road east and then south when the blood of this sorceress called to me.'

Sir Meredith looked down at the corpse at his feet. 'You wish to use her body?'

'In a manner of speaking.' Wulgreth walked over to the sack and pulled it away from Shranree. He gazed at the woman hungrily.

Sir Meredith's bile rose in his throat then, but when Wulgreth knelt down he did nothing of a carnal nature. Instead, he shoved a single finger inside the gaping wound in Shranree's back and muttered some arcane words. Moments later the sorceress's body began to *deflate*, as if her internal fluids were being leached away. Within seconds the corpse had been reduced to a withered husk, unrecognizable as anything that might once have been human.

Wulgreth straightened; his eyes shone like rubies in his skull. 'I believe that is what they call one for the road. Now, I must go. The Master awaits.'

Sir Meredith stared at the revolting thing that had once been Shranree. 'The Master,' he repeated in a daze of horrified fascination. 'You don't mean Krazka.'

'I do not.'

'Then... who? Who is your master?'

'You might call him... a weaver. He plucks the threads of countless lives and shapes the Pattern to his will.'

Sir Meredith watched Wulgreth climb back up the embankment. Fear warred with valour, and as it always did in a true knight valour won out. 'Wait,' he called. 'Let me come with you.'

The wizard's voice reached him as a sinister whisper that nonetheless carried the length of the embankment. 'You cannot walk the paths I walk, iron man. Besides, Wolgred the Wanderer always travels alone.'

Executed

THE BANGING ON the cell door startled him awake. He'd been dreaming of her again. Every time he closed his eyes and drifted off it was Monique's face that occupied his thoughts. For that small blessing if nothing else he was grateful.

There were worse things to dwell on, the night before a man's execution.

There was another bang on the door and then the rattle of a key being inserted into the lock. The Halfmage shivered despite the sweat that suddenly sprang from his brow.

It's time.

The door scraped open and a Watchman melted out of the shadows to peer into the cell. 'You awake?'

'Of course. It would be rather careless of me to sleep through my own execution.'

'You going to come peacefully? No magic?'

'That was the deal.'

At least he hoped that was still the case – Timerus had nothing to gain by breaking his word and harming Monique once this was all over. The Grand Regent would stick to his promise; he had to keep telling himself that. The alternative was too terrible to contemplate.

'You need help with that chair?'

'How very generous of you to offer,' he replied acerbically, though in truth Eremul was slightly taken aback by the earnestness in the guard's voice. The noble men of the Crimson Watch had wasted no opportunity to torment him during his incarceration. What better way to honour the last days of the condemned than to piss in his food, or threaten to burn down the depository and his life's work with it? Whatever one might say about Marshal Bracka's incompetence when it came to keeping the city safe, the new commander of the Watch was determined not to let standards drop in the arena of petty cruelty.

There wasn't any malice in this particular's Watchman's eyes. Only a mild consternation as he came and took hold of Eremul's chair and wheeled him out of the cell into the dungeons that occupied the lowest level of the Obelisk's dark bulk. Torches lined the walls, illuminating the slabs and tools Eremul knew so intimately. The person he had once been had died in this place; died to be reborn as the Halfmage. It was fitting that it would serve as his final stop now, before the maimed mockery of a man who had survived the Culling all those years ago departed this world for good.

'Why'd you do it?' asked the Watchman as he guided Eremul up the stairs leading to the ground floor. 'You were a hero. Why plot to destroy the city you helped free from the tyrant? It makes no sense.'

'Who can know the mind of a madman,' Eremul replied drolly. He was tired of protesting his innocence. It would make no difference. He and Lorganna would hang at noon; the world would carry on spinning, people would carry on fighting and fucking and dying, and no one would give two shits that he was gone. Until recently he wouldn't have done either – but now he felt an acute sense of regret that he would be leaving Monique so suddenly, without even saying goodbye. No sooner had he found something of value in his life than it was cruelly taken from him.

It's the irony that kills. It was fortunate the gods were dead, or he might accuse them of having a sense of humour.

'My old ma didn't think so,' said the Watchman unexpectedly.

'Think what?' Eremul's earlier stoicism was beginning to waver now. His stomach churned with nerves; the armour of anger and resentment that had served to keep the terror at arm's length was beginning to fail as the moment drew nearer.

'Think you were mad. She came to you seeking aid. You gave her an elixir to help with the pain in her joints. She said you wouldn't accept payment.'

Eremul frowned, trying to remember the instance the guard referred to. The weeks following Salazar's death had become a blur with all that had transpired since. 'I don't recall. How is she feeling?'

'She's walking much better.'

'Lucky for some of us, I suppose.'

They exited the stairwell and approached the Obelisk's double doors. Eremul closed his eyes for a moment, feeling the soft breeze washing down the entrance hall, enjoying these last few seconds of peace before his ignoble march – or rather trundle – to the hangman's noose. He wondered if his life would flash before him in the moment before the rope went taut. He wondered if he would see her face one last time.

The patter of rain struck his head and finally he opened his eyes. Angry clouds filled the sky from horizon to horizon. There would be no last glorious moment in the sun for him – only a thorough drenching courtesy of the late-autumn storm.

But then, I would expect nothing less.

As he was wheeled through the courtyard other Watchmen fell in behind them from the barracks on either side. Several had crossbows levelled on him.

'Ready to die, half-man?' one of the officers sneered.

Eremul ignored the guard and fixed his attention on the streets as the procession headed east and then south towards the Hook. The Noble Quarter had been ransacked months past, and things had got even worse since then as the White Lady had continued to asset-strip the city's wealth. Dorminia was ripe for insurrection, a fact the woman who had posed as Lorganna had been quick to use for her own ends. What Melissan's ends *were* exactly, Eremul still hadn't figured out. He was still confused as to why she had drawn him into her schemes. Why set up the meeting at the lighthouse? Why allow him to experiment with the prisoner and uncover the truth about the mind-controlling tattoos?

He cursed himself again for handing over the construct to Melissan back at the lighthouse. She had told him she was going to present it as evidence to the council and had apparently managed to dispose of it before the Watch arrested her. From the guards outside his cell Eremul had learned that Melissan hadn't said a thing since her capture. It was his word against Remy's evidence... and it turned out no one was inclined to believe a reputedly mad wizard.

As he was escorted to the great plaza the crowds that had gathered to watch the execution grew thicker. Young children hurled insults at him while their mothers sneered and made warding gestures. The fleeting respect he had enjoyed was well and truly gone now. He was back to being the bogeyman, the object of ridicule. It hurt more than he had thought it would.

After all I've done for this city. This is how you thank me?

He forced his hands to stop trembling and set his jaw in a grim line. He wouldn't give them the satisfaction of seeing him distressed. Let them gawk and laugh. Melissan's arrest would change nothing. Dorminia was on the brink of disaster and all it would take was one more nudge before the city plunged into the abyss.

A gallows had been erected in the Hook. As they approached the platform a huge roar went up from the crowd gathered around it. The barrage of abuse intensified and rotten fruit and vegetables began to rain down on Eremul, splattering all over his robes, striking him in the face and dribbling down his chin.

'Nearly there,' said the young Watchman who was pushing his chair. He sounded almost apologetic. A dog barked somewhere in the crowd and Eremul was suddenly reminded of an important detail he had overlooked. Filled with panic, he turned to the guard. 'Tyro,' he said urgently.

'What did you say?'

'My dog. Tyro. I left him back at the depository. Somebody needs to feed him when I'm gone.'

The Watchman looked confused.

'You said I refused payment. When your mother came to me. If she still wishes to repay her debt, she can check on my dog. He'll need a home, too.'

'I'll… I'll mention it to her.'

'Thank you.' Eremul relaxed slightly and turned his attention back to the platform. Melissan was already up there, her hands bound behind her and a sack pulled over her head. Eremul's chair was lifted onto the platform and then he was wheeled over to sit beside the rebel leader. The executioner lowered the noose and placed it around Melissan's neck, and then it was the Halfmage's turn.

He stared out over the assembled city folk as the rope settled into position, wondering how long it would take for him to suffocate once the lever that opened the platform was released. Longer than it might a whole-bodied man with the additional weight of a pair of legs to tighten the noose around his throat, he supposed.

Perhaps I won't suffocate at all. Perhaps I'll simply hang there like a stubborn turd, wasting away over the course of days or even weeks. He hoped it wouldn't come to that. The sooner he died, the sooner Timerus would release Monique from wherever she was being held captive.

With a grunt, the executioner tore the sack from Melissan's head. The woman he had once known as Lorganna was battered and bruised, but apart from the cosmetic damage to her face she looked no different than he remembered. She was remarkably plain for a woman who had inspired such loyalty in her fanatics, who had won a seat on the Council through a piece of breathtakingly audacious deception.

As Eremul stared at Melissan he had the sudden sense that something wasn't quite right. It gnawed at him with the overwhelming urgency of an itch he couldn't scratch, but just then the crowd parted and Timerus arrived.

The Grand Regent was wearing his golden robes as well as that ridiculous silver circlet atop his balding crown. Behind him trailed his personal bodyguard, the White Lady's handmaiden in her robes of purest white. Bracka was there too, the big marshal bellowing orders at his men for no particular reason, enjoying the illusion of importance it gave him. Scurrying a little behind was the spymaster Remy, as dishevelled as ever and quite possibly drunk again, though it was hard to tell with the pouring rain obstructing Eremul's view.

Timerus raised a hand and the crowd fell silent. Eremul met the Grand Regent's beady eyes and the insufferable smugness on that narrow face almost made him abandon their deal.

I could melt that smile right off your fucking skull, you Ishari snake. As if reading his thoughts, the handmaiden twitched slightly and gave a gentle shake of her head. Eremul swallowed his anger and forced himself to remain calm. It would be over soon.

'Fellow citizens,' Timerus intoned in his arrogant drawl, his voice carrying over the soft roar of the rain. 'I present to you the accused! This woman Melissan plotted the downfall of our fair city whilst insinuating herself onto its very Council. The campaign of terror she instigated through her network of fanatics caused considerable damage to the city coffers.'

'Not just our coffers! My wife was taken from me the night of the fire,' a man cried out, his voice cracking with emotion. 'She burned alive in our bed.'

A muscle in Timerus's check twitched at the interruption, but he inclined his head and his voice was grave. 'Quite. Let us also not forget the human cost this woman's villainy has wrought upon us all.'

'Whore!' someone shrieked.

Timerus uttered something to Bracka, who in turn barked a few words to his lieutenants. The guards began to fan out into the crowd and issue stern warnings to keep quiet while the Grand Regent was speaking. Eremul watched it all with a jaded eye. He'd only been in the job a few months but already Timerus was displaying dictatorial tendencies that would have made Salazar proud.

He glanced at Melissan again. She displayed no emotion on her bland face. Rather, she looked like she was... waiting for something. That sense of urgency tugged at him again, tugged at a memory that was as slippery as an eel to pin down.

'Not only did Melissan's schemes taint the aftermath of our glorious liberation,' Timerus continued, 'she also turned one of our own against us. A man once thought a hero. Alas, the wizard who sits before you was not satisfied with the great honour bestowed upon him for his role in winning the city's freedom. No, he desired more. Like all wizards, his lust for power corrupted his soul. And so he hatched a plot with the woman beside him, and together the two of them sought to tear the city apart in their quest for power. What you see before you, ladies and gentlemen, is the true face of villainy.'

'Hang them,' someone shouted.

'Traitor scum!' someone else roared. Others joined in and soon the crowd was a seething cauldron of anger and abuse. Timerus allowed the massed citizenry to work themselves into a frenzy before he raised a hand and order was restored.

'These two were foolish to believe they could dupe the Grand Council. They were foolish to believe their nefarious schemes could go unpunished. Let their fates serve as a lesson to any who would do us harm. My colleagues and I serve the White Lady's will; we carry her light in our hearts, and there is no darkness it will not illuminate when our people are threatened.'

It was too much. Eremul couldn't help himself. The snigger burst out of him before he could stop it, snot and rainwater bubbling out of his nose to run down his chin. He had to hand it to

463

Timerus; he'd heard some bullshit in his time but that last part was pure gold, one final nugget of idiocy to take with him to the grave.

'Any last words?' the Grand Regent drawled. If he'd noticed Eremul's reaction, he gave no indication.

The Halfmage attempted to clear his throat. There were many things he wanted to say. He wanted to scream his innocence; he wanted to state that this was all a big mistake, that the woman next to him had set him up. But it was too late for that. They had Monique, and if he didn't play along, they would kill her. It was a strange thing, caring enough about someone to willingly surrender his own life. Perhaps it was true what the cult of the Nameless claimed: that love was man's greatest weakness.

Perhaps it was true, but as he gazed out at the hundreds of pairs of eyes locked on him, all he saw was Monique's smile. 'No words,' he said raggedly, his voice hardly carrying above the rain. 'Just… remember our agreement.'

Melissan lifted her head then. 'I would speak,' she said, and to Eremul's ears her voice sounded more musical than he remembered, and all of a sudden that sense of urgency struck him so hard his head felt as if it might explode. He blinked away water as he stared at her, fighting against unseen forces he couldn't comprehend, couldn't rationalize except for the persistent sense that something was very wrong.

'I wish to admit my guilt.'

Timerus raised a narrow eyebrow. 'I believe your guilt is already established. We have your full confession.'

'I wish to confess to something else.'

The Grand Regent steepled his fingers in front of his chin. 'Go on.'

'Forty years ago as you count the passing of time, a ship arrived upon a distant shore. Others had come to this shore before and had been turned away – but this ship had been battered by a storm and would capsize at any moment. I took pity on the crew, allowed it entry to our port. This was my first mistake.'

As Eremul stared, aghast, Melissan's skin seemed to ripple.

'My second mistake was to offer the crew shelter while they convalesced. The youngest among us had never before seen a human. They were curious. They listened... and thus were they lost.'

Like a torrent of water rushing in to fill a burst dam, memories flooded back to Eremul. Memories of a night outside the depository, when a man he thought he knew revealed himself to be something else entirely. With growing horror, the Halfmage watched as Melissan's face seemed to take on more angular features, her skin whitening, becoming pale.

'When the time came for the humans to return across the sea, two of our kind decided they wished to accompany them. They were eager to see the world we had left behind. I warned them against such recklessness... but in my weakness I relented, eventually allowed them to go. That was my third mistake.'

All in the crowd stood transfixed by Melissan's words, caught up in the spell her voice wove.

'My kin were taken to the city you humans named Shadowport and presented to the Magelord Marius. At first they were happy to share their knowledge with him, revealing technologies your kind were still many centuries from discovering. But this human, Marius, grew more demanding. He wanted to learn their every secret. And when they grew weary of his demands, he tortured them. The suffering our kin endured at his hands is unimaginable. And for that... I am guilty.'

The pain in Melissan's voice moved Eremul to tears, and as he looked out across the crowd he saw that others were crying too, men and women sobbing in each other's arms. The 'woman' beside him was somehow manipulating the emotions of those present, forcing them to share in her grief, to sympathize with her loss. To his credit or perhaps his eternal damnation, Timerus seemed unmoved. 'What are you?' the Grand Regent demanded.

'She's a Fade,' Eremul rasped. And he knew it to be true, for he alone had encountered such a being once before. *The night Salazar fell. The confrontation with Isaac outside the depository.*

'A *fehd*,' Melissan corrected him softly. 'Fade is what we did, two thousand years ago. We gave you much before we left: the tools to build a civilization we hoped would one day mirror the glory of our own. Instead you tyrannized your own people. You killed your gods. You broke the Pattern and in doing so inflicted immeasurable damage on the world. My kind have decided that mankind is poison. A poison that must be cleansed if the land is ever to recover.'

'Tell me,' Timerus asked, his voice quavering only a little. 'What... what can I do to offer redress?'

'Redress? The one you called Salazar sought to offer redress, too. Forty thousand human lives for two of my kind.' Melissan shook her head then, each strand of her fine silver hair dancing like woven moonlight. 'It was never enough. If he had sacrificed every human on this continent, it would not have been enough.'

Timerus nodded and then turned to Bracka. 'Shoot her.'

Melissan raised her arms, and somehow her hands were no longer bound. In her left hand she carried a cylindrical device made of metal. There was a pregnant pause – and then the world seemed to explode.

When his vision finally returned, Eremul found himself on his side, suspended awkwardly by his neck from the noose above. His chair had toppled over from the impact of the blast, one wheel spinning wildly in the rain. There was a great roaring in his ears and smoke filled his nostrils. The rope was tight around his neck, choking him, and he stared at the scene before him with eyes bulging from the terrible pressure around his throat.

The headless corpse of Timerus jerked wildly for a few seconds before toppling backwards. The ruins of the Grand Regent's head were splattered all over Remy and Bracka – but before either man could react the White Lady's handmaiden pulled a crystalline sword from… *somewhere*, and beheaded them both faster than even the Unborn could move, and it was then that Eremul noticed that her eyes weren't colourless like those of the other handmaidens but rather as black as obsidian, older than the mountains and forests, so ancient that even his own choking expiry struck him as pitifully insignificant.

How? he wondered dully as the world began to darken.

'My sister disposed of one of those creatures some months back and took her place,' Melissan said, as if reading his thoughts. 'The three of us have been hiding out in this city for years. Making preparations.'

The *fehd* took a step towards him. Her free hand went to her waist, and when it withdrew it clutched a blade that looked to be made of glass. It hummed through the air, too fast for his failing eyes to follow. The next thing he knew Eremul was in a heap on the platform, the severed noose falling away from his neck as he gasped in air.

'*Three of you?*' Eremul rasped, once he had recovered breath enough to speak. The crowd had started rioting, whatever glamour that had enthralled them now shattered. The Crimson Watch were under attack from men brandishing knives and other weapons they must have secreted under their clothes. As the Halfmage took in the chaos, he realized that many of those at the heart of the commotion must be mind-controlled fanatics, strategically positioned among the crowd.

'You've met our brother Isaac,' Melissan said. 'It was he who arranged to transport our army of thralls – those implanted with our technology – into the city. Isaac is with the First Fleet now. It will arrive soon.'

There was a loud bang as the first firebomb exploded in the plaza and the stench of burning flesh filled the air.

Then the screams started.

'Why?' Eremul whispered above the tumult. 'Why cut me down? Why spare me?'

'Our brother Isaac commanded that you be unharmed, at

least for now. You should know it is but a temporary respite –
the humans we massacred at the Celestial Isles were but the first.
We will not stop until your entire race is purged from these
lands.'

Homecoming

THEY REACHED THE Greenwild just as the late-autumn snow began to fall.

Kayne wiped frost from his beard with the back of his hand and checked to see how the orphans were faring. Somehow they'd made it to the edge of the great forest without losing a single child, though Tiny Tom had fallen badly ill yesterday afternoon and others were showing signs of sickness. Every one of the orphans was cold and miserable – but against all the odds they were *alive*.

Boots crunched on the frosty grass and Brick came to stand beside Kayne. Together they stared into the depths of the Greenwild.

'He's gone, isn't he?' Brick said eventually, breaking the silence. Near a week had passed since their encounter with the gholam, and in that time the youngster had said very little. They'd been busy with seeing the foundlings to safety, true enough, but the old warrior knew there was more to it than that. The way Brick struggled to meet his gaze reminded him of Magnar in years gone by.

Kayne blinked snow from his eyes. 'Aye,' he said simply. 'He's gone.'

A gust of wind howled through the trees and Brick shivered. Like Kayne, he'd given his cloak to the orphans to help keep them warm. 'He saved us all in the end.'

Kayne nodded.

Brick turned to watch Corinn as she portioned out the meagre reserves of food that remained. For his part, the boy barely seemed to eat a thing. He'd been thin before, but now he looked gaunt, all skin and bone. 'Why didn't tell you tell him the truth?' the youngster asked.

Kayne watched his breath mist in the early-morning air, trying to think of the right answer to that question. The honest answer. 'Sometimes a lie builds until the truth does more harm than good,' he replied. 'That and I'm a bloody old fool.'

'He would have followed you to the ends of the earth.'

Kayne grunted and turned away. With considerable effort he knelt down and pretended to check the ground for tracks. In truth he didn't have a clue what he was looking for, but the movement helped hide his face from Brick. 'He was the most loyal friend a man could wish for,' he said gruffly. 'Ain't many like him around these days.'

He remembered the Wolf's final words to him. *If I ever see you again I'll kill you. That's a promise.*

Jerek wouldn't see him again; he knew that with a certainty. The gholam was a weapon forged by the gods, an unstoppable killing machine that no man could hope to outrun, not down in those forsaken ruins. The fact Jerek had bought them time to flee to safety was astonishing enough. If anyone could've managed that, it was the Wolf.

'The children are ready to move. Are you crying?'

Kayne uttered a silent curse and blinked away tears as Jana Shah Shan suddenly loomed over him. He hadn't heard her approach. The woman moved as quiet as a ghost.

'I'm fine,' he grunted. 'Damn snow getting in my eyes.' He straightened slowly, his creaking knees hurting worse than ever. 'We can build a fire once we're inside the forest. Keep everyone warm until this passes.'

'Won't that draw the attention of the Wildfolk?'

'It might, but we can fight 'em if it comes to it. There ain't no fighting the cold.'

Jana nodded and turned to help Corinn, who was trying to get Milo to eat something. The tiny orphan kept asking about Grunt. He was too young to understand that his big green friend wouldn't be coming back.

'I can hunt us some game,' Brick said. 'Jerek taught me how.'

Kayne watched the flame-haired youngster fiddle with his bow and felt a warm pride in the boy. He was turning into a man and a true one at that. If he'd done anything right these last few months it was sparing Brick's life when he'd had the chance.

With Kayne and Brick leading the way, the odd little group entered the Greenwild. As the forest welcomed them into its snow-swept embrace, Kayne offered the spirits a silent prayer for seeing them this far.

He also said a prayer for friends lost along the way. For Jerek. For Grunt. Even for Brick's uncle Glaston. He couldn't shake the feeling he would be joining them soon enough.

Days merged into each other as they followed the rough paths leading north through the Greenwild. The weather grew colder, but even late in autumn the forest canopy above sheltered them from the worst vagaries of the approaching winter. Occasionally a snowstorm would shake the trees and cover the woodland floor in a blanket of white, but there was plenty of firewood to burn and game to hunt and water to refill their empty skins. Brick brought back rabbits and deer, even a small wild boar, though Kayne almost put his back out dragging the beast to camp. They ate well, however, and soon the children were in much better spirits.

One mild evening, a week after they first crossed into the Greenwild, Corinn was attempting to start a fire without success while Kayne and Brick sat together preparing dinner. The old Highlander gave the youngster a nudge and nodded at the struggling girl. 'Seems like a good opportunity to lend a hand.'

'Huh?' Brick looked up from skinning a rabbit and pretended to notice Corinn for the first time that evening. His green eyes narrowed. 'I'm a little busy right now,' he said, fixing the tiny ·carcass with a good, hard stare as if to prove his point.

Kayne reached out and placed a firm hand on the boy's arm. 'I can take care of that,' he said. 'The girl's been through hell seeing these little 'uns all to safety. I reckon she could use a friend.'

'Jana's her friend!'

'Jana's busy.'

Jana Shah Shan was practising her combat postures at the edge of the forest clearing. A handful of children watched, though by now many were bored of the routine. Jana did the same thing for hours each night, pushing herself as hard as she could, immersing herself in her Unity.

Kayne figured he knew why. The shame in her eyes still hadn't faded. She'd frozen back there in the ruins, lost her discipline and submitted to her fear. It had happened to him once and he knew from experience that it could take years to recover, to forgive oneself for that moment of weakness.

Corinn was still struggling to start the campfire. She threw the flint at the ground and rubbed her teary eyes in frustration, the sort that wasn't solely down to the matter at hand. Kayne was about to climb to his feet and offer the girl some help when, to his surprise, Brick clambered up and went to her.

'All right?' he said guardedly.

Corinn looked at him with her pretty blue eyes. 'Yes,' she said slowly.

Brick glanced back at Kayne, rising panic on his face. He looked as though he were about to flee. The old warrior gave him an encouraging wave. '*Go on*,' he mouthed silently.

Brick hesitated, frozen by indecision. Lucky for him, Corinn took the lead. 'I'm trying to start a fire,' she said.

'Well... you're doing it wrong.'

'Bloody hell, Brick,' Kayne mouthed. *You're as bad as the*

Wolf, he was about to add, but in the end it didn't feel right. Fortunately, Brick seemed to realize something more was required.

'I can help you. If you want,' he finished lamely.

Corinn brushed a few strands of blond hair from her face and nodded. 'Okay,' she said.

A moment later the two of them had a fire going. Brick risked a satisfied half-smile, but something on Corinn's face must have startled him as it faded immediately. 'Are you crying?' he asked.

'No. Well, a little. I was remembering my father.'

Brick hesitated. 'Is he waiting for you? Up in the mountains?'

'He's dead.'

'Oh. I'm sorry.'

'It's okay.'

A moment of silence passed. 'My uncle died recently. He was like a father to me, too. I miss him.'

Kayne forced himself to stop listening at that point. He turned away and reached into the bag at his waist. He took out the small bundle wrapped in cloth, opened it and stared at the contents. At the old silver ring. At the lock of hair Mhaira had given to him when she became so sick he was certain he would lose her. The memory of those few days still gave him nightmares.

He stared at the knife he'd fashioned for Magnar's fourteenth naming day. The image of his son trapped in a wicker cage wormed its way into his mind again and he fumbled the knife. He picked it up with shaking hands and looked around, afraid someone might have seen. If any of the children had noticed, they were too young to understand. His gaze settled on Brick and Corinn. Even in his grief he managed a small smile.

They were standing side by side by the fire, their hands clasped tightly together.

*

473

The next day they came across the devastation that had been inflicted on the Greenwild during the fight between Yllandris and her pursuers.

Swathes of forest had been reduced to blackened wasteland. At one point, nothing but a thick carpet of ash covered the ground for miles. The scale of the damage was appalling, and despite everything Kayne found himself feeling sorry for the Wildfolk that had come looking for vengeance. They were just as much victims as anyone else.

They encountered no living Wildfolk as they continued north through the burned-out forest. With a heavy heart, Kayne wondered if the group that had accompanied Ryder to Mal-Torrad had been the last of their kind. The Wildfolk had dwelled within the Greenwild for centuries, before the coming of the Shaman. Their passing would be another small tragedy in an age that had already seen so many peoples fade from the world.

As they crossed yet another field of ash, Brick spotted a strange sight. A circle of trees stood undamaged in the wasteland: an island of green amidst the ruin. Corinn recognized it immediately. 'The Nexus Glade,' she gasped from where she walked beside Brick. The two youngsters spent all their time together now.

'You know this place?' Kayne asked.

Corinn nodded. 'This is where the iron man and the others caught up with us.'

'How'd it survive the fire?'

'This place is blessed,' Corinn replied. 'The spirits watch over it.'

Kayne turned and waited for Jana, who was hanging back to ensure none of the orphans wandered off. 'You mind stopping here with the children? I don't want the little 'uns seeing anything that might upset them.'

Jana called a halt, and together with Brick and Corinn Kayne made his way into the mysterious glade. He half expected a scene of mass slaughter, but what he found instead was a sight that made his old heart ache. The body of a young woman lay curled up on the grass. She had a deep wound in her chest where the killing blow had been delivered, but her expression was strangely peaceful in death. An old canvas sack lay nearby. Kayne saw it and thought of Grunt.

'Yllandris,' Corinn gasped suddenly. She rushed over, tears streaming down her cheeks.

Brick examined the sack. 'It's filled with bones.'

'The remains of the children Krazka sacrificed to the Herald,' Corinn said, cradling the body of the woman in her arms. 'Yllandris wanted to bury them here.'

Kayne cracked his fingers. 'Brick, help me find a sturdy branch. I'm gonna need to build a shovel.'

They spent the next hour digging four graves for the sad remains of the orphans and the pretty sorceress. As they laid them to rest, a thought occurred to Kayne. 'This young woman,' he said to Corinn. 'Did she know Magnar?'

Corinn started as if surprised by the question. 'She was his paramour.'

Kayne froze. 'His paramour?'

'You know. His... lover. Ever since last year. He was very fond of her. Or at least that's what all the women used to say.'

'Did... did she love him? My son, I mean. Did she love my son?'

'People used to say mean things about her. That she wasn't capable of loving anyone except herself. But I heard the way she spoke about Magnar after we fled town. She loved him.' Corinn glanced at Brick and flushed slightly.

'I never knew,' Kayne said brokenly. He was burying his son's first love – and he'd never even known her.

When finally they left the Greenwild, it was to be met by the breathtaking sight of rolling white hills. The Green Reaching was covered in snow as far as the eye could see.

'It's beautiful,' Brick said, awestruck.

'It's home,' Kayne said simply. Behind him the foundlings made happy noises and began scooping up handfuls of snow. Tiny Tom was feeling much better now, and he threw a handful of snow at Milo, squealing in delight.

Jana looked around, her eyes wide in amazement. 'It's like a white sea,' she said in wonder.

'Does it ever snow where you're from?' Kayne asked.

'Once, when I was a girl. But nothing like this.'

Kayne closed his eyes for a moment. He was remembering the morning he and Mhaira and Magnar had been playing out in the snowy fields just before he'd been called away to the war. Those had been simpler times. Happier times. His reminiscing was abruptly shattered by Brick nudging him in the ribs.

'Men approaching,' the boy hissed. 'Dozens. And they're armed.'

Kayne's eyes snapped open. 'This far south?' he muttered, shocked and dismayed. He'd been intending to see the orphans to Southaven, then find a horse and ride west and north, circling around to the West Reaching and joining up with Carn Bloodfist's army. If even the peaceful Green Reaching had become caught up in the war, nowhere in the Heartlands was likely to be safe.

Brick was readying his bow. Kayne placed a firm hand around his narrow shoulders and shook his head. 'Not here, lad. There's too many.'

'We're not going to fight?'

'We're outnumbered twenty to one.'

'But... you're the Sword of the North.'

'I'm just a man, lad. One man goes up against twenty, he gets a spear in the back and a half a dozen swords in the ribs while he's wondering which way to turn first. Twenty on one, it don't matter how good the one is. Fact is, he dies.' He remembered Red Valley, men dropping like leaves all around him. He looked at Jana, noticed the set of her jaw and the glint in her eyes. She wanted a fight, wanted the chance to regain whatever honour she thought she'd lost back in the ruins. 'Let me do the talking,' he said firmly.

The band of warriors approached slowly. They were dressed for battle, fully armoured and bristling with weapons. Many wore cloaks with fur-lined hoods covering their faces, but those that didn't looked young. Very young.

One warrior, a big fellow with a deep cleft in his chin who couldn't have seen his twentieth winter, took a step forward. He hardly seemed able to control his anger. 'Got some gall passing back this way after the evil shit you done.' He cleared his throat noisily and spat.

Kayne glanced at the yellow spittle dribbling down the front of his leather vest. He took a deep breath to calm himself, then, keeping his voice level and his hands by his sides: 'Come again?'

'Men and children slain. Women raped with cold steel and left to bleed out. The Butcher thinks we're sheep-fuckers and cowards? That he can send his Kingsmen to terrorize us and we'll bend over and take it?'

'Hang on a minute, I ain't no Kingsman—'

'Bullshit!' the warrior roared. A vein on his thick neck stood out angrily. 'You chased these kids all the way down from Heartstone on the King's orders. What, sacrificing children to demons wasn't enough for you, old man? Couldn't get you hard enough?'

'Watch your mouth,' Kayne snarled. He had his greatsword in his hands, his own anger getting the better of him now.

The cleft-jawed warrior advanced, two spearmen falling in behind him, their hoods hiding their faces. 'I'm gonna send your head back to that butcher,' the leader hissed. He sprang at Kayne, sword flashing down.

Kayne casually disarmed the young firebrand, then planted a boot in his mid-section and sent him flailing back to land flat on his arse.

The spearman on the left leaped at him, thrusting towards his chest. Kayne knocked aside the stabbing steel tip, kicked away the man's legs and sent his weapon skittering across the snow with a flick of his foot.

That left one spearman remaining, at least as an immediate threat. This bastard was good, much better than Kayne might've expected. He seemed to waver a little as if drunk, and in fact Kayne could smell the mead on the man's breath – but his spear batted aside Kayne's every attack, thwarted his every effort at subduing the fellow.

The apparent leader of the band, the big one with the cleft in his chin, clambered to his feet and turned to his men. 'Kill him!' he roared.

Out of the corner of his eye Kayne saw Brick fumbling for an arrow and Jana Shah Shan taking up a fighting stance. 'Call your men off!' he tried to yell. 'I ain't no Kingsman!' But the damned spearman kept coming at him, and any second now the other warriors would reach him. He and Jana and maybe even Brick were going to die here, all because of one hot-headed young fool with fire in his blood who'd mistaken him for someone else. He snarled and redoubled his efforts until he drove the spearman to his knees. He lined up his greatsword for a killing blow. There was no point pulling his punches; it seemed they were beyond that.

'*Kayne?*'

The disbelieving gasp reached his ears at the last possible moment. He turned his blade aside just before it cleaved through the man's neck, staring down in disbelief as the warrior reached up and pulled back his hood.

'Taran?' he said dumbly, once his brain finally caught up.

It'd been many years since he'd last seen that face, and it had changed for the worse. Taran had been handsome once, but now his skin had the ruddy, vein-threaded complexion of a man who'd drunk far too much. His eyes were yellowed and dull and his teeth, where he still had them, more brown than white.

Taran scrambled up and twisted to face the advancing warriors. 'Stop,' he shouted. 'He's not lying. This ain't no Kingsman!'

'Then who the fuck *is* he? He sure as hell fights like one.' The leader scowled and held up a hand, halting his men.

'This... this man here is the Sword of the North.'

That brought gasps and incredulous laughter from the band of warriors. 'You taking the piss, Taran?' said Cleft-chin angrily. 'The Sword of the North's ancient history. Borun hunted him down.'

'Aye,' Kayne said, reaching up and sheathing his greatsword. 'He hunted me down. But I'm still here, and Borun's dead.'

It turned out the leader's name was Carver. He was the eldest son of Brandwyn the Younger, chieftain of the Green Reaching, and he and his band had set out from Southaven as soon as his father's council had voted in favour of war against Krazka. The atrocities committed in the King's name could not go unanswered.

Kayne listened as Carver described the events that had led to the Butcher King seizing the throne whilst the Shaman and the Brethren were elsewhere, summoned down to the Trine by the Tyrant of Dorminia. Kayne himself had witnessed the moment the Shaman had received news of Krazka's audacious coup, though at the time all he knew was that Heartstone was in grave peril. The revelation that Mhaira yet lived had stunned him. It was only after he considered what Heartstone's peril actually meant that he had begun to fear for Magnar.

'Demons,' he said again. 'What kind of man bargains with demons?'

'A madman,' Carver replied. 'You never saw the things Krazka did at Beregund.'

No, Kayne thought bitterly. *I was trapped in a cage while my friends were murdered and the capital was burned to the ground.*

'What you gonna do, Kayne?' Taran asked. The one-time Warden was a broken man. Red Valley had done to him all those years ago what the horrors of the Borderland couldn't. Soon after returning from the war, Taran had been exiled from Heartstone for beating his wife to death in a drunken rage. Kayne had wanted nothing to do with his old friend after that. As Taran sat there now, breath stinking of mead, Kayne just felt pity for him.

'Krazka's placed my boy in a wicker cage,' he said quietly. 'I got no love for the Shaman, but if I'm gonna get Magnar out of there, he and the Bloodfist are my only hope.'

'Rumour is the Shaman's not long for this world,' Carver said. 'He's dying, if such a thing's possible. Hasn't been seen in months. Most of the Brethren were slaughtered outside Heartstone's walls.' The young warrior shook his head and spat. 'We can't count on the Shaman's help. Still, my father will be pleased to know the Sword of the North stands with us. We're rounding up the last of the fighting men down south before we move north to join my father's army.'

Kayne nodded slowly, still taken aback by the news about the Shaman. It scarcely seemed possible. 'Someone ought to send word to Eastmeet. Watcher's Keep's likely fallen, but Orgrim Foehammer might yet live. If it's demons we're fighting, there ain't no man more experienced.'

Taran stared at him. There was something like shame in his bleary eyes. 'Kayne... Orgrim threw in his lot with Krazka.'

'What?' Kayne felt as though someone had stuck a knife in his ribs and twisted it.

'Shortly after the Herald showed up the demons started getting more numerous. They flooded the Borderland, until the Wardens couldn't hold the Keep any longer. Krazka offered the Foehammer a choice. Stand down and be spared the demons, or... Well, you can guess the rest.'

Kayne thought back to that fateful moment on the bank of the Icemelt when Orgrim had saved his life. He thought back to the morning of his Initiation, when the Foehammer had volunteered to lead him into the Borderland together with the broken warrior sitting opposite him. 'But the Foehammer was a man of honour,' he whispered to Taran. 'He was true.'

Taran shrugged helplessly. 'There's none that are true any more. We're old men, Kayne. We bend with the world or we break.' He hiccupped, still half-drunk, and tried to hide his trembling hands.

Silence followed. Kayne watched the foundlings playing in the snow. Brick had his arm around Corinn's shoulders, the two of them staring out at the white hills. Jana was fiddling with the medallion she wore around her neck beneath her black clothing. Apparently the amulet, a gift from the Wizard-Emperor himself, would hasten her return home. According to Jana, its magic would function only for graduates of the Academy.

Brodar Kayne cleared his throat. This was it. No point putting it off any longer. 'There's something I need to know,' he said.

Taran and Carver looked at him. Behind the three men the rest of the band waited. Occasionally someone would cast a curious glance in Kayne's direction. 'Go on,' said Taran.

'Mhaira. My wife. I thought she was dead, but the truth... the truth is she was exiled by the Shaman.' He paused for a moment. Afraid to ask. Afraid to know the answer. 'I wonder if you got any idea where she might be.'

Carver looked puzzled. Like the rest of his band, he knew Kayne only by reputation.

Taran, though, was a different matter. 'I've spent the last eight years in exile,' he said slowly. 'Been all over the Fangs. Everywhere save the Heartlands, which were forbidden me by the terms of banishment. I never saw nor heard anything that might've led me to think Mhaira was close by.'

Kayne sagged.

'Except... there was this one evening...' Taran closed his eyes, as if searching for something buried deep in his drink-scoured mind. 'I was travelling back south two months ago. Returning home after I heard the Shaman got ousted. I passed near Beregund on the way. Nothing but a burned-out ruin now, but I wanted to see it for myself. Anyways, a few miles on I

481

spotted a field with a couple of houses. I remember being surprised. I couldn't understand why the army that marched on the capital had left them untouched. I saw light coming from one of the houses, and I thought to myself, this reminds me of the place my old friend told me about at Red Valley. When we was surrounded by Targus Bloodfist's army and men were dying all around us, and we was sure we'd be joining them any moment. I asked you what it was that made you keep going. That made you fight on. And you answered that it was a vision. A vision of following the long road home after this was all over and stepping from the shadows into the light.'

As Kayne listened to Taran, he began to shake. 'Two months? he said, his voice husky. 'You said it was two months back?'

'Aye, two months. Give or take a week.'

Kayne hesitated, frozen by uncertainty. He wanted nothing more than to find a horse and ride home and find Mhaira and take her in his arms. But that would take precious days of travel – and lead him away from Heartstone.

Magnar needed him. His son was in dire trouble. The promise he'd made to Mhaira burned in his chest.

'I need a horse,' he said, climbing to his feet.

Carver looked from Taran to Kayne. 'You're leaving?'

'I'm going to join your pa and his army. Ain't no more time to waste.'

'There's a farm a mile north of here. Place ought to have a horse of some kind.'

Kayne went to Brick and Corinn. They turned as he approached. Kayne hesitated, then reached out and placed a hand on Brick's shoulder. 'I'm going to join the army. My son needs me. Afterwards I'm going home to Mhaira. She's here, Brick. She's alive.'

Brick stared at him for a moment – and then his freckled face folded into an enormous smile. 'I knew you'd find her!' he exclaimed, his green eyes bright.

A snowball hit Brick on the back of the head and he turned.

Milo was grinning at them, hands dripping wet. The other foundlings were teaming up to build a big snowman. 'His name's Grunt!' Tiny Tom piped up happily.

'Corinn and me are going to Southaven with the children,' Brick said, wiping snow from his red hair. 'They need someone to watch over them.'

Kayne nodded. He'd figured as much. 'Carver says you should be safe in the capital. As safe anyone can be in these dark times. The Green Reaching's declared against Krazka. The Kingsmen that came through here looking for the younglings will be killed on sight, and so will anyone else proclaiming to serve that butcher. We're at war now.' He turned to Corinn. 'Make sure you look after young Brick,' he said, trying to keep his voice steady. 'He ain't as tough as he thinks he is.'

'I'll do my best,' Corinn said, smiling shyly.

'All right then, Brick,' Kayne said. He cleared his throat.

'All right,' answered Brick, not meeting his eyes.

They stood there awkwardly for a moment. Then Kayne leaned forward and embraced the young flame-haired archer. 'You keep safe, you hear?' he whispered. 'I'll come check on you once this is all over.'

He felt Brick nod, and something suspiciously moist trickled down the boy's cheek and landed on his hand. It might have been melted snow, except that it was warm.

Having bid farewell to the youngsters, Kayne went to say goodbye to Jana. She nodded at him and adjusted her veil. 'I'm sorry to say that I must shortly depart. There is no sign of the thief, and my betrothed is waiting for me.' The snow fell more thickly now, flecking her black hair and clothes.

'You never did tell me who your betrothed is.'

Jana looked faintly embarrassed. 'You recall I told you that he taught me much? I meant that literally. He is... was... my master at the Academy. Our relationship is forbidden by law. I thought that if I volunteered for this mission and succeeded, our indiscretions might be overlooked. But I have failed.'

'You know,' Kayne said, 'there ain't no shame in failing. There ain't no shame in being afraid. Someone once told me to master fear. Turn it into a weapon.'

'My body is my weapon,' Jana said, though she sounded a lot less certain than when they had first met. She was still young, Kayne reminded himself. She might speak six languages and be a master of Unity and an agent of the one of the Confederation's most powerful Magelords, the man her people revered as Wizard-Emperor, but she was still learning the truth of who she was.

He cleared his throat. 'Seems to me you can keep your fear closer than anyone. Turn it into your sword and your shield *and* your armour. Make it a thing nothing is able to pierce.'

Jana appeared to consider his words. 'Thank you,' she said. 'I wish you good luck. I would like to help you in your war, but I have to bring word to the Emperor. The gholam must be stopped.'

Kayne nodded and bid his final farewell to the Jade Islander. He saw Taran sitting on the snow, staring out at nothing in particular. He'd intended to leave the man in peace, but the haunted look on the ex-Warden's face was so tragic he couldn't help but go to him.

'Carver's band are heading north to join the army once they're done recruiting here,' Kayne said. 'You going with them?'

'I got a mind to.'

'You looking to die?'

'I should've died at Red Valley. Never could beat my own demons. Figure I might as well die fighting the other kind. The easier kind. Maybe I'll see my daughter again before the end. Maybe not. Don't think she'd care much either way.'

'Your daughter. That was your answer at Red Valley, when I asked you the same question you asked me.'

'Aye,' Taran said. 'I remember.'

'What was her name again? You know I ain't ever been good with names.'

Taran looked up at him. 'Yllandris,' he said.

Several seconds passed before Kayne's greatsword fell from his nerveless fingers and he sank to his knees in the snow.

The Truth of Iron

THE BLIZZARD WAS growing stronger, the biting cold working its way into his armour and setting his teeth to chattering even with the thick cloak wrapped tight around him and the hood pulled down. He hated winter. He hated this country. Gods, how he hated this country.

Why did I come back?

It didn't matter any more. He was leaving, heading back to civilization, the Duke and his men be damned. If they discovered him, why, he would kill them. He was a knight. Let those worthless curs learn why he had once earned the name the Sword Lord.

Somehow he had made it past the enemy line. The Greenmen were camped and ready to march on Heartstone, but like the rank amateurs they were they had left holes big enough for him to ride straight through. They hadn't tried to stop him. No doubt they had simply mistaken the cloaked rider for one of their own. He smiled behind his visor. Only a few more miles and the Greenwild beckoned. Soon he would be free of this hellish place, never to return.

A sudden gust of wind buffeted him with snow. His horse snorted and tried to shy away from the storm and Sir Meredith cursed, tugging viciously at the beast's reins. If the blizzard got any worse it would be near impossible to see more than a few feet in front of his face. As luck would have it, a little further on a lone farmhouse emerged from the swirling snow. The light from within was inviting, and the knight reined in his horse and led it inside the small stables at the side of the house. Then he went to rap on the door.

It opened to reveal an old man with a crown of white hair falling around a balding pate and a walking stick clutched tightly in one unsteady hand. He squinted through bleary eyes at the knight, who had little patience for such an inspection while he stood there in the freezing snow.

'Who are you?' Sir Meredith demanded, trying not to let his chattering teeth show.

'Name's Seb,' said the grandfather. He appeared to hesitate for a moment, and then he shuffled aside and pointed indoors with his stick. 'It's no evening to be out riding. You come in out of the cold and I'll get Drenna to bring you some warm stew.'

Sir Meredith grunted and entered the hearth chamber, taking a seat by the fire. A moment later a younger woman, likely the old man's daughter judging by her homely features, came and stood next to him, a steaming clay bowl grasped uncertainly in her hands. Sir Meredith lowered his hood and removed his helmet, placing it carefully down on the floor.

'Give it here then, woman. Don't stand there gawking.'

The woman handed over the bowl. Sir Meredith stared down at the contents with a deep frown. 'Where's the spoon?' he demanded. 'Do you expect me to bury my face in this inedible filth like some farmyard animal? Fetch me some wine!'

'We… we don't have any wine. My husband has some mead in the back. I… I can bring you some, if it pleases you.'

Sir Meredith gave a sharp nod, watching the wench's swaying hips as she disappeared into the other room. She returned with a tankard of mead, spilling some on the floor with her shaking hand. He snatched it off her and raised it to his lips, taking a long swallow.

'Gah!' He spat the foul liquid all over the shocked woman, then hurled the clay mug across the room where it shattered against the far wall. 'Are you trying to poison me, you stupid bitch?'

There was a tapping sound from over near the door. It was the old man, Seb, his walking stick beating a furious rhythm. 'That's no way for a guest to behave, now. You've got some nerve, coming in here and speaking to my daughter like that. I'm going to have to ask you to leave.'

Sir Meredith was on his feet in a flash. He stormed across to the old man, who raised his stick in a pathetic defensive gesture. The knight tore it from his grasp and struck the fool across the side of the head, knocking him to the floor.

'Papa!' Seb's daughter rushed across to them, but a quick backhand from Sir Meredith sent her sprawling too.

He was breathing hard beneath his armour now, the old rage prodding at the blackness inside him. They dared disrespect *him*, this family of sheep-fuckers? As if Shranree's barbs hadn't been enough. As if the way the King had humiliated him back on the hill hadn't been enough. He was tired of being treated with contempt. It was time to administer some harsh lessons.

He took a step towards the sobbing woman, but just then a small face peeked out from behind another doorway and a small boy made to dash into the room. 'Mama,' he cried, but a hand reached out to stop him and a pale-faced man stepped forward.

'Leave here,' he pleaded, his voice trembling. 'Please. We've done nothing to you. My Drenna was only trying to make you feel welcome in our home.'

'*Make me feel welcome*,' Sir Meredith echoed, his eyes not leaving the boy. 'This is how you a welcome a knight? By feeding him goat shit and pisswater?'

The man of the house, if he could even be called that, began to stutter a reply, but Sir Meredith held up a hand and cut him off. 'You're a coward. Your wife is an ugly cow. Maybe your father-in-law had some balls years ago, but they're as shrivelled as the rest of him now. Come here, boy.'

'No,' the father said, his voice a ragged whisper. 'Please.'

'Don't beg. It makes you sound even more wretched than you are.'

'What... what are you going to do to him?'

Sir Meredith smiled humourlessly. 'I fail to see how that should concern you. Worry about the few seconds you and your wife have remaining to you instead. I *might* let this child live – but I can make no guarantees.'

A long moment of terrified silence followed his words.

And then from outside there came the sound of booted feet crunching on snow. It was the only sound besides the crackling of the hearth and Drenna's sobs.

A voice called out. An older man's voice, proud but uncertain. 'Sorry to bother you, but I don't s'pose I could borrow that horse you got tied up in the stables over yonder? And if you got something to drink I'd be mighty grateful.'

A shadow emerged from the doorway, and the light of the hearth illuminated the newcomer. He was tall and powerfully built, a little diminished by age but still in good fighting shape. Bright blue eyes peered out from a bearded face covered in the grime of countless days of travel. They were slightly puffy, as if he had recently been crying.

Sir Meredith's top lip curled in contempt. 'That horse belongs to me. There is nothing for you here, barbarian.'

The grizzled old warrior took another step into the house. He wore a leather hauberk, Sir Meredith saw, and the hilt of some godforsaken savage's greatsword poked out above his shoulder. On the floor near the door, the old man gasped softly.

'I *said* there is nothing for you here,' Sir Meredith barked. His gauntleted hand came to rest on the hilt of the sabre at his belt. But as the warrior looked around the room, and his jaw tightened, and his blue eyes grew as clear and hard as a glacier on the coldest winter morning, the knight felt the briefest moment of unease.

'Everything all right?' the newcomer said slowly and deliberately. The woman at Sir Meredith's feet let out a small sob, and her husband over near the other door made a strangled sound. The old warrior met his eyes for the briefest of moments. Then

489

he nodded, and his scarred hands rose slowly to the hilt of his greatsword.

'I warned you,' Sir Meredith snapped. He drew his sabre and it whispered from its sheath like the promise of death. 'You could have walked out of here, old fool. Now you're just another corpse. A backwater savage whose faith in your legends was sadly misplaced. I am Sir Meredith, a knight of Tarbonne, champion of the Circle, known as the Sword Lord. My sabre was forged by Dranthe, the finest smith in the Shattered Realms. Who are *you*?'

'No one important.'

Sir Meredith snorted at that. 'At least you know your place.'

The old warrior had his greatsword in his hands now. 'Let me show you what happens when a barbarian meets a true knight,' Sir Meredith declared. But those blue eyes didn't waver. If anything they grew colder, and as Sir Meredith strode forward to meet this veteran he wondered idly who he was.

It hardly mattered, of course. He was a champion of the Circle. He had killed a hundred men. He was a *knight*.

He feinted and then launched a blinding chain of attacks, displaying perfect form, a masterful display of swordsmanship that would have made the Masters weep.

He didn't recall what happened next. All he knew was that somehow he was on the floor in a broken heap. He couldn't move his arms or legs. But he could *feel*: half a dozen spots on his body screaming in agony where the dripping steel above him had found the gaps in his armour and cut his flesh to ribbons. The bearded face looked down at him, and he might have been staring into the gaze of the Reaver himself.

'How...' he tried to ask, but when he opened his mouth all that emerged was a thick bubble of blood. His killer turned and sheathed his greatsword. Then the stranger reached down and, with a gentleness that seemed impossible for a man so skilled at taking lives, helped the woman of the house to her feet.

Sir Meredith's eyes felt terribly heavy now, and as he turned his head to find a more comfortable position to die he saw Seb watching him.

'You asked who he was,' the old man said as he went to retrieve his walking stick. 'That man there, I'll tell you who he is.'

Seb's words seemed to reach him from very far away. 'That man... is the Sword of the North...'

The Wanderer

THE TRAVELLER GHOSTED through the grey and deserted streets, sweeping eyes suffused with crimson over the multitude of corpses lining the avenues, piled high against burned-out buildings that still smoked gently in the pre-dawn gloom. The blood of those who were unburned called to him, but he ignored it. There would be time to sate his hunger later. The journey had been arduous and depleted much of his power, yet the Master would suffer no delay.

He sniffed the air as he wandered through the wreckage of a city torn apart first by war and then by insurgency. The stench of alchemy filled his nostrils. This city had seen so much death; he could feel it in every pore of the dark granite beneath his feet.

There was a commotion ahead. A group of men and women were marauding down the street opposite. Their clothing was singed and their faces were covered in black powder and he knew they were fanatics, roaming the streets like jackals, looking for victims who lacked the wit to have barred themselves in their homes and closed the shutters. He could sense the alien technology implanted in their flesh, though its flavour was strange to him.

The group passed him by, oblivious to his presence. The traveller walked the paths others could not see. He reached up and touched the key hanging on the chain beneath his cloak, wondering what had become of the devastating entity he had freed from the depths of the forgotten kingdom. The gholam would have pierced his shroud of concealment, he knew. Caught him and scattered his ashes to the wind had he not taken such great pains to avoid making himself a target. It had been a huge risk, activating that terrible weapon of the gods, but the Master had willed it and Wolgred had obeyed. So it had been for the last three hundred years.

He was close now; the voice in his skull grew louder, beckoning him onwards, drawing him towards the docks where a fleet of newly arrived ships the likes of which even he had never seen filled the harbour. They were magnificent vessels: massive and yet delicate, the engineering that had gone into their design so far advanced of any ship ever built by the hand of man that it was as if he been transported to a different age. Though he was himself ancient by the standards of his people, the power he possessed exceeded only by the Master and his surviving peers, he felt himself humbled. He quickened his pace, aware that if those aboard the ships learned of his presence even his magic would not save him.

The building he was looking for was situated on a nondescript street. It appeared to be some kind of book depository, judging by the sign out front. He raised a hand to knock upon the door, but before his knuckles could rap against the wood the door swung inward and the Master's words manifested directly inside his skull.

'Enter.'

He did as he was commanded. The interior of the building was dark and unlit, and though his eyes could pierce shadows as easily as if it were day there was a pool of utter blackness in the corner of the well-maintained store that even the gaze of one versed in the ninth school could not penetrate.

'Wolgred.' The voice inside his head spoke again. Something seemed to move within that unnatural abyss of light, a deeper shade of black shifting slightly to regard him. *'You bring news.'*

'Of course, master. It is my honour to serve.'

Silence followed his words, and Wolgred the Wanderer was

filled with a sudden dread, afraid he had inadvertently caused offence. But a moment later that voice slithered into his skull again.

'*Report.*'

'The Nameless stirs beneath the Spine. The hold his Herald has on the King is near complete. Mithradates is dying and will not interfere in our plans.'

'*What of the gholam?*'

'It is somewhere in the ruins still.'

Two tiny pinpricks of malevolent red light flickered in the depths of the darkness. '*You have done well.*'

Joy filled Wolgred's heart at the Master's praise, but he didn't dare let the pleasure show in his voice. 'The Ancients have arrived. We must leave soon. Are… are you strong enough to portal, master?'

'*Not quite. Soon. I require sustenance.*'

'Of course, master. I shall see to it.'

'*Wait. There is something else. A marker in the Pattern has appeared unexpectedly. One I did not account for.*'

'Tell me what must be done, master.'

'*Go to Thelassa. Find the one named Davarus Cole and kill him. Take care not to alert the White Lady to your presence, or you will place our plans in jeopardy and risk a deviation in the Pattern. That cannot come to pass.*'

'Of course, master.' Wolgred wanted to ask about Shadowport, enquire how much longer Lord Marius would need before he could resume his old form. But he dared not. Instead he bowed low, and then he left the depository to obtain the sacrifices his master had requested.

As luck would have it, a young Watchman was already on his way to the depository as Wolgred left the building. The guard mentioned something about a dog and keeping a promise to a man named the Halfmage. The Wanderer gestured at him to go inside with a warm smile.

He whistled a tuneless ditty as a high-pitched shriek erupted from the depository and was abruptly cut off by a feral growl and the crunching of bone. With the *fehd* ships now patrolling the harbour, he would need to find some other way of crossing Deadman's Channel. It would only serve to delay the inevitable.

As he had so many hundreds of others before him, Wolgred the Wanderer would hunt down this Davarus Cole and kill him without remorse.

Acknowledgements

It's often said that the second novel is the hardest; now I understand why. I would like to thank my publishers for their continued patience over the past two years as I wrestled with a succession of personal and professional challenges that made writing this book such a challenge.

My sincere thanks to my agent, Robert Dinsdale, without whom I would still be procrastinating over the manuscript that would become *The Grim Company*. Rob plucked a fledgling writer from the obscurity of the internet and into bookstores in the relative blink of an eye. He has equal claim to any success I enjoy.

I'd also like to extend my thanks to Rob's colleagues at A M Heath, who continue to represent my work in the international markets. I dread the day they find me a Spanish publisher and my in-laws are finally able to read these books...

My thanks also to Chris Lotts for all his work in North America.

Mike Brooks again provided much needed (and *honest*) feedback on early versions of the manuscript. Not only is Mike is a great pair of eyes, he's also rather a fine writer himself.

Lastly – but absolutely *not* least – in my absence of any artistic talent whatsoever, my wife Yesica stepped in to draft the map of Kayne's journey. She also helped out with last-minute proofreading. Her loving support helped ensure this book got written.